To my late aunt, whose enthralling retellings of the Indian epics introduced me, at five, to the marvellous world of mythology and blue-skinned gods.

And to my husband, R, for saying the perfect words in 2016.

PROLOGUE

THE DEATH CRIES came as they had for weeks, taking over his mind.

Wrenched from sleep, Shara sat up with a choked cry, covered in sweat. He was clawing at his neck with his left hand, to tear free of an imagined stranglehold; in his right, he was gripping the hilt of his sword that had been conjured in instinctive defence. The dark room was illuminated by the lambent blue of its fire-edged blade.

Outside the open window, the night was calm, and the scent of rain drifted in on a cool breeze that pebbled his skin. As he forced his eyes open, he unclenched his fist; the sword was gone, taking the light with it.

He pushed up to sit on the edge of the bed, elbows on his knees, holding his head in his hands. He stayed like that, shoulders hunched, pressing the heels of his palms into his eyes until at last his breathing evened. Then he peeled off his clothes and stepped out of his lodge.

Like him, his small log cabin stood alone in the middle of a glade in Nibiru's Mashu forest. The rain had let up but the wind was stronger now, cold and wet with the spray from a nearby cascade.

As he padded across damp grass to the stream, he filled his lungs with deep gulps of the crisp night air. In his weakened state, he had to labour against the waist-high current to reach the rock wall. He stood under the spray with his head bowed, palms flat on the unyielding stone behind the falls, breath shivering out of him as the cold water sluiced down his overheated limbs and drenched his hair.

He stayed that way for a long time while strange voices clamoured in his head. When at last they quietened, he scooped up handfuls of coarse mud from the banks and scrubbed himself all over until his skin felt raw. He dragged his fingers hard over his scalp, front to back, and down to the tips of his hair, over and over, in a vain attempt to wash away his visions. But the images lingered, as if burned into his mind. He saw strange men and women, their faces frozen in horror, lying cut up and bleeding as their lives leached out of their limp bodies. Their anguish felt real to him, as if every gash on their body had left a mark on his own.

The sky was lightening by the time he felt clean enough to return home. He had reached the water's edge and set one foot on the pebbled shore when it happened.

Not again.

Pain seared up his spine, folding his body into itself, arms wrapped around his ribs while his insides burned with another's wounds.

He heard it, different this time. Not the chorus of screams as before, but a single familiar voice, the shaking cry of a dying man.

When Shara was five, Nidaba had told him of a power coveted by all the gods but possessed by none, not even Anu, creator of time itself and all that followed. It was the power of foreknowledge. Shara had believed her then, for what cause would a child have to doubt the goddess of Knowledge? But today, in this moment, Shara knew that Nidaba was wrong.

Because the voice was his, only older. And he was seeing how he would be killed.

Closing his eyes only made the horror more real, with visions colliding in the unseeing blackness. He lay motionless on the riverbank, as paralyzed and powerless now as he would be in the future, when the strip of blue fire would sink through him, as though he were mere flesh and blood, with no bone to impede his own hacking sword. His mind showed him a ringed hand flinging his dismembered limbs into the heavens, his faceless killer looking down at what remained of him. *Who are you?* He moaned, then went silent. But the stream of images continued.

In the darkness of his mind's eye, a fireball arced across the night sky, leaving a trail of blue in its wake as it disappeared into the forest. He sensed a presence moving beside him. Then he saw something new.

The hilt of a sword.

Echoes

of the

Gods

A Punarjanman Novel

Gaia Sol

Echoes of the Gods (A Punarjanman Novel)

Published by Gaia Sol

Cover by Noor Sobhan © Gaia Sol

Digital ISBN: 978-1-7750786-3-0

Print ISBN: 978-1-7750786-4-7

Audio ISBN: 978-1-7750786-1-6

It was a singular weapon. A large sapphire adorned the golden hilt. Blood—his blood—was creeping darkly down the grooved length of steel, delineating in black the engraving of two serpents coiled around a winged staff.

He knew that sword, that design. He knew its master. He did not know why the killer wanted him dead.

Falling to his hands and knees, he let his head drop to his chest and stared down at his reflection in the fading ripples—fair hair gleaming like wet pearl in the moonlight, blue skin gone ashen, pale eyes touched with a strange light. The silver leaf-like birthmark on his stomach, its long stem curling around his navel, had turned blood-black.

His elbows buckled and he crumpled on the damp bank, while the grass around him turned white and wove into a soft mesh over his helpless, shuddering body.

A furious thumping on his door jolted him to the edge of wakefulness.

At once, echoes of the previous night's delirium overran his mind, snapping him upright in his bed, bare and shivering. He didn't know when he had found the strength to drag himself back inside. He couldn't hear the thumping on the door over the pounding inside his head. His heart hammered in his chest.

"Shara!" The fist on his door wouldn't relent. "Open up, Shara!"

Forcing his body out of bed, he yanked open the door and threw up a hand to shield his eyes from the glare of the mid-day sun. Through narrowed eyes, he discerned the figure of an envoy standing outside.

"What do you want, Namhu?" said Shara tersely, his voice hoarse with sleep. When his eyes had adjusted to the brightness, he caught Namhu's gaze straying over his nakedness. "Seen enough?"

Namhu smirked. "You have been summoned to the Great Hall. The Sky-Father wants you there immediately."

"Leave me alone," Shara snapped, as much to the ghosts whispering in his head as to Namhu. He made to slam the door but it thumped hard against Namhu's hand and stayed open.

"You know Enlil doesn't like to be kept waiting." Namhu allowed himself another unhurried look at Shara from head to feet. "And put some clothes on." Then Namhu turned and walked away.

CHAPTER ONE

"YOU'VE BEEN SUMMONED to Valhalla, brother."

Yngvi groaned. It was a voice he was hoping not to hear, over the rhythmic soughing of the evening surf and the cries of the circling gulls. Especially not when he had only just settled into a chair outside Midgard's optimally located seaside tavern, placed a frothing mug of the barkeep's best brew on his thigh, and begun his wait. It wouldn't be more than a few minutes, he had estimated.

Beyond his shuttered eyelids, the waning sun had been a diffuse radiance until the speaker had blocked the light. "Magne," he said, without opening his eyes. "Are you following me?"

"You weren't home, so I've come to collect you."

Yngvi sighed and looked up into a mildly reproving green gaze.

On the battlefield, Magne was considered one of the fiercest warriors in the Midgardian army of Thor Odinson, second only to the god of Thunder himself. But now he was, like Yngvi, weaponless and wearing a simple, long-sleeved linen tunic over pants tucked into leather boots.

"Who wants me there?" Yngvi took a sip of his mead and gave Magne's thigh a backhanded swat with his other hand. "Stop hovering. Was it Thor?"

Magne had nine years and six inches on Yngvi, which meant that when he settled into the chair beside him, Yngvi, though bigger than the average Midgardian man, felt every bit the younger brother.

"You'd like that, wouldn't you?" Magne grinned with the assurance of one who knew he was Thor's chosen champion. "But no. This comes all the way from the top."

"The All-Father? Why me, why now, and why not you?"

"All very good questions that you can ask him." Magne's grin widened. "If you dare."

"He only calls when he needs us to fight," said Yngvi. "Or about Loki."

"Then there's probably a war brewing—"

"War? No, no, no. Look." Yngvi pointed with his chin at the bluish-white peaks fringing the skyline on his left, far beyond the placid waters that enisled Midgard. "It's all quiet in Niflheim." Then to his right. "Nothing happening in Muspelheim either," he said of the mountains simmering against the silent evening sky. "And if ice and fire can get along, so can the rest of Yggdrasil."

"Then, as you said, it must be Loki…"

"It can't be," said Yngvi.

He was extremely disinclined to leave his spot outside the tavern. The skies were clear, the setting sun was cool, and Loki, the trickster thorn in the collective Asgardian side, was far too unpleasant a subject to dwell on right now.

"That nuisance remains where Odin put him. I confirmed it myself."

Magne was not assuaged. "That was a month ago."

Yngvi shrugged. "It must have been someone else's turn today. You know he never calls the same warden twice in succession."

At Odin's direction four weeks ago, Yngvi had accompanied Hodur, Odin's blind son, to Loki's bespelled cave. As he had every time, Hodur had taken Yngvi's arm and led him through the massive boulder blocking the entrance. Even after years of doing so, passing through solid stone and emerging whole on the other side always left Yngvi somewhat unsettled. Once inside, he had described to Hodur everything he saw— the irons that still held Loki, naked and spreadeagled, on a rock; the serpent that remained coiled on the rocky ledge above Loki's head, dripping venom; Sigyn, still holding a bowl over her husband's face to collect the venom—for Hodur to relay to Odin.

"But it's been longer than—"

"It can't be Loki, and there hasn't been a war for years." Yngvi took another gulp of his drink, placed the mug on the ground and lounged deeper in his chair. He folded his hands lightly over his stomach and tipped his head back, enjoying the stretch in his neck. "Can't we keep it that way a little longer—?"

"Yngvi, you've always taken the gods a little lightly—"

"The gods, perhaps, but never the responsibility," said Yngvi. "You know that." He puffed his cheeks and blew out a slow breath of habitual frustration through pursed lips.

"I do, brother."

Magne, like their parents and grandparents before them, venerated the Asgardians, Odin in particular. Although, in fairness to his family, that was true of most Midgardians. But Yngvi had always, and more so since his last visit to the cave, been somewhat sparing with his regard.

"It's never troubled you," he asked, lolling his head to look at his brother, "that Odin can't trust his own children to watch over Loki? That he uses mortals to keep an eye on his immortal menace?"

A muscle jumped in Magne's jaw, and Yngvi knew what was coming.

"Never. And I would not presume to question the wisdom of the All-Father," said Magne, firmly, the unspoken *neither should you* explicit in his tone. "It is an honour"—he lifted his chin unconsciously on the word, as he always did—"that our family was among those chosen for that duty and responsibility."

Honour, duty and responsibility. The Ecklundson family credo, handed down by their grandparents, that Magne recited every so often. Yngvi sighed and let his eyes drift back to the open sky, calmed by the brush of the cool breeze, wet with sea-spray, over his face and ruffling his hair. He did not want to think of Loki any longer, not when it was only a few more minutes' wait. The anticipation was strong enough to bring back his good humour, and his lips were curved when he looked at Magne again.

"Well…I can't go to Valhalla just yet. I'm busy."

"Busy," said Magne flatly, taking in Yngvi's pose.

Yngvi knew how manifestly not busy he appeared, with his legs stretched out before him, crossed at the ankles. His arms were lifted now, fingers interlaced behind his head. And his hair, which he kept braided during battle, hung loose over the chairback. Even his jawline, which Magne teased him for keeping smooth contrary to the hirsute Midgardian fashion, had a faint shadow when seen up close.

"All right, then," he admitted, "I am *going* to be busy very soon."

"Doing what?"

"This and that," said Yngvi.

He kept his expression neutral and returned his eyes to his brother's so as to not stray to the marmoreal figure of the young man who was just then striding up to the tavern. But when Magne's attention shifted, Yngvi stole a look at the long limbs, the dark hair, the expression that was tetchier than when Yngvi first espied him earlier that day. The stranger's eyes passed over them without stopping as he entered. When Magne looked back at Yngvi, his brows were raised. Yngvi's lips quirked up.

"Not this again." Magne sighed, rubbing his beard and looking very much, Yngvi thought fondly, the long-suffering older brother. Then Magne gave him an impish smile. "Weren't you…disciplining…young Halli just two nights ago, or was it last night, for knocking you on the head?"

It was Halli last night, and Ulfe's daughter the night before, but it was also not Magne's or anyone else's concern. Yngvi straightened in the chair. "Who's the carrytale—"

"But I'm glad, even if it's only Halli. I was worried there was no one left on Midgard to interest you."

Yngvi didn't want to hear what Magne was sure to say next.

"Oh look," said Magne. He was laughing now. "Here he comes."

A gaggle of youths made their way over. "Captain," they said with a nod to Yngvi, and to Magne, "General."

"Boys," said Yngvi.

"So…Halli…" Magne grinned at the sapling who was heroically keeping his gaze from flitting to Yngvi. "I was just asking my brother how you knocked the Captain of *Thor's* armies on the head."

The young soldier opened his mouth. "General, I—"

"Halli," Yngvi cut in testily, "broke the rules of sparring. And for that he had to be punished."

"Halli, how dare you!" an older boy scolded, shoulders shaking helplessly. "Apologise at once to the Cap—"

"Shut up, Vidar," Halli muttered, shoving his elbow into his brother's arm hard enough to make him wince.

"Oh, he apologised," said Yngvi, with a husky laugh. He gazed up at Halli as he thought back to the boy's enthusiastic contrition in bed.

"Thrice," said Halli, with characteristically incautious pride that devolved into slow-blooming mortification. He averted his eyes. Colour filled his cheeks.

"Yes," added Magne. "I think all of Midgard felt *those* tremors, even if they were only little ones."

Tremors. The word shook Yngvi out of the joshing, his mind reluctantly pulled back to what he had witnessed in Loki's cave.

Sigyn's bowl had brimmed that day, four weeks ago. The aftereffects themselves were not novel; he and all of Yggdrasil continued to experience them over the years with sickening predictability. But never before had Yngvi *seen* it happen.

And he would never forget how, for the few seconds it took Sigyn to empty the bowl, Loki's face had been exposed to the serpent. His beaten, resigned gaze had locked with Yngvi's for a half-second that Yngvi would remember as long as he lived. Then Loki, bound by Odin's chains, had screamed, and Yngvi, bound by Odin's orders, had stared in mute horror, his stomach twisting tighter than Loki's body as it thrashed in pain from the few scattered drops of venom that fell onto his face in that time and sank into his flesh. Fumes had risen, dark and acrid, from where Loki's pale skin had blackened and peeled away under the poison; his wrists and ankles had grown bloodied from yanking hard on the chains that used to be his son's entrails before Odin transformed them to iron.

"Have you ever seen the tremors happen?" Yngvi asked, absently watching a pair of flapping, flustered gulls that had sat out the twirling aerobatics of their flock and one of which was, for some reason, sitting on the other.

"No, and I prefer not to, thank you," said Magne, with a warm chuckle. "But I imagine you both started like those mating gulls."

Yngvi only half-heard Magne, because his thoughts had returned to Loki's cave. So violent was that fleeting torment of Loki that Yggdrasil had quaked for nearly a half hour after, the tremors rippling outwards from the ground beneath their feet all the way to the ends of their world, while he and Hodur struggled to steady themselves against the wall of the cave. Yngvi had gaped, appalled and disbelieving, as the newly pocked skin of Loki's face and the bleeding bruises on his wrists and ankles slowly repaired themselves to their immortal wholeness.

They had left then, and Hodur had again obscured the cave from all eyes but his own sightless ones. Even if he never actually saw it transpire again, Yngvi now knew exactly what would happen the next time Sigyn's bowl filled to the top. And the next time, and the time after that, for eternity.

For all of Magne's lofty ideas about *duty* and *responsibility*, standing in the cave that day and witnessing another's everlasting agony had felt nothing like an honour.

"Yngvi?" said Magne, with a lopsided grin. "You were daydreaming. Was Halli that good?"

Yngvi forced a smile, but said nothing. He picked up his mug, quaffed the last of his drink to swallow the memory down, and placed it under his chair again. Deliberately ignoring the qualm that lingered, he let himself be pulled back in by the sound of laughter from the tavern and by the boys' cheers, which were growing bawdier with each jaunty thump on Halli's back.

But Halli was staring in the direction of the tavern door. Following the boy's gaze, Yngvi understood why: the stranger had stepped out; Halli had spotted the man; and, Yngvi supposed, his own proclivities were hardly a secret. His mood already lifting, he shifted in his seat to watch the stone-faced stranger and the group of catcalling barflies who had, tankards in hand, staggered out behind him.

"He—" said one drunk, sputtering as he laughed and pointed at the stranger. "He doesn't know where the gods live!" The others joined in on the guffaws, pausing their jeers only to chug their drinks.

But the pale man held himself as though he were alone outside the tavern. He was looking straight down the long street that cut across to the opposite coast. Even if he didn't know it, he was looking in the direction of Asgard.

"Hello," said Yngvi.

The stranger turned his head, and Yngvi waited for those grey eyes to settle on him. In the background, Magne and the youths were snickering.

"I've never seen you here before." Best not be threatening. "Where are you from?"

Magne leaned in. "Not Midgard," he said, his voice low enough for only Yngvi's ears.

Clearly. With skin paler than the ice of Niflheim and hair dark as the infernal depths of Helheim, the stranger seemed to exude a cold fire, and Yngvi, given time, would enjoy discovering whether that frosty exterior concealed a volcano underneath.

The silent eyes regarded him steadily. A Midgardian rock might have been more forthcoming.

"Alfheim?" he ventured pleasantly. The fey features were certainly lovely enough to belong to a dark-haired elf, rare though they were, but even that provenance did not fit. Something about this man was different.

He stood. "I'm Yngvi Ecklundson," he said with a smile. "And you are?"

The stranger gave a slow blink and returned to contemplating the horizon.

Magne, heartily and loudly inhabiting the role of irksome older brother, proffered an answer for the stranger. "I think that means he is not interested." Yngvi decided he would choke his brother later.

To be on the receiving end of a rebuff was foreign to Yngvi, and deeply unpleasant. The laughter behind him was louder now. No matter. Time to go for the kill. "I can take you to the gods," he said.

That returned the man's attention to Yngvi and earned him a question in the almost imperceptible lift of dark brows.

Encouraged, he moved in. "I could take you to Asgard."

This close, those grey eyes were the palest he had ever seen, like the colour of ice but flecked with deep blue and ringed with black, the gaze bright and keen under dark, heavy lashes.

"Who are you looking for? Thor?" he said, optimistically naming the god closest in appearance to himself.

"Thor?" said the stranger.

Yngvi immediately liked the warm timbre of his voice, incongruous with his icy bearing. The volcano had just become a little more probable.

"Is that your god of the Underworld?" the stranger asked.

"*My* god of—? Who's yours?" How many gods of the Underworld did this man think there were? And then, with a twinge of wariness, "Underworld?"

"Yngvi," said Magne from behind, a warning in his tone.

The stranger's lack of knowledge of Yggdrasil's gods was baffling, but his particular interest in the Underworld, however…that was perturbing. "That would be Loki," Yngvi said carefully.

"Loki…" the stranger repeated, brow furrowed, as if the name meant something to him.

It had begun to disturb Yngvi, this unwelcome recurrence of Loki in conversation and contemplation today. "What do you want with Loki?"

Magne, presumably having the same qualms, picked that moment to remind Yngvi of Odin's summons. "Yngvi, the All-Father is not known for his patience."

The stranger turned to Magne with newfound interest. "All-Father?"

Annoyed by his brother's interruption, Yngvi stepped in quickly to explain, but "Odin All-Father—" was as far as he got before an ear-splitting clarion cleaved the quiet dusk, sending a flock of startled, crying gulls flapping up into the dark sky.

"Gjallarhorn!" said Magne.

Yngvi whipped his head around at the sound, then back for one last glance at arctic eyes before instinct and training took hold of him in a galvanising instant and propelled him into a tear down Midgard's streets.

Because Heimdallr, the Guardian god, was calling; because that particular call—one long note followed by two short bursts, then another long note—was intended for him and Magne alone among the wardens; and because it meant one thing, and one thing only: Loki.

As his legs swallowed the distance between the tavern and his home, the boys and the stranger put out of his mind and Magne keeping pace beside him, Yngvi allowed himself to fully confront the misgiving he had shaken off earlier.

That it had been too long since the nine worlds of Yggdrasil had last quaked.

CHAPTER TWO

YNGVI THREW OPEN his door and picked up the weapons immediately accessible on the wall by the entrance.

He fastened his sword belt around his waist and slid the steel into its sheath. He slung his shield over his back, clutched his spear in his right hand. The rest of his armour—helmet, gauntlets and mail shirt—were on the bed at the far end of his longhouse, which meant they would be left behind. There was no time to armour up. His mind was a whirl of disquiet as he exited the back of his house to the narrow shed where his horse waited.

"Snabb!" he called.

The beast looked up at the sound of its name. Pleased to see its master, it snorted and pawed the ground. He untied Snabb, wrapped the reins around his left hand, and swung up onto the glossy, bare back. There was no time to saddle Snabb. "We've been summoned to Asgard." He rolled his shoulders. "Show me your name is deserved, boy. Swiftly now."

Snabb threw its head back with a nicker and set off apace in the direction of Asgard.

As Yngvi approached the perimeter of Midgard, where the streets converged into the exit road, Magne came up beside him on Sansad, Snabb's brother. The horses were named for their masters: sober and swift. The horses tossed their heads, never breaking stride, and whinnied in greeting.

Magne and Yngvi exchanged an urgent glance, spurred their mounts, and rode onto the icy Bifröst, the shimmering rainbow bridge that connected the land of the mortals with the realm of the gods.

Asgard.

They drew up at the Asgardian end of the Bifröst, expecting to be met by Heimdallr, but the Guardian god was absent from his post.

Leaving the frozen rainbow behind, they cantered over the open green plain that encircled Valhalla's high stone walls. Since Loki's last attack and subsequent confinement, Odin had seen fit to fortify Valhalla against the prophesied destruction of the gods: Ragnarök.

On this night, Yngvi counted a dozen Midgardian soldiers, three times the usual complement, patrolling the battlements on the visible front half of the walls, arrows and spears at the ready, the first line of defence against any invading force. He assumed a similar number watched the back.

The gates were already opening for them. Their shields bore the Ecklundson family crest: a carving of Thor's hammer, Mjölnir. The guards knew those shields, knew the brothers.

Their horses slowed as they approached the gates. Yngvi nodded at the two Midgardian sentries, and they rode past them into the empty courtyard, at the centre of which was situated the majestic home of the Aesir, three times as tall as it was broad, dwarfed by its high-flung central tower arrowing into the heavens.

"Where is everyone?" said Yngvi. The pricking unease he had felt in the pit of his stomach since leaving Midgard had sharpened to a spike of worry.

On any other day, Valhalla would be throbbing with activity—carnivals, contests, commemorations, or however else the Aesir chose to spend their days—long after darkness had fallen, but now the home of the gods was nothing more than a sprawling, deserted void with a beacon of white stone standing in solitary silence at its centre.

"This feels all wrong," said Magne.

They dismounted at the bottom of the steps that led up to the large wooden doors of Valhalla.

"Wait here, boy," Yngvi said to his horse. Snabb nodded and snorted. "Good."

"Come on," Magne urged, his boots clacking on the marble steps as he took them two at a time to the top. Yngvi followed.

Two armed Midgardian sentries flanked the doors, their faces obscured by their helmets.

"You're late," said one.

"Good luck," said the other.

Magne pushed the doors open.

The heavy panels of carved wood swung inwards noiselessly on well-oiled hinges, letting them into the vast outer hall with its soaring columns and vaulted ceiling. Empty of gods and guards, the only source of sound and movement were the fires in tall bronze braziers which were placed in stolid formation before each column.

Yngvi's first memory of this hall was of a ceremony he had attended with his family when he was five. Valhalla had been bright and celebratory that day when fourteen-year-old Magne and other boys his age were initiated into Odin's youth forces, and Yngvi had been impatient for nine years to pass quickly for his turn to arrive. Since that day, he had walked this way a hundred times or more, with his parents, with Magne, alone, and yet today felt different. The air had grown heavy, and it left him with a vague sense of apprehension.

Across the width of the outer hall, a hundred paces opposite the doors, was the arched curtained entrance to Odin All-Father's throne room. It was a private chamber restricted to the immortals and a select few Midgardians, including Yngvi and Magne, who, as Captain and General of Thor's Midgardian army, enjoyed the same unimpeded access as the mortal children of the gods.

Even from this distance, faint voices carried to them, muffled by the heavy crimson drape, but Yngvi caught snatches of heated conversation as they neared.

"She betrayed me!" Odin's voice was strident in the still silence, "My own daughter, an Aesir, betrayed me. And for whom? The one prophesied to end us all and destroy Asgard!"

Closer, he could hear Heimdallr's calm refutation.

"What happened with Sigyn was an age ago, Odin." Heimdallr's words carried the authority of an elder god, the only Aesir who would dare address Odin by name. "And it was love, not betrayal. The prophecy was not known then."

Magne lifted the curtain, and Yngvi followed him inside.

The nervous flutter of torches in wall sconces had created a fraught, flickering scene of the Aesir in council: the powerful gods of Asgard, and the Valkyries, their winged battle-maidens, all primed for war in gleaming armour. But if it was war that the Aesir expected, where was the rest of the war council? Where were the elders of Alfheim with their elven elites, the Vanir and their generals? The Dwarves?

The Aesir seemed to all be present, all one hundred of them, arrayed in a semicircle around the throne of Odin All-Father. Their backs were to the entrance, and Yngvi had a view of a near-identical panoply of polished silver, except for the one figure that was wearing gold and facing down Odin.

Besides himself and Magne, a dozen guardsmen were the only Midgardians in attendance. For all that the Aesir were geared for battle, the Midgardian armies had yet to be called up.

Under the quailing torchlight, the air in the throne room seemed to shiver with Odin's rage. But Yngvi knew of no untoward happenings that would explain the friction, the *dread*, in the hall. This extent of open discord between Odin and Heimdallr, oldest of the Aesir after Odin, was rare enough that Yngvi had never witnessed it in his twenty-five years.

He waited in silence with Magne, just inside the curtain, for a lull in the exchange. But Heimdallr was not finished.

"And for marrying Loki, you took what was rightfully hers as your firstborn and gave it to Thor when you chose him to lead Asgard. What reason did she have to stay? Or return?"

"She battled against me!"

"She battled alongside her husband. And so, her father condemned her to an eternity of watching her husband be tortured. Your distrust of your family, of the Aesir since then—"

"—You castigate me, old friend? What you term distrust, I call discretion. And it is that discretion that has kept the Aesir alive all this time."

"Until now," said Heimdallr, his veneer of calm suffering a slight disturbance before he collected himself. "I have held my peace all these years, Odin, but no longer. You say your discretion has kept us alive. But I say it is what has brought us to where we are today, with the fate of Yggdrasil held in the hands of men and a blind—"

"That's enough, Heimdallr!" Odin roared. "You forget yourself."

He surged to his feet to pace the floor, his polished white armour sparking orange whenever his restive form passed under the torches. He struck the marble floor with his spear in time with the fractious beat of his boots, like the impending battle march.

Heimdallr assumed a stony, smouldering silence. None of the other Aesir dared speak.

Magne must have deemed it a sufficiently long pause, because he stepped forward to announce himself and Yngvi. "All-Father," he said, his voice hushed with respect and awe.

The Aesir turned around in unison to face the brothers, as though glad for the interruption. They neatly divided into two groups of roughly equal numbers around Heimdallr and Odin, who stopped pacing and fixed them with his one good eye.

Yngvi went up to Odin, dropped to one knee and bowed his head. Beside him, Magne did the same.

"You're late," said Odin, in an unnerving echo of the sentry.

Yngvi stood, and frowned, because Tyr was watching him with a look of commiseration, his left hand tight around the pommel of his sword. *Good luck,* the other sentry had said. Yngvi opened his mouth to answer but Tyr lifted a cautionary arm. It was his right, and it ended in a stump. Fenrir, Loki's wolf-son, had ripped off the hand in the first battle. What had the guards known of what was happening inside?

Magne, also rising, said, "We came as soon as—"

"Enough!" Odin held up a hand. "Where is he?" he demanded of Yngvi.

"Who?" said Yngvi, automatically.

"Hodur! Where is Hodur?"

Yngvi remembered Magne's reproof outside the tavern and decided that keeping his own eyes on Odin's eyepatch would appear less disrespectful. It did not help that Odin's head came up to his nose. It helped even less that Odin had opened with an unwarranted interrogatory tack.

"I don't know where Hodur is," Yngvi said. "The last time I saw him was a month ago."

"Your brother has taken to lying, Magne," said Odin, still glaring up at Yngvi, his sour expression curdling when Yngvi tossed his head.

"I'm not lying," said Yngvi. "I have no reason to."

"All-Father—" Magne started, but Thor curtailed him with a finger.

"Let me handle this." Thor fixed his cold blue gaze on Yngvi. "What did you see yesterday?"

"Yesterday?" This entire line of questioning was incomprehensible to Yngvi. "What did I see where?"

"What is going on?" said Magne. "Thor, I don't understand—"

"Your *brother*," said Thor, lips drawing back from clenched teeth on the word, "came here last night and accompanied Hodur to Loki's cave. Yggdrasil should have quaked today. It has not." To Yngvi, "Tell us what you saw. Was Loki still bound?"

The shadows had stilled, and the torches had ceased their fluttering and burned steadily now, as though frightened into immobility by Thor. But it was not just the fires. The Aesir, too, did not move. Odin's heavy breathing was audible.

"Hodur and I went to Loki's cave *four weeks ago*," said Yngvi, enunciating each word precisely to leave little room for doubt or misunderstanding. "He must have told you everything about that day already. If he went there again yesterday, it was not with me." His voice, betraying its strapped-down exasperation, echoed a little in the unnatural quiet of the hall. "I was not called yesterday."

"I *know* you were not called," Odin shouted, "because I called *Ulfe*, and when he arrived, Hodur had already left with *you*."

It was becoming increasingly difficult for Yngvi to keep his answers polite. "I—" he started to say when, at the edge of his vision, he caught movement along the wall. It was one of the guardsmen. Even across the distance, the man seemed unsettled, as though the All-Father's edginess was transmitting itself to everyone present.

"Father, please," said Tyr, clasping his father's shoulder. Odin angrily shook his hand off.

Yngvi had to fight his irritation to keep his voice level. "I was in Midgard all of yesterday and all of last night. Whoever says they saw me with Hodur is mistaken."

He heard it then, the words that would seal the Aesir's judgement against him. Later, he would remember this as the moment the Aesir's trust in him was shattered.

"I am never mistaken," said Heimdallr, his gravitas implying that his assertion was a fact as inviolate as the cycle of day and night. "*I* let you in, Yngvi. And I saw you leave with Hodur."

Yngvi followed the glint of gold and the deep voice to face the recrimination in Heimdallr's flashing eyes.

Yngvi shook his head. "That was not me." He had a passing thought that Halli could confirm that they had spent the night together, but discarded it in the next instant. If the word of the Captain of Thor's armies was not good enough for the Aesir, that of a soldier in training was worth nothing. There was only one plausible explanation. "It must be some sort of trickery… Someone must have cast an illusion—"

No sooner had he said it than he grasped its self-defeating implication. Thor did, too. An illusion strong enough to deceive Heimdallr could only be the work of two immortals, one of whom was missing and the other imprisoned.

"You mean, an illusionist like Loki?" Thor challenged.

Heimdallr laughed at that, a haughty sound. "Yngvi, if you are about to suggest that someone assumed your appearance and entered Valhalla, you are forgetting that nothing and no one on Yggdrasil is obscured from me."

Except Loki and his cave? Did the gods ever entertain the possibility that they were not infallible? "I don't know who or what you saw, but it was not me—"

"This is pointless!" Odin slammed his spear-butt on the floor. The strike of metal on marble rang in the sprawling hall.

Magne stepped forward to stand beside Yngvi. "Heimdallr, do *you* not see Hodur?"

"I do not. If he was taken to Loki's cave"—Heimdallr shot an accusatory, sidelong glance at Odin—"you know that none but Hodur can find it."

Yngvi could barely suppress the low, scornful breath that left him. He thought for a moment. Then, "Vör might know where Hodur is."

And for the third time in minutes, he knew as soon as he said it that it was in vain. Nothing was concealed from the goddess of Knowledge, except, of course, the location of Loki's cave. In the brief yet inexplicably tense pause that ensued, Yngvi's eyes searched Thor, Tyr, Heimdallr, Odin, the gathered Aesir. And then he spotted it, an absence, chillingly conspicuous now.

"Where is Vör?" he asked, almost loath to receive the answer.

"Dead!" Thor shouted. "She's dead!"

The impossible implications of that word rippled across the hall, stirring agitated murmurs among the Aesir as the tension of uncertainty rose from their rigid, armoured bodies to fill the enclosing space of the arched throne room.

"Dead?" said Magne, his voice hushed. "How can that be?"

Yngvi said nothing. He had never truly worried that Ragnarök might occur because his mind could not conceive a *dead immortal.* Was it even immortality if it was for a limited time? A full-body shudder had him clutching his spear to remain upright. But with that one word, it was as though his world had toppled, and everything he had believed all his life had been thrown into disarray.

"We don't know!" said Thor. "Sif found her a few hours ago, lying in her chambers."

"But she had been dead for two weeks," said Eir, going up to Thor. Her voice was soft where her brother's had been resonant. "But I found no wounds, or signs of a struggle. She was just lying on the floor in a lifeless heap, as if she had fallen dead. Her eyes were open and she seemed...astonished. And there was nothing I could do to bring her back."

If Vör's condition was beyond the skills of even the goddess of Healing and Medicine, she had truly died, however impossible that prospect had been a few minutes ago.

"And if Vör can die, we all can!" said Thor, giving voice to what every single Aesir was, undoubtedly, telling themselves.

"No one could have foreseen this situation with Vör," said Magne, with a hopeful, almost pleading look at Thor and Odin. "Or Hodur." But it was a wasted attempt at placation.

"My daughter is dead. My blind son is missing," said Odin. "And we don't know where Loki is. What we do know is that Hodur left Valhalla last night, and Yngvi was with him."

Every Asgardian's eyes, glimmering like hard-cut jewels, turned to Yngvi.

"There's more," said Odin. "Tell them what you saw, Heimdallr."

"The ice and fire realms have stirred," said the Guardian god. "Hel is marshalling her forces."

"Hel?" said Magne. "She hasn't left Helheim since the last war, since you captured her father."

"I have seen her fiends in Niflheim," said Heimdallr, "meeting with the leaders of the ice giants, and Hel, herself, in Muspelheim, among the fire giants. We think she is plotting Loki's escape. There is trouble brewing."

The guardsman had slinked to the edge of the group, putting him closer to the gods, close enough that Yngvi could see his eyes. They were keen and attentive. Then Yngvi turned cold. Because those eyes were also ice-coloured with blue flecks.

Yngvi's mind throbbed. He ran a hand through his hair.

On the heels of the initial alarm that the stranger had made it into Valhalla unnoticed by Heimdallr came a flood of embarrassment that he had watched Yngvi be upbraided by Odin. But it passed as quickly as it had come, because his Captain's mind took over, and in the space of a few moments, ran quickfire through the possibilities.

Was it the stranger who had impersonated Yngvi yesterday? How had he infiltrated Asgard? Where had he got the guardsman's uniform? *Why* was he here? The stranger had first started at the mention of Loki's cave, and now again at Vör's death. Was he spying for Loki? Or Hel? Yngvi recalled the darkness he had sensed in the stranger outside the tavern. Was he from Helheim?

Yngvi had taken a step towards the guardsmen to confront the man when Odin spoke. The impulse of ingrained deference turned his head in Odin's direction for a split-second, but when he looked back, the stranger was not among the guards.

"We have to prepare," said Odin. "We all know the prophecy."

They all did, even the children, who were taught the prophecy as soon as they said their first words. *When Yggdrasil ceases to quake, Ragnarök begins.*

"Then where are the Elves, the Dwarves?" Yngvi asked, and added, despite Magne's warning glare, "Why haven't the Vanir been called up? And the Midgardian army?"

Odin fixed Yngvi with his excoriating eye, his lips curling back from his teeth. He did not say a word and did not need to, because Yngvi, for all the righteous outrage at his own undeserved discredit, shrank under the All-Father's withering glare.

"Forgive me, All-Father," said Yngvi, dropping his head.

Odin drew himself to his full height. "Heimdallr, it is time."

Heimdallr nodded, and strode out of the throne room.

Yngvi exchanged a tense look with Magne, whose knuckles were white around his spear.

The Midgardian army would soon arrive in Valhalla. Magne and he had trained their soldiers for this very day, putting them through drill after drill on horseback, on foot, with weapons, and hand-to-hand combat, and pushing them past the limits of their endurance until they knew their unswerving objectives on the battlefield as well as their own names. kill the enemy; protect your fellow soldiers; and if death were the consequence, make it honourable and make it count.

Outside, Heimdallr sounded the summons. Yngvi had expected Gjallarhorn's blast to be a single extended note issued thrice at brief intervals, Asgard's loud and urgent call to its allies among the nine realms. What he heard, instead, was a truncated burst; the clang of metal; a thunderous crash.

Odin and Thor were shouting out orders, but abandoning all regard for protocol, Yngvi slapped the curtain out of his way and ran to the doors. It was too soon for this much activity. Outside, he stopped short beside Heimdallr, and saw what the Guardian god saw: that it was the summons that had been sounded too late.

Because the gates of Valhalla had been blown open. They hung like decaying teeth, held up by a single hinge on either side, swaying in the wind. Two lifeless bodies, slumped on the ground, formed small silhouettes against the dark plains beyond. The loss of lives had begun, and as it had in the first and second wars, it had begun with the Midgardians, with the two sentries at the gates.

The sky was pitch, churning chaos, moonless and starless, the hollow courtyard filled with the tormented wails of angry winds. Far beyond the walls was a diffuse, orange glow.

And Yngvi watched, aghast, as the breach in the high stone walls was filled by three unmistakable figures: Sigyn and Hel on massive war horses, and Loki's writhing serpent son, Jörmungandr.

They parted to make way for another. And through the gap, astride his colossal wolf-son, Fenrir, came the nemesis of the Aesir himself. Loki.

"Come out, you cowards!" Loki's cry reverberated in the quad. He tugged on his wolf's fur, and Fenrir bounded ahead, followed by Sigyn, Hel and Jörmungandr.

Magne came up beside Yngvi, spear and shield in battle-ready position. The Aesir streamed out around them. Yngvi could feel the gusts from the Valkyries' beating wings as they hovered above.

Before today, it would have been absurd to fear the portended massacre of Ragnarök, when confronting Loki's faction of three gods and two monsters was the entire immortal might of Asgard. Two wars Loki had waged against the Aesir after the prophecy had been proclaimed, two wars in which the casualties had been giants and monsters, demigods and mortals. Asgard's numbers had remained unchanged. Until today.

The two sides held, waiting to see who would strike the first blow. Although Loki had already struck, because the battlements showed no activity, no sign of the sentries who were presumably dead. And on the edges of Yngvi's burgeoning horror at the situation was a moribund hope that their horses had saved themselves.

The Aesir's high-strung mood was palpable, and Yngvi's own body was taut with tension.

As Odin descended the steps, flanked by Thor and Heimdallr, the luminescence from the Guardian god's golden armour revealed four partial equine shapes beside the steps. A second look showed Yngvi that they were two heads that had been sliced clean from the two bodies. Snabb and Sansad. Nausea rolled up to his throat, and he felt himself sway. He pushed down on the grief when he felt Magne's hand clasp his arm. There would be time for grieving later.

His hand tightened around his spear when Odin spoke.

The All-Father had stopped halfway between the tower and Loki. "How did you get out?"

"Did you really think," Loki snarled, "that a blind god and a handful of mortals could hold me there for eternity?"

"Where's Hodur?" Thor demanded.

Loki smiled and nodded to Hel. She reached behind her saddle, pulled a burlap sack off her horse and flung it towards the Asgardians. It was too big for its slight contents and landed with a rattling thud, rolling to a stop halfway between her and Thor. The loose cloth had dipped here and there into the emaciated hollows of the body-shaped lump inside, which was seemingly stripped of its flesh, and unmoving.

Another dead immortal.

"He begged for mercy," said Sigyn. "I gave him to your serpent for a while, then to mine." Her lips curved when Jörmungandr hissed. "There's very little of him left. Bones, perhaps—"

"He was your brother!" said Odin.

"My brother died," said Sigyn, "the day he became the architect of my husband's torment."

"I'll kill you!" Thor roared, splitting the dark sky with a loud crack and a blistering flash of white. He had begun to charge, but Odin flung out an arm, and Heimdallr and Magne bodily held him back, struggling to contain his wrathful might.

"This is the day you die, All-Father," said Loki. "All of you. Starting with Hodur."

But not Vör two weeks ago? Yngvi felt in his bones the cold certainty that today was nothing like Loki's past attacks on Valhalla. The oddly vulnerable vigilance in Odin's rigid stance seemed to have afflicted the rest of the Aesir.

"Is it?" said Odin, after a pause, his voice hard. "You come here with your family to destroy mine. Do you think I will allow that to happen? I have all of Asgard with me. The Elves and the Dwarves will be here soon.

And the Vanir. You'll be surrounded. And I will end you and your family where you stand."

Loki threw his head back and laughed. He shook his head, still laughing. "They are not coming. I killed a few of their immortals and gave the rest a choice. They saw my armies, and chose to live."

"Your armies?" asked Odin.

If even a single Asgardian was not, in that moment, recalling farsighted Heimdallr's visions, the Aesir's chances against Loki were not good.

Loki turned his head slightly and called out, "Break the walls!"

An explosion of rock and dust, and moments later, the walls ruptured, and massive boulders crashed to the ground. More and more wall fell to reveal hundreds of giants standing almost as tall as the barricade, smashing bodily through the high stone.

Wave upon wave of Loki's armies stampeded in, breaking through Valhalla's soaring, purportedly impermeable defences as easily as through sand, pummelling with fists and shoulders and feet until all around was only flat land: the marble expanse fringed by a wide circle of detritus where the walls had been, the open fields of Asgard beyond. And as far as the eye could see, lit by the glare of fire giants, blue was interspersed with orange and black, as the giants of Niflheim and Muspelheim, and Hel's shadow fiends bringing up the rear, bore down on the Asgardians.

"Kill every last one of them!" Loki shouted, and put his heels into Fenrir.

Yngvi's stomach dropped.

Because this was Ragnarök.

And all of Asgard believed that it had begun on his watch.

CHAPTER THREE

IT WAS PANDEMONIUM: the crash of giants; the Valkyries' high-pitched, ululating battle cries as the winged warriors took to the air. On the ground, a thundering collision as gods and demigods, led by Thor and Odin, met the onslaught head-on.

It was not an even fight.

Magne and he had weapons but no armour; the Aesir were all on foot, having had no time to gather their mounts; and bearing down on them were Loki's armies, which had the advantage of sheer size or being mounted on horse- or wolf-back. Even with the Valkyries swooping down to pick off fiends and rip them apart, even with Thor's hammer smashing through hordes of giants, the Aesir would be vanquished.

A sudden wet spray on his face was Yngvi's first sign that the slaughter of Asgard had begun. Sif and Tyr, who had been fighting a few feet away, now lay on the ground, sparking holes in their chests where blasts of energy from Loki's spear had cut clean through their armour, the white flagstones growing dark around them. Ragnarök was unfolding before his eyes.

Yngvi knew he still lived only because a dead mortal would not tilt the balance of power the way a dead Aesir would, and there remained scores of immortals to kill. He wiped his face on his sleeve. It came away wet and black with the blood of the dead Aesir. Seeking the thickest part of the fight, he charged. He swung his sword over his head at the giants circling him, gratified by their dying screams as he drove deeper into the claustrophobic fray.

Hours later, his shield had shattered, his sweaty tunic stuck to his body in dark patches. Long after that, his tunic was torn, his forearm slashed, his own blood mingling with that of dead monsters, his boots soddened with the watery remains of ice giants that had fallen to his sword. His mouth was dry, his chest heaved, and every breath was a burning, open-mouthed rasp. And still he fought, fuelled by a single thought that overrode all others: Loki had brought his ruin to Asgard, and for that, Loki would have to die.

When the moonless night stretched on and morning did not come, Yngvi remembered that even this was presaged: Loki's monsters had swallowed Mani and Sol, and with them the light of the moon and the sun, to plunge all of Yggdrasil into unending night. Under starlight and the glow of fire giants, he let loose with his weapons on the tumult around him to carve a gruelling channel of death through Loki's forces until he reached the gates.

By then, Yngvi's wound was a dry, powdery streak of red on his forearm, his right shoulder cramped from the unrelenting effort of shearing through the giants, and his left arm burned from repeatedly deploying his spear like a long knife to gouge out the eyes and vitals of Loki's demons.

Later, he threw his spear across the yard to impale a giant before it could pummel the unprotected head of a fallen Valkyrie. Sword and dagger were all that kept him standing, while around him, giants and monsters fell. Exploiting a few seconds' respite, he slipped his dagger into his boot and freed a hand to wipe his clumped hair out of his eyes. He hoicked up a dead giant's axe in his left hand, sword in his right, and drove back into the press of warring frost and flame.

A loud hiss from his left, then a shout. In Magne's voice.

Yngvi's reflexes sent him rushing in the direction of the cry, but Hel's shadows descended around him in a circle, attacking as one. With a shout, he put sword and axe to lethal use, cutting, smiting and thrusting until there was only the scythe-like sweep of his blades and tattered shadows falling around him, their shrieks nearly drowning out a swelling rumble, the pounding of hooves, the knocking of swords on shields.

A disturbing thought occurred: if those were Loki's reinforcements, the Asgardian resistance would crumble like sand underfoot. But as mounted figures ruptured the thicket of Loki's forces with familiar armour and battle cries, Yngvi experienced a moment of paralyzing relief.

The Midgardian army had answered Heimdallr's unfinished call.

With sword and axe, spear and sling, the Midgardian riders broke through the wall of giants, slicing their way in with the agility of foot soldiers. Minutes later, Vidar and Halli had reined in beside Yngvi. He swung up on Halli's horse behind him, gave his orders, then left Vidar to carry them out.

As Halli's horse forded a thinner part of the fighting on its way to Magne, Yngvi looked back once at Vidar and the Midgardians. Those young fighters had never faced death before; this was their first real battle, and he felt a captain's pride to watch them apply their training with killing effect.

Nimble on their mounts, the soldiers worked in pairs. One engaged an ice giant, the other a fire giant, drawing them ever closer. And when the behemoths' lumbering momentum made them unstoppable at close range, the soldiers rode hard out of the way. Fire and frost might fight on the same side, but make them collide and their natural opposing propensities would do the rest. Why fight if you can get the enemy to kill itself?

But the satisfaction was short-lived. Yngvi's stomach dropped. Magne had lunged at Jörmungandr's tail, but the monster turned swiftly on its middle and spewed a stream of noxious green. Magne fell to his knees, hands covering his face as Jörmungandr slithered closer and opened its mouth. Yngvi had seen those maws pulverise boulders. Magne's head would crack like a seed.

Had Yngvi believed in the gods' power, he would have begged them to protect his brother. But what good was it to invoke gods who could not protect themselves?

Yngvi was still too far when he caught a glint to his left. He jerked his head up just as a javelin sailed past him to find Jörmungandr's eye and sink in. Blood spurted from the monster's blinded eye. It faltered, shrieking and spewing poison indiscriminately, burning Aesir and giants alike, as it retreated to the edge of the courtyard, where the gates had been.

When Halli's mount was as close to Magne as it could get in the fracas, Yngvi gripped Halli's shoulder, and as soon as the horse slowed, swung off the saddle and rushed towards Magne, shredding whatever dared to get in his way.

Yngvi sprinted to Magne's side, looked for the thrower of the javelin, and started. It was the stranger, and he was looking at Yngvi. He nodded once. Disbelieving but grateful, Yngvi nodded back as he dropped to his knees beside his brother.

"Magne!"

"I'm all right," said Magne, wiping his reddened, watering eyes. "I'll be all right. Go!"

Yngvi thrust Magne's sword into his open hand, hefted his own sword and axe, and cut his way back to Jörmungandr, leaving a trail of bodies behind him.

Thor, holding Mjölnir aloft, also raced towards the serpent. Heeding their master's call, fraying threads of blinding light converged in the dark sky and poured into his hammer. Still running, he hurled the power-saturated weapon at Jörmungandr's head, and as prophesied, Mjölnir crashed into the serpent's skull. Thor let out a wild laugh at the awful crack of bone. The monster floundered, whipping up its tail to stay upright. But Thor was focused on the hammer, which was already rebounding to his outstretched hand. He was too close to the serpent.

"Get back!" Yngvi shouted, but his voice was lost in the din. Had Thor forgotten how that prophecy ended? Had he forgotten that Jörmungandr would kill him?

Jörmungandr's flailing tail slammed into Thor's back, shattering his armour, the scales ripping his skin.

Thor's roar of pain shook the skies as he crashed to the ground. With no hand to arrest it, Mjölnir flew past Thor and pulverised the courtyard where it fell, lodged firmly in a marble crater. None but Thor could extricate the hammer. Without it, Thor was just another Aesir. And without Thor, the Aesir would be decimated. Yngvi banished the fleeting, foolish hope that the stranger might return to save the gods.

But he had. The stranger was back beside Thor.

In one smooth move, he leaned down briefly to thrust the hilt of the guardsman's sword into Thor's loose, unresponsive fist, conjured a flaming blade and charged towards Jörmungandr on its blind side. Sensing his approach, the serpent slithered around to fix its uninjured eye on him.

Between sword strikes to fend off attacking giants, Yngvi glimpsed the stranger launch himself from a proximate body and arc through the air, holding his weapon aloft with both hands; and as he landed, he brought the strip of fire down on the serpent's middle. Jörmungandr's screech cleaved the air as its own body was cut in half and thudded to the ground in two thrashing pieces.

Pungent venom jetted wetly from the serpent's dying mouth as Yngvi ran to Thor's side, simultaneously tucking the axe handle into his belt and sheathing his blade. He gripped Thor's arm with both hands to wrench him out of the trajectory of the poison. But after hours—or days? there was no way to tell—of relentless, brutal fighting, Thor's seven feet of muscle and sinew and bone proved too heavy for Yngvi's diminishing strength, and he grunted long and loud with the effort.

When Yngvi let go of him, Thor thudded to the ground, his skin corroding where more than a few drops of venom had landed on his unprotected torso. But the serpent had been beaten; its writhing sibilance gradually faded to silence. Jörmungandr was dead.

Movement in the background. The fallen fighter who had served as the stranger's launchpad was slowly pushing off his helmet and rolling onto his back. *Her* back. Long, dark hair spilled out to stream over the bloodied marble. Her chest swelled with one last desperate breath, then fell, her head lolling to the side. It was Sigyn. And her lifeless eyes were resting on her dead serpent son.

The stranger stood with a foot on Jörmungandr, his fire-blade sizzling in his hand. As if feeling eyes upon him, he turned his head and met Yngvi's gaze. Yngvi stared.

That brief lapse in attention was a mistake.

"Behind you!" the stranger shouted.

Yngvi spun around, steel singing as he drew his sword out of its sheath. He swept the blade blindly, slicing off the leg of a frost giant below the knee. The destabilised leviathan teetered dangerously, and it took Yngvi all of his strength to dive out of its path a second before it crashed to the ground in a landslide of ice pebbles. But the relentless fighting had slowed his reactions, and he was still on the ground when another mass of looming giants besieged him. He swung his sword from a kneeling position, his flagging strength offering negligible protection against his assailants. But he was not alone. The air hissed, and moments later, the giants around him fell backwards, fire-tipped arrows lodged in their chests.

The stranger was holding a glowing bow. He opened his hand, the bow dematerialised, and his sword reappeared in his grip.

Anything Yngvi might have said was forestalled by the shock of an enormous black wolf landing before them. Loki, astride Fenrir, was staring at the stranger with—unbelievably—recognition. Yngvi registered too late that Fenrir's attention was on him, and a swipe of its massive paw sent him sprawling onto his back. His head struck the marble hard. The last thing he saw before everything turned bright white was a horde of shadow fiends flying towards him. And the last thing he heard was Loki's voice.

"So...you've caught up to me at last, Shara."

When consciousness returned, he was alone, left for dead among the strips of shadow.

He ran his fingers gingerly over his head, hissing softly when he touched the small, painful swelling where he had hit the ground. He looked about at the dark forms around him and knew the sword that had shredded them. It was the stranger's—Shara's.

Shara. What kind of name was that? And how did Loki know him?

But now was not the time for questions. From the distance came a reverberating, triumphant howl, and Yngvi jerked his head to follow the sound beyond the gates of Valhalla just as Fenrir opened its massive jaws and swallowed Odin whole.

This, too, had been foretold.

Yngvi drew his sword and ran, his beaten legs thumping onwards to the fields past the gates. Heimdallr caught up to him, and together they cut their way through to the carnage Fenrir had unleashed on the Midgardian forces.

Metal collided with rock as three frost giants assailed the Guardian god, who effortlessly hewed them into blocks of dead ice. Yngvi kept running, until a scream of pain stopped him in his tracks. As he spun around, a rope of white energy lashed itself around Heimdallr's axe-wielding arm and cut it cleanly at the wrist. The severed hand fell to the ground, twitching, its fingers still clutching his weapon. A fountain of black blood spurted from the stump as Heimdallr faced Hel, panting hard, defenceless and on his knees.

White fire sparked at the tip of Hel's unfurling whip and hit Heimdallr in the middle of his chest. His breastplate splintered into golden fragments as his body curved around the bolt, flew backwards into the bottom half of a nearby shattered pillar and crumpled to the ground. Hel strode up to the guardian and delivered the death blow.

With Hel's back to him, Yngvi dove for Heimdallr's amputated hand, wrested the axe from the tight fist and lunged at Fenrir. When he struck the beast's flank, the divine axe drew blood and a bestial whine that rent the air as the wolf thudded to the ground.

Hearing her brother's cry, Hel lifted a hand, and Yngvi was instantly hemmed in by three fire giants. He yanked Heimdallr's axe free of the wolf's flesh and started to slash at the burning blockade.

When the last giant was extinguished, Yngvi leaned his weight on the axe. His torso was heaving, and wet with sweat and blood, too much of it his own. Standing upright on his exhausted legs was proving unsustainable. As he watched Shara end a monster at the far end of the yard, the air behind Yngvi crackled as he was smothered by more fire giants.

Visible through a gap in the flaming circle was the figure of Shara racing towards him, the bodies of the dead like an obstacle course on his way. Yngvi swung the axe in a feeble, mechanical attempt at self-protection, lurching his body into an unsteady spiral from the weight of the weapon and almost falling over in the process; two flaming demons screamed and vapourised. Yngvi swung again.

But this time, it was he who cried out. A sudden, blistering agony burst over his left shoulder. A fire giant had evaded his blade and struck, searing the skin on his back. His legs buckled, and he collapsed to the ground, unarmed, watching helplessly as the monster reached down to incinerate him. But it never did.

A blue strip cut the giant into tendrils of scorching vapour. Then another giant was ribboned, and another, until all the fiery forms around Yngvi had dissipated, leaving only Yngvi, and Shara holding his sword edged with blue fire. The skin behind Yngvi's shoulder burned.

Hel fought a clutch of Midgardians some distance away, but a heavy tread approached, crunching gravel with each step.

"Why won't you die, Shara?" said a man's voice.

Trailed by a mass of shadow monsters, Loki strolled up to face Shara. Yngvi flung Heimdallr's axe at Loki's legs. The blade bounced off his flesh and clattered to the ground, but it got Loki's attention. He fixed Yngvi with an annihilating look. Yngvi glared back.

Leaving the shadows to occupy Shara, Loki sauntered up to Yngvi, clucking softly. "Did you enjoy what you saw in the cave that day, warden of mine?" He appraised Yngvi's battered, unarmed body, and touched the tip of his spear to Yngvi's chest. "I left the job half done when I killed your parents. But the Ecklundson line ends today."

Bile rose to the back of Yngvi's throat; the impotent fury of memories burned on his tongue, and his eyes stung. The dagger tucked in his boot was out of reach, but his empty hands did not fly up in instinctual self-defence. He was strangely unafraid, and in the moment he acknowledged that, he also knew why.

The shadows' shrieks had died; the blast of energy never came, and it was Loki who cried out. His spear had fallen from his open hand and a flaming arrow was lodged in his wrist. When he used his other hand to pull it out, the arrow dissipated into blue wisps. Blood oozed, thick and black, from the puncture in his wrist.

Rounding on Yngvi's unlikely protector, Loki reached for his sword just as Yngvi lunged at him, slipping the dagger out of his boot as he did, and seizing Loki by the waist. But he was a wounded mortal tackling a raving god. Loki swatted him off as he would an insect and Yngvi again crashed onto his burned shoulder.

Madness flashed in Loki's eyes a moment before pain exploded in Yngvi's cheekbone; Loki's fist smashed into his face, snapping his head to the side and splitting the skin on his cheek. That pain registered only briefly, because agony speared like fire down his body through the wound in his shoulder. Loki dug his fingers into the scorched skin while he pummelled Yngvi's torso with his other fist.

The blows rained down with no method, no finesse. It might have been less than a minute, but felt like an eternity of being battered by a manic god. Disgusted by the powerlessness brought on by physical pain, Yngvi made himself move past the sensation until it was no more than a dull annoyance in the background. He slashed his knife upwards at Loki's waist.

The blade didn't catch flesh, but Loki's grip on his wound changed, dragging on his skin as if to hold on, because he was being bodily lifted off Yngvi. A moment later, Loki arced through the air and landed on a mound of dead soldiers. Shara lowered his arm and dropped to his knees.

He scanned Yngvi for wounds and stopped on Yngvi's cheek. "Are you all right?"

Yngvi's shoulder felt like it was on fire, but he nodded. His knife had sliced through Loki's sword-belt. Blade and scabbard were within reach. "I'll free Odin. Get Loki," he said. Shara rose, but Yngvi grasped his arm, holding him back. "Kill him."

Shara pulled Yngvi to his feet, then set off towards Loki, fire-blade in hand.

Yngvi unsheathed Loki's sword and reeled towards Fenrir. The wolf lay on its side, incapacitated by the oozing wound in its flank. Yngvi brought the sword down on the groaning beast's distended belly. The furred flesh split and Fenrir let out a howl of pain that shook the ground.

With the stony detachment of an executioner, Yngvi retracted the sword and, putting the full weight of his body behind the strike, brought it down again, dragging the blade lower, relishing the sound of the monster's flesh tearing as he extended the gash and ripped it open.

The wolf's eyes rolled back into its head and its life pulsed out of its body with its blood. The lining of its dead stomach moved, peaked to a point, and a steel blade perforated the flesh. A sword sliced the beast open from the inside and the All-Father emerged, covered in blood. A wave of his hand down his body erased all evidence of Fenrir's innards and restored him to his shining self.

"Yngvi," he said, curtly. Then he raised his sword and summarily cleaved Fenrir's head from its body. Without another look at Yngvi, he charged into a nearby swarm of giants plaguing a pair of fallen Valkyries.

Panting hard, Yngvi assessed the damage. The Aesir and Midgardians had cut a swathe through Loki's armies. Loki's monster sons were dead; his wife was dead. And the remnants of Hel's forces were being dispatched by the surviving Valkyries.

Even though any utility he had on the battlefield had long since been expended, Yngvi teetered back to where Shara fought Loki. Because this was one death he needed to witness with his own eyes.

Loki still fought, fuelled by a feverish energy, his moves growing desperate against Shara, who was an inexorable force, his weapon a blur of blue fire.

Loki started to make mistakes. His heel caught on the body of a dead soldier and he floundered, arms flailing in an ungainly struggle to stay upright and exposing his chest. Shara exploited his advantage, and with ruthless precision drove his sword into Loki's heart.

Loki collapsed on the rubble, impaled by the fire-blade which was burning a hole in his chest. But he was, incredibly, still breathing. He lifted his head and put out an arm, scrabbling for his spear only to find it lying at Shara's feet. Loki's hand twitched, but Yngvi, calling up his strength for one last surge, swiped up the shaft, and invoking the image of his dead parents, plunged it with both hands into Loki's chest next to the fire-blade. Then he fell to his knees beside Loki's body.

Shara grabbed the spear and twisted it deeper into Loki's chest, his face expressionless as Loki's body went into a paroxysm of hacking coughs, blood frothing at his mouth.

Then, with a final shudder, Loki's body stilled.

CHAPTER FOUR

SHARA YANKED LOKI'S spear from his chest and regarded it for a moment, a glimmer of fulfilment passing over his face. Then he lifted his knee and broke it in two over his thigh. The weapon snapped with a small explosion of sparking energy. Its glow faded and the two halves clattered to the ground, rods of metal as lifeless as the body of their master.

Loki's torso jerked once; his mouth opened, as if pried from the inside, and a bluish plume arose to hover over his body, seemingly resolving into the shape of a man. But no more than its head had formed before Shara retrieved his sword from Loki's chest and slashed at it. The entity sundered into ribbons of vapor and vanished.

Shara's shoulders dropped; he fell to his knees and sat back on his heels. His hands lay on his thighs, palms up. His sword had disappeared from his grip.

Seeing Shara like that, head thrown back, eyes closed, chest heaving with his open-mouthed breaths, gave Yngvi his first inkling that the battle was, finally, truly, over.

It came then, all at once, everything he had not allowed himself to fully feel before now. The utter exhaustion of battle; his face, battered by Loki; his shoulder, burned by a fire giant; the gashes on his arms; his leaden, unsteady legs. His eyes burned and watered. His parched mouth wouldn't close, and grew drier from gulping in the heat and dust of battle. He would give up a limb for a cup of water. A continuous tremor ran through the enervated muscles of his arms and back. If a giant were to so much as breathe in his direction, he would fall.

Loki was dead, but only Yngvi and Shara knew that. He wanted to know why Loki's death seemed as crucial to Shara as it was to the Aesir, because Shara hadn't even known who Loki was. He would ask him that, but later. For now, there was something he had to do.

Swaying precariously, he picked his way through the bodies to the place where Heimdallr lay. A faint tingling at the back of his neck, like the scratch of an invisible nail, meant that he was being followed. He turned around, expecting to see Shara but saw something else, something he had seen Shara kill.

The blue phantasm had returned and was floating closer.

Yngvi had never seen a god die before. If this was the remnant of Loki's spirit, it must be seeking another vessel. But he would be damned to Helheim before he allowed Loki to take over his body.

It seemed to be looking at his waist. Instinct made him draw his sword and slash the air between them. But swifter than his blade, the entity recoiled and dissipated in a startled burst of blue. Yngvi's gaze swept the courtyard for evidence of blue vapour, but there was only wreckage and blood and death. The skies seemed emptier now, with fewer Valkyries in the air; the ground, too, had calmed, with fewer giants and mortals still upright.

He hefted the sword—Loki's sword. His own was lost somewhere among the bodies. And this was an excellent weapon, beautifully forged. A large blue gemstone was set in the hilt. He traced the curious engraving of entwined snakes at the base. He slid the blade into his scabbard and lifted his gaze to the sky where the roiling shadows that had plunged the heavens into enduring night had begun to clear.

A pale light was rising from the eastern horizon. It was Mani. He had been returned to the sky, and his moonbeams would soon drench all of Yggdrasil in their benevolent radiance.

Yngvi resumed his search and found Gjallarhorn still hanging from Heimdallr's belt. He drew in a deep, long breath as he lifted the horn to his lips, and blew on it as hard as his exhausted lungs could manage.

His strident proclamation of victory for the Aesir must have reached the far edges of the battle because the surviving invaders, led by Hel, began to retreat. Like a dark tide receding from rutted shores, they fled, leaving behind their ruin on a shattered expanse strewn with lifeless bodies.

Ragnarök had ended, but not as the prophecy had foretold. Loki's forces had been quelled within a few unbroken nights, not three unbroken winters. Asgard had prevailed, not perished. And Yngvi had no doubt it was because one man had fought on their side.

He looked back to find that man.

But Shara was gone.

Across the courtyard, Magne was kneeling beside Thor.

Yngvi made his way there, grunting hard as his muscles screamed in protest against the weight of Loki's body that he was dragging behind him. Odin joined them with the surviving Aesir and Valkyries. Odin placed his palm over his son's chest. Shortly, Thor's body began to convulse in a prolonged bout of retching coughs as he expelled the poison from his lungs. His eyes fluttered open and he pushed himself up with a groan. Magne helped him to his feet.

"Father, are you all right?" Thor asked, clasping Magne's shoulder to steady himself.

"I'm alive," said Odin. "Most of us are." His voice trembled, like any hoary patriarch who has had to witness the slaughter of his clan. "I thought it ended with Vör. But Hodur is gone, and Tyr. Heimdallr, too. And others."

"Sif?" said Thor.

Odin shook his head slowly.

"No!" Thor cried out. His legs buckled, but Magne slipped his arm around his back, holding him up.

Odin lifted his hands to Thor's face. "Grieve, my son," he said, with the fortitude of a father and a leader, "and I will grieve with you. But know that they have fallen as heroes, for they broke the prophecy, and their souls will receive the highest honour known to Asgard—a place among the eternal spirits of Valhalla."

Not a single pair of Aesir eyes had passed over Yngvi. Even Magne's glances at him were painfully brief. Frustration burgeoned, bitter and aching in Yngvi's chest. There was also anger that he had not been believed. But he had no evidence, and never would. Hodur was dead. Loki and Sigyn were dead. Everyone who knew the truth of Loki's escape was dead.

Still, he said, "How may I help, All-Father?"

Thor straightened, whipped his head to Yngvi. "You've helped enough." His eyes were red and raw. The skies crackled and flashed a warning. His words flung his anger, his grief, his resentment at Yngvi. "Just go!"

No one moved. No one spoke.

When at last the heavens calmed, Magne stepped between them. "Thor," he pleaded. "All-Father, please... Yngvi did—"

"Don't," said Yngvi. He didn't need Magne to intercede again on his behalf.

Ignoring him, Magne said, "There must be something more we can do, All-Father."

"*You* can," said Odin. "Help us take the dead inside. Then have Eir tend to the wounded, including yourselves."

"Valhalla is ruined." Magne's voice had shaken a little. His blond hair was matted with blood near his forehead.

"The Asgardians will easily restore our home and make it even grander than before," said Odin. "But repairing our spirits will take time."

Yngvi swept his gaze over the battlefield, taking in the magnitude of their loss. Asgardians and Midgardians helped each other up, then went searching the fallen bodies for other survivors. Bloodied yet defiant, more gods and mortals staggered to their feet. Far more did not. Loki's forces had been trounced, but at too great a cost.

The weight of battle was pushing down on Yngvi. But even heavier was the certainty that Asgard believed Ragnarök had happened because he had failed in his duty.

"Loki?" said Thor, wiping at his eyes.

"Dead," Yngvi answered, even though Thor had asked Magne. He stepped aside so that Thor could see Loki's body behind him. "Killed by the man who ended Jörmungandr," he said, answering Odin's unspoken question.

"I've never seen anyone fight like him," said Magne. "He saved me."

"And me," said Thor. "Where is he?"

"I don't know," said Yngvi.

His mind was a knot of emotions, and questions to which he had no answers. Yet. One thought overrode all others—that the day he had first seen Shara in Midgard was the day that Loki had attacked Asgard.

That was no coincidence. Shara knew something, and Yngvi wanted to know what it was. But for now, there was work to be done.

Magne and the surviving Aesir carried the dead Asgardians into the Hall of Heroes and placed them on marble altars, as his parents' bodies had been after the last war.

Yngvi lingered nearby, waiting to be called on to assist. He was given water to drink, and a wet cloth to wipe his face and dab at his wounds, but that was all. When he'd had enough of receiving less attention than a piece of shattered wall, he sought out the Midgardians who retained the ability to walk, carry or drag, and helped arrange the bodies of the mortal soldiers in Valhalla's central tower, laying them down in neat rows on the floor of the outer hall.

The families of the dead would come to claim their loved ones and bury them in accordance with tradition. He was glad no one spoke after the brief enquiries, because that allowed him to use the time to enumerate every little detail he would wring out of Shara. If he ever saw him again.

Much later, when the dead had been tended to, Yngvi joined Magne and the throng of injured mortals making their way to the goddess of Healing and Medicine. The gods who had survived the onslaught had no need of Eir's skills. They would heal.

Four Valkyrie maidens made their way down the queue of the wounded, assessing the severity of injuries and tending to minor cuts and bruises. Eir sat at a large table on which fresh bandages, healing salves and potions were arranged. Every soldier with wounds critical enough to warrant Eir's skills received her gentle and thorough care.

When it was Yngvi's turn, she gestured wordlessly to the chair beside her. He sat. She did not look at him as she cleaned and dressed his wounds, or when she placed two spoonfuls of a powder into a small pouch, pulled the drawstring tight and pushed it across the table towards him. "Take this once, all of it, with water." She lifted her eyes then, and he read the indictment in her mien before he heard it in her voice. "You'll live," she said.

Yngvi pulled on his torn tunic, inclined his head in thanks, and rose.

Halli and Vidar found him while he waited for Magne's wounds to be treated.

Halli gasped. "Captain! What happened?" He had seen the thick bandage on Yngvi's shoulder.

"Scratches," said Yngvi. "You and Vidar? Are you all right?"

"Yes, Captain," said Vidar. They had sustained minor injuries which would heal quickly under the Valkyries' ministrations.

The murk of battle had cleared, Mani had dipped below the western horizon, and the last stars were blinking out of sight in the early light of dawn when Yngvi staggered out of Valhalla with Magne, carrying in their weary arms the severed heads of Snabb and Sansad. Halli and Vidar dragged the headless bodies behind their own horses.

They buried the faithful beasts among the other animal graves in the field outside Valhalla. It was the most respect they could accord their fallen horses in the situation. Yngvi said his farewells, then mounted Halli's horse behind him. Magne rode with Vidar, and they joined the Midgardian convoy on the long ride across the Bifröst to their homes.

Yngvi searched the convoy in vain for ice-blue eyes. He ran his thumb over the gemstone in his sword's hilt.

Shara would follow. Yngvi was sure of it.

CHAPTER FIVE

THE SURVIVING MIDGARDIAN contingent, too exhausted for conversation, trundled home in bloodied silence across the icy bridge until they reached Midgard's borders. Loki's rage had been unleashed on Asgard, but Midgard had not escaped the squalls raised by Hel's fiends.

When at last they stood at Midgard's perimeter where the road forked, Vidar's horse took the path that led to Magne's house. Halli and Yngvi went the other way, navigating the storm-tossed streets to arrive at Yngvi's house.

Yngvi dismounted, thanked Halli, and entered his home. Minutes later, there was a knock on the door.

Yngvi opened the door and saw, with scant surprise, that Shara stood outside. They regarded each other for a moment. Then Yngvi stepped back, allowed Shara inside and shut the door.

He undid the sword belt and tossed it, with the foreign weapon, on his bed, and began pacing the length of the floor, edgy, bewildered. Shara's eyes snagged on the sword. Yngvi noticed, and stopped his pacing.

He poured water in a cup and offered it to Shara, who took it gratefully. He poured out a second cup for himself, drank it with his eyes closed, then placed it on the table by the hearth.

"You were expecting me," said Shara.

Yngvi didn't answer. The fire in the pit had almost died. He watched in silence as Shara looked around and located the pile of firewood.

Shara tossed a few twigs in, and the flames rose hungrily. A large dished stone, half-filled with oil and holding several cotton-grass wicks, sat by a wall. Pulling out a wick, Shara held it to the fire until it caught the flame, then returned it to the lamp where he touched it to each of the other wicks in turn until they were all lit and warm, orange light spread through the room.

Yngvi's shadow fell across the floor and folded onto the walls, a faceless, black spectre whose feet never left his as he paced. It was annoying. He wanted to kick it away. He wanted— He didn't know what he wanted.

After a while, Shara broke the silence. "Stop."

Yngvi stopped abruptly in the middle of the room, his back to Shara, and felt him approach, the warmth of his body radiating towards Yngvi.

He turned around and looked into the clear blue-flecked gaze. "I know why you're here."

Shara held out a hand. "Then you know I need it back."

"You can't have it."

Shara lifted an eyebrow.

"You can kill me and take it," said Yngvi, "or you can tell me what I want to know and I'll give it to you."

Shara sighed. "That's hardly a choice. You know I'm not going to kill you."

Yngvi nodded. He gave Shara a frank appraisal from head to toe, went around him and looked down his back, where his tunic was torn in places. "You're unhurt. But I saw you get wounded."

Shara shrugged. "I must have healed."

"Must have?"

"I healed."

Yngvi looked at him wordlessly, the silence lengthening between them. Then he asked, his voice very quiet, "Who are you?"

"You wouldn't believe me."

"After what I saw in Valhalla," said Yngvi, "I think I'll believe anything."

Shara said nothing, just gazed steadily at Yngvi.

"Your weapons…" Yngvi lifted his hand and slowly ran his fingers through his grimy hair. "I've never seen any like them."

"Your gods have similar weapons."

"Are you a god?"

The question seemed to take Shara by surprise. "I—don't know."

"You don't know?" Now Yngvi was irritated. "How can you not know what you are? You clearly have powers. Your weapons… You conjured them."

"Perhaps I'm a conjurer," Shara said, mildly.

"Conjurers don't fight like you did."

"Perhaps not." A moment later, "I am not a god."

"How did you enter Valhalla?"

"There was no one to stop me."

That much was true. If Shara had been able to enter Valhalla under Heimdallr's watch, the Midgardian sentries would have posed no challenge. Yngvi's next words were cold, an accusation wrapped in a question. "Did you know this was going to happen?"

Shara gave a slow, reluctant nod. "I expected this."

"You expected Ragnarök? How?"

"You won't believe me."

Shara had stood disguised among the guardsmen, but Yngvi had recognised him. "You knew about Vör. I saw you move when Odin mentioned his daughter's death."

"Is that your…goddess of Knowledge?" said Shara.

"She was," said Yngvi. "You heard Eir speak of it. Gods don't just die. They're not supposed to. But she did."

"When did this happen?"

"You didn't hear that?"

Shara shook his head.

"Two weeks ago," said Yngvi.

"It can't be," Shara said, as if speaking to himself.

"What can't be? Did you know she was going to die?"

"No. No, I didn't," Shara insisted.

"Loki knew you," said Yngvi, his tone sharp. "You knew Asgard was going to fall!" He didn't care that he was shouting now, or that his hands were fists on Shara's chest, grabbing his tunic.

"I came here to prevent it."

"Prevent it?" He yanked again on Shara's tunic. "Who *are* you, Shara, that you thought *you* could prevent Ragnarök? Is that even your name? Shara?"

"It is."

Yngvi let go of Shara and stepped back. His breathing was fast and shallow. "Where is your home?"

"You won't know where it is."

"What do you mean?"

"It will take too long to explain," said Shara. "And you won't believe me."

"You keep saying that!" Yngvi gave Shara a push backwards. "I've got nowhere else to be, and neither do you, until you tell me."

Shara thought for a moment. "I might be able to show you, but...it might not work. I've never...*sent* thoughts to someone else."

"Sent thoughts? What are you talking about?"

"A temporary exchange of memories," said Shara. "I will need to take you into my own mind and then…even deeper."

Yngvi grabbed his shoulders. "Do it! I want to know everything."

Shara looked around the chamber and found a sheathed knife hanging from a peg in the wall. "Our blood will need to mingle for that."

Yngvi nodded.

Shara extracted the knife, and made a small cut in his palm. Black blood oozed from it. Yngvi took the knife and made a cut in his own palm. Then he put his hand over Shara's. Black mingled with red.

Nothing happened at first. Yngvi only felt his palm grow wet and sticky. He scanned the chamber around him. His simple furnishings were sufficient for a man who lived alone: a table, a chair and a stool, a bench bed lined with straw and covered with a woollen blanket, a single pillow. They were unchanged.

"Look at me," Shara said.

Yngvi's gaze locked with Shara's.

And just like that, the air around them began to ripple, as if turning to water, but he was still able to breathe normally. The parts of his chamber still visible beyond Shara were no more than indistinct impressions. The flames in the hearth licked higher and the warmth spread through the room. Eventually, it all melded into a hazy background against which the only clear shape was Shara's silhouette.

Yngvi's perception receded from his surroundings and turned inwards, searching. He was acutely aware of the thumping of his heart, his lungs expanding with every intake of breath. He could hear the gurgle of his blood as it rushed through his veins and felt the slow descent of saliva along his throat each time he swallowed.

His palm prickled; all of this mindfulness emanated from the point where his hand pressed against Shara's. Vision had become redundant; it was as though he was seeing with his skin, sensation skittering over his nerve endings. He could feel the beat of his heart flow through him, from the crown of his head to the soles of his feet, languid and heavy.

A second string of thumps joined in, and he recognised Shara's heart beating in time with his own. It should have felt jarring, intrusive, but their cadence was utterly natural.

A blue aura had appeared around Shara. Yngvi resisted the urge to withdraw when it slowly curved and enveloped him. They stood in the middle of the room, cocooned by this translucent swathe. When a tingling current of warmth flowed from the centre of Shara's forehead to his own, Yngvi felt thin fissures form in his mind and fingers of indigo light entering through the gaps. It was Shara, reaching inside him.

This felt like an infiltration, more intimate than anything Yngvi had known. Their *minds* were touching. Distantly, he heard Shara say his name, and behind his eyes, the fractured terrain of his mind surrendered, crumbling into a void.

He was fully open.

In the next instant, a crashing flood of images invaded his mind, lighting up an invisible spider-web of impulses as Shara took him back in time.

CHAPTER SIX

A YOUNG MAN made his way through a thicket.

He emerged from the woods into an urban setting that resembled a city, and passed a long line of slaves working at a construction site. Armed guards strode up and down the line, bringing their whips down on the labouring backs with mechanical regularity and eliciting repellent cries of pain.

The young man went down a series of streets, the last of which was broad and opened onto a vast courtyard. He stopped for a moment at a towering arched entryway, covered with blue-glazed bricks. Passing through it, he went up to the sprawling palace that stood in the centre. It was encircled by a roofed colonnade of fluted columns of black marble that ended high above him in filigreed capitals.

He was stopped outside large oak doors by a dark-haired, brown-skinned guard.

"Get out of my way, Namhu," said the young man.

"Shara," Namhu sneered. "You have kept the Sky-Father waiting. Are you carrying any weapons?"

He had a knife tucked into his boot. "No."

Namhu handed him a silk scarf, his lips twisted as though he had bitten into something unpleasant. "Cover your head. You know Enlil doesn't like to see it. The Sky-Palace is a place of dignity and respect—"

Mirrored in the highly polished obsidian walls, Shara saw what Namhu saw: a truculent, blue-skinned young man wearing a tunic over thigh-hugging dark pants that were tucked into knee-high leather boots, and silver-white hair that fell down to the middle of his back.

"—and mongrels such as yourself—" Namhu was saying.

"Then he shouldn't have called me here."

Shara pushed open the heavy doors, a deep rumble echoing through the corridor as he did, and entered a large circular hall. Its dark walls were covered with intricate carvings in praise of the gods of Nibiru, chronicling their reign over the realm.

Shara sniffed. The air in the torch-lit hall was thick with the cloying fragrance of incense. He lifted the scarf to his nose.

Opposite the door, across the length of the Great Hall, was a stepped dais on which sat two thrones of ornate gold. The throne on the right was vacant. Sprawled over the throne on the left was a man in kingly robes of crimson velvet that fell in folds over the cushioned seat. A limp, ringed hand clasped a carved armrest and the other held a goblet. The man's bluish skin was slightly sallow. He beckoned with a finger.

Shara's temper further darkened as he strode towards the dais.

The man held out his right hand. His signet ring glinted in the torchlight, illuminating the engraving: a circle in which were set two perpendicular eyes in outline, intersecting over the large red jewel serving as the iris.

"Sky-Father." Shara went down on one knee, held his breath and lowered the scarf just long enough to brush his lips over the ring. Then he rose and stepped back five paces. The nearness to Enlil, who smelled of perfumed sickness, was nauseating, even with the silk pressed against his nose.

"It's Ninkur's odious medicine. My nephew is mediocre at best as the god of Healing. Or perhaps Enki has recruited his son to kill me. I wouldn't put it past him." Enlil peered into the goblet, curling his lips in distaste. "Whatever this is makes me think death might

be the preferable alternative." He placed the goblet on the cushioned stool beside his throne. "Let me see you."

Shara discarded the scarf.

"Look who it is," Enlil proclaimed to the empty hall. "The bastard son of my churlish brother."

Shara kept silent.

"Shara, Shara, Shara." Enlil's tone dripped with censure. His eyes swept over Shara's hair. "Have you given any consideration at all to covering your head for this visit? You know I find your hair distasteful."

The tips of Shara's mouth lifted. "Your man insisted I hurry."

"And yet you are late."

"It is only by the grace of your forethought that I arrived when I did," said Shara.

Enlil frowned. "What do you mean?"

"Only someone with the Sky-Father's prescience would build a terrestrial Sky-Palace."

"Insolent!" said Enlil, his voice rising. "You are as much like Enki in temperament as in appearance."

"Your brother insists I take after you, Sky-Father," Shara returned. "Is it possible that it is yourself you denounce when you insult my parentage?"

Enlil's lips drew back from his teeth, as though repulsed by the prospect. "I would never sire a half-blood such as you." But he hummed thoughtfully. "In truth, my brother and I both resemble our father. You might even be our brother if Anu hadn't left so long ago and you weren't so young. But you must be Enki's, because only he has ever cavorted with wood nymphs. Those snow-manes…he has always been partial to them."

Shara had little interest in the predilections of the Anunnaki. "Is there a point to this?"

"I refer, of course, to your mother. She must have been a particularly lovely nymph to have merited something more enduring than Enki's fleeting passion." Enlil smiled, a dead, reptilian expression that pleated his pallid skin into loose, concentric folds. "A bastard child," he added in superfluous clarification. Then he tipped his head back and looked at Shara through half-lidded eyes. "Sometimes I think he might have lain with our step-mother, too."

Shara had even less interest in whether Enki had ever bedded Ishtar. He lifted his chin, defiant despite the insults. 'Snow-mane' he had been called, like the forest nymphs, like Nidaba, and Ishtar, her mother and Anu's second wife.

Seemingly unsatisfied with the reaction he had provoked, Enlil continued, "And her energies must have been very powerful to have imbued you with so much of herself."

Shara knew what Enlil meant, but also knew Enlil would inform him again.

"Your mongrel imprints."

Shara's thoughts strayed to the silvery leaf-like marking around his navel. He sighed but held his tongue. This was no different from every other exchange with the Sky-Father.

But Enlil wasn't finished. He tapped his chin with two fingers. "That's not all she gave you. There's something unusual about your features. Something that is…not all of a man."

Interesting. That was a new insult. Something must be galling Enlil more than usual.

"Was there an actual point to summoning me, Sky-Father, or am I to stand here until you have insulted me to your satisfaction?"

"I don't loathe myself enough to suffer your presence, let alone demand it, without a point. Have you seen your father?"

"I have no father," said Shara.

Enlil tutted. "It must feel wretched not to be claimed by anyone. To be universally shunned."

Calm and toneless, Shara replied, "Not universally."

"Yes…yes," Enlil agreed. "There's Nidaba."

The name filled Shara with warmth.

"For reasons none of us will ever understand, our half-sister loves you like she would a favourite pet. You were nothing but a wildling before she found you and gave you your name. Perhaps it is that you are both snow-manes, like Ishtar, even though you, a god-spawned bastard child, impure of blood, were deservedly discarded at birth."

Shara blew out a breath. "Sky-Father, why have you called me here?"

"You never give me my fill of insulting you, Shara." He reclined against the cushions with a sigh, and ran his hand over his face. "Have you seen Nidaba?"

"I haven't visited the Great Library in a…while."

"No? I was certain you and she never went more than two days without speaking to each other. What happened?"

"Nothing that would interest you," Shara muttered.

"Nidaba hasn't visited me," Enlil groused. "Neither has my son."

"Have you considered calling on them?"

"Be quiet! Your insolence knows no bounds. It is beneath the Sky-Father to call on the pantheon," he declaimed. "They come to me to pay obeisance."

"Your eminence is boundless, Sky-Father," Shara remarked, with a smirk.

"I tire of you, Shara."

"I am ready to depart at a moment's notice."

"Not yet. I want you to call on Nidaba."

"You could have sent that message with Namhu, or sent him directly to Nidaba and saved yourself this distasteful exchange."

"I had another reason to see you in person." Enlil leaned forward and ran his eyes over Shara's body. "You seem well. Have you been well?"

Shara's eyebrows lifted in surprise. "I can't imagine my wellbeing is of any consequence to you, Sky-Father."

"It is not. I am merely attempting to establish a trend. Ninlil and I are afflicted by a peculiar malaise. A lassitude pervades our bodies down the right arm," he said, waving his left hand over the offending limb, "almost to the point of rendering it unusable." He let out a shivery breath and slumped in his throne. "Nergal sent word that he suffers the same kind of enervation. It has impaired my son's effectiveness as the god of War. In fact, most of the Anunnaki are affected." A narrow-eyed pause. "No, that's not quite right. I have not seen Enki in a while, but Ninki and Ninkur seemed hale. And you appear disgustingly vigorous."

"And you appear quite disappointed," Shara bit back.

"I shall not lower myself to trading insults with a mongrel pup, but I wish to know whether Nidaba is similarly debilitated. Or whether"—Enlil ran his eyes over Shara's body again from head to toe—"the snow-manes have also been spared this malady."

Shara said tersely, "Then I will return to Mashu and call on her."

"Do that." Enlil wagged his index finger. "Now go."

The Great Library was a pristine structure situated in the heart of Mashu forest, as white as the Sky Palace was black. Shara was striding down its gleaming marble hallways, in search of Nidaba, when a sliver of light caught his eye.

Oddly, the door to the Vault was open a fraction.

The Vault held all of Nibiru's secrets and was to be secured at all times. As goddess of Knowledge, Nidaba was also the Keeper of the Secrets of Nibiru. And she was never negligent.

Intrigued, he pushed the door open and froze. Nidaba lay on the floor of the Vault by the eastern wall. Dead. When the initial shock wore off, he rushed to her side and fell to his knees by her body.

Her white hair was fanned out over the glossy floor. A sharp wedge of clay was embedded in her stomach, and blood stained her white robes and the white floor in now-dry patches of black. Nidaba's blue skin had dulled to grey from the loss of blood; her unseeing eyes were open, her mouth twisted in a rictus of pain.

"Nidaba," Shara whispered, foolishly, desperately hoping her dead eyes would show signs of life, that she would blink and look at him. His own eyes pricked, then welled and overflowed. An aching despair filled his chest and he remained kneeling, shaking with the utter helplessness of the situation.

It was a new and altogether terrible feeling—this pain of loss.

He gazed mutely at the only person who had ever cared for him and now lay dead on the cold floor of the Vault, her hand clutching a scrap of parchment. He wiped his eyes and carefully opened her fist, unfurling her fingers one at a time. Words were scrawled on the parchment in black, as if written with a blood-tipped finger. The letters were thick and imprecise, but the message was clear. And it was addressed to him.

Sitting back on his heels, he read it. Then, he untied the leaf-amulet from around her neck and put it around his own, pulled the knife out of his boot and made a small cut in his palm.

Blood oozed out in dark droplets. He placed his palm over Nidaba's stomach wound and asked her, wordlessly, to show him her murderer's face. And through her eyes he saw the last moments of her life.

He saw Enki.

Yngvi was close to collapsing, but had a marginal awareness of Shara's hand grasping his shoulder.

That soon faded because the blue threads of Shara's mind were woven around his, drawing him even deeper. Yngvi's consciousness was in free fall, as if he were hurtling down into the pits of Helheim.

His instincts were on high alert, warning him to pull back while he still could, to sever that link. But his need to know the truth was stronger. He did not resist; instead, he let himself be sucked past the barrier of Shara's mind into Nidaba's vision.

Nidaba was staring at the figure outside the Vault. "I don't think I've ever seen you here. What could the god of the Underworld want in a library today?"

"You know why I am here," said Enki. "Tell me what happened and how."

"There's nothing to tell," she said. "Leave now and I'll keep this visit between us."

"Don't be a fool. I know you're hiding something in the Vault."

"I'm hiding nothing."

"If there's nothing, why not let me in?"

"I'm warning you. Act rashly and you'll regret it."

"Who'll come for me? Enlil? I did offer you my favour before, but you chose to throw in your lot with him. That was a mistake. He grows fat and too slow to move, sitting on a throne that will soon be too small for him."

"Shara will come for you."

"Oh yes, Shara," said Enki, laughing. "The hermit who frolics with animals and his forest family." Enki tilted his head from side to side, stretching his neck. "Nidaba. You bore me. I know it's in the Vault." He raised his sword; the sapphire in the pommel flashed a dark blue. "Open it."

"Never."

"My quarrel is with Enlil, not you. I don't wish to harm you, but you are being difficult."

Enki calmly lifted a hand and struck Nidaba's face. She fell to the floor. She was unarmed. What use did Nidaba have for weapons that could kill? Her only weapon was knowledge. She struggled to her feet and threw herself at Enki, scratching wildly at his face.

"That was a mistake," said Enki. He shoved her backwards against a shelf. It wobbled from the impact and clay tablets crashed to the hard floor, shattering into treacherously sharp fragments.

Nidaba weakly lifted her body, her horrified eyes looking down at her middle, at the dark stain blooming over her white robes. A triangular sliver was wedged in her stomach.

Enki leaned down, gripped her wrist and dragged her bleeding, gasping body to the Vault. "I did not want it to come to this, but you left me no choice."

He held her hand up against the door. Under her touch, it clicked open.

Enki strode into the Vault, pulling Nidaba with him. He flung her arm down and she crumpled to the floor. A trail of blood stained the marble tiles where she had been dragged. She lay there, whimpering.

A lectern stood in the centre of the Vault, holding a large clay tablet. Enki strode up to it.

"Ah, the fabled foretelling of Nibiru's future. You should probably have hidden it away." He studied it in silence. "Oh." He was struck by something particular on the tablet.

Nidaba was wheezing. "Get away from it!"

"Then stop me," said Enki. "But you can't, can you?"

"Shara will stop you. When he finds out what you've done, he'll hunt you down," she warned, eyes blazing, lips twisted in pain. "It won't matter where you go. He'll find you."

Enki ignored her and studied the tablet. His expression changed from grim to appalled, and finally settled into a glower. "Who else knows about this?"

"No one."

"You do."

Nidaba huffed, a sound of pain. "I have never needed a tablet to know things."

"Indeed. The goddess of Knowledge already knows everything."

Enki's lips curled into a cold sneer. With the back of his hand, he shoved the tablet off the lectern. Nidaba's eyes followed its arc through the air until it struck the wall and crashed to the floor in a starburst of red over white.

"I can't have anyone else learning the secrets of Nibiru," said Enki. "And you're going to die." He leaned down, pulled out her stylus from her waist sash, and calmly plunged it into her neck. The ivory shaft faced little resistance as it sank into her soft flesh. Enki's laugh echoed in the hollow space as he swept out of the Vault.

Nidaba remained on the floor, blood pooling under her head and torso. Broken. Waiting. With a grunt of pain, she reached up and slowly extracted the stylus from her neck. It dropped onto the tile and skidded away.

She dragged herself on the marble to a scroll that had rolled to a stop a little out of reach. She unfurled it and turned it over. Then, dipping her finger in her wound she scrawled a message on the back in her blood. When she was done, she fell back with a gasp of pain and lay like that.

Her eyes were open as life leached out of her dying body.

The pocket of space around Yngvi's thoughts had become less dense and he intuited that he had retreated from Nidaba's vision and was back in Shara's mind.

Breaking free of the horror of Nidaba's death should have been a relief, but it was worse now because Shara's sorrow ripped through him, as real and emptying as his own grief when he had wept over his parents' bloodied bodies. And he was still not free; Shara was holding him back in Nibiru. Shara seemed to be all around him, growing uncomfortably, suffocatingly close. It was not over.

Shara pulled his hand away from Nidaba's body and sat hunched, hands gripping his knees, rocking back and forth as if to soothe himself. A dark, wet patch formed on one knee. He wiped his bloodied palm on his thigh.

When the tears came again, he did not stop them. He knew who had murdered Nidaba, all for a clay tablet. He sat like that until his tear-streaked cheeks had dried and anguish had hardened into rage. Then he made himself look at her face.

Nidaba's empty gaze was settled on a bookstand by the Vault's western wall. From his position, he spotted a piece of the tablet that had skidded over the floor and slipped under there. He retrieved it and scanned it briefly.

It was a corner piece bearing pictographs etched into the clay. He had just memorised the last symbol when he became aware of his hands crushing the fragment to powder. Wiping his dust-tipped fingers on his pants, he took one last look at her body, and left the Great Library to return home.

Passing his cabin, he headed directly into a nearby waterfall where he stripped off his clothes and boots and bathed under the cascade. He entered his cabin, pulled on fresh clothing, then made his way to a massive banyan tree where he lay down on the mound at its base.

The tree, as if sensing his presence, rustled and spread over him in a lush canopy. The deep green of its leaves gradually paled to white, like the forest floor had around Shara, and a bluish tinge spread over the trunk of the tree and along its branches. The grass rose up and knitted itself over him, enveloping him in its warmth.

The spray had washed away his last tears, leaving only the certitude that he would kill Enki.

Shara clutched the leaf-amulet around his neck.

He saw the light of the stars.

And Yngvi was thrown out of Shara's mind.

CHAPTER SEVEN

THE ABRUPT, ALMOST violent disseverance from Shara's memories came as both a shock and a release.

It had felt as real as a physical shove, and its force sent Yngvi stumbling backwards. A dizzying whorl of light, hot and glaring, rose up his spine and out through his eyes, taking with it all the air from his lungs. His body folded over, and his breaths came in deep gasps.

"You pushed me out?" The words came out as a heaving rasp.

He could tell he was once again the sole inhabitant of his mind, but around him, the room still rippled. He fell on his bed, trembling, his thoughts still scrambled from the exchange of memories, his body broken by the fighting.

"I didn't," said Shara. He knelt beside Yngvi and held him by his shoulders.

Yngvi glared at him, but there was no disclosure in Shara's expression, only bewilderment. Yngvi closed his eyes. Gradually, the shaking abated and he forced his eyes open.

"You're that Shara," he whispered.

"Yes. Can you sit?" Shara's voice was quiet, and thick with concern.

"What was all that?" Yngvi coughed and tried to rise.

Shara helped him sit up. "You need to stay still."

"No! I don't!" Yngvi snapped, then hunched over while his body shuddered. The brusque untethering of Shara's mind from his had left a lingering distortion in his thoughts.

"Yngvi…"

Yngvi's words were jammed in his throat. He stared at the floor between his boots.

Shara got up and sat on the bed beside him.

Yngvi stared at the dark hair, pale eyes and paler face. "You're—You're blue."

"Yes. I know you have questions. I'm not going anywhere until I answer every last one."

Yngvi staggered up and stood. "I'll kill you if you do." That made him laugh, a low, mocking sound directed at himself. "How can I kill you? Can anyone?"

Shara was looking up at him. "Yes," he said, so softly that Yngvi almost didn't hear him.

"Who?"

Shara only shook his head and rose.

Yngvi didn't press him for an answer. He poured water in a bowl to splash on his face and dipped his shaking hand in, sending curlicues of red through the ripples. He looked at Shara. Shara held up his hand; it was healed.

Yngvi nodded slowly. "I need a little time. It's too much." He ran his hand through his hair.

"I understand," said Shara, gentling his tone.

"No, you don't."

"No, I don't," Shara agreed tolerantly.

A long silence followed, but it felt safe to Yngvi. There was an ordinariness to the way they moved in each other's space, and an ease that he knew could only be the result of the union of their minds.

He could feel Shara's concerned gaze on him, as though Shara sensed the dissonance between what Yngvi had known all his life and the sheer impossibility of what he had just learnt. The memories Shara had shown him wouldn't stop. They passed behind his eyes in a continuous loop, and each time he noticed something new.

"Enough!" Yngvi muttered to himself. Only a few minutes had passed, but it seemed longer. He stood in the middle of the room, drawing in deep breaths. Finally, he was ready to talk.

"You're not from…here. Not from the nine worlds of Yggdrasil." Yngvi sorted through the facts as he knew them. "You're from…"

"Nibiru."

"Where is Nibiru?"

"Somewhere up there." Shara pointed skywards. "In the heavens."

"How is this possible?"

"I don't know. Until a week ago, I only knew Nibiru."

"When did Nidaba die?"

"Two weeks ago," said Shara.

"This is going to take time. Sit," Yngvi said, and Shara settled on the bed.

Yngvi's questions tumbled out of him, urgent and unrelenting, and Shara answered them all.

"You have gods and goddesses, like we do. The Sky-Father…that's Enlil. And Enki is the god of the Underworld."

"Yes."

"Like Odin and Loki… When I saw you in Valhalla, among the guardsmen, I was certain it was you that night with Hodur. But it was Enki, wasn't it?"

"Yes."

"How could he know to take my form? He had never seen me before."

"I don't know. Probably like I know things."

Yngvi snorted. "*You* know things? You didn't even know who you were looking for or where."

"I did," Shara insisted sharply, before dropping his voice and conceding, with obvious reluctance, "eventually."

"Eventually," said Yngvi. Was there more behind that word? Was Shara thinking what he was? The past, with its dead and unalterable happenings, was something Yngvi seldom pondered, yet the thought couldn't be ignored: how much of this ruin might have been prevented, or at least minimised, had Shara known earlier?

The part of him that knew he was shunned by Asgard wanted to hold Shara culpable, but that same part knew that Shara had left Nibiru to stop the scourge of his world, that Shara was the only reason Asgard still stood, and Yngvi was here, and Magne back with his family, with all their limbs attached to their bodies. He shook his head tightly to reject the question for the pointless distraction that it was, and returned his thoughts to what he had been shown.

"Ninki and Ninkur are Enki's wife and son," said Yngvi. "And Ninlil and Nergal are Enlil's family."

Shara nodded.

Yngvi repeated the names a few times in his mind to commit them to memory. He'd had a hard enough time keeping the Aesir hierarchy straight in his head—although there were far fewer names to remember now.

"Nidaba—" he said, remembering that Enki had left her bleeding and dying in the Vault. "How could you leave her there like that?"

Shara flinched. "What else could I have done? She was gone. Time was of the essence. If I carried her body back to the Great Hall, Enlil would have either accused me of her murder or held me back to be interrogated. If I didn't return, he would have to send an envoy to the Library. Neither of those options would bring her back. But I could follow Enki and avenge the one person who cared for me."

Yngvi regarded Shara for a long moment, regretting his question, because he would have done exactly what Shara had. "I know that feeling of helplessness, of wanting retribution."

"Your parents," said Shara. "Loki killed them, didn't he?"

Yngvi didn't think Shara had heard Loki. He closed his eyes, remembering. "My parents died defending Valhalla from Loki in the last war."

His eyes opened when he felt Shara's hand on his unhurt shoulder.

"You have your brother," said Shara.

Yngvi nodded. "I… I am sorry about Nidaba."

Shara dropped his hand.

"I want to see you as…you."

Shara sighed. He lifted a hand and moved his fingers minutely, like a twitch.

Before Yngvi's incredulous eyes, Shara's body changed. He remained as tall and as broad as he had been, but now his skin was blue, like the evening sky. And his dark hair had turned opalescent.

It was Shara's face from the tavern, but it also was not. His eyes held a hint of the truculence that had stolen Yngvi's breath. But underlying the clear gaze was the ferocity of the warrior who had levelled Loki's forces with cool, dominant ease.

Despite all the unanswered questions, despite all his misgivings, Yngvi had never reacted this intensely to anyone. He said, with whispering amazement, "You're…" He searched for the right word. Exquisite, he wanted to say, but settled on, "Incredible."

And despite the horrors they had survived and the gruesome vision he had just shared with Yngvi, Shara's lips stretched around a breathless laugh, quite shy, very pleased.

Yngvi laughed with him, but there was a solemnity to it. With a mind of its own, his hand rose to stroke Shara's hair. He held there, waiting. Shara nodded his permission, and Yngvi ran his fingers over the snow mane, as Enlil had so appropriately called it. It was shimmering white and soft, like snow fox fur. How could anyone think to deride this? He could not believe that Shara was allowing his touch. His heart thudded in his chest as he pushed his next words out. "I want to see it. The mark that Enlil hated so much."

Shara could have lifted up the hem of his tunic but instead reached behind himself to pull it off and toss it aside. It landed on the chair. "It's torn," he said, with a shrug.

He stood facing Yngvi, arms at his side. Yngvi dropped his gaze to Shara's torso and slowly traced the shape of the leaf with his forefinger, liking the sharp intake of breath and the subtle tightening of Shara's abdomen at his touch. He held his finger over Shara's navel for a moment, then followed the stem down over the soft hairs until he encountered the waistband of Shara's pants. He looked up at Shara. "This is extraordinary," he said. *You are extraordinary.*

A sudden surge of feeling pushed Yngvi back bodily; he withdrew his hand and put some distance between them, because his interest in this stranger from a strange land was turning into something else, something far stronger than the attraction he had felt when he first saw Shara.

It was part fascination with his implausible origins, part awe for his calm superiority on the battlefield. But beyond that, it was desire, stronger and more visceral than anything Yngvi had ever experienced.

"What is it?"

Yngvi said, sounding as helplessly wonderstruck as he felt, "I…can't believe you're real."

Shara's answering smile felt like the touch of a warm hand, so gentle, so genuine. But there was something else: the flare of his pupils, the way his lips parted when his gaze dropped to Yngvi's mouth, then flew up to meet Yngvi's waiting eyes. Encouraged, Yngvi placed his palm on Shara's bare chest. When there was no demurral, he passed his hand slowly up to Shara's neck, attentive for the smallest indication of unease in the body under his palm, feeling the strong, rapid beat of Shara's heart beneath the plane of muscle, tracing the sharp collar bone, gently thumbing the dip in his throat, then slipped his hand behind Shara's neck and pulled him closer. Shara was pliant, and the faint flush on the sky blue cheeks pleased Yngvi very much. Slowly, carefully, he drew Shara's face towards his.

But as his own lips parted, he felt a minute stiffening in Shara's neck against his palm. Yngvi lifted his hand, still holding it over Shara's shoulder. Shara took a sudden half step back, his neck taut and corded, his shoulder now touching Yngvi's palm again, pushing against it. His eyes were wide, his whole body had gone rigid.

All right. Too soon, thought Yngvi.

In anyone else, Yngvi would have written this off as push-and-pull teasing, a game he enjoyed playing. But the wariness on Shara's face made it seem the almost panicked reaction of a naïf, which Yngvi was struggling to reconcile with the near-godly fighter who had won the battle for Valhalla. Or perhaps it was a rebuff.

Forcing a smile to keep his own expression casual, he lowered his hand and turned to the table to pick up a water pitcher and pour out a cup. He drank slowly with his eyes closed, allowing himself time to recover from this rare misstep. He could not remember the last time he had misread another's cues. His attraction, therefore, must be nothing more than the residual rush of battle and these new fantastical discoveries.

He filled another cup and offered it to Shara.

Shara drank, his eyes never leaving Yngvi's from over the rim of the cup, then handed it back to him.

"More?"

Shara shook his head, and moved closer to the fire.

Yngvi leaned against the table, fingers curled around the edge, while Shara resolved whatever conflict was inside him. After a long silence,

Shara turned and lifted his eyes to Yngvi. He looked like himself again. Yngvi let out a breath.

"I want to know…" He didn't know where to start.

"What do you want to know?" said Shara. His tone was as cooperative as his expression, the openness in his eyes as real as his reticence had been.

"Everything."

Shara smiled. "Everything?"

CHAPTER EIGHT

YNGVI PICKED UP a block of wood from the fire pit and held it out. "Show me what you saw on the tablet."

Shara placed the wedge on the table, smooth side facing up, picked up the knife and began to etch the pictographs from memory. When he stood back, he had created a series of five rectangular sections, each bearing a different symbol.

Fascinated, Yngvi ran his fingers over the indentations. "It reminds me of our own writing, yet it's also different." Struck by a sudden realisation, he jerked his head up. "You're speaking my language. How did you learn our words?"

Shara hesitated. "I don't know… They…come to me."

With his finger, Yngvi traced the partial symbol at the top left. "What is this?" He pointed at two slanting lines.

"This is incomplete, but here, where they taper upwards, I think they would've ended like this." Shara etched a small angled wedge, like a roof atop the two vertical lines. "If I'm right, this could be read as *Babylon*." Then he carved a bowman's figure beside Babylon. The arrowhead ended in a small circle.

"Who is the archer?" said Yngvi

"This is *Sipa-Zi-An-Na*, the Archer in the Sky. It is said that his arrow"—he tapped on the circle—"points to Nibiru."

Sipa-Zi-An-Na. Strange, but still not the strangest thing he had learnt today. "We have an Archer in the Sky. Oruwandil. His arrow is said to point to Polaris. I suppose that is…Nibiru?"

"It must be," said Shara.

Yngvi drew a finger over the three other sections. "And these are?"

"*Apsu* and *Marduk*…and this is…" He looked at Yngvi, waiting.

"Yggdrasil," Yngvi surmised, running his finger over the imprints. "Did Enki go to these two realms?"

A slow nod. "I followed him there, but I was too late reaching Apsu. On Marduk, I narrowly missed him. But here, we were able to stop him."

"How does he travel across the realms?"

Shara held out the leaf-amulet around his neck. "He probably has one like this. I think of where I want to go and I am there."

"And how do you know where to go? Or does that also just…come to you?"

"Yes."

Yngvi searched Shara's face for signs of deception, but the blue eyes were clear and unguarded. Still, he gave a disbelieving huff. It was getting to be too much. He poured himself another cup of water and quaffed it in a single gulp. He rubbed his face, feeling the grunge of battle under his palms. He needed to bathe. But later.

"I knew you wouldn't believe me," said Shara.

"All right, I'll believe you. For now," said Yngvi. " *You're* here chasing Enki. But why was *he* here?"

"He means to destroy all the pantheons."

"Pantheons?"

Shara said, "Each realm so far has had a pantheon of gods identical to the Anunnaki, the gods of Nibiru."

"Loki," said Yngvi, recalling something. "The apparition that rose from him…it was blue. That was Enki, wasn't it?" Reading Shara's question in his eyes, Yngvi said, "I know Loki's weapon. It's a spear. But that"—he pointed his chin at the sword lying on his bed—"isn't his. I saw it in Nidaba's vision."

He picked up the sword and held it to the fire. It might have been a trick of the light, but something moved inside the blue stone, a shadow worming along the inner circumference. He gripped the hilt and squeezed. The skin on his palm tingled, as though the weapon was transmitting a dark energy to him. The day's events were tricking his senses. He shook his head and tossed the sword back on the bed. "That's Enki's sword."

"It was," Shara said, his eyes narrowed, assessing.

Yngvi frowned. "I don't understand… How can one god from Nibiru destroy an entire pantheon of gods?" He stared at the floor, momentarily lost in thought. Then, looking up at Shara, he said, "Loki's spear. You sought it specifically and destroyed it."

Shara nodded. "It appears that each of these realms has a weapon powerful enough to kill its gods. On Asgard, it was Loki's spear."

Yngvi took a moment to insert that information into the mental catalogue he was building, then, almost as an afterthought, asked, "Where's the weapon on Nibiru?"

"I…don't know."

"But there has to be one." Yngvi was animated now, gesturing with his hands. "If everything related to the Anunnaki exists on these realms, an equivalent god-killer weapon must exist on Nibiru. You must have known this."

"You're right to assume its existence, but I didn't know of such a weapon before leaving Nibiru. I wasn't even looking for one." Shara seemed to be thinking aloud. "If it exists, Enki mustn't have discovered its location or he wouldn't go to all this trouble otherwise."

"Your sword," said Yngvi. "I've never seen anything like it. Who gave it to you?"

Shara was silent for a moment before he spoke. "No one."

"No one?"

"It… It came to me when I was nine. I remember I was running through Mashu forest. I was being chased by a pack of wolves. The sky had lit up. My hand…" He looked down at his open fingers. "The sword appeared in my hand. It was too big for me then. I needed both hands to hold it up, but it scared the wolves. Since then, it comes when I call."

Yngvi lifted an eyebrow. "You don't know your parents, but you knew you were nine when the sword came to you."

"When I told Nidaba about the sword, she was not surprised. She said I was born nine years earlier on the day Sipa-Zi-An-Na shoots a fireball into the sky."

Having no reason to doubt the goddess of Knowledge on any realm, Yngvi nodded. He leaned a shoulder against the wall and faced Shara, arms folded over his chest, legs crossed at the ankles. "What happens now? Will you return to Nibiru?"

"Yes."

Yngvi shook his head. "You won't go back. Not yet."

"And why is that?" said Shara.

All right. "There's another realm. I saw it in your visions." When Yngvi received no indication whether he was right about what he had seen, he added, "And…Enki isn't dead. At least, I don't think he is, if what rose from Loki's body was Enki."

"You saw me kill it—kill him," said Shara.

"Yes." Yngvi pinched the bridge of his nose. He knew the reaction his next words would elicit. "But I saw it again…that same man-shaped blue cloud. It followed me but I warded it off with Enki's sword, and it disappeared."

"Why didn't you tell me this!"

"You had left!" Yngvi returned, feeling his lips twist. He'd had enough of people holding him responsible, without justification, for everything that went wrong on Yggdrasil. "And I couldn't find you." Shara's hands had curled into fists, but Yngvi didn't care. He ran a hand roughly through his hair, pushing it off his face. He had not had time to braid it and it was clumped with the grime of battle. "I think I know why Enki wasn't killed."

Shara glared, his jaw set in a clear challenge to Yngvi to supply a plausible explanation.

"Nidaba..." Yngvi softened his tone, wishing he did not have to remind Shara of her death. "Enki had his sword, but he used her stylus to kill her. It was her implement, the...weapon...she wielded as goddess of Knowledge." Yngvi paused, searching Shara's face for a reaction. "I think...Enki can be killed by his sword. I think that's why his spirit recoiled when I threatened it with his sword."

He waited while Shara considered that, his eyes never leaving Yngvi's. Something had shifted in Shara's gaze, as though he was not looking at Yngvi anymore but inwards, into some private corner of his own mind, and Yngvi wondered if it was something he had been shown when he was in Shara's memories.

"I think," said Yngvi, taking his supposition to its conclusion, "that the Anunnaki can only be killed by their own weapons."

An extended pause.

"Yes," Shara said at last, anger ceding to a new approbation in the way he was regarding Yngvi, as if Yngvi had, somehow, surprised him. "I think you might be right."

"The other realm," Yngvi gently reminded him. "What was it called?"

This time, he got an answer.

"Aegyptus."

Aegyptus. Yngvi added the name to his catalogue.

"It is dark already. You can stay here tonight," he said, and added, very casually, "and we can leave tomorrow morning." It did not work.

"We?" said Shara.

"We. Take me with you."

"No."

Yngvi passed a hand over his face. He had expected resistance. "I can help you." Hearing Shara's cynical laugh, he added, "I said *help*, not *protect*. I've probably given you the solution to killing Enki. I can fight. I can be useful to you." He rubbed the back of his neck. "You don't have to do this alone."

Shara cocked his head and put his measuring gaze on Yngvi. This, too, was expected.

"You want to know what's in it for me," said Yngvi.

Silence.

Yngvi took in a deep breath, held it for a few moments, then exhaled through his mouth. "Redemption."

Shara raised his eyebrows. "Redemption?"

He must have expected Yngvi to want *revenge*. It was what Yngvi himself had expected to say.

"I am no longer welcome in Valhalla. They hold me responsible for Ragnarök." He stared at the dying fire in the hearth. It hurt to speak the words, because they made it real. "Odin. Thor. The rest of the Aesir. Even Magne—" Cutting off the thought, he looked up at Shara. "What I need is Enki's scalp. Like you, I want him dead. We can help each other. And when Enki is dead, you can have his sword."

"When he's dead?" said Shara. "You've changed the terms of the agreement."

"So you're agreed?"

Shara did not answer. His face showed nothing.

"You could kill me any time you want and take it," said Yngvi.

The moments ticked by as Shara watched him wordlessly, as though he could see into Yngvi's mind. "You are very ready to die."

Yngvi flinched. He had considered the possibility that parts of his own mind were revealed to Shara. Had Shara felt the weight of the anguish Yngvi carried inside at his own survival when so many had died? Did Shara know that if Yngvi could have chosen the time of his death, he would have chosen to die in battle?

"But you're right," said Shara, lightly. "I could always kill you." He let out a breath that was not quite laughter. "Very well."

Yngvi stared at him while Shara looked about the chamber casually, like a guest getting ready to make himself comfortable.

"Just like that?"

"You are very persuasive," said Shara, dryly, but his lips were no longer pressed into a thin, hard line. "And I don't yet know where to go on Aegyptus. What do we do until morning?"

There's a river behind the house," said Yngvi. "I need to bathe. As do you. Then I'll make us some food. We drink. Then we sleep. In the morning, I'll need to go see Magne before we leave. You can come with."

"All right," Shara said, with a tentative smile that seemed to unknot something inside Yngvi.

"All right." Yngvi brought a set of his clean clothes for Shara. "Can you..." he indicated Shara's body with a wave of his hand "...change back?"

Shara's reaction was no more than a twitch of his lips that Yngvi almost missed.

"I didn't mean—"

Shara cut him off with a little flick of his fingers. And as before, Shara from the tavern stood there, restored to his pale appearance.

"Better?" Shara asked. Without another word, he stepped out through the back door and headed down to the river.

"I didn't mean right now," said Yngvi, but he was speaking to an empty house.

He hurried out after Shara, troubled by the sudden change in his mood.

Shara didn't acknowledge his presence, just stripped off his boots and pants and entered the water. Stomped into it, Yngvi thought. He hurried out of his own clothes and waded in, careful to keep his bandaged shoulder dry.

It was dusk already. Where had the day gone? Shara swam some distance away and bathed as though he were alone in the stream. Yngvi didn't approach him; he washed in his own little section of the water, but followed Shara's every move.

Shara scrubbed the dirt and sweat of the battle from his limbs with brisk efficiency. He submerged his head, then surfaced like some otherworldly river creature, wet hair streaming down to the middle of his back.

Yngvi wished Shara would turn and look at him. Their eyes met once more and held for a moment, then Shara turned away.

A short while later, Shara emerged from the river, water trailing down his bare body. To Yngvi's enamoured eyes, he was a moon-kissed, wet-pearl figure, yet Yngvi's mind wouldn't let go of its memory of Shara's blue form. And in that moment, Yngvi understood what had upset him.

Shara's gait was more languorous now; the swim seemed to have calmed him. Or perhaps he had made peace with his own assumption. He stood naked in the night air, eyes closed, head thrown back, as he unselfconsciously dried himself in the breeze.

Yngvi lingered in the water, his breath catching at the play of the rising moonlight on Shara's body, all planes and sliding muscle and long limbs. He told himself that this attraction to Shara was unhelpful and patently unrequited, even if it provided a distraction from the horrors of battle. He turned in the water and tipped his head back, letting his gaze sweep the dark sky. He did not watch Shara pull on his borrowed clothes and head back into the house. They had still not exchanged words.

Alone in the stream, Yngvi started to replay everything he had learnt from the exchange of memories with Shara. But his mind took him back to the battle, to its brutal finality and the staggering loss of lives, to Shara's participation in it which had given the Aesir a fortuitous advantage, and despite his hand in the death of Loki, to Yngvi's own ignominy at the end. He was not welcome in Valhalla any longer. But worse than that was the unmistakable disappointment he had read in Magne's eyes.

Yngvi splashed water in his eyes, feeling the burn, then rubbed his face and swam to the shore. There he put on his own set of clean clothes and padded back inside.

CHAPTER NINE

SHARA STOOD BY the fire pit, his back to the door.

Yngvi's tunic hung off Shara's slimmer frame and fell down to mid-thigh. Yngvi found it charming.

He settled onto the stool, drumming his fingers on the tabletop, weighing his next words. "What was that?"

"What was what?"

"Just now, by the river. You marched off. Why?"

Shara turned to face him. "No reason."

"You thought…" Yngvi drew in a deep breath, let it out. They both knew what Shara had thought. It was laughable, and he wondered how to convince Shara of just how wrong he was. He shook his head. "If I ever meet Enlil or Namhu"—he heard the earnestness in his own voice—"I will…make sure they behave better towards you."

Shara's breath of laughter was just the reaction Yngvi wanted, because it was more than amusement. He had taken Shara by surprise.

"But…" said Yngvi.

"But?"

"But," Yngvi continued with a smile, "there's no one in all of Yggdrasil who looks like you. If you came with me to Magne's looking like you do…"

Shara nodded slowly.

"Good." Yngvi caught the softening in Shara's gaze and switched to the subject of food, with the smallest bit of apprehension about his skills and supplies, both of which had served him well enough as an unattached man who had never before needed to feed his visitors, even those that stayed the night. "I don't know what you eat on Nibiru, but I have some bread, meat, salted fish."

"That sounds appetising." Shara's stomach gave an anticipatory rumble that made Yngvi irrationally relieved.

"And there's mead," Yngvi added.

"Even better."

They ate in companionable silence, Shara seated on the chair by the table, Yngvi on the floor by the fire. When their plates had been put away, Yngvi brought out two deep cups and a pitcher of mead.

"You haven't taken Eir's medicine," said Shara.

"How closely were you watching me?"

Shara only smiled and poured water into Yngvi's cup. Yngvi emptied the contents of the pouch into it, stirred it with his finger and drank it in a single gulp. It was bitter, so he washed it down with mead.

The fire burned bright. Shara refilled Yngvi's cup when he held it out, and drank some more himself. The mood was warm and comfortable. Occasionally, Yngvi would glance at Shara and find himself trapped in the steady, crystalline gaze. Shara watched him openly until Yngvi averted his eyes.

The few times Shara studied other things in the room, Yngvi would study Shara, keen to capture and preserve the smallest particulars of his fine features, the languid elegance of his long limbs as he lounged in the chair, the fall of his hair down his back, his slender fingers hanging limply over the edge of the table and— He looked away, choosing, instead, to learn more about the man behind the marvel.

"Tell me about Nibiru," he said. "About your life in Mashu forest."

Shara smiled. "A bedtime story?"

"I doubt I'll sleep tonight," said Yngvi.

Shara was quiet for a while, gazing at the fire. When he spoke, his voice was low. "My first awareness was of the trees of Mashu. I was alone. One morning, a few years later, I woke on the ground in the forest and I saw Nidaba looking down at me. She was much older, but she smiled and took me in her arms and said that we had the same skin, the same hair and so I was going to be her little brother. And from that moment on, I was Nidaba's brother. She gave me my name and…" He stopped, shaking his head.

"I'm sorry," said Yngvi.

Shara nodded slowly.

Yngvi heard himself saying, with a sincerity that surprised even himself, "You should know, I would never ask you to cover your hair."

He wondered if their memory exchange had exposed his own thoughts, because Shara looked at him for a moment, as if caught off guard, then gestured minutely with his hand. And Yngvi watched in amazement as Shara returned to his blue form. So pleased was Yngvi that he felt the need to thank Shara. "You're…" He shook his head. "Go on."

"She used to take me through the halls of the Great Library, show me books and tell me tales."

"Bedtime stories?" Yngvi teased gently. He wanted to see Shara smile again.

Shara gave a soft snort. "Something like that. The legends of Nibiru, the origin story."

The absurdity of the situation pulled a laugh out of Yngvi. "Some hours ago, I only knew of Yggdrasil, and never really learnt its own legends. Yet I'm now about to hear the origin story of another world."

Shara's smile widened. He seemed to have a need to share as great as Yngvi's own need to know.

"The Anunnaki, the gods of Nibiru, are descended from Anu."

"So…Anu's the root of all your troubles," said Yngvi, smiling.

"So it would seem," Shara agreed, with a soft laugh. "Legend has it that Anu was the first consciousness, existing before time itself. He created Ki to be his consort, the female aspect of his male energy. They were the fount of all life. From Anu's seed, Ki bore the twins, Enlil and Enki."

"Why do the brothers hate each other?"

"Not just each other," said Shara. "They hated Ishtar, too, Anu's second consort."

"He made himself another wife?"

"Ki did. The creative force in her was so strong that her own twin came forth from her, independent of Anu, a fully formed woman. It is said that Ishtar's emergence left Ki as a lifeless, withered pile of skin that faded away soon after. But Ishtar was dark and beautiful like a clear summer's night."

"And she was a snow-mane?"

"She was said to be the first," said Shara. "And Anu desired her more than he had ever desired Ki. When they mated, Nidaba was born. The brothers have never been too fond of their half-sister."

"No one likes the mistress, or her spawn," said Yngvi. "Where is Anu now? And Ishtar?"

"No one knows when Anu left Nibiru. It is said that Ishtar was so heartbroken that she wept until she was no more. Her tears swelled the rivers of Nibiru and her eyes became its lakes. Mashu forest sprouted from her bones, her hair changing into the leaves and the grass, and from her limbs were born the forest nymphs. Her lips bloomed into flowers; her breasts became the hills. And from her womb were born the first men and women of the human race on Nibiru. Those men and women mated and bore children who, in turn, mated and bore children. That continues to this day."

"So much mating on Nibiru," Yngvi mused, giving Shara a significant look.

"As it is here, I would imagine," Shara returned, with a half-smile of his own.

Yngvi wasn't about to let that opening slip. "Yes. Humans here seek companionship with each other. Women and men mate. But not only to make children."

Shara was silent.

"Sometimes just women. And sometimes…"

Shara swallowed, and Yngvi felt his own pulse quicken.

"Sometimes…just men." He could tell Shara was holding himself very still, but he had to know. "Are you one of them?"

Shara blinked, but took a second too long to answer. "The humans?"

Too soon. "The Anunnaki," Yngvi said, quickly recovering.

"I don't know. I don't think so. But I don't think I'm human either, because they are not blue-skinned. Perhaps they once were, but now they are like Namhu."

Yngvi retrieved the memory of Namhu's face to renew his dislike of the envoy.

It was cold outside, but inside Yngvi's home, the firelight poured over the room, thick and golden, like warm honey.

Later, when the fires were dying, Yngvi tossed more kindling into the hearth. The flames jumped with a sputter.

Shara stifled a yawn.

Yngvi rose at once, dragged the large fur rug from its place in the middle of the floor and dropped it closer to the fireside. He improvised a long pillow from a rolled fur coat. From a wooden chest, he took out two wool blankets, tossed one to Shara and dropped the other on the rug.

"You can take the bed," said Yngvi.

"I can sleep on the rug," Shara offered.

"It's a cold night. You're my guest. Take the bed." But Yngvi's perpetual optimism pushed an invitation out of him, barely audible over the hissing fire. "Or we could share the rug," he murmured.

Shara sat on the edge of the bed, watching Yngvi with an unreadable expression. Then he lay down and pulled the blanket over his body.

Yngvi turned to his side so as to not strain his bandaged shoulder. His back was to Shara. His head sank into the pleasingly soft coat-pillow. His limbs still carried the strain of the earlier action in Valhalla; carefully, he stretched his body on the thick fur, tensing his muscles, holding them in their flexed position for a few seconds, then letting them go limp with a groan.

He smoothed the provisional bedding, rumpled from his movements, over the floor until it lay flat and spread to its full width, sufficient to accommodate two bodies. And because it was more agreeable than thoughts of death, his imagination obligingly supplied a picture of two heads resting on a single pillow, one gold and one white—or even dark, as before; he didn't mind, as long as it was the same man.

A subtle shift in the air. A muffled sound from behind told him that Shara had picked up his blanket and risen from the bed. Perhaps it wasn't too soon. Yngvi's shaking breath misted in front of his face.

He listened to Shara's progress across the floor. He felt Shara's soft tread through his body, the thump of the blanket when it hit the rug, the thrill of Shara's nearness as he lowered himself between Yngvi and the fire. Yngvi looked up at him, waiting.

Shara's cheek hollowed as he bit the inside. "I'd like to be close to the fire. It's a cold night."

"Should I take the bed?" Yngvi made to sit up but Shara's hand on his arm kept him from rising.

"Or we could share the rug."

Yngvi went very still.

Shara's throat jumped. "Unless you want the bed."

The air grew hot as the distance between their bodies shrank. The mood was changing. What had been cozily impersonal now felt treacherous.

"No," Yngvi said. "But—"

"Then it's fine."

And Yngvi found he could not speak, because Shara had stretched out on the rug and turned to his side, sharing the makeshift pillow, facing Yngvi. With the fire behind him, Shara's face was cast in shadow. Only the steady lamplight was reflected in his eyes. A lock of his hair, pale and thick, had slipped forward to snake down his smooth neck. Shara's eyes dropped to Yngvi's lips, and lifted after a long moment. They were gazing at each other.

Looking at Shara now, so close that he was able to see the sweep of lashes veiling the pale blue eyes, and the way Shara's lips pressed together under Yngvi's gaze, was a different experience from what Yngvi had imagined.

The flames in the hearth flared bright in Yngvi's vision, hissing like the fire giant that had burned his shoulder. He closed his eyes and listened to the young wood sparking and snapping, loud in the quiet chamber, like the crunch of ice on bone, the crackling blast from Loki's spear. The winds outside had grown restless, whistling through the gap below his doors, like Hel's shadow fiends.

He wanted to forget it all, but the horrors of the battle filled his mind, as real as if he were standing in Valhalla's courtyard again surrounded by the dust-covered bodies of gods and mortals, the stench of blood pervading the thick air, Snabb's severed head, Thor's corroded chest, the screams of the Valkyries. And after, the desolate march of the wounded, the recrimination in Odin's gaze, the disappointment in Magne's. He wished he could forget, if only for one night, and opened his eyes at the sound of his name.

"Yngvi…"

Shara had a faint frown, but his expression was open and searching.

A moment of understanding passed between them.

"There was nothing," Shara said, quietly, gently, "that anyone on Yggdrasil could have done to stop Enki. It was not your war to stop. There was nothing you could have done, and still you fought."

Yngvi could not speak because of what was welling inside him. Somehow, Shara had known that he needed to hear this, and only Shara could have said this with certitude. Shara's words seemed to drift through the air between them and settle over Yngvi's body, like the touch of a warm hand. He nodded again wordlessly, dropping his gaze, his throat thick with everything he wanted to say. He knew it wasn't over. He knew Enki would kill again.

"But we will stop him," said Shara, resolutely, putting a hand on Yngvi's chest, "you and I—"

Yngvi lifted his eyes and before he knew it, he had taken Shara's head in his hands and was kissing him. He felt the hard ache inside his chest with the first press of lips, soft and warm and alive. If desire had been a part of it, it was subsumed now in the overriding, desperate gratitude inside him. Shara had given him what no one else had: a reprieve, kindness. And hope.

He did not know how long he had been holding Shara that way, but the instant he realised where his lips were, shock at his presumption made him jerk his head back. Shara's hand, which had been resting gently on his neck, fell abruptly onto Yngvi's chest. The pale blue eyes came open in surprise at their separation. The full lips were still parted, but slowly closed.

There was nothing to say but, "I'm sorry." Yngvi shifted onto his back and put a handspan of distance between them. "I don't know what came over me."

Shara showed no reaction, simply lay on his side of the bedding staring up at the ceiling. After a while, he closed his eyes. He was silent for a time, so long that Yngvi thought he slept. Then his lashes lifted, and Yngvi saw him gazing at the still night outside the window. The stars had come out and the kindling was almost ash when he turned on his side to face Yngvi and spoke, his voice quiet and grave.

"On Apsu and Marduk, it was all over when I reached. I— I only saw what was left of the gods. Which was nothing—worse than nothing... I imagine it must have been like this. If I had known earlier, I might have— " The words were bitter, his eyes cast down to Yngvi's chest.

"You didn't know," said Yngvi, tipping Shara's chin up, "and still you ended Ragnarök. You saved Asgard. You saved Magne, you saved me. You've been pursuing him alone all this time, but I'm with you now. And we are going to stop Enki before he kills again. Together."

Another long silence stretched out between them.

"Shara..." Yngvi started to say, but it was his words that were cut off this time because Shara was cleaving to him and kissing him as though he needed it too, the solidity of a warm, living body in his arms. What else could Yngvi do but give him what he wanted.

He pulled away only long enough to gasp, "On your back," and push down on Shara's shoulder.

Shara obeyed, and in the next moment, Yngvi was leaning over him, lowering his head to capture Shara's lips again. Desire came flooding back, and there was a different kind of desperation to the kiss this time. He ran his hands over Shara's body, his long, lithely muscled limbs, the span of his chest, the dip below his ribcage, the plane of his taut stomach, the curve of his hip as the inside of his thigh, lifted now, pressed against Yngvi's waist.

When Yngvi's lips parted, Shara echoed the movement, and a shiver ran down Yngvi's back at the first wet touch of Shara's open mouth. He held still, then in a moment of daring, of irrepressible need, slid his tongue inside, finding Shara's and tangling. They kissed, and kissed again, drawing relief and reassurance from each other.

Yngvi was gasping when they separated. He rolled onto his back and stared at the ceiling, his chest rising and falling rapidly with his breaths. It had felt strange, like a dream in which he had been allowed to touch Shara, to kiss him. When he turned, he found Shara on his side, touching his lips, gazing at Yngvi. The crackle of the fire was barely audible over the blood beating in Yngvi's ears as Shara's gaze locked with his.

Then Shara said, into the stillness between them, "I've never—done that." He shifted his head closer on the pillow. "I—" His breathing hitched, and Yngvi felt a throb of proprietary satisfaction that he was the cause of that minor tumult in Shara.

Shara's eyes were wide and dark, the black swallowing up the blue, leaving only a thin bright ring to remind Yngvi of the crystal gaze that had so entranced him outside the tavern. Shara was holding himself carefully, perhaps a little nervously, as though expecting Yngvi to laugh at his words. Desire seemed locked in battle with disbelief on the lovely and eager blue face.

"I'm glad," said Yngvi, unduly gratified by Shara's surprise. He lifted a hand to cup Shara's cheek and slid it behind his neck to pull him even closer. Shara's lips parted, but Yngvi took his time to kiss Shara's closed eyes, his cheeks, his neck, before returning to his lips.

When they pulled apart, Shara shifted back onto the pillow, but only so far that looking at each other was not uncomfortable.

Yngvi smiled. "You were right that I wouldn't believe you."

"I meant that," said Shara, frowning.

Yngvi pressed his finger to the point between Shara's eyebrows until the frown smoothed. "And I meant that I can't believe no one on Nibiru has done that to you before."

The colour rose on Shara's face, and Yngvi watched it helplessly, wishing he could do more, so much more. But the events of the past days had left him exhausted, even if Shara showed hardly any signs of fatigue. And they had time, didn't they?

"I would have died today if it wasn't for you."

Shara's smile was forlorn. "Then I am glad that I was there."

After that, the words seemed to run out. Their breaths were slow and deep, the fire too loud, the air too still, their faces too far apart.

When Shara finally shifted onto his back, Yngvi's world narrowed to the shape of his sharp profile silhouetted against the light of the dying embers. Moments later, Yngvi closed his eyes and let sleep claim him.

CHAPTER TEN

YNGVI AWOKE WITH a shiver.

The fire had died. The improvised pillow had slipped off the rug and unfolded. The fur rug was now askew. He had shifted in the night and was lying on his stomach, his tunic pushed up, exposing his skin to the chilly, bare floor. But one stretch of skin was not cold, under one arm. The arm which was thrown over a warm body.

Lifting his head, he blinked slowly, then deliberately a few times, to push the sleep out of his eyes and clear his vision.

He had awakened to the unreal fact of Shara lying beside him, all blue skin and pale hair. A drowsy smile tugged at Yngvi's lips and he allowed himself the small pleasure of gazing at Shara, at the face of a warrior in deep sleep, peaceful and even younger in repose, arms stretched out over his head. Shara's lips were slightly parted, his breaths long and slow.

Yngvi lifted his arm carefully, so as to not disturb, but Shara stirred. Yngvi watched the thick lashes flutter open as Shara made his way back to wakefulness. He waited while Shara's gaze flitted over the room, placing his surroundings, and then landed on Yngvi.

Shara blinked a few times, and Yngvi wondered if he was replaying the events of the previous day, which had culminated in the quiet, private exchanges of the evening. He waited while Shara's eyes cleared and he came fully awake.

" *Yngvi.* "

Uttered in Shara's sleep-soft, husky voice, the sound of his name felt more intimate than their joined memories. Shara's expression was relaxed and open, and he wore the grateful smile of an exhausted fighter who has been allowed to rest.

"Shara," said Yngvi. "It's evening."

The pale eyes widened. "Evening?"

Yngvi laughed softly. "We slept one whole night and one whole day."

"Oh." Shara shifted his gaze to the waning sun sheeting in through the window, then back to Yngvi.

"Slept well?"

The corners of Shara's mouth curled up; his eyes crinkled with mischief. "Can I sleep another week?"

It welled again inside Yngvi, that feeling he couldn't name. The only bedmates who had woken up beside Yngvi had gone to sleep in his arms. And those bedmates would be naked now, and kissing Yngvi, on his lips or elsewhere on his body. But this was Shara and he was fully clothed, which was why, even after last night, Yngvi would not presume anything.

He rolled onto his back. His laugh was a cynical breath in the still evening. He had slept the weary sleep of the dead, and now felt somewhat rested. He lolled his head to look at Shara, who had pushed himself up on his elbows.

"I should leave." Then, catching Yngvi's disputing look, Shara amended, " *We* should."

Yngvi gave him a smile. "Bathe first?"

Shara nodded.

Yngvi closed his eyes for a moment. When he opened them, Shara was already walking out towards the back door that led to the river. His skin was pale again, his hair dark. Yngvi gave himself a moment to clear his mind, then rose and followed Shara to the stream.

A pleasurable languor saturated Yngvi's limbs as he washed. He dipped his head below the surface, closed his eyes, and started when the water around him moved and Shara touched his shoulder. Together, they swam up to the surface.

Yngvi pulled on a tunic and buckled his sword belt around his waist.

The scabbard was heavy with Enki's sword, now his. "We'll stop by Magne's. I have to tell him I'm leaving."

They were back in the house. Shara had on his own pants and boots under another of Yngvi's tunics. Yngvi pressed his lips together, because the tunic's shoulder seams were hanging just above Shara's biceps, and Shara had rolled the sleeves up to a manageable length.

Shara gave him an unamused glare. Yngvi allowed himself a laugh then, and pulled on his boots.

When he straightened, he found that Shara had come dangerously close and was holding his gaze. As Shara lifted his hand to Yngvi's shoulder, he dropped his eyes to Yngvi's lips. Yngvi, who thought a continuation of last night a most propitious way to begin the parlous travels that lay ahead of them, pulled Shara in again. Shara's hands slipped down to Yngvi's chest. Their lips had barely touched when Shara pushed against him, the pressure not forceful, but not quite playful either.

"No?" Yngvi found he had taken a step back.

The blue face was closed and frowning slightly, the full lips pressed in a thin line; the clear eyes that had hidden so little last night were impenetrable now, and Yngvi confronted the first stirrings of doubt in his ability to interpret the unspoken language of new lovers. He felt, in this moment, somewhat less charitable about Shara's equivocation, because it was easier to accept than the prospect that yesterday had been nothing more than the aching desperation of two men plagued with their own personal agonies, and Yngvi had, foolishly, ascribed significance to it.

"We should leave," said Shara.

"All right," Yngvi said, when the sting of insult had passed.

They had a murderous god to stop, and Aegyptus awaited.

The last of the sun's light had leached out of the sky and taken with it the remnants of Yngvi's good humour by the time they stood outside Magne's home.

He lifted his hand to knock, but his fingers curled into a fist. This would not be pleasant. He drew in a deep breath and knocked.

The door opened into a foyer. A woman faced them. She was almost as tall as Shara; she wore her golden hair in a braid that sat heavy on her shoulder and reached down to her thick waist.

From inside, Magne asked, "Who is it?"

Ulla's lips were pressed into a thin line as she regarded Yngvi.

"Ulla." Yngvi inclined his head in greeting.

Two blond boys, mirror images of each other, ran up to crowd around her legs. "Uncle Yngvi!" they chirped.

Even Ulla's reserve could not dampen the joy that welled inside Yngvi. "Come here, you little imps! Oof!" he said, as his nephews leapt into his arms. He weathered Ulla's blue-eyed hostility. "I need to see my brother, Ulla. I'm leaving."

"Good," was all she said.

Yngvi inwardly added Ulla to the growing list of those who blamed him for Ragnarök. But her disapproval felt more wounding, because she was family, and if things had gone differently, she would have lost her husband, her children would have lost their father, and Yngvi would have lost his brother.

Ulla stepped back, soothing her swollen belly with one hand as she opened the door wider. Magne's sons slithered out of Yngvi's arms and down to the ground, and scampered off to play.

In Yngvi's longhouse, bed, kitchen, table and hearth all occupied the same undivided spare enclosure, as was sufficient for a man who lived alone. Magne's house, in contrast, had been sectioned into a series of rooms with doors and furnishings, as befitted a family man. The foyer led to the main sitting room which, in turn, opened into the kitchen at the far end. Behind the kitchen were two bedrooms, the smaller one for the children, the bigger one for Magne and Ulla.

Yngvi followed Ulla to the sitting room, where Magne sat at the head of a large table near the fireplace. They waited while she went into the kitchen. The boys were running in semi-circles around Yngvi and Shara, smacking each other on the shoulder, then darting off in the opposite direction to avoid being hit. He hadn't yet determined which of them was winning when they ended that game abruptly and leapt at him again, clambering up his arms.

Magne's left shoulder, head and both forearms were swathed in Eir's bandages. Ulla returned with a plate piled with bread and meats, and a cup of mead, both of which she placed on the table before Magne. She exchanged a questioning look with her husband, then directed her flinty gaze at Yngvi.

"Will you eat?" said Magne.

Yngvi's shoulders were awkwardly flexed now with the effort of holding up his giggling little nephews who were hanging on to his outstretched arms. He had been swinging them about lightly while they squealed with delight and Ulla watched in frosty silence. He lowered his arms so that the twins could slide off safely.

"We ate already."

He and Shara had eaten the stew Yngvi had prepared, which had used up the meats and potatoes in his house. They had drunk the final half pitcher of mead. Yngvi had shoved his entire supply of clean clothes— four pairs of tunic and pants—into a large cloth pouch with a drawstring which he'd slung over his shoulder. Finally, he had taken one parting look at his house, fully aware that he might never return to it. Then they had left.

Magne took Ulla's hand, which was resting gently on his bandaged shoulder, and held it to his lips. Then he kissed her belly and smiled up at her. She gave him a wan smile in return. Leaning down with effort, she kissed the small section of uninjured skin on his forehead. She straightened slowly and looked at her sons. "Come," she said, then turned and slowly followed her boisterous sons to their bedroom where they continued their play.

"The boys miss you," said Magne. "You don't visit as often anymore."

"I miss them too. I can't believe I'm going to be an uncle for the third time."

"Or fourth, if Ulla has twins again."

"How long?"

"About three weeks. I'm hoping for a sister, or sisters, for the boys."

Yngvi smiled. "You wouldn't know what to do with girls."

"Ulla will teach me," said Magne. But his smile faded as his eyes stopped on Yngvi's shoulder. "That looks bad." He nodded at a chair and Yngvi sat across the table.

"It was. Eir's powder nearly killed me with its taste, but I'll live." The throbbing in his injured shoulder was negligible. He had peeked under the bandage, and was gladdened to see that his skin had started to heal. "I'll be all right."

Magne glanced over Shara's body, looking for signs of injury "Your friend…he looks unharmed."

"I was fortunate," said Shara.

"I don't think fortune had anything to do with it. Sit. You were part of all of it."

Shara took the chair beside Yngvi.

"What are you called?" said Magne.

"Shara."

"Shara," Magne repeated. "I've never heard that name before. We looked for you. Where did you go after the fighting ended?"

Shara was silent.

"Where have you been since then?" Magne pressed.

"With me," Yngvi interjected.

Magne nodded, as though he had expected that. "Shara. You saved my life."

"I was just a soldier helping another," said Shara.

"You needn't be modest. I saw you fight. I don't think you're a soldier at all."

In Magne's narrowed eyes were all the questions Yngvi himself had wanted to ask Shara when he had first opened the door to him. But they didn't have time for that now.

"Magne," said Yngvi. "I'm leaving."

"Leaving? Where are you going?"

"It's not important," said Yngvi.

"Not important?"

"I can't tell you… But I came to see you because I don't know when I'll be back."

"Is he going with you?" Magne inclined his head in Shara's direction.

"Yes."

Magne was quiet for a long time. Yngvi glanced at Shara, who had been keeping silent.

" *Will* you be back, Yngvi?" said Magne.

That rankled. "I'm not running away after Rag—after what just happened, if that's what you mean," Yngvi snapped. "I told you then and I'll tell you again—"

"That is not what I meant." Magne looked at Shara with weary eyes. "I wish my brother wouldn't always misunderstand me."

To Yngvi's disbelief, Shara nodded that *he* understood. "You worry about him."

"I worry about him." Magne returned his gaze to Yngvi. "A lot. Yngvi, you're twenty-five. I worry that you're going to do something impulsive and reckless. I think it's time—"

"I know what you think. You want me to be like you."

"If not me, then know that it's what Mother and Father would want for you. A family of your own."

"What for? You're keeping the Ecklundson line going," said Yngvi. "And I'm all right the way I am."

"Am I not allowed to wish for you to have some…constancy…in your life?"

"Magne—" The concern in his brother's eyes was breaking through the hardness in Yngvi's heart.

"We have just been through so much, all of us. And already you're leaving to go somewhere—you won't tell me where—with a stranger who fights like no one I've ever seen." Magne kept his eyes on Yngvi. "Is it because you find him attractive?"

"Magne!" Yngvi would never get used to how abruptly his brother could go from reasonable and mature, even lovable, to puerile and highly annoying.

Now Magne looked at Shara. "You know that, don't you?"

Irritation promptly became mortification, because Shara nodded once, keeping his eyes on Magne.

"Can you stay?" Magne asked Shara.

"Magne! Stop this!"

"I—" Shara's pale skin had turned crimson. He blinked rapidly, and glanced at Yngvi. "No, I can't."

"You see? *This* is why I don't visit," said Yngvi, feeling his own face flush.

"Is there anything I can say to change your mind?"

"I have to do this," said Yngvi. "It's the only way."

"Only way? For what?" Magne demanded, his voice rising in both pitch and volume, as it did when Yngvi worried him. Redundantly, he said: "You're worrying me, Yngvi."

In the long silence that followed, Yngvi considered, and decided against, telling Magne what he had learnt from Shara.

"Please," Yngvi said, softly. "Let me go. Just…wish that I succeed."

Magne's shoulders dropped. He closed his eyes and let out a breath, but when, long moments later, he opened his eyes again, there was no argument in them, only acceptance. He stood and came around the table to stand beside Yngvi, who rose to his feet. Shara, too.

"I might not always show it," said Magne, holding out his arms, "but I love you. More than you know."

"I know," said Yngvi, letting Magne ruffle his hair as if he were ten. He dropped his head on Magne's shoulders and breathed in his brother's scent, but it was mixed with Eir's salves. Another memory to carry with him to…to wherever Shara took him. "And I love you. I wish it didn't have to be like this."

Over Magne's shoulder, Shara was observing them in silence. Their eyes met. A shadow passed over Shara's face just as he looked away. Yngvi remembered Nidaba and stood back.

Magne took Yngvi's face in his hands and pressed his lips to Yngvi's temple. "I know, and I will wait for you to return. May I have a word with Shara?"

"Alone?" said Yngvi.

"Alone."

Yngvi looked from his brother to Shara and back, trying and failing to divine Magne's intentions. "All right," he said. "I'll wait by the door."

He left the room but stopped in the foyer just out of sight, waiting close enough to hear them talking.

"Shara," said Magne. "I don't know who you are or where you come from. But I've seen you fight. I know you have no need of protection, but Yngvi might. So...I ask if you will watch over my brother."

"I will," said Shara.

"Do I have your word?"

"You have my word."

Magne spoke after a pause. "Be safe, and be well, Shara."

CHAPTER ELEVEN

YNGVI LED SHARA away from Magne's house and down a narrow deserted alley. Even though it was already night, he did not want any curious Midgardians spotting them.

"Now?" he said.

Shara nodded. "Hold on to me."

Yngvi held on to Shara's shoulders. "I'm ready."

Shara just looked at him for a moment. Then, sounding as surprised as Yngvi felt, he said, "I'm glad you're coming with me."

Yngvi had to consciously mask how unreasonably pleased that made him. "Stay here or go with you?" he said, evenly. "It's not the toughest choice I've had to make."

Shara nodded. He put one hand on Yngvi's forearm, and curled the other around his leaf-amulet.

"How does it feel," said Yngvi, "to travel across realms?"

"It's quite indescribable."

Yngvi gave Shara a flat look. "That's very helpful. Now I know exactly what to expect."

Shara smiled. "You'll be disoriented when we arrive. But I'll be with you. Keep your eyes on me."

Yngvi gave him an unsteady smile of his own. "I'm not taking my eyes off you." He was only half-teasing because his legs felt like water.

"Good," said Shara, just as his blue aura reached out again, enveloping Yngvi as if it recognised him from before. A thin shiver ran through Yngvi's body. The vibrations began slowly, intensifying with each passing moment until Yngvi felt his physical form coming apart. But there was no pain, just a feeling of weightlessness, and a spike of mild panic at the realisation that their bodies were becoming amorphous. He was transforming into a faintly golden cloud, his consciousness the sole force binding his corporeal particles into a single entity.

For fear that he would drift into nothingness, he willed his vaporous arms to hold the bluish form before him. That was a timely decision, because they were ascending into the heavens. Higher and higher they rose, and when he glanced down, Midgard's houses were no more than a wide scattering of bright dots. Without warning, his head snapped back and he was shot down a long tunnel of light, the vivid points stretching out into snaking trails of white in his vision.

Yngvi couldn't tell up from down as he barrelled headfirst along the endless cosmic strip. A low, loud drone filled his ears. When he regained a little equipoise, he opened his eyes just a fraction but shut them as soon as he grasped that the highway was in fact a celestial funnel that was rapidly contracting to the size of a pebble.

So this was how he would end—in the heavens, his particles dispersed like stardust. But incredibly, like everything about this mad journey, his formless body slid through that tiny aperture and came out on the other side.

Before him lay an endless expanse of black, dotted with nebulous patches of colour and countless tiny, pulsing lights. The stellar tunnel had exploded into infinity.

Yngvi found himself alone, drifting across the darkness. A tiny ring of light appeared in the distance, growing larger as he hurtled closer. It appeared to be a threshold to somewhere else. A split-second later, it was around him and then behind him as the portal spat him out.

He knew he was flesh and bone again when his body lurched painfully onto a dry surface and came to a stop face down in coarse powder.

He stayed that way, surrounded by a cloud of crackling energy while his body fully coalesced into its own shape. When he finally felt whole, he pushed himself up with one arm and flopped onto his back. He lay like that for a long time, breathing hard and staring up at the endless span of dawn sky, the very skies he had just traversed in the space of— How long had it been? A few seconds? Hours? It had been night when they left Midgard. Time had lost meaning.

Was this Aegyptus? His vision was unfocused, and he blinked to banish the dark haze.

Endeavouring to sit up while the skies still wheeled would be overambitious. He stayed flat on his back, racked by diminishing aftershocks, while his mind seesawed towards equilibrium. But his body was back inside his skin and his lungs were drawing breath. He was still alive.

Blinking dazedly, he noticed that the purple and orange sky had turned a shadowed blue. *Strange. The sky has eyes and a nose and lips. The sky's lips are moving. They are sweet lips.* He smiled. *Idiot. It's Shara.*

The name felt like sanctuary. Yngvi's face felt warm.

Shara was leaning over him, calling his name, his hand cupping Yngvi's cheek. He sounded remote but his face was very close. So close that Yngvi could see, under the light of the stars, that Shara's forehead was creased, his eyes wide with concern. Yngvi liked what he saw. He gave Shara a dreamy smile. Then he frowned.

"You're blue," he said.

Shara laughed. "Only to you. I'll appear like a native to the people here. As will you."

Yngvi groaned, pushed himself up to a sitting position, and swayed.

"It will take a few minutes to feel normal," said Shara.

Yngvi nodded, and immediately regretted doing so. "The sky is still spinning."

Shara waited while Yngvi leaned forward shakily, his hands on his knees. Long minutes passed before he looked up at Shara.

"I think I can stand now."

Shara held out a hand and helped him up.

Yngvi looked around the dark field, then at Shara, who was watching him intently. "Gods!" He ran a hand through his hair. "That was something."

"The first time is always the hardest. You'll get used to it."

Yngvi lifted his eyes. "The sky looks different."

"We are very far from Yggdrasil, but that, there"—Shara pointed to a bright cluster of stars hanging low over the horizon—"is Sipa-Zi-An-Na. Oruwandil in your language. So not all different."

"Where are we?" Yngvi was still breathing heavily.

Shara was looking in the direction of a glow in the distance. "In a desert on the outskirts of Saqqara."

"Saqqara," said Yngvi, testing the unfamiliar combination of syllables on his tongue. "This *is* Aegyptus, isn't it?"

"It is."

"What is in Saqqara?"

"Answers, I hope," said Shara. "And Enki."

Yngvi frowned faintly. "You didn't know of Saqqara when we were in Midgard. How do you know all this?"

Shara's shrug said that he had wondered the same thing. "There's something inside me, like a part of my mind I have not fully seen before. I'm not sure… With each realm I visit, more of my mind seems to open. So…I…just seem to know." He didn't elaborate and Yngvi didn't press him.

"When you're ready," said Shara, "we have to walk some distance to the city. That's where we'll find the oracular goddess."

"Let's go."

The desert extended many miles out, and after a few hours of his boots sinking into the sand, Yngvi began to long for the stability of firm terrain underfoot.

Their arrival in the desert's dawn coolness had left him unprepared for its soaring daytime temperatures. Worse, hailing from Midgard, which was dark and frozen for the first half of the year, bright and pleasant for the latter half, Yngvi was acclimatised to the cold, and sorely ill-equipped to withstand the desert heat, which was all around him now, like a dry, smothering blanket of fire. His body was throwing off water to keep itself cool. His hair was wet, his tunic damp and stuck to his body in long, sweaty patches. Thirst was another growing hardship, and he wished he had thought to carry a waterskin from Midgard. Swallowing to keep his throat wet could only go so far. He let out an involuntary rasping breath.

Shara looked over at Yngvi and raised his eyebrows. Unsurprisingly, he seemed unaffected by the elements.

"I've never seen so much sand and absolutely no water," said Yngvi.

"Nibiru doesn't have deserts this large," said Shara, conversationally, "but there are rivers, mountains and trees." Then, realising what Yngvi had meant, "We are almost in Saqqara. We should be able to find water there."

Yngvi nodded. Under the blinding light of the sun, he looked out at the vast, tranquil sheet of greyish gold stretched over the ridged desert floor. Smooth mounds of sand shifted with sinuous grace under the warm breeze. In this austere, infertile expanse, the only signs of foliage were scattered tufts of blackish green.

He felt something crawl up his legs and looked down to investigate. Audacious insects were making their way up to his knees. Yngvi brushed them off with care.

They seemed to have walked into a nest. Here and there the loose sand peaked, then fell away around small hard-shelled creatures that had channelled their way out. They skittered over the surface erratically and with comical urgency, stopped to inspect some miniscule particle and then, their curiosity apparently satisfied, burrowed back into the sandy depths.

"Even the creatures here seek answers," Yngvi said as he stepped over a small mound.

Shara flung out an arm before Yngvi. "Stop."

Yngvi froze in mid-step. He hadn't seen the snake swiftly sidewinding across their paths.

"It might have been venomous," said Shara.

Yngvi grinned weakly. "You know how to get snake venom out of someone, don't you?"

Shara's glare held no heat. They walked the rest of the way in silence, Shara pulling slightly ahead, Yngvi following.

CHAPTER TWELVE

ANOTHER HOUR HAD passed before Saqqara came into view.

In the foreground was a small clump of specks, some of which seemed to be moving. Behind the clump was a long and thin sand-coloured strip that curved at either end. And debouching through the clump were long queues of ant-sized black dots.

As they drew closer, the ants turned out to be people, and the strip a wall. Large caravans were spreading out into the desert. Some of the travellers rode odd-looking beasts with orange-brown skin stretched over strange humps and long, gangly legs. Despite being saddled and harnessed, the beasts' wobbly gait and the large, colourful blankets loosely spread out over the saddles surely meant that riders were in perpetual danger of slipping off. And the prospect of falling from that height, even if into the yielding sands of the desert, could not be pleasant because these beasts appeared to be almost three feet taller than a horse. Given the choice to ride one of these or walk, Yngvi knew which mode of transport he would pick.

Shara scanned the men in the convoy, then moved his hand minutely.

"What are you doing?" Yngvi asked.

"Making us look like the locals," said Shara.

"Are you putting us in skirts, like those men?" The Aegyptian men wore pleated white skirts and leather sandals. Most were shirtless, but a few wore tunics of white linen.

"No. And they're called shendyts," said Shara, absently.

"How do you know they're called shend— Never mind." Yngvi smiled. "Are you sure we won't be found out?"

"I'm sure. At any rate, we're going to put our disguises to the test very soon."

They passed the caravans without incident. A few beasts turned their long, curved necks to regard them with heavy-lidded, indifferent eyes, jaws moving hypnotically as they chewed on wads of green. One spat in their direction. A group of young boys trailing the caravans pointed and laughed at that, at them. The disguises had worked.

As they neared the city, a medley of scents wafted towards them— spiced meat and freshly baked bread, fresh fruit and other prepared confections. Sounds of civilisation were audible, because the desert was bordering what looked like a marketplace. It appeared to be the zenith of business hours, with farmers and vendors hurrying to their stalls with replenishments of merchandise, setting up their wares, shouting out products and prices and competing to be heard over the general bustle.

"And I expect," said Yngvi, in the Midgardian tongue, "that we'll be able to converse with the locals."

Shara only smiled.

Yngvi shook his head with a smile of his own. *Of course, we will.*

They dodged the beetling populace and trundling caravans, earning curses if they were too slow in getting out of the way, and finally cut across to the opposite side. The city of Saqqara lay beyond the market, on the other side of the high-flung wall. Yngvi understood, from the span of desert they had just traversed, and from the outflow of men and beasts through the market, that this would be the departing travellers' last opportunity to stock up on food and supplies until they reached their destination.

Looking around for an approachable face, Yngvi found two: two boys leaning against the mud wall of a small shack. Their sun-darkened bodies were bare but for white loincloths, their smooth skin gleaming with sweat in the noonday heat. And they were watching him and Shara with interest.

"Come," said Yngvi, making his way to the boys. Shara followed.

"Hello," Yngvi said. Up close, they seemed less welcoming than they had from afar.

"What do you want?" said the taller boy, pushing up from the wall and drawing himself to his full height. He came up to Yngvi's chest.

"Water," said Yngvi, meeting the boy's dark, unfriendly eyes. "We have come a long way and are parched."

"Where do you come from?" said the younger boy, whose attempt to emulate his taciturn companion's manner was unsuccessful, because excitement danced in his eyes.

"Far away," said Shara. "Is there somewhere we could get water to drink?"

"How far away?" the younger boy asked.

"That's enough, Shai," said the taller boy. He seemed to be around Halli's age. Eighteen or nineteen.

"No one ever talks to us!" said Shai, in sweet protest.

"Shai," said Yngvi, pleasantly. "Is that your name?"

"Yes!" Shai's wholesome grin showed very white teeth. He looked to be around twelve.

"And why does no one talk to you?" Yngvi asked.

Shai's smile faltered, but his words did not. "We are low born. We are only allowed to work for people like you, not talk to you."

"People like us?"

The older boy flicked his eyes sceptically over Yngvi's body. "Are you not scribes?"

Yngvi glanced at Shara. What kind of clothes did they appear to be wearing?

"Yes…we are scribes," said Yngvi. "And what are you called?"

The boy crossed his arms over his chest. "Why do you want to know?"

"Ineni…" Shai chided his grouchy companion, with charming naivete.

"So, you are Ineni," said Yngvi, with a laugh. "We mean you no harm, Ineni. All we want is some water."

"Shai," Ineni said to the grinning younger boy, "you are an idiot." To Yngvi: "There's a well behind the shop there." He pointed his thumb to his right, where a jewellery stall stood at the edge of the market.

"I'll get it for you!" said Shai. He ducked into the hut and reappeared with something tucked under his arms. Then he scampered off in the direction of the well, returning a few minutes later with two distended waterskins which he offered to Shara and Yngvi.

"Thank you," Yngvi said. He drank, and drank, putting out his tongue to collect the last drops, nearly falling to his knees from the relief of the unexpectedly cool water travelling down his throat. The water seemed to have refreshed all of him from the inside. He felt certain he could run ten miles.

Beside him, Shara had taken his fill of water and handed his waterskin back to Shai.

"Thank you," said Yngvi.

They made to leave, but Shai's voice held them back.

"Why have you come to Saqqara?"

"We are seeking the oracular goddess," said Shara.

"Wadjet?"

"Can you direct us to her temple?" said Shara.

Ineni shook his head. "You're too late. The festival ended yesterday."

That explained the mass egression of caravans.

"We are not here for the festival," said Shara. "There is a matter of worship that we must discuss."

"*He* would be able to help you!" said Shai, showing even more teeth in his happy, helpful face. "Look! Ow!"

Ineni had swatted the back of Shai's head lightly. "You talk too much!"

But Yngvi had already turned to follow Shai's finger and spotted an all-male throng of around twenty Aegyptians streaming into the market from the city. It appeared to be a royal contingent led by an imperious man. He sat erect against cloth-covered cushions in an ornate palanquin held aloft at shoulder height by four slaves. From his bearing and the respect accorded to him by his retinue, Yngvi surmised that the Aegyptian ranked high in society.

"That's the High Priest, sitting in his high chair," said Ineni, dryly. "Hemiunu. Talk to him."

"Thank you," said Shara.

"And keep our names out of your discussions," said Ineni.

"We will," said Yngvi. "And thank you for the water, Shai."

Ineni scowled, but Shai grinned and waved to them. Yngvi found that endearing and grinned back, eliciting a darker glare from Ineni.

As they turned, Ineni muttered to Shai, "If we get in trouble, it will be your fault."

Yngvi smiled.

They wove through the departing travellers to make their way to Hemiunu's coterie.

A linen canopy enclosed Hemiunu's palanquin on three sides and above, to shield him from the sun. He had been spared the harsh living conditions of his dark-skinned slaves and attendants. High cheekbones and a proud brow lent him a particular kind of aristocracy. His eyes were bright and outlined with black, and his skin was lighter and of a single tone all over—from his shaven head down to his bare torso and legs. His only attire was a snug, pleated skirt—*shendyt*, Shara had called it—which was held at his waist by a gold belt. It might have been longer standing up, but now it ended several inches above his knees.

As they walked, Shara whispered, "Someone should tell him to bring his knees together."

Yngvi smirked. "These men are all a foot shorter than you. Fortunately for them, they have a different point of view."

A sidelong glance showed him that Shara's shoulders were shaking.

"Stop it," he said, even though his own lips quivered.

They walked up to the gathering and stood before the leader.

"Greetings," said Shara. "We seek an audience with the High Priest of Saqqara."

"For what purpose?" said Hemiunu.

"We seek guidance on a matter of historical significance, and were told the High Priest is the foremost authority on such matters in Saqqara. Especially those that require the wisdom of the oracular goddess."

Shara's affected humility appeared to have met with Hemiunu's approval.

"You have come to the right place," Hemiunu proclaimed. "I am the High Priest of Saqqara."

He held up a hand. At once, his obedient followers formed tidy columns and knelt as one. The five men who remained standing were dressed in full-length tunics of unadorned white linen, and were closer in appearance to Hemiunu than the slaves and attendants, with shaven heads and eyes contoured with black paint.

Leaning forward, Hemiunu issued a quiet command to his palanquin-bearers. They carefully lowered his chair to the ground, and in one smooth move, he rose from his seat and stepped off his vehicle, his sandaled feet pressing into the loose sand.

On closer inspection, the lightness of his skin appeared to be the effect of gold paint. He was smeared with it. Except for the decorative patterns traced around his biceps in black, there was a preponderance of gold: the orange-gold linen wrapped around his hips, the golden belt, the broad gold necklace adorning his muscled chest, his skin paint, all set against the backdrop of the desert sands.

"Identify yourselves," he said. His inflection commanded respect and he exuded power, both innate and conferred. Standing before Shara and Yngvi, however, he wasn't as tall as they were and appeared far less formidable than he had while on his perch.

"I am Shai, and my companion is Ineni," said Shara, and Yngvi heard the words with a throb of admiration for his quick thinking, and an apology to the real Ineni. "We are apprenticed to a historian who has sent us here on a quest."

"What is your quest?" said Hemiunu.

"We seek an artefact. It has no intrinsic value except its age; it is ancient. We were told the oracular goddess would know its location."

"I also seek Wadjet's counsel," said Hemiunu, straightening as he prepared to introduce himself. "I am Hemiunu, High Priest and chief architect of Pharaoh Djoser. I seek the location of Pharaoh's pyramid. I have been entrusted with preparing for the journey of Pharaoh's soul to the Afterlife. It falls to me to first ascertain, within a week, where Pharaoh's pyramid should be built, then supervise its design and construction."

"Would it not be Pharaoh's decision to pick the location of his pyramid?" Yngvi asked.

Hemiunu looked aghast. "As scribes, surely you know that the location is preordained by the patron god! If Pharaoh's pyramid is not built where Djehuty intended, his safe passage through the portals between life and death is in jeopardy." Hemiunu lowered his voice. "And with it, my own life and that of my priests."

"Could you obtain the location from Djehuty himself, or his temple?" said Yngvi.

"Why does every scribe I encounter assume that I have not attempted to speak to Djehuty already?" said Hemiunu, spreading his hands in a gesture of exasperation. "Djehuty has gone silent. He does not speak to his priestess anymore."

"Priestess?" said Yngvi.

"Yes, the Chief Physician's daughter is Djehuty's priestess," said Hemiunu, adding, with a subtle straightening of his back, "and my own daughter, Tausret, is Ra's priestess." The paternal pride passed quickly, and he gave a heavy sigh, as if to purge his frustration with the entire matter of pyramid-construction. "Time is running out. I would have preferred a safer way, but his daughter, Wadjet, is my last hope."

"Safer?"

"What kind of historian's apprentice are you? Do you not know about Wadjet?" Hemiunu had spoken with a slight tremor in his voice, and a shocked murmur had risen among his priests.

Yngvi glanced at Shara and said, "Our master keeps us in the dark about many things, especially our gods."

That appeared to assuage Hemiunu. "Many have sought answers from the goddess, but none have returned alive. Or those who survived have never spoken of it. But I have no options left. I *will* die if I do not get my answer, but I can hope that I survive Wadjet." He pressed his lips into a thin, tight line. "It is a chance I must take, and alone, for my priests fear for their lives and will not accompany me inside."

Yngvi was about to suggest that Hemiunu could persuade his priests to accompany him on pain of death when Shara spoke. "Then as our quests are not secrets, perhaps we could call on the goddess together."

"Very well," said Hemiunu. "We shall."

CHAPTER THIRTEEN

THE TEMPLE OF the oracular goddess, Wadjet, stood in the desert to the east of the city.

That meant returning to the shifting sands for another hours-long trudge in the enervating midday heat. But Yngvi and Shara had been given a turgid waterskin each, and Hemiunu had also instructed a servant to offer them a leafy umbrella to hold over their heads. Shielded thus from sunburn and thirst, Yngvi glanced over at Shara beside him under the shared parasol and felt hope rise inside him—and, inexplicably, excitement.

When his arm started to cramp from holding the sunshade, Yngvi handed it to Shara. As with their journey to Saqqara, their sinking feet made for a wobbly gait, and Yngvi now felt an unexpected kinship with the ugly, gangling humped horses that had accompanied the caravans leaving the city. Occasionally, his shoulder would bump Shara's under the narrow ambit of the shade. Sometimes, when that happened, Shara would turn to him and smile faintly. Then he would return his gaze to the endless gold of the desert, lost to his own thoughts, and whatever Yngvi had wanted to say to Shara would die on his lips. It made for a long, tedious and silent slog.

An hour into their journey, Yngvi's waterskin was half-empty, his hair was damp, and he was yearning for the mead of the tavern and the frost of Niflheim.

An hour later, they stood before Wadjet's temple, and Yngvi's breath caught in his throat.

Nothing on Yggdrasil even remotely resembled the pair of soaring obelisks and immense pyramidal gates fronting the temple. They drew the eye to the blinding sky, all straight lines and angles. The only curves in the gates belonged to the two towering statues of seated deities in front of each pylon. Each deity was carved wearing a pleated shendyt like

Hemiunu's, and sitting upright with their hands on their knees. One statue was unambiguously female, carved with a long head cloth whose flaps on either side hung in front of the shoulders and reached down to the tops of bare breasts that ended in points. It took Yngvi a second, startled look to infer the significance of the large protuberance in the other statue's lap, after which he decided that it was unambiguously male.

Hemiunu's coterie stepped through the massive rectangular archway between the pylons and onto a courtyard, with Yngvi and Shara bringing up the rear. Walking over firm ground felt like a long-denied luxury to Yngvi's tired legs.

The courtyard was a vast, walled quadrangle, and at its centre stood the temple of Wadjet: a tall, broad structure that looked like an extension of the desert, as though the sand had risen and coalesced into that shape. Behind the courtyard was an area that, Yngvi estimated, was at least thrice as large and in which were situated two enormous stepped triangular structures.

Hemiunu's servants lowered his palanquin at the bottom of the steps that led up to the temple's plinth. He alighted from his perch and called for Yngvi and Shara to join him at the front, and together they ascended the steps. The entrance to the temple was a doorless rectangular archway that led to the first of several concentric halls which were connected by a single enclosed corridor that, Hemiunu told them, led directly to the inner sanctum.

Hemiunu's party remained in the outermost hall, where they were sheltered from the blazing sun. A servant handed Hemiunu, Yngvi and Shara each a flaming torch.

As they followed Hemiunu down the lightless corridor, their path illumined by the torchlight, they surveyed the flickering carvings on the walls. Shara walked alongside Hemiunu, and Yngvi followed close behind.

Hemiunu, apparently glad to have company on this dark and perilous task, seemed agreeable to answer questions. And Yngvi and Shara had many.

"Djehuty," Hemiunu explained, "wanted Wadjet to be his wife."

Yngvi said, "But didn't you say she was his daughter?"

"Yes, Djehuty wanted her for his daughter-wife. She was born of his union with a mortal woman, who gave Wadjet the gift of foreknowledge, but also her mortality."

Daughter-wife? Yngvi recoiled a little at that.

"When Wadjet came of age, Djehuty offered her deathless godhood if she married him. But she chose to marry Min, our god of Fertility."

Yngvi allowed himself a grin, because he walked behind Hemiunu. That explained the statue.

"Min could not bear the thought of losing Wadjet to death, and gave up his own godhood for her, choosing to live out a mortal life with the woman he loved. But Djehuty was enraged by her betrayal and cursed them both to be forever separated. He cursed Min, sending him back to his father to spend all of eternity in the Underworld. Osiris, god of that realm, pleaded on his son's behalf."

At the mention of Osiris, Yngvi and Shara looked at each other.

"Was Wadjet trapped in the temple?" Shara asked. "Or was she cursed too?"

Hemiunu gave Shara an appreciative nod. They walked on, and Hemiunu continued.

"Djehuty would not relent. Osiris was furious about the curse laid upon his son, and cursed Wadjet to live forever as a wraith, imprisoned in the temple sanctum's vault with his own demons standing guard. Wadjet would have the head of a falcon and the body of a cobra, and a tongue as twisted as her serpentine nether."

"What does that mean?" said Shara.

Hemiunu gave a weary sigh. "It means that she would never be able to provide a straightforward answer to any question."

Yngvi had a passing notion that the motivations and retributions of Yggdrasil's gods—power, betrayal, vengeance, killing—seemed somewhat rudimentary in comparison.

"But Wadjet's statue outside the temple—" said Shara.

"—was carved before she spurned her father and incurred Osiris's wrath," Hemiunu explained. "She was still a woman then."

They had passed another three halls when Yngvi stopped in front of a carving of a man with a disc above his head. The disc was encircled by a snake, its hood and tail almost touching at the top. "Is that the god of the Sun?"

"Yes, that is Ra."

"Who is this he's fighting?" Shara asked. In the image, Ra held one end of a palm leaf while the other end was in the hands of a man with a white semicircle over his head. "The god of the Moon?"

"Yes," said Hemiunu again. "That is Djehuty. At the time, Ra and Djehuty were struggling for dominion over Knowledge."

"It is a fascinating tale," said Yngvi, breezily.

"It is no *tale*," said Hemiunu. He had adopted the reproachful tone of a disappointed parent. "These are our gods, and these carvings illustrate their *lives*. Your master's instruction is sorely lacking! I suspect he is less historian and more charlatan."

Yngvi dipped his head in apology, but Hemiunu only gave him a chilly look and continued down the corridor. Yngvi decided against asking Hemiunu who had won.

Two halls later, they arrived at the centre of the temple and stood before Wadjet's sanctum, a square enclosure that Hemiunu said housed a statue of the goddess. But the door was shut and Hemiunu had gone down on his knees before it, beseeching Min for forgiveness for what they were going to have to do. Yngvi experienced some difficulty stifling a laugh when he saw what had shocked Hemiunu into obeisance.

"Is this Djehuty's doing?" he could not resist asking.

Hemiunu nodded nervously. "He wanted a way to demean Min in perpetuity."

"I think Djehuty's design is a rousing success," said Yngvi, sobering his expression too late and receiving a black look from Hemiunu. For carved into the sandstone was the door-high, embossed figure of Min. Great attention had been paid to etching the features of his face, the folds of his shendyt, the musculature of his limbs. Even more meticulously carved was the door handle, which was positioned at the centre of Min's hips. It was Min's erect member, and it was available for any ordinary temple visitor to hold and pull on to open the door.

Hemiunu's hand reached for the handle, then recoiled. Shara had come up beside him and was staring at the object.

Yngvi playfully inclined his head at the door. *Open it.*

Shara put out a tentative hand, pulled it back.

Yngvi grinned. Holding Shara's eyes, he transferred the torch to his left hand and with his right, clasped the stone shaft as teasingly as he would any lover's. Min's figure was larger than life, or perhaps representative of the gods' proportions, and the door handle was of a commensurate size. His fingers could barely encircle it. Shara's gaze dropped to Yngvi's hand, which Yngvi slid down to the root. Then back up to the swollen head. Down again. Then up, to run his thumb in a slow circle over the tip, then down, up, down; ran his palm over the entire head, cupping it with his hand, then down again, up, down; as he would if he were pleasuring Min; as he himself liked to be pleasured. All the while he watched Shara, and all the while, Shara stared at Yngvi's hand.

Shara's eyes had darkened as Hemiunu's prayers loudened. Yngvi stilled his hand, and when Shara's scandalised gaze lifted to meet his, he grinned, then pulled the door open.

The motion sucked a gust of wind out of the sanctum, causing their torches to flutter. They stepped in. A statue stood against the left wall; it was a woman with the head of a falcon, the body of a serpent. Wadjet. Torchlight provided the only illumination, and directly across from the statue, Yngvi discerned the faint outline of a single locked door.

The vault.

No sooner were they inside than the door slammed shut behind them.

Hemiunu spun around and pushed on the handle in vain. Unlike its spiteful counterpart on the outside, this was a staid and more utilitarian construction—a carving of Min's face serving as the doorknob, and the chin extending into a cylindrical beard that provided a better grip. Hemiunu let out a tense breath. "Wadjet is keeping us inside," he said ominously.

The only sounds in the vault were the hiss and sputter of the torches and a low, urgent clacking, which had swelled to an anxious rustle. The glow from the fires poured yellow-orange light over the walls of the crypt, bringing colour to the lifeless figures of men etched into the stone.

Yngvi held the light up to the walls, the ceiling and finally the floor, which was dark and showed signs of movement. When he lowered his torch, the lump-filled carpet over the ground began to pull back in smooth waves, unveiling what lay beneath.

Despite the heat from the flame, Yngvi felt a touch of cold horror.

The carpet turned out to be a swarm of beetles. Their feeding disrupted by the firelight, they moved like a thick black fluid, converging into a triangular mass whose tip advanced towards a small hole in the wall through which they flowed out of the sanctum. The tiny creatures had been feasting on three bodies. Dried blood stained the floor in dark patches.

The skin on the corpses was still somewhat supple. Yngvi estimated the bodies had lain there no more than a few days, even though they were missing entire sections of flesh and bone that the rapacious insects had devoured. These men had probably come to Saqqara for Wadjet's festival.

Hemiunu must have drawn the same conclusion because he shot his arm out and grabbed the handle again. "What horror is this? Wadjet has killed these men!" His back hit the door and he sagged against it. "How are mortals to defend themselves against a force that attacks from beyond the grave?"

Shara touched Hemiunu's shoulder. "Are you all right?" he asked gently, taking Hemiunu's torch and handing it to Yngvi.

Yngvi placed the two torches in sconces in the wall, then took Shara's torch and placed it in a third bracket. Hemiunu was pressed up against the door, his eyes wide in his ashen face, but Shara was back in the centre of the crypt, calmly taking in the scene, from the grisly floor to the carvings on the wall. Yngvi went up to Shara, his own hand tight around his sword hilt, ready to draw.

"What about him?"

"I can put him to sleep," said Shara, in a low voice, "but he must not suspect anything."

A wordless understanding passed between them. Yngvi gave a terse nod and returned to Hemiunu. "Can you try opening the door? Do you know any prayers—any…chants that might work?" That earned Yngvi a sour look and a shake of the head.

"Chants?" said Hemiunu. "You are truly hopeless."

Yngvi kept his face expressionless and waved a hand at the mangled bodies on the floor. It worked.

Hemiunu shuddered, and pushed on the doorknob. It did not budge. He clasped the beard with both hands and tried turning the knob, like a key in a lock. It did not move. He leaned a shoulder against the door and pushed. "Am I to do this myself while you two strapping young men watch? You're worse than my priests," he spat.

With a quick glance at Shara, Yngvi raised his sword and struck the back of Hemiunu's head with the pommel, applying just enough force to cause pain but not injury. But he must have miscalculated, because Hemiunu dropped to the floor with a cry, one hand holding onto the beard. Shara immediately strode forward and touched him on the shoulder. Instantly, Hemiunu's eyes fell shut, his fingers slid off the handle, and his body went limp and folded into itself.

Yngvi held his hand under Hemiunu's nose to make sure he was still breathing. A small swelling had appeared on the smooth head. Yngvi carefully propped him against the door in a secure sitting position so that he would not slide down to the floor. Then Yngvi straightened, nodded at Shara, and they stepped further into the sanctum.

He drew his blade as Shara called up his own sword, the blue fire throwing an eerie glow over the walls. They treaded cautiously through the large chamber, stepping around and over the corpses of the truth-seekers.

Yngvi glanced over his shoulder at Hemiunu. "How long will he stay that way?"

"Long enough, I would hope," said Shara. He blew out a breath. It misted in front of his face.

Intrigued by the sudden drop in temperature, Yngvi blew out a puff, then another. The first breath hovered like a cloud of white, then slowly dissipated. The second was blown away by a gust.

The air in the crypt began to churn, slowly at first, then rapidly, as an unearthly apparition whipped around them in circles, trying to impede their progress and push them back towards the door.

"Wadjet? Is that you?" said Shara. "Stop!"

The wraith obeyed and hovered before them, a faceless, limbless column of wispy grey. As Yngvi stared, the faint outline of a head appeared, and at its centre, a beak. The sides of the wraith drifted up from its body, like wings.

"Are you Wadjet?"

Yes. Wadjet's sepulchral response echoed in the hollow chamber. *No one has called me by my name for an age.* "Goddess," *they would plead.* "Goddess, we seek answers."

Yngvi smirked. "We seek an answer, too."

That is the only reason anyone comes to me, said Wadjet, miserably. *Answers.*

"Was it you who shut the door?"

No.

"Why did you kill these men?"

I did not. I warned them but they would not listen. Then I tried to save them, but I could not. You must leave, the wraith urged. *Your life is in danger.*

"From what?" said Shara.

Osiris's men.

"We are not afraid. We know your story and want to help you."

Osiris will unleash his forces if you linger. I cannot save you from them. Go while you still live.

Yngvi was about to tell Wadjet that her reputation for a twisted tongue was quite undeserved when her form whirled around to face the wall.

Look!

Something moved to Yngvi's left. He jerked his head to the side. Then he turned fully, in unblinking shock.

The walls had come alive.

The symbols of men from the top few rows of etchings were dropping to the floor, one by one, leaving behind smooth stone. They arrayed themselves in a tiny column of black outlines stretched across the base of the wall. And before Yngvi's bewildered eyes, the figures grew in size, the outlines filling out to become the fully developed bodies of soldiers made of mud and bearing weapons designed for close combat.

The tallest and broadest of them, the evident leader, took a step in their direction. In the next moment, footfalls filled the crypt as the remaining soldiers advanced. They marched closer and closer in formation, quickly converging upon Yngvi and Shara.

Yngvi raised his sword. "Shara," he said in a low voice, "these soldiers have no faces, no eyes."

"Doesn't mean they can't see. They are a god's army."

Yngvi shrugged. "And this is a god's sword." With a shout, he ran towards the leader and sliced the head off before it could deploy its mace. Then the arm of a second lumbering demon followed by its head, a third head, then a fourth's leg, and a clean slice across the waist of a fifth. Within a minute, an impressive heap of bodies lay in pieces at his feet. He had ended the first wave of Osiris's dead guardsmen.

"Twelve," he counted, with a grin, then pointed his chin at a second troop approaching Shara from behind. "Your turn."

Shara's sword cleaved through eight undead bodies with ease, beheaded another three, then sliced the limbs off seven more. Maces, cudgels and swords flew into the walls, hit the floor and disintegrated in bursts of mud.

"Eighteen," he stated.

Yngvi said, "You have the better sword," but he knew his grin told Shara what he actually felt.

But it had only just begun, because the walls continued to peel and drop more demons to the floor.

Burn them, or they will keep coming, Wadjet said.

Yngvi immediately moved to retrieve a torch, but Wadjet said, *Ordinary fire will not stop them. Burn them with that blade.*

Then Wadjet threw herself into the fracas, her dark form whipping around the demons as she dismembered and decapitated them with her ghostly beak and talons.

Shara was at the closest wall, sweeping his blade along the small shapes of soldiers at its base, beheading them before they could grow into men. Then he made his way up the wall, running the tip of his flaming blade in straight lines over the illustrations, back and forth, cutting through the images, making sure he burned every figure that had yet to drop to the floor. He repeated the process with the three other walls.

In the centre of the crypt, Yngvi employed his sword, the steel of his blade ringing over the swish of Wadjet's spectral form darting through the crypt, the dying cries of Osiris's demons and the thump and burst of stone shattering to dust. But too many undead demons were already awake.

With a shout, Shara cut his way into the fight, put his back against Yngvi's and together they cleaved through Osiris's guards.

When the last demon had fallen, Yngvi lowered his sword and looked about the crypt, assessing the aftermath.

The walls were scorched in straight lines running horizontally across, and the sliced images of men had begun to decompose into smudged black stains.

All of Osiris's soldiers who had been awakened now lay in lifeless hunks of stone on the floor. A demon's head was impaled on the tip of Yngvi's sword; he shook it off with a laugh and kicked it at the wall. It shattered on impact and floated to the floor in a spray of powder.

"Are you all right?" said Shara.

Yngvi nodded. He noted, with a pang of worry, that Hemiunu was still unconscious and hoped that he had not caused serious injury.

"Wadjet!" said Shara. "Stop!"

The vaporous column returned to hover before them. *Who are you?*

Ignoring her question, Shara said, "Is your husband behind that door?"

Yes, said Wadjet. *And my own body.*

Shara strode up to the door, lifted his sword and brought it down diagonally across the middle. But his blade bounced off and the door stayed shut. Shara turned to Wadjet. "How do we open the door?"

You must answer the riddle of the oracle.

"That's your riddle," Yngvi pointed out. "Can't you give us the answer?"

I can only ask you the question, and it is the only question I can ask.

"What is it, then?" said Yngvi, sharply.

Wadjet's ghostly breath came out in a quivering plume.

There is a thought, a word, that precedes all other thoughts, even when one is not aware of thinking it. What is it?

"*I* don't know, but you do! Give us the answer," said Yngvi, "and you'll be reunited with your husband."

I wish I could tell you. But Osiris's curse prevents me from doing so.

Frustration tightened Yngvi's hand around his sword as he took an unconscious step forward.

Wadjet's form jerked back, but Shara stepped between them and faced Yngvi.

"Calm down," said Shara, with quiet authority. He put two fingers on Yngvi's raised blade and lightly pushed down on it. "We have made it this far. The answer will come to us."

"Don't ask me to calm down," said Yngvi, sullenly. But he lowered the sword. "I'm tired of gods. I'm tired of their riddles and their curses. I want to get out of this...this tomb and I hope I haven't injured Hemiunu."

I, I, I! Wadjet's amorphous form blew out in a burst of grey, thickening the air. *All anyone cares about is themselves! What of me and my husband? What of the torture I have undergone for centuries only because I fell in love?*

Yngvi blinked. Her sudden, plaintive outburst had broken through his black temper. He felt a pang of remorse as he considered her predicament, and sheathed his sword. "Wadjet—"

"That's it!" said a fourth voice from behind, interrupting his apology.

Turning around, Yngvi saw Hemiunu sitting up, rubbing his head.

He groaned as he tried to stand. "Something knocked me unconscious."

Yngvi quickly averted his eyes, glad that Shara had hurried over to Hemiunu and was helping him to his feet.

An enigmatic smile played on Hemiunu's lips. "I thank you, goddess."

Wadjet responded with a wispy nod.

Yngvi looked from Wadjet to Hemiunu. "Why are you thanking her? What has she told us?"

"The answer," said Hemiunu.

CHAPTER FOURTEEN

HEMIUNU SHOT YNGVI a mordant look as he passed him to the vault.

Placing his palm on the door, he said in a sombre voice, to no one in particular, "The thought that precedes all other thoughts is *I*."

In the brief pause that followed, Yngvi intuited the meaning of Hemiunu's simple words and smiled at the cunning of Wadjet's question.

Hemiunu seemed to have cast off his fear of death and was expounding with a grandiosity behoving a High Priest. "It is one's own self that one must acknowledge," he declaimed, "instinctively if not explicitly, before expressing any thought. Every thought requires a thinker, for without a thinker, there can be no thought. The answer...is *I*."

When Hemiunu finished, a muffled scraping echoed in the chamber, which must have been the bolt on the inside sliding open. The door slowly opened inwards with a loud creak. Beside him, Wadjet gasped.

Hemiunu pushed the door open and looked over at Wadjet.

Thank you, said Wadjet, a tremor in her voice. A touch of red had infused her dull form, as life returned to her undead spirit. *I am grateful to you all.*

She floated towards the vault but Yngvi put his arm out, barring the doorway.

"We need to know where the artefact is located on Aegyptus before we allow you to enter," said Yngvi.

I will give you your answer if you step aside, said Wadjet, her wraith-form shuddering with yearning. *I promise. Please, allow me to see my husband. I ache for him. It has been so long since I have laid eyes on him.*

"Ineni..." said Shara.

"Very well," Yngvi muttered, and stepped aside.

Wadjet's eager soul floated into the chamber and gazed upon her dead husband. Min's body lay beside hers on a slab of stone. Wadjet placed a soft kiss on his forehead, his cheeks, his lips. Then her grey form infused her own body, her back arching with a deep intake of breath and flattening with a sigh.

Thank you, she said. *What you seek is buried under Djoser's pyramid.*

"Wait!" said Shara, but the air around the bodies shimmered, and Wadjet's and Min's bodies gradually faded from view, leaving behind a stone altar in an empty vault.

From behind them came the sound of a latch opening. The door to the sanctum had unlocked.

"That's perfect," Yngvi snapped. "We went to all this trouble and still don't have the answer. I won't listen to you again."

But Shara was staring at the altar, because a ripple ran over its surface. "Did you see that?"

There was another ripple, then another. The ripple became a wave that crested, stretching the slab's surface upwards, pulling the liquid stone up around a man's shape and then falling away like a speckled veil to reveal a god. He wore a feathered white crown; his torso was bare and he wore a shendyt similar to Ra's in the carvings.

Hemiunu went down on his knees at once. "Great One, we thank you for blessing us with your presence."

"And I thank you, Hemiunu, for solving Wadjet's riddle and reuniting her with my son."

My son. Yngvi's shock was reflected in Shara's eyes. So, this was Osiris. And he was watching them with kind eyes. *You're nothing like the other gods of the Underworld we know.* Another thought, darker, a confirmation: *Enki lived.*

"I could not have done it without them," said Hemiunu, nodding at Shara and Yngvi.

"Yes, I know." Osiris was smiling. "They killed my guards. It's a good thing they were already dead."

Shara said, "Has your son been returned to you?"

"He has," said Osiris. "Min has joined his wife in the Afterlife. Wadjet was imprisoned in this awful crypt for an age, hovering between life and death because of my own heartless curse. Even I could not revoke the curse, because it was the word of a god. But today, I have you to thank for his release. What are you called?"

"I am Shai."

Osiris was watching Shara steadily, as if peering beyond his exterior. "Are you keeping a secret from me?"

"Shai is my name."

"Perhaps it is a secret that is kept from yourself too," said Osiris, an inscrutable smile curving his lips. "One day, soon, the whole truth will be revealed to you, Shai." He looked at Yngvi. "And what do you call yourself?"

It was an odd way to phrase the question. "I am Ineni," said Yngvi.

"Ineni and Shai," said Osiris, and his smile told Yngvi that he did not believe them at all. "I know you sought answers from Wadjet. What did she tell you?"

"She told us what we seek is buried under Djoser's pyramid," said Shara.

Shara's response had been calm, but Yngvi was less composed. "And you know as well as we do that Djoser's pyramid does not yet exist!" *It was your curse that twisted her tongue.*

Hemiunu added, casting an apologetic look in Yngvi's direction, "Will the Great One reveal its preordained location?"

"Like Wadjet, I, too, am constrained by Djehuty from revealing too much, but I might be able to light your path."

"With what? Another hint?" said Yngvi, just as Shara said, "You know the location?"

"Yes, another hint, and yes, I do know the location," said Osiris. "I can tell you that when you find your artefact, you will find all the knowledge on Aegyptus. Be well, Hemiunu. Farewell—Shai and Ineni."

With that ambiguous and unhelpful message, Osiris's form faded and Yngvi and Shara were left alone with Hemiunu in the crypt.

"All is for naught," Hemiunu lamented.

He had put out a hand to support himself against the wall but pulled it back. His palm had come away blackened with burned sandstone. "I will be put to death by Pharaoh. Wadjet was my last hope." He stared at the ground, running his other hand over his smooth scalp.

Shara touched his shoulder. "There is still hope. Are you able to speak to the gods? Or perhaps one of your priests?"

"Not my priests," said Hemiunu, looking up at Shara with the desperation of a drowning man whose last lifeline had just drifted out of reach. "But I am able to communicate with the gods. In indirect ways. Why? I have already told you Djehuty has gone silent."

"Does his priestess know why he doesn't speak to her anymore?"

"All of Aegyptus knows. Djehuty is in mourning for his dead wife, Seshat. Her passing was most unexpected."

"Seshat? Your…goddess of Knowledge?" Yngvi ventured, anticipating Hemiunu's answer.

"If you know already, why do you ask?" Hemiunu said irately.

Shara gave a little shake of his head, and Yngvi swallowed his retort.

"That is most unfortunate," said Shara. "How did Seshat die?"

Unsurprisingly, Hemiunu said, "She fell to the floor one day and was no more. It was a shock." His forehead was furrowed. "Goddesses do not just die."

Yngvi needed no reminder of his own shock at Vör's death. "No, they do not... Wadjet said: *What you seek is buried under Djoser's pyramid.*"

He caught a brightening in Shara's gaze and knew that he had picked up on Yngvi's train of thought, because Shara added, "And Osiris said: *Find your artefact and you will find all the knowledge in Aegyptus.*"

"*All the knowledge in Aegyptus.* Do you see?" Yngvi was openly excited now. "He meant Seshat! I am sure of it!" His enthusiasm was overloud in the hollow crypt, but Shara was grinning in response.

"Show some respect, young man!" said Hemiunu with a reproachful glare at Yngvi. "Our goddess has died."

"Forgive me." Yngvi assumed an air of solemnity. "I grew overeager because it occurred to me that if we discover where Seshat is buried, we will find the artefact and the location of Pharaoh Djoser's pyramid."

"That might be," said Hemiunu, still sounding discouraged, "but only Djehuty knows where Seshat is buried."

That was not quite right. Osiris knew, too. Shara was looking at Yngvi, as if he had had the same thought.

Then Shara said, "Could we speak with your daughter?"

Hemiunu's eyebrows drew together at the forthright request. "What do you think Tausret would tell two strangers that she has not told her father?"

Hemiunu's reluctance to introduce them to his daughter was not lost on Yngvi, but if Shara thought that might help somehow, he would not let Hemiunu deny them that chance.

"We won't know until we talk to her," said Yngvi. He added, perhaps a little unkindly, "Unless you have other options."

"You know very well that I do not," Hemiunu conceded, too dejected to glare at Yngvi. "You may accompany me to my home."

They retrieved their torches and made their way back to the outermost hall where Hemiunu's entourage waited, then down the steps to the courtyard.

The evening sun cast its light over the polished flagstones. The oppressive heat of the noon had given way to a comfortable warmth, made cooler by a gentle breeze.

Yngvi pointed to the two pyramids behind the temple. "What are those?"

"That is the Necropolis, where Pharaohs are laid to rest," said Hemiunu. "The two mastabas you see hold the sarcophagi of Pharaoh Djoser's father, and his father. I know what you are thinking," he said to Yngvi, tersely. "It is true that Djoser's mastaba will be situated in the Necropolis, but its exact coordinates are what I seek."

"On our way here," said Shara, "we saw similar structures, but with straight lines and smooth sides. These have steps."

"You have so much to learn," said Hemiunu, with a look only slightly less withering than those Yngvi had elicited. "The structures you saw belong to the old ways. The Pharaohs of that time thought themselves descended from the gods and assumed that granted them a direct path to the heavens." He gave a sniff of derision. "They were punished for their arrogance. Since then, Pharaohs, wise to the ways of the gods, have commissioned stepped pyramids. Each step represents the demands of life's different stages that they must fulfil before they are deemed worthy of an afterlife in the heavens."

Yngvi decided he preferred the uncomplicated Midgardian ways. An honourable death in battle was, after all, a far easier path to an afterlife in the Hall of Fallen Heroes.

Hemiunu's slaves waited while he stepped onto his palanquin and arranged himself against the cushions, then hoisted him up to their shoulders. Yngvi and Shara were given fresh waterskins from which they drank gratefully. Then the throng began the long march back to Saqqara, to Hemiunu's home.

Shara and Yngvi had been asked to walk behind the palanquin, which meant that any retrospective of the events of the temple would have to wait until they were alone.

Two hours later, when the sun had sunk in its westerly grave, the urban skyline reappeared against the purpling sky. A short while later, they re-entered the city of Saqqara, passing the now-quiet marketplace, and made their way to Hemiunu's home.

CHAPTER FIFTEEN

'HOME' WAS A gross understatement, in Yngvi's opinion.

Hemiunu lived in a broad, pillared mansion with high sandstone walls and a flat roof. Six attendants, clad in simple knee-length tunics of white linen, led them through a torch-lit antechamber into a sprawling sitting room. Then they retreated to its periphery where they stood as still as the stately figurines placed in the corners and the plants that adorned the walls on either side of the tall, curtained windows.

Illumination was provided by flaming torches that leaned out from carved sconces on the pillars. A heady scent filled the air, and Yngvi, seeking its source, spotted lazy tendrils of vapor rising from coffin-shaped incense burners. The scent reminded him of the flower oils of Midgard; this one smelled like lavender, sweet but light enough not to overwhelm. The entire setting had a halcyon ambience.

While Hemiunu conferred with his priests, Shara and Yngvi waited in the middle of the chamber. Eventually, the priests took their leave and Hemiunu joined Shara and Yngvi, gesturing with a finger as he approached them.

The attendants promptly scurried closer, arraying themselves in single file, heads bowed and hands folded demurely over their stomachs, awaiting their master's orders.

"Shai, Ineni, welcome to my home," said Hemiunu. "It was a hot day and you must be weary. Rest awhile. My servants will look after your comfort. A bath, meals, then sleep."

"When might we speak with your daughter?" said Shara.

"Tausret has only just returned from the temple of Ra, after her evening prayers. I will take you to her in the morning. We have all earned ourselves a night of rest, I think."

Hemiunu lifted a hand. At once, the head servant came forward and bowed before him. "See to my guests. They are to be given every comfort. And Nenwef," he said to a tall, thin man whom Yngvi had seen watching them on their way back from Wadjet's temple, "attend me in my chambers."

With that Hemiunu swept out of the room, leaving Shara and Yngvi faced with six respectful attendants.

"Please come with us, Masters," said the head attendant.

He led them up a broad staircase to two adjacent chambers and opened one door. "Master," he said to Yngvi. Then he opened the other door for Shara.

"If Master wishes to keep his belongings in the room and change—" He indicated a small pile of white cloth neatly folded on the pillow. It was a towel.

"Master does wish that," Yngvi said, with a smile.

He nodded once at Shara, entered the chamber and shut the door behind him. He tossed his bag on the bed, unbuckled his sword belt and slid it under the mattress. Then he stripped his clothes and boots, and tied the towel around his waist. He carefully unwound the bandage and reached over his left shoulder. He felt nothing, no salve, no pain, no scars. Just skin. Eir's medicine, although resentfully administered, must have been very potent to have healed his burns so completely. When he opened the door again, the attendants were waiting outside. Shara was with them, wrapped in a towel, looking perplexed.

They followed the attendants down the stairs and deeper into Hemiunu's home, past a large dining room, and then out through a curtained archway to the connected bathhouse.

It was a wide chamber, walled for privacy but open to the sky, sectioned into sunken brick-lined rectangles, some of which were filled with water. A few servants, wearing loincloths, were industriously filling up one of the larger baths with water heated on wood stoves set up along the walls. Two attendants placed soaps and fresh towels on the edge. Another, once the bath had filled to a certain level, tossed in flower petals and poured scented oil over the water.

The attendants split into two groups of two girls and one youth. One group attended to Yngvi, the other to Shara. The oldest was probably eighteen or nineteen. Yngvi stared at his attendants and they stared back at him.

"Masters," said Yngvi's male servant with a deferential bow, "we have instructions to bathe you and then serve you meals."

"Bathe us?" said Shara. That came out sharper than he had probably intended.

The attendant straightened but kept his eyes lowered. "Master, it is our duty to serve you. Does this displease you?"

"No. It does not," Yngvi said, smiling at the nervous youth who was now meeting his eyes. Shara led a solitary existence in Mashu forest. And washing himself in the stream was as sophisticated as Yngvi's own ablutions got on Midgard. "We are…not accustomed to being served," he said, truthfully.

The attendant glanced at the girls, then gave another brief bow. "Your towel, Master?"

Yngvi grinned. "Turn around," he said, teasingly. One of the girls gave a coy smile. But she didn't turn around. Perhaps this was part of their training. He took off the towel. "I'm ready," he said.

Shara, too, stood naked. Yngvi wondered what kind of Aegyptian the attendants saw when they looked at Shara, because he saw the same stunning composite of blue skin, fair hair and ice-blue eyes. And he wouldn't have it any other way. Well, maybe one other way: Shara's pale, elfin appearance at the tavern. That had been a rather lovely sight.

At the attendants' invitation, they stepped into the bath, padding on bare feet down the six steps and into the comfortably hot scented water.

They sat on the bottom ledge against opposite walls, facing each other. The thin layer of bath oil and petals strewn over the surface broke into small islands around their bodies.

Two girls each stepped into the water with them and began to scrub their fronts and backs with an earthy paste.

"What is this?" Yngvi asked.

"Clay and ash, Master," said one of the girls.

"This is very nice."

It was. In fact, the entire experience in the heavy, scented steam of the bath felt like a dream.

Seeing hands roam everywhere on Shara's wet skin was bringing up vivid and problematic images in Yngvi's mind. His limbs were starting to feel languorous; he rested his head against the wall of the bath and closed his eyes. He permitted himself to indulge the fantasy that the sensation of scented oils and earthy pastes being rubbed over his skin came not from the soft hands of servant girls, but from the sword-calloused palms of a warrior from another world. A warrior who wanted him. He shook his head to banish the fanciful thoughts, and opened his eyes. Shara's lidded gaze from across the bath was on him, steady and intimate. And Yngvi wondered again if Shara could read his mind.

When the girls were satisfied that their skin had been adequately sloughed, they dipped small jugs into a second tub and poured water over them, washing off the residual paste. Then Shara and Yngvi stood and were wiped down with lush white towels. Finally, the two youths helped them into fresh tunics, which they tied around the waist with a sash, and wooden sandals.

"Thank you," said Yngvi.

"Please come with us, Masters," said the head servant. "We will have your meals sent up to your rooms."

They went back into the house, past the dining and sitting rooms and up the staircase. Yngvi nodded once at Shara, and entered his room.

Minutes later, a knock sounded on the door, and he opened it to two attendants.

One held a large plate on which were placed meat and breads and some kind of hot stew. The other held out a tray with a pitcher of wine, and a cup. Yngvi's mouth came alive at the sight. He let them in and waited while they placed the plate, pitcher and cup on the small table beside the bed, bowed to him, and left.

He ate quickly and drank all the wine.

Opposite the door, he had seen an archway that seemed to be open to the night. It was a balcony. Stepping out, he drew in a breath, awestruck by the view of Saqqara laid out before him, silhouetted against the black of night under the mournful light of the moon. Tiny lights winking in the dark distance flickered out one by one as the retiring populace grew quieter and the city fell asleep.

Looking out at Saqqara now, Yngvi was thinking that he wanted to know how many more worlds had evolved independent of each other, yet connected in intangible ways, when he heard his name, turned his head and smiled. Coming up beside him across the linked balconies was his favoured tangible connection to another world.

"Good wash?"

"I've never felt this clean," said Shara, rubbing his forearms. "It's as though they scrubbed my skin off."

Shara's arms and neck had a sheen; he looked fresh and relaxed, and like Yngvi, smelled faintly of rain-wet earth.

"What is it?" said Shara.

"So lovely," he said, eyes still locked with Shara's. After a beat, he returned his gaze to Saqqara. He leaned over the balustrade and looked out at the skyline. "Beautiful city, isn't it?"

A pause. Then, "Yes, it is."

Beyond Saqqara's borders, the pylons of Wadjet's temples were dim shapes against the dark sky, and looming behind them, the two lonely mastabas.

"Hemiunu's daughter," he said. "That's an interesting angle. You think she might know something?"

"She might not," said Shara, "but I think Ra will."

Yngvi waited, but Shara had gone quiet, his eyes fixed on some point in the distance.

"Am I supposed to guess why Ra will know something?" said Yngvi. "After Wadjet and Osiris, I've had quite enough of Aegyptian riddles." He remembered the tale Hemiunu had told them. "Daughter-wives," he said, undisguised antipathy in his voice. "We don't have those on Yggdrasil."

Shara shrugged. "Enlil and Enki have taken sister-wives to keep their godhood within the bloodline. I think perhaps things work differently with the gods," he said mildly.

"Perhaps," said Yngvi. "What makes you think Ra knows?"

"Do you recall the carving of Ra and Djehuty holding on to the opposite ends of a palm leaf?"

"Yes. What of it?"

"Hemiunu interpreted it as them fighting for godhood over the domain of Knowledge," said Shara. "But I think they were fighting over the *goddess* of Knowledge."

"Why do you think that?"

"Because Seshat was Djehuty's wife, not Ra's, which means Djehuty won."

Yngvi wasn't convinced. "You're speculating, Shara."

"Perhaps," said Shara, seemingly untroubled by Yngvi's lack of confidence in his reasoning, "but we'll find out soon enough."

"I suppose we will."

Shara looked at him a moment, then shifted his gaze to the horizon.

"Osiris is alive," Yngvi said, his voice quiet. "That means Enki is alive. That's good."

"That's good?" Shara had turned his head fully and was watching Yngvi very directly now, with incredulity.

Yngvi ran a fretful hand through his hair as he prepared to say something Shara was sure to reject outright. "I think..." He blew out a breath. "I think we can't...we *shouldn't* kill Enki."

"What?"

"If we do, I think all his counterparts will die." Yngvi paused for the weight of that realisation to settle on Shara. It was a long pause.

"Go on," said Shara, finally.

"I think I understand now." Yngvi straightened in instinctual preparation for Shara's resistance. "Vör, Seshat and Nidaba—all goddesses of Knowledge on their realms. Nidaba was killed. Vör and Seshat died. I can't be certain of the exact timing, but they died inexplicably around the same time. It's enough to make me suspect Nibiru is—" He stopped, because he was about to say something ridiculous.

"—the original realm," said Shara, completing his thought. "You think anything that happens to the gods on Nibiru has an almost immediate effect on the related pantheons." He shook his head. "But you're speculating with even less evidence than I presented."

Yngvi shrugged, equally unperturbed by Shara's lack of confidence in his reasoning. "If I'm right about Nibiru being the original realm, I think the reverse might also be true."

"What do you mean?"

"You said Enki destroyed the pantheons on Apsu and Marduk. That could have had an effect on Nibiru. The destruction of those pantheons might have affected your gods."

Shara waited, eyebrows raised with interest.

His conviction burgeoning, Yngvi elaborated. "In your vision, Enlil complained about a lassitude that affected most of the Anunnaki. If it's possible that when an Anunnaki dies, the equivalent gods die, then maybe when a counterpart god dies, the Anunnaki...original...is weakened."

Shara's gaze flickered, and Yngvi knew his words had made an impact.

He offered one more observation. "You...have the same skin, I've seen you fight, your weapons, Enlil said you might be Enki's son, and yet you're not affected."

Shara's lips pressed into a thin line. "I told you I'm not an Anunnaki," he said, an edge to his words.

"Maybe you're not. Or...maybe...there's no one like you on the other realms." Yngvi would have said more had the subtle stiffening of Shara's body not marked the end of that line of discussion. Instead, he said, "We have to stop Enki. Where is he?"

"I...don't know."

"He has to be on Aegyptus. He saw the same tablet you did. He's here somewhere. Can't you locate him?"

"No."

"*Shara*. How are you not worried about this?"

"How do you suggest I demonstrate worry?" Shara snapped. "What good will that do?"

It was a long time before Yngvi spoke. "We're here now, so let's try and find the weapon. And Enki. So if you think Hemiunu's daughter might bring us the answer," he said, hearing the earnestness in his own voice, "you know I'll help however I can."

Shara was watching him steadily. "If you look at her like this," he said, unsmiling, his tone solemn and stripped of all teasing, "I think we will have our answer."

Yngvi blinked, dropped his hand and took a step back. How *had* he been looking at Shara? When he lifted his head, he was snared again in that pellucid gaze. What he read in it was not quite encouragement, but it wasn't denial either. In the next moment, everything changed, because Shara was coming forward, the air between them was growing warmer with their breaths, and Shara's hand was sliding inch by inch over the balustrade towards Yngvi's. Another step. Even Shara had to know this was too close for casual conversation in a foreign land in someone else's home.

Yngvi stayed rooted to his spot. The only sound was the noisy flapping of the torches in the breeze, their light casting fluttering shadows on Shara's face. Another step closer. The look in Shara's eyes was unmistakable. Yngvi's entire body was taut with anticipation. The words, when he pushed them out, were husky and intimate. "What do you want, Shara?"

"I don't *know* what I want," said Shara, and in his eyes was a spike of dark panic. "What do *you* want?"

Shara's lips were parted, his breathing shallow, and his eyes. Gods, those eyes. They were even darker now, with whatever Shara was feeling. Desire pulsed through Yngvi's body; he felt weak with it. It was a warm evening, yet he shuddered. Shara had asked him, and so he uttered the words he had wanted to say since the day Shara had come to his house and shown him impossible things.

"Don't you know?" he murmured. "I want you." He hooked a finger under Shara's chin to tip his face up, and ran his thumb over Shara's lips. "I want to kiss you. But—"

A pause. "Then kiss me," said Shara.

"Here? Are you sure?" Yngvi asked. His room had a bed and a door that locked, but if this is where Shara wanted to kiss, then this is where they would kiss.

"Yes." The word was more breath than sound.

Yngvi closed his eyes and found Shara's lips with his own. Shara's manner might be skittish but his lips were soft, warm, yielding. Yngvi was careful, still unable to believe what was happening. He drew Shara close until their bodies were pressed against each other from chest to knees and Shara went pliant in his arms. He smiled against Shara's mouth when warm hands slid up his face and into his hair, pulling his head down in invitation. With a low groan, he ran his tongue across the seam of Shara's lips, seeking entry.

And found himself bodily thrown back.

"What—" Yngvi took three stumbling steps backwards before he could regain his balance. Embarrassment was averted when he stayed upright by grabbing the balustrade.

Shara's body had gone rigid and his eyes flashed with warning. With his set jaw and implacable expression, he looked like an austere, older version of himself. The man facing Yngvi now was the sort of man who would have shoved Yngvi out of his memories without a second thought, and had shoved him now.

Any hopes Yngvi may have had that Shara, in his inexperience, thought this was a provocative game were obliterated when the icy, unyielding eyes settled on him. Yngvi's chest heaved with his breath. Focusing his thoughts was proving to be a challenge. What had he done to merit this…this humiliation? It was disorienting. He grabbed the railing to have contact with a tangible object. He returned Shara's glower as stupefaction hardened to anger. He had kept his distance after Shara's cool response before they left for Magne's house. He had been affronted then, given their closeness the previous night, but now? Now he was furious.

"You asked for this," he gritted out.

"I changed my mind," said Shara, in a different, harder voice.

Yngvi's hand was clenched around the railing; his other hand was a fist at his side. He kept his eyes on Shara, the hurt and anger rising inside him. "You changed your mind?"

Even as the words left Yngvi's lips, Shara seemed to be changing his mind again. His expression was already softening, growing more recognisable, almost penitent. He blinked, appearing as mystified by what had happened as Yngvi was livid.

He reached out a hand. "Yngvi—"

Yngvi recoiled. He didn't care what Shara felt; didn't care that he needed Shara to kill Enki, to return home. Had anyone else manipulated him like this, teasing him into a reaction, then slapping him down, his response would have been a fist to the jaw. But Shara had saved his brother's life and his, and had saved Asgard. It was that debt alone that stayed his hand.

He grabbed a fistful of Shara's tunic. They were both breathing hard.

"You want me," Yngvi ground out, his lips twisted in a snarl. "When you can admit that, you come to me and you ask for it. And I'll decide if I want you."

He released Shara with a hard push, satisfied that he stumbled backwards as Yngvi had. Then he turned with finality and stomped into his room.

He fell on the bed, pulled the sheet up to his chin, and consigning every last thought of Shara and his eyes to the pits of Helheim, sank into sleep.

CHAPTER SIXTEEN

IN THE MORNING, after a light meal that was delivered to their room, Yngvi and Shara were summoned to the sitting room.

Even though the events of the previous night seemed distant now, Yngvi kept his eyes on Hemiunu, who was seated on a cushioned couch. Shara had attempted to speak to him on their way down the stairs, but Yngvi had ignored him.

"Tausret is ready to receive us," said Hemiunu, rising. "I will take you to her."

He led them through what Yngvi had mistaken for a window last night, a discreet archway, curtained by a reed mat, that led out of the sitting room and down a long hallway of polished stone, buttressed by tall, smooth pillars. The walls were lined with stone representations of Djoser's antecedents: Pharaohs and their queens, seated straight-backed on spare thrones with their hands on their thighs.

At the end of the corridor, Hemiunu stopped before a heavy reed-mat tapestry. It appeared to be at least twice as thick as the curtain in the sitting room, and bore numerous images of birds, animals, people and other symbols of Aegyptus. At the centre was a large representation of Ra.

"Tausret, daughter," said Hemiunu. "May we come in?"

"Come," a young female voice responded from inside.

Shara lifted the mat for Hemiunu and Yngvi to enter, then let it drop behind him.

Yngvi scanned the room. It was large and furnished with a reclining couch and four cushioned armchairs. Two chambers flowed out of this one, both concealed behind gauzy curtains of white linen. The wall opposite the door had a window which framed the mid-morning sky. A woman stood there, her head bowed, apparently to the sun. She turned to face them.

Ra's priestess was young, very beautiful, and very bare under her dress.

It was not so much a dress as a patterned network of cylindrical beads. Broad shoulder straps ended just below her chest and held up a floor-length skirt. The criss-crossing pattern did little to conceal her naked breasts or nethers. Still chafing from Shara's rebuff, Yngvi, who enjoyed women almost as much as he did men, and whose last view of a woman had been censorious Ulla in her severe long-sleeved woollen dress that was closed to both air and eyes, decided that he much preferred Tausret and her well-ventilated dress.

Shoulder-length black hair framed her oval face, and her skin glistened like dusky brown silk in the slanted sunshine; her eyes, large pools of brown lined with black, held his gaze. She had her father's regal nose, and her soft, bow-shaped lips were likely her mother's gift.

If Hemiunu coughed uncomfortably, Yngvi didn't hear him because he was admiring Tausret and she was returning his interest. It had not escaped his notice that she had scarcely looked at Shara. Given Shara's actual appearance, the only explanation was that Shara had assumed the veneer of an unappealing Aegyptian.

Tausret shifted her attention to Hemiunu and dipped her head in greeting. "Father."

"Tausret, my child," said Hemiunu. "This is Shai, and this is Ineni. They are helping with my search for the location of Pharaoh's pyramid. We had an unfruitful day yesterday."

"Not wholly," said Yngvi. "We do have a way forward and need your help, Priestess."

"You may address me by my name." Her eyes were impassive, but the corners of her mouth were slightly tipped up. Unlike her father, Tausret, thankfully, seemed amused by Yngvi's forthrightness.

Hemiunu's throat must have been quite congested because he cleared it twice in succession, rather loudly, but Yngvi grinned.

"In that case," Yngvi said, "we need your help, Tausret. Have you asked Ra?"

"What—" Hemiunu started, but Tausret was responding.

"Why would Ra know?"

Shara stepped forward determinedly. "Has Ra also been silent since Seshat passed?"

Tausret considered that for a moment. "He...has." She came towards them, her small, bare feet stepping delicately on the stone floor.

"And what is it that you seek?" she asked Yngvi, but Shara answered for him.

"My father seeks the same information," she said. "Why do you suppose Ra would know?"

"Because I suspect that Ra and Seshat were lovers," said Shara, "and that Ra is mourning her passing, just as her husband is."

Tausret gave Shara a brief look and returned her attention to Yngvi. "And what do you think?"

"I think he might be right," said Yngvi. "Can you persuade Ra to speak to you? Even if it is only to tell you where Seshat is buried."

"I have tried to make him speak to me—" she admitted, then held his gaze a little too directly and a little too long to be a coincidence.

"Tausret—" Hemiunu rasped. He was coughing in earnest now.

"—but I cannot do it alone."

"I find myself at a loss. I don't understand," said Yngvi.

Hemiunu stepped between them to look squarely at Yngvi. "You wished to meet my daughter and so you have. As you can see, she has no information for us. You may rest now, and tomorrow we will resume our search for the location of the pyramid." He directed a stern look at Tausret and issued a peremptory clarification: "In the scrolls of the sacred texts in the library."

Shara nodded in agreement, with enough enthusiasm that Yngvi wondered if Shara had changed his mind about speaking to Ra.

But Tausret was not ready to give up. "Ra speaks to me in the language of the gods," she said, "which I can only understand when I...when he...possesses me. A hidden part of my mind is opened in those moments, then is shut again when he leaves."

A few beats of silence as the three men interpreted her words.

Yngvi had only ever known Asgard's straightforward exercise of power: those who pleased the Aesir, like his family, were granted positions of authority and access to Valhalla; those who displeased the Aesir, like Loki's family, were dealt with on the battlefield. But he was learning that the gods of Aegyptus seemed partial to priapic expressions of their divine favour. Or disfavour.

For lack of anything better to say, he asked, "Does Ra not know the language of the common man?"

That pulled a breath of amusement from Tausret. "Perhaps he feels the language of the common man lacks the solemnity demanded by the gods," she said wryly. "I shall ask him when he next visits me, whenever that is." She inclined her head and looked at Yngvi significantly. "But—"

"Tausret—" Hemiunu cautioned.

"—there is another way to speak to Ra. A ritual invocation through a mortal vessel—"

"Tausret, that is *quite* enough!"

"No, Father," she said, gravely. "You know that there is no one in all of Saqqara who would dare participate in the ritual and incur Ra's ire."

Before Yngvi could open his mouth to speak, Shara said, "We are not from Saqqara." And added, truthfully but impetuously, in even Yngvi's opinion, "We don't fear the gods."

Shara seemed eager, and Yngvi stared at him now, with flat incredulity. Did Shara truly understand what Tausret meant? And if he did, was his reaction yesterday because he realised that he preferred women? That possibility, disheartening though it was, went some way towards placating Yngvi.

"Father... This could save your life."

Hemiunu shook his head. "I need to think about it." He strode out onto her balcony, leaving Yngvi, Shara and Tausret to exchange uncomfortable glances while they waited. When he returned, his expression was resigned. "Very well. Shai will do it."

"Yes," said Shara at once. "What must I do?"

Tausret's expression wavered. Was that disappointment in her eyes?

"You will take the spirit of Ra into you and lie with me," she said, with scant enthusiasm, "while I invoke Ra and speak to him."

"Lie— With you?" Shara whipped his head to Yngvi.

But after last night, Yngvi was not above letting Shara suffer for a few exquisitely tense moments and took his time before saying, "Excuse us, please," and walking out of earshot of Hemiunu and Tausret with Shara hurrying behind him.

To an onlooker, they might appear to be conferring. But the ice-blue irises were dark. Yngvi stifled the urge to laugh. The killer of Loki was apprehensive about coupling with a woman. Shara should have kept his mouth shut. In the insulted corner of his mind, he wanted Shara to have to endure the ritual, which was, after all, a self-inflicted ordeal. But it was a small corner, and shrinking with every unnerved flutter of Shara's lashes. Yngvi shook his head at Shara, and went back to where Hemiunu and Tausret waited.

"Shai cannot lie with a woman," he said.

"Why not?" Hemiunu demanded.

"He reminded me that he has taken a vow of celibacy for a month. Our master has chosen Shai for a ritual of his own. Master has not," Yngvi said, to pre-empt any further inquiries, "told us anything beyond the requirement of abstinence."

"And you?" Tausret asked. "Have you also taken the same vow?"

Yngvi gave Shara a sideways look, then smiled at Tausret. "I am under no such constraints."

Hemiunu's smooth forehead furrowed so hard his entire scalp seemed to move. "You..." he pushed out through clenched teeth. "You are a disrespectful young man, Ineni. I saw what you did to the door. And I know you knocked me unconscious in the temple—"

"That was for your own protection," Shara interposed. "Ineni knew that Osiris's guards would not think to kill someone they thought was already dead."

Hemiunu shook his head. "He mocks the gods! I worry that Djehuty—"

"Father, there is no time. You must permit me to carry out the ritual with Ineni. It is the quickest way, the *only* way." Tausret put a gentle hand on Hemiunu's forearm. "You know I will not stand by doing nothing while your life is in danger."

It took Hemiunu a long time to marshal his composure. "I will allow it," he said at last, "but I am not happy about it."

Tausret smiled faintly for the first time since they had entered her chamber. It was genuine, and Yngvi read hope in it.

"You will return to my chamber an hour before sunset," she said to Yngvi. "My maidens will prepare you for the ritual. And precisely at sunset, we will begin."

Hemiunu was scowling at Yngvi. To Tausret he said: "Make sure he keeps his hands to himself." To Shara: "Only Tausret and her maidens may be present at the ritual. I will have Nenwef arrange for other entertainments for you."

With a bow to her father, Tausret turned, pushed the white curtain aside and disappeared into the room on the right. They had been dismissed.

They left Tausret's chamber and made their way down the long corridor in silence. Hemiunu said he would retire to his rooms for the afternoon and suggested that they do the same. Then they were alone.

"It's a pity you won't be there," Yngvi said through his teeth, as they ascended the stairs. "You might have learnt what it is that men do."

Shara paused outside his door. "Yngvi—"

Yngvi slowly turned his head. "Are you about to thank me?" he asked, letting Shara hear the resentment in his voice.

"I—"

"I'm not doing it for you," Yngvi said. Then he entered his room and shut the door behind him.

CHAPTER SEVENTEEN

YNGVI ANSWERED THE knock on the door.

The male attendant who had served him in the baths had come to take him to Tausret's chamber. The attendant was punctual, because, seen from the balcony, the sun was a placid ball of light hovering the length of a hand above the horizon. Shara's door was shut. He was, no doubt, enjoying the entertainments Hemiunu had offered him.

The youth led Yngvi down the stairs, along the hallway to Tausret's chamber, where he held the reed curtain open for Yngvi, bowed, then left. Yngvi waited in the empty sitting room, considering which room to enter when a young girl lifted the gauzy screen on the left and gestured that he should follow her. He went.

And was again struck by the strangeness of where he was and what he was about to do.

It was a ritual room. One windowed wall, one with carvings, and two walls with ledge shelves. By the window was a waist-high stepped altar of polished sandstone. Carved into the surface, in black, was a pair of wide concentric circles inscribed with evenly spaced arcane patterns, some of which resembled the images on the tapestry at the main entrance. Drawn across the width of the inner circle was the figure of Ra.

Yngvi was the only man there. Five young maidens, presumably priestesses-in-training, were diligently preparing for the ritual. None of the girls spoke to him, or to each other. They were all dressed in floor-length tunics of white linen. Their faces were painted with black patterns, most prominent around the eyes and cheekbones.

While one of the girls arranged and lit thick candles and incense sticks along the wall shelves, another girl came up to Yngvi and tugged lightly on the shoulders of her tunic. He understood, and reached behind himself to pull off his tunic. Then he removed his sandals. She folded the tunic, placed the sandals over it and laid them neatly on the floor by the wall.

Two girls came up to him holding small jars from which they poured scented oil into their cupped hands and began smearing his legs with it. He had to kneel to give them access to his upper body. They continued until his face, both arms, his torso and back, his posterior, his legs and feet glistened with the same kind of gold sheen that Hemiunu had when Yngvi first saw him. They had left his front untouched. He rose to his feet.

By now, the air was sweet and heavy with incense. Candle flame cast long shadows on the walls, accentuating the deep grooves in the wall carvings.

The girl who had taken his clothes had now tilted a large jar over the altar to shake out a fragrant red powder all over until the entire circumscribed area was covered with it. When that was done, she replaced the jar on a shelf to pick up the pitcher that sat next to it. She poured out a white liquid into a clay goblet and held it out to him. Yngvi took the goblet and inhaled its aroma. Its sweet, floral scent was reminiscent of the herbal compounds used on Midgard to enhance the male partner's vitality. His lips curved. Not that he had ever required that form of assistance, but he drank the contents in a single swallow and handed the goblet back. The girl inspected the cup, as if to ensure he had imbibed it all, then returned to her other duties.

The fifth girl approached with a bowl containing a black paint-like substance and a thin white application stick that appeared to be bone. She assessed his height, then indicated with a hand that he should sit on the altar, inside the circle. He complied, keenly aware that he was sitting on Ra, or at least the image of him. And that, when he lay down, his entire back would be covered in red dust. The girl knelt before him and he weathered the application of the black paint around his eyes and on his cheekbones. He wished he could see what he looked like. Ludicrous, he was certain. Still, he found these strange practices diverting.

The girl then held out a mask. It was a highly polished likeness of Ra, painted in red ochre with an orange disc serving as the headdress. He nodded, thinking that she need not have taken the trouble to paint his face only for it to be concealed. The girl placed the mask carefully over his face and fastened the ties behind his head. Then she pushed down gently on one shoulder, and he lay across the altar on his back, over the image of Ra, and waited for Tausret.

While the girls continued their preparations, he interlaced his fingers over his bare stomach and lolled his head to conduct a torpid study of the carvings on the wall to his right. It reminded him of the carvings in Wadjet's sanctum, except that these images were all contained within a floor-to-ceiling embossed rectangle, like a door. It must not have been important to any ritual, because some of the images in the bottom half were faded.

Unable to decipher the symbols, he tilted his head back to look up behind him. From this angle, only a sliver of sky was visible through the window: inky blue with cirri of pink and yellow cloud. Sunset was minutes away, and the firelight in the chamber seemed to have shifted, making everything in his view halcyon and hazy. The white drink must have taken effect, because his limbs felt loose and languid, and there was a mellowing inside him, a slowing of his breathing and heartbeat, as if he were approaching sleep.

A quiet commotion among the girls. He lifted his head just as a sixth maiden hurried in and stood off to the side, observing the other girls, her hands clasped in front of her. She seemed uneasy, as though she was late and wanted to stay out of the way. Her first such ritual, Yngvi assumed. Like his. He waited for her gaze to reach him and smiled, then remembered that he was wearing the mask. She looked away, and his gaze swung to the movement at the entrance.

Tausret had entered the chamber. Her eyes were already painted with black, and her skin gleamed with gold dust. She was naked under a thin linen robe which she was about to shrug off when her eyes stopped on Yngvi's front. She did not appear stimulated in the least. And he was still inert there. And dry. Her scathing gaze scrolled over the five girls and came to rest on the sixth girl, who was standing a little apart from the others.

"Well?" She raised a painted eyebrow to indicate Yngvi's hips. "Make yourself useful."

When the girl stared at her, uncomprehending, Tausret gave a whiff of impatience.

"Prepare him," she ordered coldly.

One of the girls leaned over to whisper in the maiden's ears and handed her a bowl from the wall shelf. The maiden started, then nodded, and cautiously approached the altar. She knelt beside Yngvi, keeping her eyes lowered as she scooped out a viscous blob with two fingers and reached down to his quiescent flesh.

He hissed in a sharp breath at the touch of the cool paste. The girl's fingers curled tentatively around his cock and slid down to the root. Then back up to the swelling head. Down again. Tightened around him with growing assurance. His breath shivered. He felt the first pulse of stimulation there. His eyes closed as he gave himself up to sensation. Her hand moved. Up, down, up. Her thumb made a slow circle over his tip. His back arched slightly. She slid the cup of her slick palm over the head, then down, up, down. A little faster now, a little tighter. Just as Yngvi liked it. Just as he had—

Yngvi's eyes flew open. He grabbed the girl's wrist, but dropped it when he saw her panicked, brown eyes blown wide. A glance downwards confirmed that he was magnificently roused.

"That will do," said Tausret, sharply.

The girl scrabbled to her feet and made to retreat to the wall, but Tausret stopped her.

"By his head," she instructed the girl. "Make sure he does not touch me." She slipped her robe off her shoulders, opened the stopper of a small clay jar and held it out to Yngvi. "Breathe this in."

"What is it?" he asked.

"A single breath's worth of Ra's life force, his *ka*," said Tausret. "If the ritual is successful, he will speak to me through you. When we are done, you will return it to this jar."

Yngvi propped himself up on an elbow, and took the jar with the other hand, using it to lift the mask. He held the jar to his lips. It seemed to contain nothing more than air. Nevertheless, he tilted it to inhale through his mouth.

And was knocked onto his back. A force unlike anything he had experienced was gushing into him, hotter than a flood of fire, like life itself, through his limbs down to his fingers and toes, in his blood, behind his eyes, his mind. His body spasmed in one long, hard undulation from shoulders to hips to feet. And then he went still.

He felt different, powerful beyond comprehension, but was still able to see as himself even if only through a small opening in someone else's blindingly bright consciousness. Surrendering the rest of his awareness to Ra, he focused on that opening, because it was enough for him to see that the girl had moved to the windowed wall and now knelt on the altar by his head. She lifted his hands to rest by his ears, clasped his wrists and held them down. One of her palms was still slippery.

She was looking down at him and he was looking up at her through the mask.

He felt warm skin around his thighs, felt a slight weight settle over his hips. And still his eyes were on the girl. The weight lifted. A shock, as something snug and hot enclosed his flesh. The weight rose and fell, and he slid in and out of the slick heat. Over and over. Strange words filled the air. They were uttered in Tausret's voice. A rhythm developed. The pace sped up. Faster and faster. Tausret's words were a series of breathless unintelligible sounds. And all the while, Yngvi was snared in the girl's gaze, and she was looking at him as if, like him, she could look nowhere else.

His mouth had fallen open behind the mask. He had been looking at the girl, but the image behind his eyes had changed; another face came into view, sending a sudden, unstoppable flood of pleasure surging up his spine.

His body jerked; his back arched. He struggled to free his hands to reach for the woman straddling him. But the hands on his wrist tightened with startling strength. And then climax was rolling through him and he bit off a groan as he spent inside Tausret. Pulse after pulse of release, some of it his, most of it someone else's, then his back flattened.

Through it all, his gaze had been locked with the girl's. Her brown eyes seemed paler now, touched with a strange light.

His body was shuddering, whether from climax or the sudden drop in temperature he didn't know. He closed his eyes and only opened them long after the weight had lifted from his hips and his wrists were freed. Tausret had left the ritual chamber.

Someone was wiping down his nethers with a wet towel, the moisture cooling his heated skin. He returned the mask to one girl, who then wiped the gold and black from his face. He sat up and took the proffered small jar. He inhaled through his nose, lifted the jar to his lips and exhaled hard into it through his mouth, feeling his body emptying of Ra's life force. He was, finally, alone inside himself. Another girl helped him to his feet, and he kept still while she wiped off the gold oil and red dust from his body. Then she handed him his tunic and sandals. He thanked her and dressed.

Their duties to him concluded, the girls turned to the task of clearing the room of all signs of the ritual: picking up the incense burners and guttered candles from the wall shelf, gathering the empty bowls of face paint and oils, cleaning the altar of the red dust. They did not look at him again.

And just like that, the ritual was complete, his utility expended, and he had been, wordlessly, dismissed. There was nothing to do except return to his room, lie in bed and wait for morning.

He hoped the ritual had shown Tausret the answer, because it had been, as he had expected, a most perfunctory coupling that had required from him nothing beyond the use of his body. His strongest impressions of this day were the maiden's hand around his flesh, and her gaze holding his throughout the ritual. He resolved, bitterly, to never again think of the first pulse of pleasure, and the blue face that had filled his mind in the moment before.

He turned around for one last look at the chamber. There were five girls in the room.

CHAPTER EIGHTEEN

THE MORNING MEAL was brought up to Yngvi's room.

After, an attendant had knocked on his door to summon him to the sitting room.

Shara was already there, seated straight-backed on a reclining couch to the left of Hemiunu's armchair. Yngvi sat on the couch beside Shara, keeping two feet of cool, cushioned distance between them.

"It is a fine morning," said Hemiunu. "I am hopeful that today is the day we find our answers."

"I am as well," said Yngvi, even though Hemiunu had spoken to Shara.

Hemiunu only nodded gloomily.

They waited in uncomfortable silence until Tausret emerged from the curtained archway. "Father," she said, then acknowledged Yngvi with a thin smile. "Did you have a good rest?"

"I did, thank you," said Yngvi. "And you?"

A pause. "I did." She inclined her head at Shara, then addressed Hemiunu. "Ra spoke to me yesterday, Father."

"Oh! Tausret!" said Hemiunu, his voice going a little breathless. "That is wonderful news. What did he say?"

"Ra has given us...a partial answer. A puzzle."

"What new torment is this?" Hemiunu rubbed his smooth head with both hands in a gesture of resignation. "What is the puzzle, my child?"

"It is in the ritual room, Father. Will you come? Ineni and Shai as well."

"Very well," said Hemiunu.

In the ritual room, Tausret unfurled a scroll over the altar. It bore a set of symbols in still-damp black ink.

"You did this?" Shara asked her.

"Yes. This morning."

"May I?"

Tausret nodded.

Shara leaned over the scroll to study the symbols.

The first was clearly Ra, facing right. Djehuty was drawn next to him, but his figure was half the size. Djehuty was looking to his right at a circle that contained a tree, a bird, an animal and a man. *Aegyptus.* Abutting the inside of Aegyptus' periphery was a seven-pointed star cradled between a crescent moon and a palm leaf.

"These symbols came to me," said Tausret, "after Ra spoke to me."

Yngvi knew by now that Shara was better at symbology than he was, and stayed silent.

Shara looked up at Tausret and pointed to the palm leaf. "Is this Seshat?"

"Yes."

"And this?" he asked about the symbol above Djehuty, an upside-down horseshoe over a rising sun.

"Fifteen," said Tausret. "That means *fifteen days.*"

"Do you see?" Shara asked Yngvi with bright eyes and the beginnings of a smile.

Yngvi felt a familiar pang. He would never admit that he had missed Shara's smile. He nodded, even though he did not see what Shara did.

Then Shara looked over at Tausret and Hemiunu. Tapping on the horseshoe, he said, "After fifteen days of mourning, Ra will seek his dead lover. Djehuty will not permit that. He will come between Ra and Seshat and turn day into night."

Hemiunu was incredulous. "Seshat died exactly fifteen days ago," he said. Then, as another thought struck him, he lifted his eyes from the scroll to look at Tausret in panic. "He means the moon will occult the sun. This is a bad omen."

"Not necessarily," said Shara. "Ra is bigger and more powerful. These symbols tell us that he will look past Djehuty"—he traced a line from Ra's eyes, tangential to the top of Djehuty's head, and extended it to Aegyptus, where it ended precisely at the star—"to fix his gaze upon Seshat where she is buried."

Hemiunu and Tausret were nodding now.

"And today," said Shara, "Ra will show us where she is buried so that we might unearth her and allow him to look upon her one last time. That is where we will find the artefact. That is where Pharaoh Djoser's pyramid should be constructed."

Exultant ice-blue eyes met Yngvi's gaze, and he found that he was, once again, helplessly captivated. He forced himself to look away.

"Father," said Tausret, "we must hurry to the Necropolis."

"We shall leave at once," said Hemiunu.

Shara and Yngvi proceeded on foot, alongside Hemiunu's priests, to the Necropolis of Saqqara.

As before, they were given a leafy sunshade, which compelled them to walk closer than was comfortable to Yngvi.

Six slaves shouldered a large shaded palanquin, bearing Tausret and Hemiunu. The remaining servants carried water, refreshments and digging implements.

As they neared the Necropolis, an insidious dusk began to slowly consume the sky. Clouds had rolled in from all sides, their vast, opaque swirls of grey spreading across the expanse above as their shadows darkened the ground. The sun's brilliance was being slowly but inexorably blotted out by a black shadow creeping over it. As the scroll had envisaged, Djehuty had begun to occult Ra.

By the time they arrived at the mastabas, torches had to be lit because the moon had almost completely obscured the sun, leaving only a thin yellow crescent visible behind it. And as the moments crept by, before their startled, gaping eyes, the entirety of the moon moved in front of the sun, plunging all of Saqqara into an unearthly twilight made eerier by the ring of Ra's light, like a flaming hole in the dark sky.

A low, loud roar from above rumbled through the ground. Hemiunu's servants huddled closer as the dark expanse grew restless, and the air crackled and flashed. The moon continued its angry arc across the sky, creeping away from the sun. Yngvi's hand flew up to shield his eyes when a sharp point of the sun's light appeared at the edge of the moon, and a single, blazing ray of white fire arrowed down to the earth, burning a shallow hole in the sand. Ra's questing gaze had found his dead lover. But Djehuty's rage had lit up the darkness; the sky roared and sparked, and forks of light speared the ground.

The slaves had lowered the palanquin and all the Aegyptians, with Hemiunu and Tausret at the front, had fallen to the sand and were prostrating themselves before the turbulent elements. Only Yngvi and Shara remained standing. Yngvi wondered distantly about the prudence of that, but something inside him, something hard and bitter, would not allow him to kneel.

His instinct for self-preservation suggested belatedly that they could have waited inside Wadjet's temple where he would have asked her if Ra might burn him to a crisp for what he had done with Tausret last night. Not only would that be a disreputable death, but if he died today, he was too far from Valhalla to receive a burial.

Louder than the crash of lightning were the terrified, arcane chants of the priests, with Hemiunu and the attendants joining in.

But Tausret's body jerked upright and her head was thrown back, as if in a trance. Yngvi wove his way through the prone priests and attendants to kneel beside her. She had gone mute. The wrathful moon was mirrored in her open, petrified eyes; her lips moved but made no sound. Gradually, her body slackened and fell back into his arms.

As abruptly as the lightning had struck, it stopped. The moon had voyaged beyond the sun, Ra had burned away the last of Djehuty's clouded chaos, and the sky was restored to its clear, brilliant blue. Casting worshipful looks heavenwards, the Aegyptians rose to their feet. Then they looked around, shocked into silence.

A square area, around four hundred feet on each side, had been demarcated by crystalline shapes that glittered under the sun. The lightning had blasted the sand into glass.

"We have it!" Hemiunu rejoiced. "Ra has shown us the location of Djoser's pyramid and the precise dimensions of its base!" He embraced Shara. "You have saved my life!"

"It was Tausret who gave us the answer," said Shara. "And Ineni."

Yngvi remained beside Tausret, helping her up to a sitting position, indifferent to Hemiunu's priests and servants muttering about the impropriety of his actions.

"We only gave you half the answer," Tausret said to Shara. Her face was drained of colour. She sounded weary, almost fearful. "You inferred its true meaning. My father and I are grateful to you." She looked up at Yngvi and said, her voice very quiet, "He said he will come for us."

Yngvi was about to ask who she meant but Hemiunu clapped him on the shoulder.

"We are," Hemiunu agreed. "We are very grateful. Shai, my men will dig this entire area to search for your artefact."

"That won't be necessary," said Shara. "Ra specifically looked upon Seshat. He has told us where she is buried. Come." He strode to the hole at the north-eastern corner. "This is where she will be. And the artefact."

"Very well," said Hemiunu, and instructed his slaves to start digging there.

While the slaves toiled, the servants spread out a large blanket over the sand with a canopy for Shara, Yngvi and the priests to seat themselves. Hemiunu and Tausret joined them.

Occasionally, the excavators received water and refreshments from the servants. It was early evening by the time the slaves had dug a trench deeper than the tallest of them.

A call went up from the slaves. A servant scrambled to his feet, ran to the trough and knelt over the edge to speak to someone inside. Then he ran back to the canopy to give his message. Hemiunu, Shara and Yngvi hurried over.

"What is it?" said Hemiunu, looking down into the trench.

"I have found something, Master!" said a slave, tapping his spade on the ground between his feet. His legs were spread in a territorial pose, as though claiming the discovery for himself. "There is something underneath."

"Don't just stand there!" Hemiunu snapped at the other slaves. "Help him!"

The four other slaves cursed and redoubled their efforts under the critical eye of their master and his two guests. A short while later, the detritus had been cleared to reveal a long, rectangular casket. Ropes were lowered and fastened around the casket to hoist it to the surface. The servants dusted off the mud to reveal a wooden casket painted with Aegyptian symbols and held shut by a simple latch in front.

Tausret had joined them at the excavation. At once, the men stood aside to let her pass. She knelt before the coffin and ran her fingers over its length. Then she snapped the latch open and lifted the cover. It unlocked with a loud creak. Inside, its only contents were a papyrus scroll wrapped in white linen.

"Is this the artefact you seek?" Hemiunu asked.

"It is," Shara said, but he sounded sceptical.

Was it? What kind of god-killing power could a mere scroll possess? Yngvi's confusion was reflected on Shara's face.

Hemiunu picked up the scroll and held it out to Shara. "I should like to see what it contains."

Shara took it a little hastily, cradling it in his arms. "Our master cautioned us that the scroll is so ancient that any disturbance to it, any rash attempt to unfurl it and view its contents, might cause it to disintegrate."

"How ancient is the artefact supposed to be?" Hemiunu probed.

"Very," Shara said.

Hemiunu held his gaze for a moment, clearly dissatisfied with that non-committal answer. He might have pressed further if he didn't need his own answers here. "All right," he said, grudgingly, "but where is Seshat?"

"*This* is Seshat, Father," said Tausret, looking up. "All of this." She pointed to an inscription spanning the length of the lid. "*Here lies all the knowledge of the land of Aegyptus.* Seshat possessed all the knowledge in the land. She *was* all the knowledge."

Tausret drew her finger across the symbols of a woman in a leopard-skin robe with a seven-pointed headdress, writing on a palm leaf with a palm stem. "These symbols illustrate her life: Seshat's birth, her marriage to Djehuty, her untimely death. She became a star after she died."

"We should return Seshat's sarcophagus to its resting place without delay," said Hemiunu. "My priests and I will begin designing Pharaoh's pyramid tomorrow, after I convey the good news to him. You may accompany me to see Pharaoh."

"Ineni and I are honoured," said Shara, "but we must depart at the earliest."

"Very well, I shall not compel you to stay. But perhaps you would consider departing tomorrow, in order that I may extend my hospitality for one more night. Tomorrow morning, my servants will prepare for your journey. You are welcome to return at your leisure. My doors are always open to you both."

"You are most gracious," said Shara. He looked over at Yngvi, who nodded, and said to Hemiunu, "We gratefully accept your offer. We will resume our journey tomorrow."

"Wonderful!" Hemiunu clapped his hands in delight. "Let us make haste then!"

His slaves promptly knelt by his palanquin, grasped the horizontal poles once he and Tausret had seated themselves, and carefully hoisted it to their shoulders.

The servants rolled up the large blanket on which they had been sitting and gathered the digging implements in a cloth sack. Seshat's coffin was returned to its place in the ground.

The sun's passage across the sky was nearing its end when a smaller group began the journey back to Saqqara; a contingent of slaves had stayed back to refill the hole and restore it to its original state before the excavation.

Yngvi fell behind, and Shara kept pace with him.

"That was good," said Shara. "We found the weapon." He looked relieved to be holding the scroll. He was smiling, as though he was happy that Yngvi was beside him.

"You found the weapon. If a scroll or its contents can somehow be used as a weapon."

"*We* found it," said Shara. "And I did want to thank you."

"For what?"

"For last night. The…ritual. I—"

"Did you enjoy yourself yesterday?" said Yngvi.

"What?"

Yngvi turned his face and looked at Shara with intent.

"Yesterday— I—" A fraught pause. "You mean the…entertainments…Hemiunu mentioned?"

Yngvi's lips tightened. "Surely you weren't just watching." It gave him a perverse satisfaction to see Shara's lashes flutter. "I hope you at least touched a thing or two."

"I—" Shara's gaze flitted away from Yngvi's and wandered off to some point among the group. "I declined the entertainments. I slept."

"That's a shame," said Yngvi, neutrally. "You might have seen what you were missing."

They did not speak the rest of the way.

Their steps quickened as they neared Hemiunu's mansion.

Inside, they were greeted by attendants. Tausret had retired to her chambers without a word to anyone.

Hemiunu said, "Tausret will not eat tonight. And you must both be tired. My servants will bring your meals to you in your chambers."

"Thank you," said Yngvi.

Hemiunu summoned Nenwef. The tall man approached them and gave a respectful bow.

"Nenwef is my Keeper of Slaves. He will provide entertainment for the night. Sleep well." With that parting remark, Hemiunu swept out of the hall.

Nenwef bowed to Shara and Yngvi. "It is my privilege to serve you tonight. I will have your meals sent up to your rooms and will return with your entertainment after."

Yngvi said, "I am grateful for your courtesy. I find that I am tired and should like to rest after my meals."

"I would like that, as well," Shara hurried to add.

Nenwef, seemingly accustomed to the whims of guests, bowed his head. "As you wish," he said, then withdrew to an inner chamber.

At the top of the stairs, Yngvi sensed that Shara was watching him, but did not turn to look at him. He opened his door and stepped inside.

CHAPTER NINETEEN

FINALLY ALONE, YNGVI lay on the bed, staring at the ceiling in dreamlike solitude while the events that had followed his first sighting of Shara scrolled past his mind's eye.

For as long as he could remember, everyone around him—the gods, leaders, elders, his parents and Magne—had always cautioned him against his inclination to act with immediacy rather than, as was their tendency, to reflect first. But he had no doubt that had he reflected too long this time, he would still be on Midgard with rumination, regret and resentment as his only companions in the aftermath while Asgard's doors remained closed to him and all of Midgard turned away.

He had been right to accompany Shara, even though he was being taken into inconceivable unknowns, to worlds where Shara himself was a stranger. He knew that because there was a lightness in his chest, as though the pressure he had carried within since Midgard had, even if only to a small degree, been released.

Where earlier he had felt only grief and powerlessness after Ragnarök, he now saw a thin thread of possibility, even hope, because there were developments, and he had been instrumental in bringing them about. A new vim flowed through him, a tenuous but growing conviction that they would find Enki and stop him. He trusted that Shara had been able to decipher whatever symbols the scroll contained, even if it seemed improbable that a scroll was a weapon.

Then there was last night's ritual.

He closed his eyes, remembering every detail. The girl, Tausret, the experience of unimaginable power contained in that one breath, the warm pressure at his hips, Ra's release mingled with his own. The girl's eyes, throughout, gazing down at him, and changing at the end into the pale eyes he would recognise anywhere.

Last night had provided a respite of a more fundamental nature, a corporeal assuagement of his lingering, and growing, frustrations with Shara, and himself. The desire that shivered beneath his skin was stronger than it had been in Midgard. He wanted Shara. And he knew now that Shara, despite his callous caprice on the balcony, still wanted him. Yngvi let out a breath of bitter amusement. He was a patient man. He would wait.

A knock on the door disrupted his thoughts. He opened it, expecting a servant with his meals, but it was one of Tausret's maidens. She must have knocked on Shara's door as well because he was standing in the doorway, looking at them both.

"The Priestess requests your presence in her chamber," the girl said.

Yngvi shared a look with Shara, then followed the girl.

Tausret and Hemiunu were waiting for them in the ritual room.

Tausret stood by the carving in the wall, which Yngvi had thought looked like a door that led nowhere.

Shara asked, "What is this?"

"It is a false door," said Hemiunu. "A threshold between Life and the Afterlife."

"Look at this, here." Tausret had leaned down to point to a set of symbols in the bottom half.

Hemiunu offered Yngvi a lamp as Shara went down on his haunches. Yngvi bent over him, holding out the lamp to illuminate the area Tausret had indicated. This was the same section he had noted while he waited for the ritual to begin. It had seemed poorly maintained in comparison with the rest of the door.

It was disturbing from up close, unlike the other figures on the door, or even in Wadjet's temple. A right arm, right leg, a man's chest, stomach, left leg and left arm. No head. Like a body hacked into pieces and decapitated. He felt a frisson at the thought and decided against ascribing sinister significance to symbols that were probably innocuous.

Shara, too, was studying the etchings, his eyes shielded from Yngvi by long, thick lashes. But his jawline was clenched, like his hands on his knees.

"These symbols," said Tausret, "have always been on this door. But something has changed." With her finger, she underscored the two symbols that were scuffed: the right arm and the right leg.

"What are we looking at, Tausret?" Shara asked, curtly. "These are body parts, a few of which have faded."

"They are body parts," said Tausret, "but they have another interpretation. According to our sacred texts, they represent the worlds of the universe. The right arm and right leg are known as *Abzu* and *Maardokh*. The left arm is us, Aegyptus. The left leg is called *Ished*. World-tree." She stopped, and Yngvi realised it was because he had started.

Yggdrasil! Shara's eyes met Yngvi's, and Yngvi, who was expecting a similar excitement in them, saw mere acknowledgment of the familiar. *You knew.*

"How do you know there are seven worlds?" Shara asked.

Hemiunu tapped on the starburst symbol that preceded the first arm: six circles arranged in a larger circle and connected to six rays that met at the centre. "This is interpreted as 'the seven worlds of *Baabil-um.*'"

"Baabil-um," Yngvi repeated, knowing what Shara was thinking. *Babylon.*

"Six lines, six circles," Shara remarked, sounding unimpressed. "Six body parts. Six realms."

"The head is missing," said Yngvi.

"That's still only six circles," said Shara.

"Seven," said Hemiunu, with a glance at Yngvi. He pointed to the centre of Babylon, where the lines intersected over a small indentation. "Seven realms."

Shara peered. "Are you telling me a chip in the wall is a realm?"

"That is no chip," said Hemiunu. "That is *Neb-Heru*, the seed of all life in the universe. It is what we call the symbol of the stomach, which contains the navel. And the missing seventh symbol, the seventh realm, must be the head, which is not represented here. We have studied this door for years but have not been able to spot it."

"Were these always faded?" Shara asked, pointing to the symbols for Abzu and Maardokh.

"They were intact until fifteen days ago," said Tausret. "Something happened."

Shara said, "Seshat died."

"Yes." Tausret nodded slowly. "First Seshat died. Then Abzu faded, followed by Maardokh. Ished was only partially erased."

Yngvi crouched beside Shara. "Because you saved Asgard," he said, his voice pitched for Shara's ears. "This is too close to be a coincidence. There is definitely a connection. Nibiru *has* to be the parent realm."

Shara nodded slowly. "And when the pantheons on these realms were killed, the Anunnaki were weakened. The lethargy ran down their right side." Shara gave Yngvi an oblique look. "It would seem you were right about that." Returning his attention to the door, he said, "There are two new realms. The head and the chest."

"Yes," Yngvi agreed. "We must find the other weapons."

"I will, after I take you back to Midgard."

" *What?*" said Yngvi.

"Not here," Shara warned. "What realm does the head represent?"

"I do not know," said Tausret. "It does not exist on this wall or in our sacred texts."

Shara tapped the image of the chest. "And this?"

"Graecia."

Two more weapons to find and destroy, on Graecia and the unnamed seventh realm, and then the last weapon on Nibiru.

Yngvi needed to go to Graecia. He was not letting Shara go without him.

Shara stood, mumbled his thanks to Tausret and Hemiunu, and strode out of her chambers. Yngvi hurried after him.

"You're not taking me back," Yngvi called from behind him. Shara was half-way down the corridor before Yngvi caught up and grabbed his arm to stop him. "I'm going with you to Graecia."

Shara spun on his heel to face Yngvi. But whatever he was about to say was bitten off when a scream shattered the silence. It had come from Tausret's chamber.

Rushing back to her room, they slapped the reed curtain aside and pulled up short.

The air in the room glinted silver-white. Tausret was cowering beside Hemiunu, who was prostrated, his nose touching the floor and an outsize sandalled foot holding his shaven head down. Yngvi's eyes ran up from the foot, taking in the muscled calves, corded thighs and looming body of a man with a milky halo and wrathful eyes.

Djehuty.

He will come for us, Tausret had said.

"You cling too dearly to life, Hemiunu." Djehuty's voice was a deep rumble that seemed to emanate from the walls. "Ra may not care that his priestess is a whore, but you deserve to die for what you allowed your daughter to do to me."

"Forgive us, Great One," Hemiunu beseeched in a high-pitched, timorous voice. "There was no other way!"

Yngvi had had enough of vengeful gods. "Get away from them!" His shout cut through Hemiunu's loud supplication and caught Djehuty's attention.

The god of the Moon lifted his foot from Hemiunu's head, walked around the trembling High Priest, and fixed his gaze on Yngvi and Shara.

"No!" Yngvi heard Shara shout a moment too late.

If there was a lesson in the pummelling he suffered at Loki's hands, Yngvi had not learnt it because he found he had flung himself bodily at Djehuty. And he was, once again, an unarmed mortal attacking an enraged god. He had just grabbed Djehuty's arms when the god's hand slammed into his shoulder and threw him clean across the room. He crashed into a wall and thudded to the ground just as Shara rushed in. He had a vague awareness that the pain in his shoulder was not the broad, dull ache that a blow from a fist or palm would cause, but a concentrated, stinging sensation radiating down his arm and chest.

"That was a mistake," Shara snarled.

No, no, no. "Don't kill him!" Yngvi groaned.

But Shara was not listening to him. His eyes were cold and implacable; he looked older, and his body seemed to have broadened. Even his voice was deeper. Yngvi stared at Shara and recognised the man who had pushed him away two nights ago. Shara in this moment triggered a feeling that Yngvi had not expected: awe.

"You'll kill me?" Djehuty seethed. "Who are you, mortal filth? I am a *god!*"

Shara's jaw was set. "And I can kill gods," he stated, dispassionate and icy.

Tausret and Hemiunu still knelt on the floor, their foreheads touching the ground. They could not see Shara fingers curl, or the flaming blue shaft that appeared in his fist.

Djehuty flicked his hand again, to swat Shara away, but his hand hadn't completed its sweep when it was yanked back by a flaming arrow. His body tottered backwards and hit the wall.

With Djehuty fully occupied by Shara, Yngvi lunged across the room to Hemiunu and Tausret, dragging them to their feet and into the ritual chamber.

"Stay here," he ordered. "We won't let him come through."

Father and daughter nodded mutely, huddling against the wall. Terror had creased Hemiunu's brow as he put a protective arm around Tausret and held her close. Tausret's wide, stricken eyes welled and overflowed.

Leaving them in the ritual room, Yngvi planted himself at the entrance to the chamber and waited while Shara did what Yngvi had, by now, accepted that he could not: overcome a god.

The arrow in Djehuty's hand had dissipated into vaporous strips of blue, but a wet hole remained where it had entered. Stalking up to Shara, Djehuty towered over him.

"Why do you protect that whore and her father? Do you know what they have done?"

The pejorative made Yngvi recoil, but Shara's calm was undisturbed. "They did what they had to do to live. And for that, you want them to die."

"The shameless harlot broke her vows, and her father allowed it," Djehuty thundered. "She is Ra's priestess. Yet she lay with a mortal man and desecrated the resting place of *my wife*. For *that*, they must die." He turned his blazing eyes to Yngvi. "For that, *you* will die."

Djehuty took a menacing step towards Yngvi but found himself faced with Shara's flaming blade.

"Leave him alone, Djehuty!" Shara cut the air with his sword.

Yngvi's heart pounded in his chest. If he survived today, it would be because of Shara. Again.

He felt faint. And a little wet. The sharp, burning sensation had intensified above his chest, and he sank to the floor and looked down at himself, at the blossoming stain on his left shoulder where Djehuty had struck him. He touched it gingerly. His fingers came away wet and red. It slowly became clear: Djehuty had stabbed Yngvi with bare fingers. And was sauntering up to him now to deliver the killing blow.

There was a flash of blue, a scream of pain. Blue fire ripped the air, and through Djehuty. A flurry of strokes that lasted no more than a few seconds. Shara lowered his sword, and Djehuty floated before them, his white body ribboned by the fire-blade. Djehuty's shredded head, held together by what remained of his godly power, turned towards Yngvi, his white face splitting in a baleful smile as he faded from view.

Yngvi saw Shara see that smile, saw the moment when Shara's eyes registered the stain on Yngvi's shoulder. In the next instant, he was on his knees beside Yngvi, his face soft, his eyes wide and worried, his hands gentle on Yngvi's arms.

"I have killed you." A whispered warning, spoken in Djehuty's voice.

"You're bleeding!" Shara sounded hoarse.

Yngvi managed a trivialising smile. "Scratches."

Shara seemed overly upset about what felt like a minor wound, but Tausret and Hemiunu, having ventured out of the ritual room, were staring at him with guilt and, worryingly, horror.

Tausret knelt before Yngvi. "Ineni," she said, softly, looking at his wound. "Ineni."

"You're looking at me as though I'm about to die."

"Ineni…" she said again, dropping her head.

"What is it?" Shara snapped. "Say it!"

"Calm down—" Yngvi said.

"Don't ask me to calm down." Shara glared at him, then looked at Tausret. "Is he going to die?"

Tausret lifted mournful eyes to Shara.

"*Tausret!*" he snapped.

"Shai! That's not helping," said Yngvi, because Tausret had shrivelled under Shara's anger.

Her lips moved soundlessly, and Yngvi had a strange feeling he knew what she was going to say, but it was Hemiunu who confirmed his fears.

"No mortal wounded by a god has ever survived." He touched Yngvi's arm. "I am sorry."

"That—" said Shara. "That can't be. No!" He was shaking his head. Then, peremptorily: "Take us to your god of Healing."

"Shai…" said Tausret, her voice hitching. "Don't you know? *Djehuty* is our god of Healing."

Yngvi felt all the breath leave him. The wound burned, but was still far from debilitating. He had not imagined that this is how it would end for him. If only he had a little more of Eir's salve. How much more, he wondered distantly, would his left shoulder have to take? First burned from behind by fire giants. Now stabbed in the front by the enraged Aegyptian god of the Moon. He held onto the doorway and tried to stand. Shara grasped his forearm and helped him up, making him lean on his shoulder.

"How long do I have?" Yngvi asked.

"I can't say. Your wound needs to be bandaged," said Tausret. "I have some herbs that can delay deterioration. I will need some time to prepare the salve."

"You do that," said Shara, sharply. "I'm taking him back to his room."

CHAPTER TWENTY

WITH SHARA'S ARM around him providing superfluous but agreeable support, Yngvi made it back to his room. Shara forced him to lie on the bed while he paced the floor. His hands were fists.

"What were you thinking!"

"You saved me," said Yngvi. "Again."

"And as soon as your wound has been bandaged," said Shara, "I'm taking you back to Midgard. Eir might be able to heal you. Keep you alive."

"No."

"You're not listening."

"No, *you* are not. I told you the doors of Valhalla are closed to me. And what makes you think I'll go crawling back for Eir's help when she holds me responsible for the ruin of her family?"

"You will *die*." Shara almost spat the word out. "Do you understand?"

"That is what it is to be mortal. Do *you* understand? I will die one day. I just didn't expect it would be so soon, or like this. But I don't want"—*my death*, he wanted to say—"all this to be in vain. Without you, I have no hope of stopping Enki."

"You're forgetting that you're wounded."

"In my left shoulder. I'm right-handed. I can still be useful."

"I'm taking you back." Shara's eyes had gone as hard as his tone. He looked like he had on the balcony. "You're slowing me down."

This again? "Am I really?" Yngvi said, his lips twisting. "Maybe I should have let you partake in the ritual. After all, you volunteered."

He watched the words hit, saw Shara flinch. It gave him a small, spiteful satisfaction.

His wound throbbed, and he bit off a groan. "Shara, we did things on Aegyptus together that we could not have done apart. You know that. We need each other. I'm going with you."

The reed curtain rippled as a hand pushed on it, and Tausret announced herself from the other side.

"Come in," said Shara.

She entered, carrying a tray with thin cotton strips and several bowls with odorous contents. She sat down on the bed beside Yngvi. Shara hovered while she cleaned and bandaged the wound. Yngvi had to ultimately accept that no amount of glaring at Shara would make him stand down, so he looked, instead, at Tausret.

"I thought you would send one of your girls," he said to her gently. "But I am glad you came."

Tausret's eyes were wide and wet with remorse. "It will turn black soon. That's what happens with a wound inflicted by a god." She sobbed softly. "I am truly sorry, Ineni."

Yngvi touched her arm and smiled up at her. "I agreed to the ritual. And it worked, didn't it?"

She nodded sadly. "You saved my father's life," she said. "And mine."

"I… It was Shai who fought off Djehuty. I could not have done it."

Tausret looked up at Shara with a wan smile and received a terse nod in response.

She finished bandaging the wound. From the tray, she picked up two small stoppered jars and handed one to Yngvi. "Drink all of this now, and take the other with you. This medicinal potion will keep your strength up for a few days. After that…"

"A few days is all I need," said Yngvi. He took the jar, drank it down and gave it back to her. He took the second jar. Stared at it, as an idea, faint at first, grew distinct. The ritual. There was a way.

"Tausret," he said, his voice a little breathless, "can you make us two jars like the jar that held Ra's essence? His ka?"

Shara, he noted, had not asked for an explanation.

"I can, but— The jar is meant to hold a specific ka," said Tausret. "It will need their likeness carved on the outside, which my potter can do. And then I'll have to perform a ritual to prepare it to hold that life force." A moment's hesitation. Then: "Whose ka do you need it to hold?"

A murderous god on a rampage. He said, "Shai can tell you."

"I can," said Shara, "but we only need one jar."

Yngvi put his hand on Tausret's forearm and smiled. "Tausret, we need two."

Tausret left the chamber with Shara. Yngvi lay on the bed, looking about the room.

It was an hour before Shara returned alone with two jars carved with Enki's likeness.

"This is a waste of time," he said. " *You* are a waste of my time."

His voice was hard, and Yngvi decided he had tolerated Shara's mercurial temperament long enough. But Shara was not finished.

"Do you really expect that Enki is going to voluntarily breathe his life force into this?"

"Enough, Shara. If you have a better idea to trap Enki without killing him, let's hear it. Otherwise, this is what we have."

"I should never have taken you with me." Shara's voice had deepened like it had when he had faced Djehuty. There was that same coldness in his eyes, the hard set of his jaw making it clear that he resented having to do this, resented Yngvi. "All I'm doing is saving you from angry gods. You're a liability."

It hurt. So much that it stole Yngvi's breath. But he needed Shara to find Enki. He told himself that, in time, he would be inured to this vitriol, that repetition would diminish its impact. And realistically, he would not have to listen to this much longer, considering the fatal wound in his shoulder. He turned gingerly on the bed to face the wall. That position was easier on his body. It also meant he did not have to look at Shara. "You retain the option to let me die the next time a god attacks me."

Shara was keeping silent, and Yngvi wished he could read that acrimonious mind.

"In any case," he added, bitterly, "you'll be rid of me soon enough. Tausret's potion will keep me alive for a few more days. After that, you can throw my body to the animals, for all I care, and forget that we ever met." He pressed his eyes closed for a moment, wishing he could see Magne one last time. "Now, if you have expressed all the ways in which I am slowing you down, I'd like to be alone."

The stony silence that followed was a relief because Yngvi had had enough of Shara's peevishness. Shara had probably returned to his room already, leaving Yngvi talking to himself. Yngvi glowered at the bricks in the wall, vented his frustration by thumping them hard with an open palm.

From behind him a second later, an answering thud. Like an echo. But then, a groan.

Yngvi rolled onto his back to determine the source of the sound. He didn't see Shara. Craning his neck to look over the bed, he saw him lying on the ground. Before he knew it, Yngvi had swung off the bed and was kneeling beside Shara. He pulled Shara into his arms, winced when the wound in his shoulder pulled, but tightened his arms when Shara started shaking.

"What's happening to you?"

Shara bit off a cry.

"Is it another vision?"

"Leave me alone," Shara rasped.

Ignoring his objections, Yngvi lifted him with effort and carried him to the bed. Shara's eyes rolled back into his head and then closed.

His body was jerking, but Yngvi held him down. It took a long while for his body to still. It took longer for his eyes to open, and for him to come back to his surroundings.

"Yngvi," he said, sounding like himself again.

"Was it Enki?"

Shara didn't respond, just gazed at him.

Yngvi knew Shara's thoughts were somewhere else. "That was your vision, wasn't it? Enki killing the gods on Graecia?"

"No."

"It wasn't Enki, then?"

"It wasn't the gods on Graecia." Shara looked down at his hands, folded limply over his stomach.

"I don't understand. Did you see who he was killing?"

Shara kept his eyes lowered.

Yngvi's patience was running thin. He held Shara's chin and tipped his face towards him. "Who was Enki killing?"

Shara said, very quietly, "Me."

Yngvi went still. His hand slipped down to Shara's chest.

"I suppose I shouldn't be surprised," said Shara, wryly. "I have been trying to kill him for some time now."

"We are going to Graecia," said Yngvi, hearing the iron in his voice. "We are going to destroy the weapon there, and then capture Enki in the ka jar before he can get to you."

"How?" The question came as a throb, Shara sounding young and lost.

"I don't know…but something will occur to us," said Yngvi, meaning it. Shara's forehead was damp with sweat. A white lock of hair was stuck to his skin. Yngvi gently pushed it off his face. "I'm with you till the end." What end that would be, or whose, he did not know. Either he would die first, or they would capture Enki so that Shara would be safe. "Did you decipher the scroll?"

"No."

"Where is it?"

"I burned it."

"What! Why? Did you at least memorise the symbols?"

"I might have."

"*Shara.*" Irritated now. "What were the symbols?"

"If I couldn't interpret them, I doubt you'll be able to."

It took conscious restraint not to grab this smug, stubborn difficult man by the shoulders and shake the puerility out of him. "I know I won't," Yngvi muttered, "but Hemiunu or Tausret might."

Just then, a male voice called Yngvi's name from outside the door. It was Hemiunu.

"Come in," Yngvi called.

Hemiunu entered with Tausret. "I will have to see Pharaoh early tomorrow morning and wanted to see you before you leave. We owe you both so much."

Tausret wore a quizzical look. "When I left," she said to Yngvi, "you were lying on the bed. But now, Shai is?"

"He felt faint. It's nothing serious," said Yngvi. "He needs you to interpret something. Is there—" He looked around. "This should work." He reached for the candle placed on the window sill, snuffed it with his fingers and snapped its wick. He held out the rigid black wick to Shara.

With the singed tip, Shara smeared three powdery symbols on the corner of the bedsheet. "What does this say?"

A speculative glance passed between father and daughter.

"This is very curious," said Hemiunu. "It is not a word but a phrase."

"If the sounds that these symbols represent were spoken together," said Tausret, "this would say *Sh aa-raa*. The closest interpretation would be...*older than time*." She looked questioningly at Hemiunu who confirmed her interpretation with a nod.

Yngvi swung his head to Shara, to see if he was equally confounded, then went still. Because horror had flashed in Shara's eyes.

Shara dropped the sheet. "Thank you," he said, sitting up slowly. "I should return to my room. We will leave tomorrow morning. I am very grateful for your kindness."

"We came here to thank *you*," said Hemiunu. "You both," he added, with a glance at Yngvi. "You have saved our lives. I will have two camels prepared for you in the morning. It is the least I can do to ease your journey."

The wobbly, humped beasts? Not only was Yngvi averse to the idea of riding one of these *camels*, but they couldn't possibly take them along to Graecia. "Our master's instructions are that our quest must continue on foot, or the gods will be displeased," he said. "But we are grateful for your generosity."

Hemiunu frowned. "I've never heard of such a requirement. I suspect your master cares little for your welfare. He truly is a—"

Tausret touched her father's arm, and Hemiunu bit down on whatever else he was about to say about their invented master.

"If that is what you must do," she said, "we will leave you to rest. Farewell, Shai and Ineni."

With that, they left.

As soon as they were alone, Yngvi rounded on Shara. "There's something about the scroll."

"There's nothing about the scroll."

"I saw your face when Tausret told you what it means. You know something. What is it?"

"I told you, it's nothing."

"It was your *name*, Shara! Don't you want to know why your name was written on a scroll buried on a world that a few weeks ago you didn't even know existed? And *older than time*? What does that even mean? It can't mean *you*. You look no older than twenty, twenty-one. How old are you?"

"It doesn't matter—"

"Does your name have a meaning on Nibiru?"

"Stop this."

"Nidaba named you, didn't she?" said Yngvi. "The goddess of Knowledge herself. *She* knew something."

"But *I* don't! I don't know what *any* of it means."

Yngvi grabbed Shara's arm before he could turn away. "I think you do."

Shara pulled his arm free. "I don't," he repeated coldly. "And if I did, I am certain that it does not concern you."

Yngvi pressed his eyes closed for a moment, pushing down on the vexation that Shara so effortlessly and frequently caused him. He tried another tack, and gentled his voice. "I want to help. I can see this is troubling you."

Shara turned his head away.

"You showed me your memories on the day we met. Don't you trust me enough to tell me what this is? After everything we've been through?"

"I don't need your help."

Once again Yngvi felt the urge to shake the intractability out of Shara. Instead, he dug his nails into his palms, waiting for his exasperation to subside. When he could trust his voice to be even, he said, "We should leave."

"You're dying," said Shara. He was watching Yngvi with an unreadable expression.

Yngvi did not need reminding. "Are you celebrating already?"

Shara glared at him. "We should leave."

Yngvi said nothing. He opened his bag of clothing and they changed into tunic, pants and boots. He fastened his sword belt around his waist, placed Tausret's medicine and ka jars in his bag, safely wrapped inside a tunic, and slung the bag diagonally over his shoulder. This time, they carried the waterskins with them, mementos from Aegyptus. Then they stepped out onto the balcony. The moonless sky was a black sweep with pinpricks of light as far as the eye could see.

Yngvi asked, running his thumb over the gemstone in his sword's hilt. "What were the weapons on the other realms?"

"I didn't find the weapon on Apsu," said Shara. "But on Marduk, Enki had taken over the body of his counterpart, and was killing Marduk's gods. Like Loki was."

"I don't believe there is a *specific* god-killer weapon on each realm."

"There has to be," said Shara.

Yngvi shook his head. "If Loki's spear was the weapon on Asgard, if it was really that powerful, it would have worked the previous times he attacked Valhalla. On both occasions, Odin and Thor overcame him. But this time, his spear had a different kind of—" he searched for the right word, simulated ripples with his fingers, and settled on "—energy. And he seemed almost invincible. Until you came."

"You think it's because Enki was inside him."

Yngvi nodded. "I think it's the force of an Anunnaki that infuses a weapon with the power to kill other gods. And yet, you were able to kill Loki…"

"You think I have Anunnaki blood in me."

"I do."

Shara shook his head slowly. "If I did, my sword should have killed Enki."

Shara was right. Yngvi thought about that, about the deaths of the gods of Babylon and the other realms. The glimmer of a connection appeared, fragile as spider silk. "I could be wrong…"

"You haven't been wrong about much," said Shara. His gaze was open now, and his voice carried no trace of cynicism. "So? What are you thinking?"

"Nidaba was killed on Nibiru. The gods of Apsu and Marduk were killed on their own realms…"

"Loki, Vör and the other Aesir died on Yggdrasil, Seshat on Aegyptus," said Shara, completing Yngvi's thought. "You think gods only die on their own realm."

"Yes. At least, that would explain what's happened."

"It would." Shara's gaze held an echo of their intimacy after the exchange of memories in Midgard.

Yngvi looked away, turning back when he heard Shara's halting words.

"There's something—happening inside me. Something is changing, and I feel less and less able to control it, control what I say."

"I noticed."

Shara nodded slowly.

"It's just as well then," said Yngvi, "that I'm going with you."

Another slow nod. "About what you said, and what I said, before—" said Shara, gravely. "I would…prefer that you did not die."

Yngvi let out a breath. He and Shara were in agreement about that. Gazing out at Saqqara, he said, "We could go to the god of Healing on Graecia."

"We will," said Shara. "Are you ready?"

"I'm ready." Yngvi held on to Shara's arms, and as it had in Midgard, the blue halo enveloped him. They rose into the dark sky and hurtled across the stars to Graecia.

CHAPTER TWENTY-ONE

GRAECIA, OR AT least this city, was celebrating.

They found themselves on the periphery of a vast town square. Graecians of all ages were milling about, dancing and drinking. Shara caught the arm of an inebriated young man who was exiting the square, causing the drink in his cup to slosh a little.

"Hello," Shara said. "What is this place?"

Catching the man's look of disorientation, Yngvi said, "We are lost."

"There you are, Inachus!" shouted another man who was coming up the road to the square.

"Impatient fool," Inachus muttered, taking an unhurried sip of his drink as the other man marched over to them. "This is Athens, city of Athena," he slurred obligingly through a slack mouth. A little wine dribbled down his chin. "Athena, the—Wise," he added with insincere gravitas.

Wise? "Is Athena the goddess of Knowledge?" Yngvi asked, just as the other man reached them.

Inachus's companion was older than him by several years, and unquestionably sober. "You didn't know that? You must be Spartans, if you're that ignorant."

"*I* would like—to be a—Spartan." Inachus was swaying slightly now. "They can—fight."

"But you can barely stay upright. You're drunk again," said the man. He grasped Inachus's arm roughly, causing him to spill more of his wine. "I'm taking you home."

"I'm not a child, Nikos!" Inachus protested, wiping his mouth with the back of his hand as he was pulled away. He looked back at Yngvi and

Shara with an apologetic smile. "My brother," he said in farewell, and it was explanation enough for Yngvi.

When he looked at Shara, he imagined they were having the same thought. If Athena was the goddess of Knowledge, and if they were right about the connection between the realms, she was dead. Why, then, were her citizens celebrating? Did they not know? Or did she still live?

"Shara," said Yngvi. His shoulder throbbed. His bandage was damp.

Shara took one look at his shoulder and said, "We have to find you a healer." He accosted another Graecian, this time picking an elderly woman who was entering the square and had not yet got her hands on drink because she appeared to be in control of her faculties.

"Excuse me, lady. My friend is injured. Is there a healer nearby?"

Her eyes crinkled, and her kindly lips stretched over very pink gums. "Yes, my boy," she said, but her smile disappeared when she noticed the black stain on Yngvi's shoulder. "You are fortunate, young man," she said. "Athens is home to the foremost of all healers in Graecia. Take that winding road and pass eight houses on the left. The ninth is his infirmary. Hippocrates is his name."

"Thank you, lady," said Shara.

"Be well, young man," she said. Looking at Yngvi: "I hope Asclepius can help you." Then she waddled off into the crowd.

They passed the first eight houses.

The ninth, as the old woman had said, was a sanatorium. With most of Athens gathered in the square, there were only a few patients waiting for the healer, and within a half hour, Yngvi was being looked over by Hippocrates while Shara loomed. Remembering from Saqqara the futility of glaring at Shara while he glared at a healer, Yngvi ignored his frowning minder to endure Hippocrates's fingers palpating the area around his wound, hissing softly when the pressure became painful.

"I am Inachus," Yngvi had said, "and this is Nikos."

"Your brother?" Hippocrates had asked.

"My—friend," Yngvi had answered.

The physician had hummed knowingly. He was a thin man who moved with a wiry energy. He might have been forty, possibly older, and had the manner of a kindly but efficient disciplinarian, reminding Yngvi of his father.

Hippocrates was careful when he peeled off Tausret's bandage, and did not baulk at the wound, even though it was turning black.

"Ah, Inachus, your blood is changing," he remarked with a complete lack of surprise, but he was humming again. "I haven't had one of these today." Then he looked at Yngvi, and informed him, with clinical precision, "You have a wound from a god."

Yngvi smirked, but said nothing.

"Who did you cross? What did you do?" Hippocrates asked with rapid-fire interest, and Yngvi had no difficulty imagining the physician among the gossiping fishwives of Midgard.

"I...don't know who it was."

"Oh, I think you do." Hippocrates flashed him a conspiratorial smile. "Never mind, you don't have to tell me. No one who comes in with a wound like yours tells me anything. But I find out in the end."

"In the end?" said Shara.

"When they are dead, of course!" said Hippocrates, chuckling to himself.

He busied his hands with some sort of salve. Yngvi hoped its odious smell, nothing at all like Tausret's lavender-infused paste, was not a reflection of its efficacy.

"Unfortunately," said Hippocrates, "I cannot save you. If you don't have your own pollux, only Asclepius can."

Whatever a pollux was, Yngvi was fairly certain he didn't have one. Asclepius, he assumed, was the Graecian god of Healing.

"Apollonius, my dear!" Hippocrates gave the summons a singsong rendition. Moments later, a young boy hurried in. His hair was gold, his eyes green and the simple white tunic he wore did nothing to diminish his epicene beauty. "This is my youngest son, and newest apprentice," said Hippocrates, with evident pride. "I'm teaching him my skills."

Yngvi smiled at the boy. "Hello, Apollonius. I am Inachus, and this is Nikos."

"Hello," said Shara.

Apollonius gave them a sweet smile in return. "Hello."

"He likes you," said Hippocrates, "because you remind him of his brothers. And you like him now, but wait till he gives you your medicine." He tipped his head back and laughed.

"Can you delay...it?" said Shara, grimly, killing the mood. "So that I can go see this Asclepius."

Hippocrates's cheer faded. "*This* Asclepius? If that is the respect you accord the god of Healing, he might not be easily persuaded to help your friend."

"I apologise," Shara said immediately. "I worry, that is all. Please, where can I find Asclepius?"

"In his temple, my boy," said Hippocrates, his lips curving up. "Where else?"

Shara looked from him to Yngvi and back.

"I suppose you are new in Athens," said Hippocrates, and paused.

"We are Spartans," said Yngvi. He had wagered that the real Nikos's disparaging assumption about them would satisfy Hippocrates. It did.

"Spartans. All right," said the physician. "I shall tell you the way to Asclepius's temple and how to invoke him. I will also treat your friend's wound so that he draws breath until you return."

"Thank you," said Shara. "You are very kind. But we have no coin to—"

"You don't? That is quite the predicament." Hippocrates was smiling widely now. Apollonius, too, was covering his mouth. "I might be mistaken, dear boy, but I did not demand coin, did I?" He clapped Shara on the shoulder. "What gifts of healing I have were given to me by Asclepius to help our people, not to profit from their ailments."

"We are very grateful," said Shara.

Hippocrates squeezed his shoulder. "You should be. I'm about to keep your wayward friend alive just a little longer than he probably deserves." He tutted. "You young men, always getting in trouble with the gods. Like Apollonius's brothers. They are about your age, and as handsome. I caution every young man like you who comes in here with wounds such as yours to stay away from the nymphs." He brought his head close to Yngvi's and lowered his voice. "Was it a nymph?"

"No," said Yngvi, "but I wish it was." He found he was smiling.

Hippocrates's medicine tasted fouler than his salve smelled.

And there was a lot of medicine. One whole deep cup, which took three swallows to finish. Yngvi's lips untwisted only after he had chased it down with copious amounts of wine that Apollonius had presciently brought with him.

Yngvi was alone on a bed by a window. He felt fine, but Hippocrates, employing the tone a parent would use on a five-year-old, had instructed him to rest. It was twenty years since Yngvi had been five. And no one had told him what to do since his parents had died. Magne might try, but it never worked.

He had, in fact, opened his mouth to say all of those things, but Hippocrates had held up a finger, and Yngvi was now obediently horizontal on an Athenian bed, looking out at the Athenian sky while Athenians celebrated in the square. On his way out to attend to his other patients, Hippocrates had said that Asclepius took a little coaxing before he appeared to supplicants. Which meant that Shara could be gone a few hours.

They had argued about it.

Predictably, the first words out of Yngvi's mouth once Hippocrates exited the healing room were, "I feel fine. I can come with you."

Also predictably, Shara had said, "You heard Hippocrates. You'll stay here," and then clammed up.

Shara had paced the room after that, fists curled, jaws clenching, his silence feeling violent, as if he was waging a battle within himself.

Yngvi had understood. He had said, tolerantly, "You're thinking that you should have left me behind in Midgard, aren't you?"

Shara had stared at him.

"And that it wasn't in your plans to carry around a dying man who is only a liability slowing you down?"

He had watched the words penetrate.

"Something like that," Shara had eventually admitted, his voice quiet.

Yngvi had shrugged. "I suppose I should thank you for not saying it out loud."

Shara had stopped, looked at him a moment, then resumed pacing.

"Shara," Yngvi had said. "I told you. I am going to die, if not soon from this wound, then another day. It is going to happen. But if I am alive long enough to capture Enki, I'll go to the Afterlife willingly."

"You're not going to die," Shara had said, and then asked him to stop talking.

After that, Yngvi had not said a word, choosing, instead, to observe the city outside the window. He wished he could anticipate these startling changes in Shara. When Shara said he was leaving for the temple, Yngvi did not stop him.

It was early evening by the time the activity outside the healing room subsided.

When he felt reasonably confident that he would not be intercepted by Hippocrates or his staff, Yngvi threw off the thin coverlet and swung his legs off the bed. He retrieved one of the ka jars Tausret had given them, and tucked it in his belt. Then he strode out with the verve of a man who stood on the brink of death, but had one last thing to do before the moment arrived.

On his way to the main door, he spotted Apollonius and asked him to inform Hippocrates and Shara that he was going to the celebrations and would be back soon. Before the boy could express any objections, Yngvi was on the winding street heading back to the town square.

CHAPTER TWENTY-TWO

THE TOWN SQUARE—*agora*, Hippocrates had called it—was teeming with activity and lively music.

It was a sprawling hypaethral quad paved with marble, and delineated on three sides by towering arcades with permanent shops and stalls under their arches. High-flung banners fluttered cheerfully in the wind.

Two thrones stood on a dais that must have been assembled while Yngvi was fending off Hippocrates's pokes and interrogations. Lounging on the thrones were two Graecian men—two striking Graecian men. Yngvi discerned a glow around them. These were not men, but gods.

"Beautiful, aren't they?" said the man beside him. He had lifted his cup to point out the frenzied, naked maidens dancing in front of the dais for the gods' entertainment, their long hair loosed about their shoulders, bare breasts bouncing, hips swinging with wanton grace. Cries of delight and bawdy cheers went up among the onlookers when a group of Athenian youths threw off their garments and joined the revelling girls.

"Beautiful," Yngvi agreed, watching the golden-haired gods on the dais. They were swathed in dark fabric that ran in loose folds under one arm and was held up at the opposite shoulder by a golden pin. The excess fabric overhung the girdles tied around their slim waists, and the skirt reached mid-thigh with difficulty. "I like what they are wearing."

"It's just a chiton," said the man. "But," he granted, "blue is a rare colour. Only gods and the rich can afford it."

Chiton. The garment left much of their bodies exposed. It also left just enough to the imagination, and Yngvi found the suggestion of nakedness underneath the dark cloth far more appealing than the nude forms of the dancing Athenians.

"Yes," said Yngvi. "I like the blue chitons." He wondered what he looked like to the Athenian, what appearance Shara had given them. "Is this how Athenians mourn their gods?"

"Mourn the gods?" said the man, with a derisive laugh that implied Yngvi was mad to suggest that the gods could die.

But Athena had to be dead. Yngvi was sure of it. And then came the alternative: if this was how Graecians grieved, with dancing women and wrestling boys and meats and wine, how joyous were their celebrations? No renegade gods of the Underworld? No fighting? Just cavorting with fun-loving immortals and beautiful mortals? He would not mind living here—his wound pulsed as a reminder—if he did not die here.

"Then what is this celebration about?"

"This is the Spring Festival. Don't you know?"

"I'm Spartan," said Yngvi, smoothly.

The man turned his head to look at Yngvi from head to toe and back up again. He had to tilt his head back to meet Yngvi's eyes. He nodded, as though that provenance explained Yngvi's ignorance. Then he gave a shrug that said he did not care. His tongue loosened by the wine, he said, "That is Dionysus, the god of Wine and Festivities." Dionysus had made identification easy by helpfully plucking grapes from a heavy sprig and popping them in his mouth. "And that—"the man tilted his cup to indicate the god seated beside Dionysus"—is Hermes, Messenger of the gods."

"Messenger?" said Yngvi. Hermes's winged sandals and winged wand marked him clearly as the flying messenger. But he looked most unqualified for the task, draped as he was over his throne in an indolent sprawl, idly twirling a winged wand in the long fingers of one hand while his other wrist sat elegantly on the armrest. "He must keep the gods waiting. He doesn't look like he's going anywhere fast." In fact, the only sign of urgency around Hermes came from the nervous little owl that sat on his shoulder, its head swivelling about, and its large yellow eyes nictitating rapidly as it took in the scene.

"Don't be fooled by what you see today," said the Athenian. "Hermes is the swiftest of the gods, almost as fast as thought itself. He's also one of the few liminal gods."

"Liminal?"

"He can traverse the borders between worlds."

Yngvi was growing more impressed with Hermes, and also heartened. "So, he can take me to the Underworld?"

"Underworld?" The man gawped at Yngvi as one would at a mad man. "Only heroes and fools are in a hurry to get to the Underworld. Which one are you?"

Enki would be drawn to the Underworld on every realm, which his counterpart would oversee. If Yngvi and Shara could get there before him, they might have a chance to force him out into the open and capture his spirit in the ka jar tucked in his belt. "Probably not a hero," Yngvi said.

The Athenian laughed. "Hermes could take you there when you die. He's also the Shepherd of Souls." Then his voice changed. There was fear in the whispered, "Oh…look. I think the Underworld has come to you."

It had. And it was angry.

The agora had gone dark, as though the sun had been swallowed, and a single gust had extinguished all the fires in Athens in an instant. Banners flapped hard in the violent wind. Above, the skies were a churning mass of twilight, and closer to the ground, there was a rip in the air, which was opening as if torn apart by hands. Out of the rupture stepped a woman in black. Her skin was pale as moonlight, her eyes blacker than night, yet she possessed an otherworldly beauty. She was unmistakably a goddess. Trailing behind her black mane were three massive snarling black hounds and an indeterminate number of screaming ghouls.

"*Hecate*," the Athenian whispered in a trembling voice. In the next instant, he had joined the rest of the celebrators, tearing down the agora and scurrying towards the exit.

But the courage of experience nudged Yngvi closer to the dais; he stopped a few paces from the steps. The skies looked like they had in Saqqara, when Djehuty had occulted Ra, but he had survived that tumult.

"Dionysus!" the goddess screamed, making the ground shake. Her hounds raised their heads and howled.

"Do quiet down, sister," said Dionysus. He popped another plump grape in his mouth. Hermes leaned over, said something to Dionysus and they both laughed.

Hecate floated onto the dais. "How dare you!"

Dionysus jerked back minutely, but Hermes remained admirably unruffled.

"You're always complaining about us, Hecate. What is it that we've done now, sister?"

"Athena's dead! Your sister is dead, and you're celebrating?"

Graecia's goddess of Knowledge was dead. Yngvi experienced a moment of grim satisfaction at having his theory borne out.

Hermes, his eyes wide with surprise, swung his head to Dionysus, who himself looked baffled.

"What?" said Hermes, turning to Hecate.

"Athena is dead! The Sisterhood mourns." She pointed her staff accusingly at her brothers. "And yet here you are, celebrating, in her *own* city!"

Dionysus lifted a sculpted naked shoulder in a careless shrug. "We didn't know."

His green gaze was heavy-lidded, his mouth slack, and Yngvi realised that the god of Wine was drunk. Dionysus tossed the grapes aside. They missed the dais and landed on the floor of the agora, the berries at the bottom bursting wetly on impact and staining the white marble tiles with crimson juice. In contrast, Hermes's eyes, black like Hecate's, were keen, and more than a little amused.

Neither of them had asked a single question about Athena's death.

"But now you know. Stop this celebration," Hecate ordered. "And Hermes, you will give me Athena's owl."

"No, I won't," said Hermes, with an airy wave of his hand. "She lost the owl in a bet, then lost her life before she could win her bird back. You can hardly blame me for that."

"Hermes," said Hecate. "You know she cannot cross over to Elysium without the bird."

Hermes only tilted his head and gave her a cold smile, reminding Yngvi very much of Loki's nonchalant taunting of Thor and Odin.

"Hermes!" Hecate yelled.

Dionysus cringed, and held his hands up to his ears. "Please, sister, stop shouting," he muttered miserably.

Yngvi sympathised. He knew from experience how sensitive one's hearing could be in a state of drunkenness. "And quiet your beasts, I pray you."

Hecate turned her head slightly. At once the snarls turned to whimpers, the fiendish screaming quieted to a chorus of hisses.

"Thank you," said Dionysus. "We are gods, Hecate. We do not need to settle matters like the ghouls under your watch."

"Then what do you suggest?" she snarled.

"You could fight me for the owl," Hermes suggested, pleasantly.

"I won't lower myself to your level," she said, her mouth twisting on the words.

"You're the one who's *under* everyone else," said Hermes, making a face at Hecate that Yngvi remembered employing to great effect during his own adolescent quarrels with Magne. "How much lower can you go?"

"Please, grow up, both of you," said Dionysus. His eyelids were struggling to stay open, and he was listing in his throne. "Well," he drawled, "I was going to suggest that you settle this the old-fashioned way. Get the mortals to do it for you."

Hermes leaned forward, interested. "What do you mean?"

"A contest," said Dionysus, lazily. "Pit your champion against hers."

"Go on," said Hecate.

"You can both set the rules. Three bouts, perhaps? Just use what the boys were using earlier." His gaze followed the languid sweep of his hand over the agora and landed on the makeshift ring erected to the left of the dais.

And that was when the three gods looked out at the evacuated agora and their eyes landed on the only mortal standing there.

Yngvi found that he had taken a few steps back.

"Oh look. You've put an end to the celebration yourself, sister," Dionysus observed. "You've scared everyone away."

Hecate floated down the steps of the dais towards Yngvi.

"He's mine!" said a male voice. It was Hermes.

She spun around, her hair making trails of black in the thick air. "What?"

"My champion." Hermes sashayed down the steps with divine insouciance. "I choose him." And then, in the next instant, as if he had flown the distance that separated them, he was standing before Yngvi. But his eyes were not on Yngvi; they were on his sword.

"He has no one to fight!" said Hecate.

"I'm feeling generous, sister. Choose the contests, go find your champion. I think this one will win them all. And if he doesn't—" Hermes grinned over his shoulder at Hecate "—you can have the owl."

Then Hermes turned his smiling gaze to Yngvi and opened his hand. The sword slid out of Yngvi's scabbard and flew to the messenger god, settling gently on his palm. Hecate had come up beside Hermes and was raising her hand, but it was moving in half-time. The seconds seemed to stretch out, and Yngvi could do no more than watch in mute, struggling shock as Hermes's long fingers closed around the hilt. The fingers of his other hand drifted over the engraved snakes on the blade. Then his lashes dipped slowly as his eyes settled on the blue stone and his thumb traced unhurried circles over the glimmering bulge, as though following the hard-cut facets on its surface.

His thumb pressed down, made a little crack in the gem. Pressed again. The gem shattered, some of it caving into its gold setting in specks of blue, the rest rising in blue mist. A light passed over Hermes's eyes, giving them a fleeting grey aspect, and the mist hovered before his face. As if commanded by another, Hermes parted his lips, opened his mouth, and took the blue mist into himself. His shoulders jerked once. Then he was smiling again, and time was restored to its pace.

Yngvi's stomach dropped. Shock had frozen his limbs. He had seen that blue mist before, on the bloodied grounds of Valhalla. His mind quickly arranged the facts of the previous protracted seconds into a coherent thread, and he grasped what had just happened, and the part he had played in it. *Heroes or fools*, the man had said, and Yngvi had been a fool.

It was so exasperatingly clear. He had carried Enki, when Enki couldn't carry himself, from Midgard to Aegyptus and finally to Graecia, where he was now free. Yngvi closed his eyes. He told himself he still had the ka jar, that he was one step closer to capturing Enki. He told himself, shakily, that Shara would not be furious with him for wandering off wounded and dying and without Shara's god-killing protection, because he had brought Enki out into the open. That had to be worth something.

He heard voices. Men's voices. He turned his attention outwards.

"I'm keeping this," Hermes, or Enki inside him, was saying about the sword, but Yngvi was watching three Graecians who had clustered beside Dionysus on the dais. He had not seen them arrive. But Hecate had.

"I have my champions!" she proclaimed.

"Champions?" said Hermes, turning to face the dais. "Oh. There you are!" he called out to the three men. Then he laughed. "You're too late for the celebrations. Hecate scared everyone away."

"What are we to do for entertainment?" said the shortest of the three, a frowning, swarthy boulder of a man.

"You fight," said Hecate. "All three of you. For me. Against Hermes's champion." She nodded at Yngvi.

"Three of us? Against one? That one?" said the tall, bearded man who was built like Thor.

"Yes. Yes. And yes," Hecate affirmed. "That one."

"He looks like he'll fall any minute," said the shining, golden-haired beauty with the youthful, glabrous face and slender limbs. He laughed, and the sound floated to Yngvi like peals of music. "I think Hermes *wants* to lose."

"What's the bet?" asked the swarthy man, who seemed to be spoiling for a fight.

"Athena's owl, unless my champion wins every contest," said Hermes.

The bearded colossus raised his brows. "Every contest? Hermes, you're going to lose."

"It's just an owl," said Hermes, indifferently.

Dionysus laughed at that. "And what contests have you picked, sister?"

Hecate floated over to the ring. "A round with swords, a bout of wrestling, and an archery contest," she said when Yngvi and the Graecians had joined her there.

There were training swords and shields, bows and arrows placed on a large table, and an arrangement of bars that Yngvi did not recognise, probably for some form of acrobatic sport. This section of the ground was not paved. It was red earth, the soft, muddy surface making it ideal for physical competition.

"Are you ready?" Hermes asked Yngvi.

The answer was delivered in a new, steely voice. "He is not."

Yngvi closed his eyes. This was going to be unpleasant.

"I need to speak with your—*champion*," said the same irate voice, and Yngvi winced. Shara had marched over to the training area, eyes flashing with barely repressed ire, all of it directed at Yngvi.

"Very well," said Hermes. "But be quick." He turned to confer with the three Graecians while Hecate stood a little apart.

"Asclepius?" Yngvi asked.

Shara shook his head. Yngvi absorbed the implications of that response. All right. He would fight with what strength he had left. And when strength failed him, his skills would have to keep him alive, until they no longer could.

Shara said, through gritted teeth, "What were you thinking, coming here alone?" His eyes dropped to Yngvi's chest. "You're bleeding again."

Now was not the time. "Enki has been with us since Midgard," said Yngvi.

Shara's eyes narrowed. "How is that possible?"

"He was waiting, in his sword, in the blue stone," Yngvi said, with a sidelong look at the Graecians. "That's Hermes, with the wand. He's a god. He broke the stone, and took Enki into himself. This is what we wanted! Enki's out in the open now!"

Shara's unyielding gaze remained fixed on Yngvi.

"I have Tausret's jar here," Yngvi said. "This is our chance, Shara! And I'm not dead yet."

"I won't allow it." Shara's voice was hard.

" *Won't allow* it?" Yngvi's hands curled into fists. "You've wanted to be rid of me for some time now. This is your chance. Why don't you take it?"

"No."

"Why not? I never asked you to protect me!"

"You didn't. But—" Shara cut himself off.

Yngvi remembered standing in the foyer of a Midgardian house. "You're doing this for Magne."

"How—"

"I know my brother. And I heard him ask you." Magne's ability to interfere even while absent was enough to make Yngvi growl. "When I see him—" This time, Yngvi cut himself off, because he could not be sure that he would see Magne again.

"I gave him my word that I would—" Shara shook his head.

Now really was not the time. "I can fight these men."

"You think you can fight three men while you bleed from a fatal wound?"

"They won't come at me all at once," Yngvi bit back. He closed his eyes to give himself a moment, and drew in a calming breath. "I know I'm dying. But I want to go down fighting." He hoped Shara would relate to that.

But Shara's eyes were cold, his response colder. "No."

And that was the end of that argument, because Shara was striding back to the waiting gods, leaving Yngvi alone with all his unexpressed protestations jammed in his throat.

Overriding every sensible thought came the urge to hit Shara, hit *something*. It took every last shred of restraint to tell himself that there were three gods and three Graecians waiting for them, and that this was as good an occasion as any to reflect instead of react. He knew what Shara was going to do. Five deep breaths later, he came to the conclusion that Shara would prevail against the Graecians, and also that he was more use to Shara alive than dead.

"My companion is wounded," Shara was saying. "He cannot fight."

He cannot fight. That rankled so much Yngvi was tempted to challenge Shara to a fight then and there to prove him wrong. He had never thought to hear those words spoken about himself. At least not since he was appointed Captain of Thor's Midgardian forces at eighteen, the youngest Midgardian to have held that position.

"That is disappointing," said Hermes, with a grin that left no doubt that he was gladdened by the news. "No matter. Can you?"

"Yes," said Shara.

"I'll allow it," said Hermes, cheerfully. "I'll have you as my champion."

Of course he would. Enki would want Shara to fight.

"Did your companion tell you that you have to win against all three of Hecate's champions?"

"No."

"Never mind," said Hermes. "I have faith in you."

"Hermes," said the dark Graecian, in a moment of unsolicited compunction. "Look at us. Look at him. He's a reed. We'll blow him down. This is not right."

"Then be gentle, don't hurt him," said Hecate. "And make it quick." She floated to Shara. "Don't worry, they won't kill you. Probably. Tell me, have you swung a sword at all?"

Despite his irritation with Shara, Yngvi laughed at that. But no one heard him, because no one was paying him any attention, even though he stood a mere five paces away.

"Once or twice," Shara said.

"That should do quite well," said Hecate. "Let's get on with this."

CHAPTER TWENTY-THREE

THE SWARTHY GRAECIAN stalked up to Shara. His lumbering bulk loomed over Shara's slighter frame.

"Be gentle with my champion, Heph!" said Hermes. But he was laughing.

Heph picked up a pair of wooden swords and tossed one to Shara. Next, he threw Shara a round wooden shield and picked up another for himself.

"Let's see you swing that sword," Heph said, his dark beard parting to reveal very white teeth.

Shara's fingers squeezed the hilt. It was a training sword, with a leather strap wrapped around the hilt to provide a grip. It would not draw blood, but Yngvi had seen it break bone. His heart was in his throat. His wound throbbed.

Eyes fixed on his opponent, Shara hefted the weapon and cut the air between them with calm, swift strokes. Heph mirrored his moves, grinning. Shara frowned.

Heph said, "First contact with the neck, ribs or midriff counts as a win."

He knocked his shield twice with his sword, signalling the start of combat. Shara knocked his own shield twice. They were ready.

Hunched and wary, they circled each other. Yngvi looked desperately for faults in Shara's footwork and posture to predict missteps. But this was Shara, the god-killer. Who was tiring of him.

Heph's arm was tucked against his side, his torso protected by the large shield. He attacked first, thrusting his sword, but Shara calmly sprang aside. His shield swung up, caught the edge of Heph's blade and knocked it off its trajectory. Heph staggered.

A second later, Shara slapped his blade lightly on Heph's unprotected thigh. Laughter from the spectating Graecians. Curses from Heph as he crashed the rim of his shield on Shara's forearm. Shara swore; his fingers flew open in reflex and his sword fell to the ground, slewing over the dusty surface before coming to rest a fair distance from them. But an effortless somersault on one shoulder landed Shara by his sword; a spry jump and he was on his feet again, sword in hand.

Heph charged, blade lowered and body bowed, attacking Shara's legs with a flurry of strikes. But Shara's footwork was consummate. Skirting the Graecian's assaults with the poise of a dancer, Shara led him around the full area of the training section, staying just out of striking range and thwarting Heph's frustrated hits with glancing twists of his wrist.

They were as dissimilar in technique as they were in physique. Heph's expansive manoeuvres were proving ineffective against the disdainful economy of Shara's defence, which entailed strokes administered as indifferent afterthoughts, as if Heph didn't warrant the effort. Heph's infuriated grunts and growls seemed to have invigorated Shara.

It was fascinating to watch him provoke his opponent with untroubled grace now as he had not been able to when the battle was upon them from all sides and swift, efficient killing was the objective.

Heph pressed forward with cold intent. Blade caught blade and the dull scrape of wood was loud in the empty quad. Putting his considerable weight behind his blade, Heph forced Shara to the ground, but Shara surprised again. He pulled back subtly, dragging his blade along the length of the Graecian's, and rolled out of range just in time to avoid Heph falling on him.

An instant later, Heph was upright again, but his dignity was askew and dust caked one side of his face. Spinning around without warning, he raced towards Shara. They collided over a clash of wood. When they stepped apart, Heph was still cursing, Shara still unperturbed.

Shara charged, shield held close to his chest while his sword swung up to his right. Heph's own shield came up to deflect the impending blow, but it was a feint; Shara's arm made a smooth, wide arc down the left and abruptly veered up in a backhanded strike. He caught Heph's unprotected right rib in an expertly controlled ascending strike.

It was over. Shara had the first win. He moved closer to Heph, panting. "Yield."

Heph's sword and shield clattered to the ground; he kicked them away with a growl.

Shara dropped his own weapons. His hair was slightly damp. His tunic was dark under his arms and between his shoulders. He looked at Yngvi, then at Hecate.

The gods' gaze on Shara had a different quality now. They were surprised. They were displeased. They were paying attention.

"Once or twice," said Hecate, her eyes narrowed.

"That..." said Hermes, "was most unexpected."

"Let's wrestle, mortal," said the tall, muscular Graecian. He was laughing at Heph, and showing something akin to admiration for Shara. "I'll try not to crush you like an insect."

"Don't hold back, Ares," said the humbled Heph.

Shara was slimmer than Ares and not quite as tall, an exquisite column of alabaster facing the granite wall of Ares's muscle. Yngvi felt a twinge of worry, because Ares was built like Thor and moved like him, and Shara's skills with weapons would not serve him in this round. Ares approached Shara, paused before him and raised his hands, palms facing outwards. Shara lifted an eyebrow. Ares placed his hands on Shara's shoulders. And shoved him without warning.

Shara tottered backwards and fell. His head hit the sawdust hard. He attempted to sit up but was knocked down again by Ares straddling him. Ares fought to pin Shara's flailing arms down on each side and locked his thighs around Shara's thrashing legs. But Shara, drawing on some unseen reserve of strength, jerked his knees up, lifting Ares's hips, and threw him off. Ares somersaulted over the marble and was back on his feet.

But Shara was as quick. A nimble flip upwards and he had righted himself.

Bodies braced, they circled each other.

Ares attacked again. He dove at Shara's legs, but Shara swerved out of his reach, sending Ares sprawling face down. Ares's palms were flat on the ground to lift himself up when Shara leapt and landed on his back, slamming his chest into the ground, knocking the breath out of him. Ares's startled inhale must have pulled in more dust than air, because his torso jerked with his coughs. He turned his head to the side.

Shara splayed his hand over the exposed side of Ares's face, pressing his head into the ground. An interval of quivering tension. Then Ares thumped his palm thrice on the ground, yielding the fight.

Shara made an unhurried fist and pressed it to Ares's jaw. He had won round two.

He got off Ares and stood. Then glanced at Yngvi as Ares lifted himself to his feet, and shoulders drooping, joined the other Graecians.

The youthful, golden-haired beauty stepped forward with mincing elegance, as if this were a dance, not a contest in which his companions' performances had embarrassed. His physique was a match for Shara's. They were of a height and possessed the same kind of lithe, refined musculature, unlike the bulky Heph and the towering Ares.

Ares clasped the blond man's shoulder. "It's up to you, Apollo. He's a wily one."

"Unlike you and Heph, I prefer not to have to touch my opponent." Apollo turned to Shara with a broad smile. "Are you trained in archery?"

"No."

"I suspect," said Apollo, pleasantly, "you would say that you weren't trained in sword fighting and wrestling either. And yet, we saw what you did."

Shara kept silent, but Yngvi realised that this Apollo was more percipient than the others.

"In any case," said Apollo, "I enjoy a challenge. Shall we shoot a stationary target from fifty paces away?"

"All right."

"Or…we could make it more interesting."

"How?"

"A moving target. From a hundred paces away."

"All right."

Apollo's dark gold eyebrows arched in surprise, but he said nothing.

Yngvi, Shara and the Graecians followed Apollo to a large wooden wheel which was pegged between two thick posts. The six large, equidistant white circles painted along the rim were pocked. Longbows and quivers with arrows lay nearby.

Apollo handed Shara a bow and three red-tipped arrows. Then he picked up another bow and three yellow-tipped arrows for himself.

He pointed to the six white circles. "Those are the targets." He pushed down hard on a spoke. The well-oiled wheel began to spin on its pivot. "Whoever hits the most targets wins. Simple." He paused. "I know what you're thinking, but this game has never ended in a draw."

Shara said, mildly, "You should go first."

Apollo drew an arrow. "Ares, stop the wheel. Let me get ready. Then spin it however fast you want."

Apollo and Shara walked a hundred paces away and stopped. Shara stepped to the side.

Apollo aligned himself with the centre of the wheel, pointed the bow down, and nocked the arrow. Squaring his shoulders, he spread his legs in an open stance and in one fluid motion, raised his bow and drew the bowstring back. Ares stepped up to the wheel, lifting a hand to grasp a spoke.

"Wait!"

It was Hecate. In the distance, Apollo lowered his bow.

"Hermes, your champion has shamed two of mine," she said. "I fear that he will overcome Apollo, too. You play for petty stakes, but it is Athena's journey to the Afterlife that hangs in the balance. It's only fair that I give Apollo a fighting chance, wouldn't you agree?"

"I have full confidence in my champion." Hermes's expression was as bored as his tone. It was clear that he cared little about the outcome. "You may make any adjustments you wish."

A hundred paces away, Apollo and Shara waited out of earshot.

"Very well," said Hecate, and Yngvi felt a touch of cold horror, because she had put her black eyes on him. What could she possibly want with him?

"You, mortal. Do you trust your companion's skill?"

That was easy. "Implicitly."

Hecate laughed. "Then you wouldn't object to being tied to a post while we assay your trust and his skills, would you?"

Before Yngvi could answer that he did, in fact, fervently object, Dionysus stepped up to his sister.

"Hecate, what are you doing?"

The goddess shrugged. "A wheel does not bleed. There's nothing like a little flesh-and-blood distraction as motivation."

"This is not right, sister. The mortal could die." Hecate's callous disregard for Yngvi seemed to have sobered him up enough to allow his sense of fairness to protest.

"The mortal will die eventually. But if I don't get her owl, Athena will exist in the shadows for eternity."

"What's the delay?" Apollo called across the distance, but his question went unanswered.

"Is that not the old-fashioned way of the gods, brother?" said Hecate, throwing Dionysus's own words at him. "Get the mortals to do it for us, you said. That's exactly what I'm doing."

Dionysus, Heph and Ares looked to Hermes to intervene. The Messenger god had remained silent, letting the situation unfold, detached from its consequences. But now he spoke, and Yngvi wished he hadn't.

"I'll allow it," said Hermes.

"Good." She turned to Heph and Ares and waved at hand at Yngvi. "Would you prepare the...motivation?"

To their credit, the Graecians appeared reluctant to comply, if only for a moment. Ares grabbed and uprooted a proximate training post, aligned himself with the centre of the wheel and slammed the thick wood into the ground a few feet in front of it. A metal ring was hammered into the front of the post, near the top, and a thick rope was looped through it, hanging loose.

Shara was marching back to the Graecians, but he was too late. Ares and Heph had already grabbed Yngvi's arms and taken him to the post.

Cooperation was the only choice when they pushed Yngvi back against the post. He could not suppress a hiss at the sharp twinge in his shoulder when Ares winched his arms and tied his wrists to the post above his head. They left his legs free.

"Don't move," Heph instructed, redundantly, but the earnestness in his tone came as a surprise. "They're aiming at the wheel."

"You'll be all right if you don't move," Ares added. "Apollo's very good."

"You expect me to take your word for it?" Yngvi snarled. "I've seen how *very* good you both were."

Shara had broken into a run. "What are you doing!"

"I don't trust your champion not to miss and kill me!" Yngvi shouted at Hecate.

But it was Apollo himself who reassured Yngvi. He stood a few feet from the post, smiling at Yngvi as he would at a belligerent child. When had he crossed the distance?

"You needn't worry about me. My aim is true. I have never shot a wayward bolt, and I won't today."

"No!" said Shara, rounding on Hecate. "This is wrong. As soon as you agreed that I could take his place, his part in this ended. I agreed to all your terms, but this is against the rules of fair play."

"What is against the rules of fair play, champion of Hermes," said Hecate, "is you pretending to be mortal."

"I make no pretence!"

"We all saw what you did to Heph and Ares."

Why should that mean anything? Shara had killed gods. What were two men?

Hermes was smiling. "You'll just have to be very careful, both of you. Let's get this over with."

Arguing with the Graecians was pointless. Yngvi knew that, and Shara did, too. Enki was inside Hermes, and he had the sword. There was only one way to end this.

Shara stepped close to Yngvi and put a hand on his chest. "Trust me."

Yngvi gazed into those clear, concerned eyes. "I trust you."

"Are you sure you want me to go first?" said Apollo.

Shara gave a brusque nod and strode off to cross the hundred paces again. He stood aside while Apollo positioned himself directly in front of the wheel, in front of Yngvi.

Apollo nocked his arrow again, drew the bowstring and nodded.

A moment later, Yngvi picked up a hum. He did not have to look behind himself to know that it was the wheel, spinning fast on its peg.

"Now!" Hecate called out.

Stretched out on the post, Yngvi could do no more than watch, with a clenched stomach and rigid limbs, as Apollo flippantly loosed his first arrow. Yngvi forced his eyes to stay open, closing them only after he heard the arrowhead *thunk* into the wood. Relief made him sag against his bindings.

Then it was Shara's turn. Apollo stepped aside, and Shara took up his position where Apollo had stood. From behind came the tranquilising drone of the wheel as it spun on its dull, circuitous route.

"Now!" said Hermes.

Shara let his arrow fly. This time, there was not the nauseating dread Yngvi had experienced when it was Apollo shooting. Another *thunk*, but it had been preceded by a thinner, scraping sound. What followed was the clatter of wood on tile, a collective gasp, and six stunned Graecians staring at Shara.

This time, Yngvi turned his head and looked behind him.

A yellow-tipped arrow had flown off in two insulted strips to land on the tile. Shara had had five empty targets to pick from, but he had chosen to send the Graecians a message by splitting Apollo's bolt down the middle, from nock to tip.

Even Yngvi, when he had said—and meant—*implicitly*, had not expected this. Even after everything he had seen in Valhalla, Shara was still surprising to him. Yngvi closed his mouth.

Apollo's turn again. He shot his second arrow. *Thunk.* Moments later, *thunk.* Shara had split it.

Apollo's final turn. He shot his third and last arrow. *Thunk.* Shara let his bolt fly.

Yngvi watched with half his mind as the shaft sailed through the air towards him. He was already thinking ahead to when this was over and they were back to trying to capture Enki.

He felt a small gust of air, no stronger than a heavy exhalation. Time seemed to slow enough for Yngvi to detect an infinitesimal shift in the trajectory of Shara's arrow on its way to the wheel. And then, another fractional veer. It was as though someone wanted him to follow the arrow's flight.

He shifted his eyes to Hecate. Just as her lips smoothened from a pucker, he cried out. The arrow had speared his body at the centre of Hippocrates's bandage, and he heard the muffled bursts of his own convulsive breath.

Pain tore through his body, radiating outwards in waves from the wound around the protruding arrow. His half-open eyes had a blurry view of six Graecians watching him. He wished he had taken the rest of Tausret's medicine; it might have kept him standing a little longer. He blinked once, then again, and again. Dropped his head. The tiles at his feet were growing wet with black fluid that dripped thickly from his shoulder.

A face was at his waist now, looking up at him. It was blue, and pinched with shock. Hands gripped Yngvi's legs, the lips were moving. Yngvi couldn't understand the frantic words, couldn't hear them. Words of condemnation, no doubt. What else would they be? At least Shara would be free of him now.

"I'm sorry," Yngvi said.

And surrendered to the darkness.

CHAPTER TWENTY-FOUR

SHADOWS AND SIGHS shrouded Yngvi when he opened his eyes in dark and dank surroundings.

He was drifting through a gloomy channel. Black walls on either side were passing him in leisurely silence. Below and around him was a shell of wood. It was quiet, but for gentle smacking sounds, like the lap of waves. He lifted his head to look over the edge.

He was in a boat, floating down a murky river in which silver wraiths leapt alongside him, like ghostly fish lit from within. They looked up at him with deep sockets where eyes would have been, and reached out with feathery arms and tendrilled fingers, as if thirsting for whatever fading life still ran in his veins. With a shiver, he fell back in the boat.

He had died in the agora; he knew that because he had felt the life leave him. Yet, it did not feel real because he was…awake somehow. His body felt lighter, too light to have resulted from only the loss of blood, even though it had been a lot. He touched his eyes to make sure that they were still there, and had not been turned to empty hollows. Even with closed eyes, he had a blurred view of the outside, of the passing stone walls glinting with the silver of the wraiths, as though he was seeing through his skin.

A low, loud growl reverberated through the hollow. Growls. There was more than one beast; they sounded angry and they sounded close. Very close. The boat rocked to one side, rolling Yngvi onto his shoulder, and fishtailed to an abrupt stop. His eyes flew open.

Holding the boat down on that side was a massive paw with long, black nails. Three enormous heads leaned over Yngvi; six ears perked. He stayed flat, frozen in place, as six curious long-lashed brown eyes studied him. Three short, fat muzzles sniffed, then opened, snarling, frothing maws with canines exposed.

"Hush, boy," a woman said. "It's only me." The heads swung as one to the speaker, the ears flopped, and the growls immediately softened to whines of affection. Then the heads and the paw retreated, the boat wobbled back to equilibrium and sailed on.

Yngvi pushed himself up on his elbows and looked over his shoulder at the beast. All three heads were connected to one colossal body. This beast was like three of Fenrir.

Straight ahead, a woman stood at the prow. Her back was to him. She was tall and slender, with a cascade of black hair that floated in the air like thick ribbons in water. Her feet hovered a few inches above the boat.

A bird sat on her shoulder. He had seen it before, in the agora, perched on Hermes's shoulder. Its body faced front, but its head was turned all the way around, its large, yellow eyes fixed on him. He lifted his hand and wiggled his fingers to see if they worked. The owl gave a surprised blink, and hooted.

The goddess turned, her long black dress swirling sinuously around her. "You're awake," said Hecate. Her face was pale and placid, like a veiled moon.

"You!" Yngvi scrabbled to sit up. "And what do you mean 'awake'?"

"I meant you're awake on this side now. You should know, this is a special service I'm providing you. Anyone else would be sailing with the boatman."

He watched her warily. "What was that thing?"

"That little pup? That was Cerberus. We put him at the gates because he looks and sounds ferocious. But he's really just a sweetheart."

"*Sweetheart?* He looked ready to take my head off."

"Don't be afraid."

The affable woman before him looked nothing like the terrifying goddess who had thundered at Hermes and Dionysus.

"I'm not afraid." It wasn't a boast. She could not have known that he had battled and killed Loki and his giants. A smiling goddess was not quite on the same level, even if she could scream louder than Hel's shadow fiends. "But I heard you scream at your brothers, and I'd like to protect my ears."

Hecate's smile widened to a grin, and he was put off by the mirth in her black eyes. But her next words surprised him, because they touched a wound inside his heart.

"If you had a brother like them, you'd want to scream too sometimes, you know?" She huffed, and scrunched her face exactly like Yngvi knew he did when Magne asked him to do...well, anything.

"Yes," said Yngvi, and his voice shook a little. "I know. I have— I had a brother." A brother he would never see again.

His throat ached with everything he wanted to hurl at Hecate. Ulla would hate him forever. His nephews would forget him in time. Odin and Thor would remember him as the man who had allowed Ragnarök to happen. He had left Yggdrasil in infamy, only to die an anonymous death here on Graecia, worlds away from home. He would scream if it would change anything.

"I'm sorry," she said.

"Are you?" he snapped, feeling the anger like acid in his blood. "I know what you did!"

"I am sorry. I truly am. It is not my function to actually kill mortals. Can you stand?"

Scowling at her offered hand, he held onto the side of the boat and levered himself to his feet.

"But you do know you were dying, don't you?" she said. "What happened just sped up the process. I hope it didn't hurt too much."

" *What happened?* You mean, what you *did*."

Her attempts to placate Yngvi were annoying him, because he could not shake the sense that they were genuine. His body had hurt, but far less than it had to see Shara's face.

"All for that little thing," he said, pointing his chin at the owl. "I hope it was worth it."

"It was," she admitted. "I could not afford to lose the wager."

"Couldn't you have simply made the arrow miss the target? You would've got your owl. Did you have to kill me?" Enki still lived, and Hecate had denied Yngvi his only chance to kill him. It was up to Shara now.

"I didn't mean to! Believe me! I— I seem to have miscalculated the force of my breath. I am sorry."

Her brows were drawn together over her wide and sincere dark eyes, and her right hand was placed over her heart, if gods had hearts, as if to swear the truth of her words. An earnest, remorseful goddess of the Underworld was not something Yngvi had expected to encounter on this journey.

Hecate pressed a kiss to the owl's wing. "Don't be angry with me, please. You've got this sweet little thing worried."

She was right. The bird swung its head from Hecate to him a few times, appearing distressed by the friction between goddess and dead mortal. Then it fixed its round eyes on him, blinked, and gave three long and loud hoots. Yngvi supposed it was saying hello.

"Hello, little owl," he said, apathetically.

Another hoot, which earned it another kiss from Hecate.

"Hermes gave him up after you—died."

"You mean, after you…induced my death."

"I said I was sorry. But you do know this was to be the end of your journey, no matter when or how it happened. Every mortal eventually sails down this river."

"Are you saying that for my benefit, or yours?"

"Most people in your position"—she waved a hand in the general direction of the boat, but he knew she meant *dead*—"aren't quite as feisty."

"I don't feel any different."

Hecate gave a sad nod. "It takes a little time."

"How much time?"

"Three days."

He nodded, and fell silent.

"So…" said Hecate, long moments later. "Which god did you cross?"

"What?"

"Come now, we both know you bore a god's wound. What did you do? Sleep with a goddess? A god? A nymph?"

Yngvi glared at her, but despite the anger boiling inside him at being trapped in this desolate cavern with no way of getting out, he let out a breath, part anger, part disbelief, part amusement. "Is this what everyone on Graecia does?"

"And what is that?"

"Gossip," said Yngvi. "You sound like Hippocrates. He, too, wanted to know if it was a nymph."

Hecate flashed a provocative, oblique glance at him. "If you've seen the nymphs, you'd understand why."

He gazed at her, this goddess who had terrified Athens, plucked him from the agora and then apologised profusely for dropping him into Death's arms, who was sweet and teasing now, like the sister he didn't have. He couldn't help smiling. "Then I'd like to see them."

"You'd like them," said Hecate. "But…"

"But I'm dead. I know. What happens now? Where do I go from here?"

She inclined her head and looked at him like he was a puzzle to solve. "You're not like any other dead mortal I've met. Most beg me to let them go back."

"Do they?" said Yngvi. "Maybe…they have people who'll miss them."

"Don't you?"

"It doesn't matter." Yngvi didn't want to think about all the people who would not miss him.

"You're still upset."

"Of course I'm upset!" said Yngvi. "I did not want to die like—like *that*." His lips twisted on the words as his mind showed him his last gasping seconds in the land of the living.

"I know…" she said gently. "It came earlier than you expected."

"That's not… No. I always thought I would go down with my sword in my hand. Not tied to a post as a target, bleeding out, helpless to do *anything*. Who would want that kind of weak, dishonourable death."

"There's nothing you can do about the past."

The ringing truth of her words, and the irreversible finality of his circumstances, made him want to strangle Hecate. *She* was the reason he was in this boat now.

It took long moments of watching the unchanging walls go by before Yngvi had calmed enough to speak. "What happens to me now?"

"Well, you *are* dead; you cannot return to the land of the living, or cross over to the Afterlife yet."

He nodded slowly. "When can I go to the Afterlife?"

"Once someone from the living world acknowledges your passing and says the words of farewell. But there is a time limit."

"Three days?"

"Three days."

Yngvi was fully alert now. "And what of those who don't receive the words of farewell?"

"You have your friend…"

Yngvi did not answer, just shook his head. He did not want to think of the anger he had seen in Shara's eyes. Shara was unwavering in his pursuit of Enki; and now that he knew Enki was inside Hermes, he would not be thinking of Yngvi. He would be trying to get Enki out of Hermes and into the ka jar.

"Most people have someone," Hecate was saying. "If not family or friends, then…a neighbour, a landlord, a physician, a servant, a…a baker?"

"I know you're trying to help, Hecate. But please. What happens?"

She sighed heavily, and tipped her head at the sorrowful silver spirits swimming alongside the boat. "They roam the in-between. They become the shades, the half-lifes."

Yngvi closed his eyes. So, this was his end. Only it was not an end. Just a suspension of life in mid-breath, with only memories to keep him company. Had he died on Midgard, he would have asked to go back. He would have asked to see Magne again. And Ulla and the twins. Halli and Vidar. Even Thor and Odin. And although it was not possible, Shara.

"I never thought this is how it would happen for me," he said. "So far away from home."

"Far away?" said Hecate.

"I'm Spartan." The lie was automatic by now. He opened his eyes and saw her nod in understanding.

"Everyone comes here in the end. Even Spartans."

He rubbed his face, blinked hard and rapidly to stop the stinging in his eyes. Why did it have to feel like this? He had only wept once in his life, over his parents' battle-bloodied bodies. He would not weep over his own death. He ran his hands through his hair, pushing it off his face as he pushed the thoughts away.

"My friend. Is he…all right?"

She was quiet for a long moment. Then: "No."

No, no, no. "Does he live?" *Please…don't be dead.*

"He lives."

Yngvi went weak from the enormity of his relief. "Good," he said. "That's good."

"But he was so…angry…when I took you. He even threatened to kill me!"

"He wouldn't."

"I'll admit I thought him capable of it. I had to fly from there, with you, before he could chase me. But he can't come in here. Not alone, anyway." Hecate sighed. "He's something special, your friend. Those three men he fought? They are not mere Athenians. They are gods, and my half-brothers. Heph is Hephaestus, god of the Forge, Ares, the god of War, and Apollo's the god of the Sun and the Hunt and Music."

That explained the lilting enunciation and melodic voice. "Really?" said Yngvi. "Shouldn't Apollo have been too busy with his godly duties to come down to the agora?"

"He makes time for his entertainments," said Hecate, laughing. "But surely you know your friend has a god's blood in him."

"I suspected that, but he says he doesn't."

"Then he doesn't know. I've never seen him before today, but that's not surprising. Our gods are quite wanton about siring children with mortals. Sometimes they pick up the girls and take them to Olympus for a night or two of passion, never returning for the inevitable whelping.

Other times, they set their sights on youths. They'll take beauty wherever they get it."

"So they abduct helpless mortals against their wishes?"

"Mortals are shrewder than you'd think. They court divine attention, especially from the beautiful gods. Apollo is the most popular with maidens and youths alike. Heph, less so. You've seen why." She said it easily, as though sharing a joke with a friend. "Sometimes, if the gods are especially pleased, they send their young conquests back with coin. Generous coin."

Yngvi nodded, but he was distracted by the wraiths swimming along in the boat's wake. His last memory of Shara would be the shocked face looking up at him in the agora. "Three days until I'm one of them."

"I am not"—Hecate's black eyes glinting with mischief—"without compassion."

Yngvi looked at her, unamused and uncomprehending. "What have you done now?"

Hecate only smiled, but did not clarify.

Yngvi shook his head. "You smile too much for a goddess of the Underworld." And that elicited a grin.

The boat had bumped against something solid and come to a stop.

"This is where you get off."

"What is this place?" Yngvi looked around. "It could do with more light."

The tunnel had terminated in a wide table of stone walled on all sides like a cave, a damp and dismal cave. The river continued on its plashing course, disappearing into the ground under the dark platform.

Hecate floated out of the boat and hovered over the stones. "This is a waypoint. Transiting souls must wait here until they can be taken to the Afterlife." She smiled at the handful of waiting spirits that had drifted up to her. "It won't be much longer," she said to them. To Yngvi: "They've been here two days. It used to be busier than this. But ever since Hippocrates opened his infirmary with Asclepius's patronage and started sharing his methods with physicians in other cities, traffic into our realm has dwindled. Before Hippocrates, the boatman used to make multiple trips up and down every day, but now I'll just leave the boat tied here for him to take when he's called again, which could be days later."

Yngvi stepped out onto the stone platform, and stared at the boat that had borne him to the end of his life worlds away from Yggdrasil. He thought of Hippocrates and Apollonius, who had tried to keep him alive. He thought of Shara.

Hecate was watching him with a puckish gleam in her black eyes. "I know what you're thinking. As soon as I leave, you're going to row back to the land of the living, aren't you?"

He still resented her, even if her good-natured banter was breaking through his bitterness. He affected a mocking laugh. "So, you're a goddess of the Underworld *and* a reader of minds. Impressive." After a moment, "Is the Afterlife as dismal as this place?" Asgard's Hall of Fallen Heroes was said to be a vision of golden splendour and peace, a dreamland worthy of the souls that dwelt there, but that was another thing he would never see.

"It is not!" said Hecate, her dark eyes lighting up. "I think you'll enjoy it there. The Afterlife is under my supervision, and I've made it much prettier than this dusky pool of sadness. I've had it livened up. I mean, whoever comes here is already miserable that they are dead; there's no reason we, the keepers of the Underworld, should perpetuate that misery. You know, we are not cruel."

"I know *you're* not," he said, gazing at her bright face. He would never forget that she had killed him, but the rage had subsided and given way to a strange detachment.

"I must go see Athena and the Sisterhood now. I will be gone four days. I hope you are not here when I return."

The owl blinked.

"Goodbye, bird."

Hoot-hoot.

"And you," he asked Hecate, "will I see you again? In the Afterlife?"

"I'll visit, wherever you go," Hecate said, with a smile. Then she turned, her hair and her dress drifting around her, and floated out of sight

Having no one to talk to and nothing to do but wait, Yngvi scanned his surroundings.

The river burbled along, taking with it the splashing spirits that had been abandoned to eternity in the shades. The cavern's glistening walls disappeared into the shadows above, but there must have been a ceiling because a few illuminated sections had unexpectedly appeared, created by openings through which starshine streamed in. Perhaps the night was clouded over when he first arrived.

He sat on the wet stone in one of those pockets of light, close to the water's edge, drawing his knees to his chest and slinging his arms around them, and looked up at the stars. It was pointless. He would never be up there again, on living land, or among those stars. He sighed, dropped his gaze to the river.

Three days, and he would either be in those waters, trying to leap into the boat, or, if his luck held better than it had in the past weeks, he would be in the Afterlife. Occasionally, he reached out to the spirits and touched their ghostly hands. His own body was becoming translucent; the stone floor was faintly visible through the gaps between the bones of his hand, which fanned out in pale white under his skin.

His body had started to fade. How long before his thoughts died away?

Would he forget his life on Midgard? Would he forget Shara? He missed Shara. It might have been a different outcome had he not ventured into the agora alone. But he had. And in the process, had lost Enki's sword, lost his chance at redemption, lost his own life like the hapless, bleeding, ordinary mortal that he was.

Would Shara have agreed to return to Yggdrasil and tell Magne he would not be coming back, and explain everything to Odin and Thor? Would Shara say the words of farewell, and remember him after? He shook his head like a wet dog, to close the door on these foolish fanciful thoughts. He would never see Shara again, because no living soul could enter the realm of the dead. Hecate had told him that.

Around him, the waiting souls drifted aimlessly, their vacant eyes seemingly fixed on some memory from the living world. A few of them looked at him with blank pools of black, and he wondered what they saw. Did he look like them, a grey approximation of a man's form, or did he still retain anything of himself?

The air shifted. Another spirit, probably. But he heard distant words. A man's voice. He knew that voice; he remembered that mocking laugh. He rose to his feet, looked out at the river, at the approaching radiance. Thumping footfalls shook the ground. A snarl echoed down the winding darkness. Cerberus. A growl, then a soft whine, then silence. Someone had calmed the guardian dog. Someone the beast recognised, someone who frequented the Underworld.

The glow brightening. Two figures. Two men. Floating along the river in a luminous swathe. They alighted onto the stone, the man in winged sandals stepping forward with territorial authority, the other man more tentative, searching, holding up a glowing winged wand that scattered light over the cavern.

"You came!" Yngvi shouted, but what came out of his mouth was air.

He ran towards Shara. And through him.

CHAPTER TWENTY-FIVE

"THERE'S NO ONE here," Shara said to Hermes. He brandished the wand. "Show him to me or I'll break this."

Hermes let out a snarl of exasperation. In his right hand, he held Enki's sword. He waved his left hand.

Yngvi's feet, which had started to skim the ground as he grew lighter, were now fully planted on the stone. He felt weighted with muscle and bone. He held his hands up before his face and saw skin and fingers, and nothing beyond. Colour returned to his vision in stages. Black became shades of grey; grey became blue skin and white hair. And those familiar, unforgettable ice-blue eyes.

"I'm here," Yngvi said, and heard his own voice. "You came." He would be allowed into the Afterlife now.

"You're alive!" Shara rushed to Yngvi and pulled him into a hard embrace. "I thought— I thought— Forgive me. You're alive!"

Yngvi put his hands on Shara's chest and stepped back. "I'm not."

"What do you mean?"

"I'm not...alive. I think this"—he waved a hand down his front, indicating his body—"is temporary. But you came. He brought you here?"

The Shepherd of Souls, the Athenian man had said. The liminal god.

Shara held up the wand. "I made him."

Hermes laughed at that, low and mocking. "Mortals don't *make* gods do anything. I wanted you both here, so that I could dispatch you cleanly. Although Hecate did half of that herself."

"What do you mean?" said Yngvi.

"Oh...I added my breath to hers on your friend's last arrow, that's all," said Hermes, nonchalantly. "Made sure it didn't miss. Still, she is going to regret swiping my wand."

Yngvi pressed his eyes closed, and opened them with a rush of gratitude. He remembered Shara's last arrow shifting again before it impaled him. Hecate had not miscalculated the force of her breath.

But he can't come in here. Not alone, anyway. Hecate had said that. *I am not without compassion.* If Hecate were here, Yngvi would have kissed her cheek.

"I didn't think you'd come," Yngvi said.

Shara looked at him as if he had said something unspeakably foolish.

"Please, I need one more thing," said Yngvi, "one last thing from you."

"Anything." The ice-blue gaze gleamed, incongruous in the dark Graecian underworld, bright like the waters of a glacial lake.

"Say the words of farewell for me. It's the only way—"

"What words of farewell?" Shara's expression slowly changed as comprehension bloomed, and then there was horror in his eyes, and adamant denial. "No! No. You're here. I can *feel* you."

"That's only temporary," Hermes confirmed, from behind Shara. "He is dead. Irreversibly so."

"It's all right," Yngvi said, very softly. "Please, say the words for me. But after. You know what we have to do now." He tapped his sword belt and saw that Shara understood.

"My wand," said Hermes, "if you don't mind. I'd prefer not to tarry in this cesspool of sad souls."

"The sword first," said Yngvi, to goad Enki to reveal himself. "Give it back. It's not yours to keep."

Hermes's hand tightened around the hilt. "It's not yours, but it is mine."

Shara held up the wand. "I'll break it."

"Will you? All right. Go ahead, I don't need it. And you bore me." A flick of Hermes's fingers sent Shara flying backwards. "You've always been such a truculent boy, Shara."

Hermes had called him Shara. It was happening.

The messenger god rolled his head unhurriedly, and before Yngvi's waiting eyes, his golden skin gradually took on a bluish tint, his yellow hair darkened, his black eyes turned silver-grey, and his face transformed, feature by feature, into the likeness of the man carved on the ka jar. The face that bore a faint resemblance to Enlil, and to Shara.

Shara had risen to his feet but now he took a step back. Because the god before them was no longer Hermes.

"Enki!"

The cavern reverberated with Enki's laugh. A grey vapor floated, like thick smoke, over the sylphlike dead drifting down the stream.

Shara tucked the wand into the waistband of his pants and called up his sword. "This ends now, you murderer," he said, and charged towards Enki.

"Oh, do slow down," Enki drawled.

He swiped his hand, and Shara was again thrown backwards, as if yanked by an unseen hand, and crashed against the wall. He had fallen to his knees, but rushed to his feet to charge at Enki again. And encountered air, because Enki had exploited the swiftness of the messenger god whose body he was inhabiting and, in a split-second, come up behind Yngvi. He grabbed a handful of Yngvi's hair with one hand while the other held the sword to Yngvi's neck.

"Drop your sword," Enki said to Shara, "and kick it over to me, or he dies. Again. You let it vanish, and he dies."

"Leave him alone!" Shara shouted.

Enki pressed the blade to Yngvi's neck, and Yngvi hissed at the sting of its hairbreadth edge when it nicked his skin.

"Stop!" Shara shouted again, but he dropped his sword.

"Don't think about me, Shara!" said Yngvi. "You have to stop him!"

It was too late. Shara had already kicked his sword towards Enki, the steel ringing on the stone as it skidded over the wet surface until it came to a halt by Yngvi's boots. Extending a leg, Enki hooked a sandalled foot under the hilt and kicked it up, releasing Yngvi's hair to snatch it out of the air.

"Where did you get this?" said Enki, still holding his own sword to Yngvi's neck.

"It's mine," said Shara.

"Is it?" A sinister smile stretched over Enki's lips. "Then you know I can kill you with it."

Yngvi remembered Shara's vision in Saqqara. "We know you will try."

"I won't *try*, Yngvi Ecklundson." Enki rounded on him and flung him against the wall, and Yngvi found himself staring at the tip of three feet of steel. "I would have killed you in Valhalla if it wasn't for this irritant. And then you killed Loki." Enki jerked his head to the right and pointed Shara's own sword at him. "Don't try anything, or he dies."

Shara took a step back, and Enki returned his attention to Yngvi.

"It was you in Valhalla," said Yngvi, his lips curling back from his teeth. "You impersonated me."

"I did," said Enki, with a laugh. "Finding Loki was easy enough, but I couldn't get into the cave. Sigyn told me what to do. Here," he said, pressing the tip of his sword into Yngvi's shoulder wound. "I don't need two swords. You can have this one, a gift from me to you, since you seem to like it."

Then Enki ran Yngvi through.

"Keep it." He let go of the blade with a push, moved Shara's sword to his right hand and hefted it.

Pain speared through Yngvi's shoulder and he dropped to the ground, rolling onto his side. Half of the blade's length was lodged in his body, sticking out like a skewer from the point where Shara's arrow had been. And before that, Djehuty's hand. The hilt was close enough to his chest that he could reach it. He put his palms against the cross-guard, and pushed as hard as he could, grunting loudly with the effort. But little more than an inch of steel emerged from his body before his strength gave out.

Shara had lunged at Enki, shouting Yngvi's name, shouting at Enki, swearing revenge. But all that outrage made little difference, because Shara was too slow. Enki moved with preternatural speed. *Almost as fast as thought itself,* the Athenian had said to Yngvi. The winged sandals glinted as he flew across the cave, too swift to catch, almost too swift to see.

Disgust rose inside Yngvi, disgust for his own helplessness. He was bleeding, but the sluggish flux provided a welcome reminder that he was already dead and could not be killed again. All he had to do was stay conscious for a little longer. They didn't have much time. This had to end quickly.

"I am going to kill you," Shara shouted, but it was another toothless threat. His eyes darted about, trying to track Enki.

"Why?" Enki asked. "What have I ever done to you? I never meant you any harm." His voice hardened. "Until now."

In the next instant, several things happened at once: a gleam of golden sandals, a sweep of blue fire. Shara shouted. A rip opened in his sleeve, and turned wet. He clasped his bleeding arm with his other hand.

The pulse around the sword embedded in Yngvi's shoulder was a dull throb now. The cavern was wavy, and fading in and out of his vision.

"I don't care if you kill me," Shara was saying. "But give me Yngvi and let me take him out of here."

"Give you Yngvi?" Enki sounded amused. "He told you—he's already dead."

"Not as long as I can do something about it."

"Oh Shara. Sometimes I forget you're so young." Enki slowed and floated down to the ground. "There's nothing you or anyone can do about it. Your sword. A fine weapon, isn't it?" Enki held it up and admired the blade. "Do you know who wielded it before you?"

"No one before me."

That made Enki laugh. "Then you don't know what it can do." He slashed the blade down.

Shara cried out again. A slit appeared down his other sleeve, turning wet and black. He folded in on himself, grabbing both bleeding arms.

Another flash of fire-edged steel, another shout, another split in the fabric, this time on Shara's back. His body jolted up, his back arched. A slash down the front lacerated his exposed chest.

"Leave him alone!" Yngvi screamed. Shara was being sliced open, and there was nothing Yngvi could do but scream impotently. *Don't die!*

"He should have left me alone first," said Enki, turning his flashing eyes on Yngvi. "Look at you both, bleeding to death on a world so far from home. Is it worth it? Don't you wish you had just stayed on Midgard?"

Yngvi crawled on the wet ground towards Shara while Enki watched, his lips curled in a cold grimace. It was slow, excruciating progress, but Shara's muffled moans and shivering breaths kept Yngvi moving forward. *Don't you dare die!* Shara was weakening, and Yngvi had to distract Enki.

"I know why you're doing this," he said.

"You do?"

Yngvi nodded weakly and moved by will alone, the pommel of the sword dragging on the stone as his body inched forward on all fours.

"You hated Enlil because he took over as Sky-Father, didn't you?" he ventured. "And relegated you to the Underworld?"

Enki's cold, grey eyes gave Yngvi his answer.

"Jealousy, greed, power. It's the same everywhere. You gods," he said, his chest heaving. "You're just like us mortals, but with powers and eternal life. Although..." he laughed, a harsh, contemptuous sound "...it turns out that even eternal life can be made temporary."

"Jealousy, greed, power. That's very good," said Enki, a touch genuinely, "but you left out murder."

"Murder?" Yngvi had to keep Enki talking, to get close enough to do what he had come to Graecia to do.

"Enlil accused Ishtar of Anu's murder and threw her in the dungeons. He must have assumed I wouldn't try to stop him. In fact, I almost gave up. Then I remembered that nothing was hidden from Nidaba, but when I asked her, she was...reticent."

"If you hadn't broken the tablet," Shara gasped, hollowed out by pain, "you wouldn't have escaped me in Marduk and Apsu. I would have been there before you."

Enki turned to look at Shara with slightly narrowed eyes. "Did you believe the fables that the tablet foretold Nibiru's future? You foolish boy, there is no force in the universe that can see the future."

"I have."

Enki laughed. "Perhaps your wounds have made you delirious. Not even Anu could augur the future. If he could, don't you think he would have evaded his own murder?"

Yngvi watched helplessly as Shara crumpled further, but he believed Shara's vision.

"I knew I couldn't bring Enlil down single-handedly," said Enki. "Not when the entire pantheon on Nibiru had rallied behind him. But the tablet showed me a way to progressively weaken him to the point where he would be powerless against me."

"You exploited the connection between the realms," said Shara.

"You should thank him for unravelling that." Enki had pointed Shara's sword at Yngvi, but he dipped his head towards Shara, as if he were about to reveal a secret, adding, "And for bringing me here. Did he tell you that?"

Shara's eyes flashed. "He told me everything."

Enki stalked up to Yngvi and kicked him lightly in the elbow, causing his arm to buckle. Yngvi collapsed to the floor and fell, mercifully, on his uninjured side.

"This fool took my weapon in Valhalla, carried me with him to Aegyptus and finally to Graecia. He let me take my sword, let me free myself from it, and drew you down here, where I am at my strongest. And when I'm done with you, I'm going to kill all of Graecia's gods. I'm going to ruin Aegyptus. Then Asgard. And finally, my own dear family— the Anunnaki. Tell me, Shara, aren't you glad he's dead?"

"Leave him alone," Shara ground out.

Enki turned to Shara. "I was planning to let you bleed out. But I think I'll just kill you,"

"No!" Yngvi shouted.

He dove at Enki's legs, but his fingers had just brushed the wing on a sandal when Enki disappeared, only to reappear a second later beside Shara.

And before Yngvi's horrified eyes, Enki calmly drew the fire-blade across Shara's neck.

Yngvi could do nothing as the smooth blue skin opened, as though submitting to the power of the sword. Blood poured in a thick, steady stream onto the glistening ground, indistinguishable from the black of the stone. He heard the wretched sound of his own sob.

"Shara!" he cried out, but his voice was weak. "Shara! No, no, no! Get up! Shara. Get up!"

But Shara had fallen on the stone in an unmoving heap of limbs. Hermes's wand stuck out from his waistband. Enki stood over Shara, looking down at his prone body.

Rage burned through Yngvi, his muscles spasming with a final burst of white-hot, hate-fuelled strength, but it was the futile, cadaveric twitch of a dead animal. Still, he pushed himself up, biting off any sound of pain that he might utter. Slowly, painfully, he stood, the weight of the sword causing him to sway slightly.

"Fight me," he gritted out, even though it was a pathetic, empty threat from a dying warrior. "Fight me. Like a man, not a god."

Enki had looked up from Shara and was regarding Yngvi with unlooked-for admiration. "Really? Why?"

Shara was gone, and with mere minutes of capacity left, Yngvi gave Enki the truth. "I don't want to die like I did."

"All right," said Enki.

Yngvi looked pointedly at the winged sandals. "You're still a god. I don't have a fighting chance against you like this."

"Very well." Enki unlaced the sandals and kicked them aside. "How about now? In fact"—he tossed Shara's sword to the ground—"I don't need this either."

Yngvi grunted and put one unsteady foot before the other as he made his way towards Enki, pushing on the sword that was, unwieldy and unyielding, still embedded in him.

"I'm not going to help you with that," said Enki, taking an unconcerned step back.

Yngvi's eyes were wet and sweat ran down his face, but he ignored Enki's snigger and pressed on, one agonising step at a time, his body rocking, his palms against the cross-guard. The blade would not move. Enki stepped back, laughing now. Yngvi grimaced, took a step forward. Enki went back, Yngvi advanced. Again, and again. Until there was nowhere for Enki to go. The moment Enki's back hit the cavern wall and his eyes widened, Yngvi broke into a run.

He charged on trembling legs, and when he was a foot from Enki, feigned a stumble to spin on his heel; before Enki could react, he fell back against Enki's unprotected front, simultaneously changing his grip on the cross-guard to pull where he had been pretending to push.

With a long, loud cry, he drew on every last mote of strength that still flowed through his dying muscles to jerk the sword towards him. He had no more to give. In moments, everything he had theorised about the connections between the realms would be put to the test. He had never thought himself a hero, but had he been a fool all along? He pulled on the sword, hoping desperately that his gamble was sound.

This is Graecia, not Nibiru. Enki cannot be killed here.

Yngvi strained so hard that the keen blade slid easily through his own submissive flesh to sink into the unprotected body behind him until the tip hit the wall.

I am not an Anunnaki; I cannot kill Hermes with Enki's sword.

This was the moment he had been waiting for, the moment of vengeance for all the dead souls on Yggdrasil, on Apsu and Marduk, Nidaba. Shara. His vision blurred. Shara.

But I can wound Hermes and force Enki out. In Valhalla, he had fled Loki's wounded body.

Shara had been able to kill Loki. But Hermes will heal.

As Enki's head rolled onto his shoulder, Yngvi reached down to his sword belt. Enki was coughing now, but not into the air, because Yngvi had pushed his head up and slammed the open ka jar into his mouth. He ignored the blood streaming from his own wound, because behind him, Enki coughed and jerked, as Loki's body had; the jar grew heavy.

Yngvi waited to snap the lid shut and slip the jar back into his sword belt. Waited until the hair hanging over his shoulder had turned back to gold and the strangled noises came in Hermes's voice.

Only then did he grab the hilt of the sword and take four slow, agonising steps forward, feeling the blade behind him come free of Hermes, and unbearably long moments later, his own body. Enki's sword clattered onto the wet stone. With nothing to keep Yngvi standing—no strength in his drained legs, no sword pinning him to another upright body—he crashed to the ground.

It was done.

The jar juddered in his belt.

Some distance away, Shara's body was moving; he was pushing himself up, blinking slowly and looking around, as if orienting himself.

Shara's gaze locked with his. "Yngvi!" He surged to his feet to rush to Yngvi's side and dropped to his knees. His eyes were wet, his forehead furrowed. He was saying Yngvi's name over and over, like a chant, or a whispered prayer for the dying, his words of farewell.

Yngvi smiled at Shara, reached up to touch his throat. It was smooth; the gash was knitted, leaving only unbroken skin.

Your friend has a god's blood in him. Hecate had seen what Yngvi had only suspected. And Yngvi understood now.

An Anunnaki had sliced open Shara's throat using Shara's own sword.

This was Graecia, not Nibiru. Shara could not be killed here, but Enki had not known that. Yngvi pulled the jar out from his belt, and held it out to Shara.

"You're safe now," he said, his words coming out as a breathless rasp. "Shara..." Then he closed his eyes, surrendering to the experience of the Afterlife, or eternity in the in-between.

But what he did experience was shock, confusion, and tearing.

He was being ripped from himself, was rising from the stone and hurtling towards the stream of souls. Something was wrong. It was too soon. He had more time. He had three days. Hecate had said so. The waters splashed over the rocky sill. Silver wraiths reached out to him, grabbing at his ankles, this new resident in their realm. Not yet, he wanted to say to them, but he was sinking into the flow, and when he looked up, Hermes was staring at him, eyes flashing with divine rage.

"You tried to kill me? A god?" Hermes's black eyes reflected the glow of his wand. The wound from Enki's sword was gone, restored to smooth muscle and skin. His body was golden again, his hair as bright as Apollo's.

Hermes sneered. "No farewell will do for you now, mortal, no Afterlife. Enjoy eternity in the shades." With his shining godhood returned, he had reverted to his breezy indifference, cursing mortal fools and their games, and muttering about the tricks he would pull on Hecate; already he was twirling his wand and winging out of the cavern the way he had come, floating up the river and taking the light with him.

It was Hermes who had torn Yngvi out of his body and flung him into the river. Yngvi considered giving himself up to the current, and letting it pull him in, but something made him hold on to the sill. He did not care that he was behaving like the desperate souls hoping for a second chance. He only wanted one last look. At Shara.

Shara had not stopped Hermes. He was kneeling by the edge, peering down into the murky waters. Searching. Did he see Yngvi?

Shara stood. Was he leaving? At least he had tried to look for Yngvi.

But Shara lingered by the river's edge. Viewed through the watery veil, his body seemed to ripple. His hands were fists at his side, and he was shouting at the cavern. There was no one to hear him. Only Yngvi listened from the thick waters of the river.

The words reached him in fragments, muffled at times, clear at other times.

"I don't care! I don't—"

Shara's head jerked from side to side, as though he were battling something inside him; his face was twisted.

"I have to do this. I can't let him—"

It went on for a while.

"—can't let it end like this."

He paced the river's edge, hands holding his head.

"I won't—"

Yngvi gaped up at him through the water.

"I won't let anything or anyone stop me."

Shara straightened. His sword appeared in his hand.

And he dove into the river.

Shock detached Yngvi's hands from the sill, letting the river carry him deeper.

But Shara was coming after him, beset by silvery souls. The energy throbbing in Shara's veins must have lured the dead, because they swarmed around him, thirsting wraiths drunk on the scent of life. They had plastered their dank forms to him, covering his face and hair with their spectral hands. They seemed to be begging Shara to rescue them from this purgatory.

The current was stronger now. Yngvi was drifting backwards, his eyes still on Shara. He reached out a hand, only to see the water dissolve it into wisps. Shara's arm was labouring against the strong undertow, running his blade through the swathe of spirits. Their mouths opened in terrified soundless shrieks and they retreated, but only a little.

He was kicking at the spectres, turning about in the water and slashing his sword, cutting the flow with bizarre streaks of blue light, until they withdrew and waited a few feet away from him. He swam closer, while the dead followed at a safe distance.

How did it feel to be alive in the river of the dead? Did Shara's eyes burn, his arms ache? Was the water eating at his skin, pulling his own life out of him? Why was he here?

When had he come so close?

The clear eyes were looking right at Yngvi. Hope flowed anew through his transparent limbs and he propelled his feathery body forward, kicking hard against the strong current. But it was no use. The water passed through him. Shara would have to come to him.

As soon as they were within touching distance, Shara called his name. He would tell Shara he was an idiot to follow him in here. He would, if they ever made it to firm land again and his voice was returned to him.

But now, Shara was swimming beside him. He blinked and opened his mouth to speak, but Yngvi moved his lips first. *Farewell,* he said. *Thank you.* His words made no sound or bubbles in the stream. Shara was saying something. *I won't let you go. This is not over.*

Yngvi drew back in surprise but Shara pulled up close and pressed his mouth to Yngvi's. Was it a kiss? Yngvi tried to kiss back, but only tasted water. He was disappearing. And then he was somewhere else; the spirits swirled around him, but at a distance, as though held back by an impermeable membrane.

He was, inexplicably, drifting against the current. Time passed, slow and hypnotic. He was emerging out of the river, and moments later, its waters were behind him, with the splashing, grasping wraiths.

Shara's mouth, warm, wet and vital, lifted from his own. He felt himself convulse, once, again, and a third time. Then he went still.

CHAPTER TWENTY-SIX

CONSCIOUSNESS EBBED AND flowed.

Yngvi's eyes first opened to the sight of a ceiling with crisscrossing wooden beams.

In the next snatch of lucidity, he registered that he was on a bed under a clean sheet. He seemed to be naked. Then, his mind went dark. The next time he woke, he was able to place himself in a room with wooden walls and two windows, one that went from ceiling to floor, and the other that ended at waist height. Darkness again. Then, the awareness that he was alone in the room. Once more, darkness.

When, at last, consciousness returned and stayed, he pushed himself up to sit on the bed, feeling the sheets against his bare skin.

His first thought was that he was, indeed, naked. Following that came the awareness that he was, inexplicably, alive. And whole. His bandages had been removed and a quick scan of his limbs confirmed that his skin had healed. He felt no pain anywhere. There was no sign that he had ever been wounded.

He looked around for the object for which he had ended his own life and located it. A muffled rattle was coming from the bag that held his clothes, the bag that was knocking against the wall, and he knew it was Enki struggling to break free from the ka jar that confined him. Shara had remembered to conceal the foreign-looking receptacle away from Graecian eyes.

The door was slightly ajar and from outside the room came the voices of two men, which he recognised as belonging to Hippocrates and Shara. They were talking about him. Then the voices stopped, and footsteps led away from his room until they faded.

Minutes later, the door was pushed open. Apollonius entered, clad in his simple white chiton. A towel was draped over one shoulder, and he carried a large, shallow bowl in which Yngvi could hear liquid sloshing as the boy approached the bed.

"Brother Inachus!" Apollonius said, brightly. "You are awake!"

"I am awake," said Yngvi, sounding equally surprised. Apollonius seemed nervous, and Yngvi realised he was scowling, and also why. "I'm sorry," said Yngvi, forcing a smile. It wasn't the gilt-haired, green-eyed boy's fault that he was named for the galling god of the Sun. "How long have I been asleep?"

"Three days."

"Have you seen Nikos?"

"He went to the agora to watch the celebrations," said Apollonius. "Father had to order him to leave this room. He hadn't moved from your side since he brought you here." The boy placed the brimming bowl on the small bedside table, pulled the towel off his shoulder and dipped it in the water. "Father has asked me to wipe you down." He squeezed out the excess water and applied the towel to Yngvi's shoulder.

Yngvi gently clasped the boy's wrist. "And for that I thank you, Apollonius, but I feel well enough to stand. Is there somewhere I can bathe?"

"I will have to ask Father if—"

Yngvi tossed the sheet aside, and in one smooth move, swung his legs off the bed and stood. That was premature. His head swam, and he shot out his arm to grasp Apollonius's shoulder to stay upright until the dizziness passed.

The boy gaped at him with consternation. "You should rest," he urged.

"I've rested enough, dear Apollonius," said Yngvi. "I need to bathe. Would you do me a favour?"

"I am at your service."

"I should be very grateful if you could get me a clean chiton, and some food and drink."

"At once. There is a bath chamber behind that curtain." Apollonius was pointing to what Yngvi had thought was a tall, curtained window. "I shall have it prepared for you."

With that, Apollonius left the room and a few minutes later, three youths entered, carrying large buckets of steaming water. They disappeared into the bath chamber and emerged with empty buckets.

"It is ready, Master," said one boy.

"Thank you," said Yngvi. He pushed the curtain aside to find a large tub filled with fresh water that was just this side of steaming, and placed on a broad stool beside the tub, three varieties of soap, a sponge and fresh towels. He had just lowered himself into the tub when Apollonius returned with a fresh chiton and sandals.

"This feels divine," said Yngvi. It reminded him of the hot springs of Valhalla that only a chosen few Midgardians were allowed to access.

He did not demur when Apollonius poured soap onto the sponge, dipped it in the tub, built up a lather and started to wash Yngvi. "You can go harder." Apollonius scrubbed with greater force.

Yngvi closed his eyes, imagining each stroke of the sponge was sloughing off another decayed layer of death from his skin until what remained was life. A short while later, the boy moved his hands to Yngvi's head. Yngvi felt the young fingers expertly massage his scalp, lather his hair from root to tip. Then Apollonius scooped water with a jug and poured it over Yngvi. He did this a few times until all the soap was washed away.

Finally, Apollonius touched Yngvi on the shoulder. "Brother, if you will stand, I will dry you."

Yngvi smiled and grudgingly opened his eyes. "I doubt the gods have enjoyed care as rejuvenating as this, young Apollonius. You will make a fine healer."

The boy flushed and lowered his eyes. Then, in a hushed voice that revealed a very private wish, he said, "It is my hope to one day serve the gods."

"Gods, or one god in particular?" Yngvi teased, receiving his answer in the boy's bashful smile.

Yngvi stood up in the tub and stepped out onto the mat Apollonius had laid out on the floor. The boy patted his body with another towel until he was fully dry. Then he helped Yngvi into the chiton, loosely wrapping the long stretch of fabric around him, taking the folds from under one arm to the opposite shoulder where, once Yngvi bent forward, he pinned it. Next, he knotted the sash around Yngvi's waist. When he had done up the laces of the sandals and tied them around Yngvi's calves, he stood back to admire his work.

Then, he stepped out into the main room and indicated a plate and cup on the bedside table. "I have brought you bread and meats, some fruit and some wine."

Yngvi ate and drank with the voracity of one imbibing the nectar of the gods after a long privation. When he was finished, he said, "If you take such good care of me, Apollonius, I might never leave."

The boy flushed at the praise.

"And for that I thank you. But I do want to see if these legs still work. Would you tell your father and Nikos, if he arrives before I do, that I have gone to the agora and will return by nightfall?

"But—"

"Please? And if they have any objections, they can address them to me."

"Very well," said Apollonius, with a sigh.

CHAPTER TWENTY-SEVEN

WHEN YNGVI HAD first passed the agora with Shara, the celebrations had yet to reach this level of fervour, and Yngvi had been close to death.

It felt like a lifetime ago, because it was. Because three days ago, he had, in fact, died. Yet he now found himself alive by some manipulation of his lifespan, his fingers straying absently to his navel to trace the newly formed leaf mark that had appeared there, which could only mean that Shara had something to do with it.

And which was why he was here: to seek out Shara among the celebrating Athenians and ask Shara how it was that he still lived.

Shara must have been looking for him also, because it was not long before a hand clasped his shoulder. He turned, and was caught in the now-familiar crystalline gaze.

"Yngvi!" Shara's eyes were bright with sun, and something else. "You're here."

"I'm here."

"You were sleeping when I left," said Shara, with a slight frown, his gaze flitting over Yngvi's body.

"You can stop examining me. I thought I left Hippocrates and his boy back at the infirmary."

"Did he say you were well enough to get out of bed?"

"I'm all right," said Yngvi. "I'm alive. Somehow." He searched Shara's face for any acknowledgement of his part in Yngvi's impossible recovery, but found nothing beyond genuine gladness.

"You're alive," said Shara, a breathless quality to his voice. His smile had transformed his face; gone was every last trace of the cold stranger who had scowled at Yngvi outside the tavern in Midgard.

"How did you do it?"

Shara's smile faltered, but only a little, and he bit the inside of his cheek, as Yngvi now knew he did to give himself time to prevaricate.

"I pulled you out of the river," said Shara.

"I know that," said Yngvi. "But how am I alive? How did you get me out of the Underworld?"

"There was a boat."

Yngvi should have remembered. If he ever saw Hecate again, he had much to thank her for.

"We don't have to think about that now." Any further interrogation was forestalled by Shara taking Yngvi's arm and pulling him forward. "There's so much happening here. Athens is like nothing I've ever seen. Come."

Shara led Yngvi through the lively crowds and along the arcade at a leisurely pace, as though they had all the time they wanted. And Yngvi went with him, knowing that they didn't.

Enki was captured in a tiny jar; Yngvi was, inexplicably, resuscitated; and Shara would return to Nibiru. But for now, Shara was still here, beside him, and Yngvi wanted to hold on to every last moment of this time together which was, inexorably, drawing closer to the end.

When Shara remarked every so often on things that had piqued his interest, he sounded faraway, because Yngvi was aware only of the warm clasp of Shara's hand around his wrist, the slide of Shara's open hand over his palm, the pressure of Shara's long fingers as they clasped his own. And when Shara looked at him, the openness in his gaze was new, as if some shadow had lifted and revealed a previously shrouded part of himself to Yngvi.

Shara had stopped before a fabric stall, fronted by curtains of vibrant colours and a variety of clothing. He disengaged his hand to pull from a stack of folded fabric a chiton made of deep blue linen. It had a patterned gold border. He held it out to Yngvi. "This is nice."

"Two hundred drachmas," the vendor quoted.

The Athenian had said that blue was rare and expensive but Yngvi, having no notion if two hundred drachmas for that chiton—or anything else, for that matter—was a score or a scam, felt his eyebrows rise.

The vendor must have mistaken the involuntary gesture for a negotiation, because he hurried to add, "It's made from the finest linen in all of Athens and dyed with woad ink. Very rare." He was talking fast, eager to make the sale. "Reds and yellows you'll find everywhere, but not this. Only I carry blue linen."

Reds, yellows, blues—the colours meant little to Yngvi. He had no need of mementos of Graecia. He was not going to forget anything about his time with Shara. He smiled at Shara, and shrugged.

As if sensing that he was losing his customers, the vendor sweetened the deal. "One ninety is as low as I'll go."

Shara had been sampling the texture of the cloth, but now he handed it back to the vendor with a sheepish smile. "We were just looking. We have no coin."

"No coin?" The vendor snatched the chiton back from Shara. "Move along, then! You're blocking paying customers," he griped, as they left the shop laughing.

"No matter," said Yngvi, when they were out of earshot, indicating Shara's garb with his hand. "This is nice. Very nice," he murmured, and felt the spreading flush on Shara's neck and cheeks like the warmth of the sun on his own bare limbs. Wanting more of that, he added, with aching honesty, "I like you in this."

The diagonal arrangement of Shara's short white sleeveless chiton unhelpfully drew the eye to the long column of his neck, his collar bones, his bare shoulders, and the exposed half of his torso.

Desire hit, like a pang in Yngvi's chest, but was chased away by an unexpected emotion. It was bitterness, but at himself, and its force surprised him. His pulse was pounding in his ears; he was angry that Shara still had such a hold on him. He knew he should temper his expectations, no matter how proprietary Shara's hold on his hand had been.

"I... I thought of the chiton for you," said Shara. Then, a long moment later, "It goes with your eyes."

My eyes? When did you notice my eyes? Don't say things like that. As if you...

"Is that so?" Yngvi looked straight ahead as they continued their stroll down the line of shops. Shara slowed in front of a stall selling swords and bows and arrows, but Yngvi took his arm and kept him moving. Reading the question in Shara's raised eyebrows, Yngvi said, "I've been jabbed with enough of those to last me a while. We are not stopping here."

"What about here?" said Shara.

He had paused in front of the adjacent shop which sold masks. And his attention was on the most eye-catching display: a bright yellow mask of a youthful man, wearing a laurel wreath and a radiate crown.

Yngvi flinched. It was, unmistakably, Apollo, god of the Sun. He remembered the helplessness of being tied to the post, the drone of the wheel behind him while Apollo and Shara took turns shooting at the whirling target and, eventually, at him.

"I am sorry," said Shara, watching him carefully. His eyes dropped to Yngvi's hand, which had strayed to his shoulder, unconsciously feeling for the wound that had killed him.

"I wish I had coin," said Yngvi, to change the subject. "I think Apollonius would like that." He picked up two smaller masks, sized for children. One was an owl, which made it Athena's bird; the other had a headdress shaped as three canine heads. Cerberus. "My nephews would look very sweet in these."

But Shara did not seem to have heard him. He was staring miserably at the masks.

Yngvi shook his head. He needed to see the brightness on Shara's face again. He touched Shara's shoulder, and Shara turned to him. Forcing his lips into a grin and looking directly into Shara's eyes, Yngvi said, "I remember putting another Sun god's mask to rather pleasant use in Saqqara."

Shara knew what that meant, even if he would never admit it. And Yngvi had just spoken of Sun gods, in the plural. A month ago, both of those things would have seemed impossible.

Shara gave him a feeble smile, for effort if nothing else, then fell silent again. Yngvi felt the mood change. He was aware of the feelings growing inside him—frustration, longing, resignation. The silence stretched on and he was glad for the respite. It was a long time before Shara's voice came to him again, quieter this time.

"You could have—" It was bitten off.

All right, they would talk about it now.

"But I didn't," said Yngvi. "You brought me back. And you won't tell me how."

"I told you."

"I know there's more you're not telling me. I don't know what kind of god you are—"

"I'm no god, Yngvi! And I don't want to be one!"

The force of Shara's words hit Yngvi like a physical shove. He did not like the ragged weariness in Shara's tone. "It's all right—"

"I've had *enough* of gods," said Shara. "They are everywhere. Around us. *Inside* us! I just…"

"We don't have to—"

"I don't know what I am," said Shara, the words sounding raw, as if they hurt him. "But right now, I'm me and I'm with you."

"Not for long," said a jaunty voice from Yngvi's left.

Immediately resentful of the interruption, Yngvi turned to banish the interloper with a sharp word, but was blinded by the brilliant, beaming face of Apollo.

"You live!" Apollo said to Yngvi, giving him a cheerful but cursory appraisal before shifting his luminous attention to Shara. "Hermes said you had something to do with it, my lovely boy. He's very cross with Hecate, but I'm impressed that you brought your friend back. And curious about what other secrets you hold inside you."

Apollo was regarding Shara with frank appreciation which was rapidly changing to outright lust. Shara was weathering Apollo's admiration with a sort of bemused detachment. And Yngvi might as well have not been there at all.

"Shouldn't you be up in the sky?" Yngvi snapped. "It is not yet night."

"Oh, my horses know what to do," said Apollo, dismissing Yngvi's attempt at a dismissal with a breezy wave of his hand at the sky, his eyes never leaving Shara. "And I did want to see you again."

"Brother, we talked about this," said a second man.

Yngvi turned towards the familiar voice. It was Ares. Yngvi had not seen him approach, but had grown accustomed to Aegyptian and Graecian gods appearing and vanishing. Ares was smiling knowingly at his sunny brother, and Yngvi wondered, with a prickle of resentment, if the Graecian gods ever had a bad day.

Apollo waved Ares off.

"What more could you want with us, Apollo?" said Shara.

"Not us," said the glimmering god. "*You.*"

"Me?" said Shara.

"Can't you tell?" Apollo sounded utterly charmed. "I've hardly looked at your friend." He did, just then. The air around him seemed to glint somewhat as he appraised Yngvi.

Ares looked, too. "Why would you? He's quite like you when he's not two breaths from death," he said. "Golden hair, pleasing form…" his lashes dipped a little, his gaze slowed over Yngvi's body "…very pleasing form. Deep blue eyes—"

"I prefer my own green, thank you," said Apollo. "Whereas you, my pretty boy, are different." His voice dropped and turned husky. "I want *you*. I want to take you to my bed."

"Bed?" said Shara. He had physically withdrawn from Tausret at the prospect of lying with her. But now, even though alarm had flared in his eyes, he stayed where he was.

"Leave him alone, Apollo," Yngvi said, in a token effort to intervene. He was resigned to being disregarded by both the god and Shara, because he had noticed, with a sinking feeling, a growing flush over Shara's chest and neck and face. That should not have surprised him. A god's attentions could turn anyone's head, and Apollo's careless beauty outshone any god Yngvi had seen. Even, he had to admit, Thor.

"You both dare address a god by his name? For that I should strike you down," said Apollo, but his rebuke sounded not at all displeased. "Still…you…" he glanced at Yngvi "…you've been struck down already, quite terribly, so I think I'll just take him."

" *Take* him?" Yngvi found that he had moved to put himself between Shara and Apollo.

But he was talking to himself, because they were both gone.

"My brother can be persistent," was Ares's gravelly explanation.

"Persistent?" Distaste for Apollo rose up to Yngvi's throat. "He's an abductor." He realised, as soon as he said it, that it was a redundant condemnation because Hecate had told him about the gods' weakness for mortal beauty.

"Abductor? He's a god." Ares grinned like one who had never faced disapproval in his life. "He likes to have beautiful things." He shrugged. "Like your friend. But he's harmless."

"My friend is not a *thing*." Yngvi didn't know what Shara would do, but had no fear of him injuring Apollo or allowing himself to come to any harm. All he could do was wait for Shara to return so that they could get away from the gods. "And he can take care of himself."

"Oh, I know!" said Ares, his laugh rumbling like distant thunder. "It's not him I'm worried about, but you."

"Me?"

"You're standing here all by yourself while your friend is about to experience delights of the flesh he could never have imagined."

Yngvi did not doubt that in the slightest. Apollo had made his intentions quite clear.

"I'm not interested in your godly amusements, Ares." Yngvi was fast wearying of Graecia and its gods. "Why are you here?"

"To help you."

"I don't need your help."

"I think you do." Ares sighed. "For the god of the Sun, Apollo can be a little…dim. We Olympians do…on occasion…invite mortals to lie with us—"

"*Invite?* That was no invitation."

"Nonetheless, we brothers have pledged—only recently, I admit—to never come between lovers…"

"It's not…like that with us."

"But you'd like it to be," said Ares, with wounding perspicacity.

Yngvi felt the urge to pummel him, because Ares was right, and was regarding him with a smile that was patient, indulgent, and achingly reminiscent of the brother he had left behind in Midgard.

"Gods can see into mortal hearts. There are no secrets from us. I can take you to your friend." Ares placed his hand on Yngvi's shoulder. "And if we hurry, we can get to him before my brother has his way."

Yngvi was no stranger to the *delights* one enjoyed during godly celebrations. He had lost count of the number of times he had been one of the sweat-covered bodies stretched out on cushioned couches and thick rugs in Valhalla, in lazy tangles of skin and limbs, while auras had blended and flared around him as the Aesirs' divine bodies rippled together with his, drawing breathless sighs and moans. Yngvi shook his head.

"I did not take you to be a man who gives up so easily," said Ares.

In this, too, Ares was right. But Yngvi considered that. Shara might not think he was a god, but there was no doubt he was. It was fitting that Shara should lie with his kind—the god of the Sun, no less.

"I'm not. But— He knows where to find me." Yngvi blew out a long breath. "Thank you."

"You know," said Ares, with a benign tenacity Yngvi had not expected from a god, "my brother *will* have his way."

"He might, if that's what my friend wants and allows." It was easy to imagine golden arms wrapped around Shara, green eyes closing as their mouths opened to each other. He pictured Apollo on his knees before Shara. It was too much.

"Very well," said Ares.

And once again, Yngvi was alone in the boisterous agora.

With Shara gone, the festivities seemed grey and drained of their appeal.

Yngvi left the agora, rounding a corner down a path that opened into a network of streets. He walked, and walked, the unfamiliar pathways passing in a blur, his mind filled with thoughts of the next morning, when everything could change, would change.

Dusk had settled on Athens by the time he made his way back to Hippocrates's infirmary, passing the town square where the revelries had lost none of the exuberance to the dimming light; perhaps the Athenians drew their vigour from Dionysus's wine.

Soon the sounds of celebration dropped away and he was outside their room, eyes fixed hopelessly on the handle of the closed door.

The empty silence inside was punctuated by a muffled rattle, and Yngvi's lips stretched grimly. It was Enki, still struggling inside the jar that held him. The scourge of gods everywhere, more ancient than every other realm; a *god* born with all that *power*, reduced to the insignificance of a squirming worm confined to a little jar of clay. He couldn't help the bitter vindication he felt at that. This was, after all, what he had left Midgard to do.

If it weren't for Enki, Asgard would still be standing, the gods would be alive, and Yngvi's life would have continued in its contented normalcy.

If it weren't for Enki, he would never have met Shara.

An image appeared behind his eyes, with hateful clarity, of Shara in a pool of divine bodies.

Yngvi grasped the handle, pushed the door open to face the emptiness inside. And stopped short.

CHAPTER TWENTY-EIGHT

SHARA STOOD AT the window, one hand on the wall. At the sound of the door, he turned to face Yngvi, waiting.

Yngvi's words crowded in his throat as he closed the door behind him. They gazed at each other across the room. Over the long silence that Yngvi decided Shara would have to break, he searched Shara's face, the way he held himself, to see if he could spot the change in him, the change that Apollo would have wrought.

"I went back to the agora," said Shara, "but couldn't find you."

Yngvi had a sudden urge to take Shara's hand and keep him here a little longer. This stranger from a strange land. Only he was not a stranger anymore. And he would return to his home, tomorrow or the day after, or the day after that. It was inevitable.

"Ares said he offered to bring you to Apollo's palace. And that you didn't—"

"I didn't—" Yngvi's attention was caught by a bright yellow object on the bed. Even across the room, he could tell it was the mask of Apollo. Beside it were the masks of Athena's owl and Cerberus. And they were placed on folded blue linen. "Where did you get the coin for those?"

"From Apollo."

The implications of Shara's answer hurt too much to be ignored. But Apollo was a god, and Shara his conquest. Yngvi remembered Hecate's words and felt the bile rise to the back of his throat. *Two hundred drachmas. Is that what he thought you were worth?* He didn't need to hear anymore, but Shara was still speaking.

"I—" said Shara. "I want…" he gestured in the general direction of the sky "…that." He dropped his gaze.

"Didn't you get…*exactly* that?" Yngvi could hear the resentment in his own voice. "With the beautiful *god of the Sun*?"

"No. I left—" Shara shook his head, looked up. "I want that," he said, his voice quiet, "with you."

"With me." Yngvi struggled to keep his tone flat, stripped of emotion. Shara had made his feelings about Yngvi clear in Saqqara when he had broken their kiss with what Yngvi could generously only describe as aversion. Despite Shara's contrition after, despite his disguised role in the ritual, the rejection still stung. "Why are you back here, really?"

"I didn't—with Apollo."

Yngvi raised his brows. "Why not?"

"His eyes were the wrong colour." Shara came forward. "In Saqqara you said—"

"I know what I said."

You want me, Yngvi had seethed at the time. *When you can admit that, you come to me and you ask for it. And I'll decide if I want you.*

The memory still hurt, like a knife wound. "You know it didn't end well—the last time."

"No, it didn't..." Shara met his gaze again, and there was regret in his eyes "...but I wasn't...myself...that day."

Yngvi watched him approach slowly, carefully, his eyes cast down as if picking his way through broken pottery that might wound him.

"And who are you today?" said Yngvi coolly, even as hope spread its stupidly expectant warmth inside his chest.

"Today? I am... Me. Just me." A pause. "I want—you."

Then Shara was before him, separated by no more than a handspan. "I want you." His eyes dropped to Yngvi's lips, then swept up to meet Yngvi's gaze.

Yngvi was glad when Shara spoke, because his own mouth was dry. It was as though Shara's words had taken the air from the room.

"Do you still want me?" Spoken like that, with hushed vulnerability, it was devastating. Shara lifted a hand to touch Yngvi's shoulder, and Yngvi leaned in, hope and desire obliterating his last, lingering hesitancies.

"Will you kiss me?" Shara whispered.

Any choice Yngvi thought he had in the matter vanished in that moment. His hand rose with a mind of its own to tip Shara's face up as Shara's hands slid warmly to Yngvi's chest.

The first brush of lips was softer than the flicker of breaths, insubstantial, almost not-there. If Shara went still, Yngvi didn't notice. There was a tranquil period of dry lips sliding gently over each other. Shara stood there, his hands on Yngvi's chest, letting Yngvi kiss him.

Yngvi started to pull back, but Shara made a sound of frustration and cupped Yngvi's head, holding him in place, his grip tight in Yngvi's hair. The tug on Yngvi's scalp was thrilling, and he finally kissed Shara like he kissed his lovers: open-mouthed and fervent.

There was an aching tenderness in Yngvi's chest when Shara opened to him, flesh skating over warm flesh, tongues seeking, rediscovering and stroking, breath exchanged for breath, as hands roved over chest and back and hips.

When they separated, Yngvi leaned against the door, head tipped back. He was breathing heavily, with a raw ache in his chest and an agreeable strain in his cheeks from an incredulous smile that wouldn't fade. But then it did a few moments later, because their mouths met again.

Shara's fingers sank into Yngvi's hair as Yngvi curved his hands around Shara's neck and shoulder. They kissed, chest to chest, legs tangling as thigh slid over thigh and hip and breathing for each other became preferable to solitary breathing.

When they pulled apart, Shara's fingers stayed in Yngvi's hair. He hadn't pushed Yngvi away; he hadn't left; he was, in fact, gazing at Yngvi, eyes nearly all pupil, lips parted. Yngvi's mouth tipped up, lazy and triumphant.

Shara's face was grave, his gaze searching. "Why did you stop?" he asked, very simply.

"I didn't want to," said Yngvi.

"Then don't." He reached for Yngvi again.

"We have time, Shara, we can take it slow," Yngvi murmured, kissing Shara's hands. "Because there's so much more to show you."

"Show me everything."

Shara kissed with a gentle, cautious artlessness that Yngvi feared would turn his bones to water. *Gods, the things you do to me.*

"Stop." Yngvi's voice was muffled against Shara's mouth. He tugged at Shara's chiton. "Off. Take it off."

Unhesitating, Shara unpinned his chiton and untied the sash at his waist, letting the fabric drop and pool at his feet while Yngvi did the same. They unlaced their sandals, kicking them aside. Yngvi had a new appreciation for the simplicity of Graecian clothing because, as soon as the last stitch of fabric was discarded, they were kissing again.

Yngvi murmured, "I want to touch you. On the bed."

"Anything you want," said Shara. Then, "I've never—"

"You did say." Yngvi pulled back. "Still, no dryads from Mashu forest ever tempted you?"

Shara dropped his head a little. "A few did try."

Yngvi allowed himself a moment to experience the pang of possessiveness that gave him. He put his hands on Shara's shoulders, ran them down his long arms, feeling the swells and dips in the slender musculature. "I'm glad," he murmured.

He looked around for anything in the room that might ease the act, and spotted the small bedside table on which were placed two towels and a stoppered vial. The relief that brought pulled an incredulous breath of laughter out of him. But in the next instant, a question rose in his mind; he indicated the vial with a glance and raised his eyebrows.

"Hippocrates had come by to look in on you, but you weren't here. I said I was waiting for you. He looked at me strangely. He didn't say anything, just went away and came back with...that." Shara was frowning faintly in the direction of the vial. "He said you would know what to do."

Yngvi dropped his head on Shara's shoulder, feeling the joy and laughter rise up inside him. He would thank Hippocrates later. "He was right. There's so much I want to do."

He considered all the wonderful ways he would make love to Shara, who was watching him, eyes wide and holding very still, whether with anticipation or apprehension Yngvi could not say.

He took Shara's hand, led him to the bed and pushed him gently onto the sheets. "I want to kiss you..." he said, his joy bubbling out of him when Shara immediately lifted his chin, offering his mouth. "All over." Shara swallowed hard at that, then gave a tight but decisive nod.

They kissed. Yngvi took his time with Shara's mouth, then drew his lips down to explore Shara's body, attentive for the subtlest hint of disinclination. There was none. But there were also few signs of his enjoyment. After the initial stiffening of his body, Shara was staying quiet and motionless.

It was only when he slid a hand over Shara's stomach and the other down Shara's thigh that he realised he had missed the signs: the taut abdomen shuddering with shallow, hitched breaths, the tremor in Shara's muscles, bunched with the effort to keep still. Looking up, he saw Shara's head turned to the side, hands clutching the pillow, eyes closed and mouth open.

The rush of satisfaction Yngvi felt at that was different; with any other lover, it would have provided predictable proof of his talents in bed, but with Shara, he experienced it, unexpectedly, as thankfulness for what he was being allowed to do. Shara, who had never done this before, was giving himself to Yngvi. Shara's body would be his tonight, and Yngvi wanted, desperately, to give him everything.

Pushing Shara's thighs open, he settled between them and drew his lips down from Shara's navel until they came to rest against iron wrapped in hot silk. And all Yngvi wanted in that moment was to unwrap Shara with his mouth. Bend him, melt him with pleasure, then melt over him. He couldn't have enough.

He ran his tongue over the tip, tasting the musky bead shimmering there. Then, with a groan, he took it all in, his head and lips and tongue moving in a hard, teasing rhythm. One hand was curved around Shara's cock, the other flattened over his clenched stomach, holding him down. And when he swallowed Shara fully, Shara arched his back with a cry.

Yngvi felt Shara's heft in his mouth, furling his tongue around the head and suckling gently before sinking back down.

Lost in his own enjoyment, he retained only a peripheral awareness of Shara's reactions and registered too late the press of Shara's thighs against his shoulders. A sudden jerk of Shara's hips thrust deeper than expected and yanked Yngvi out of his bliss. With a closed-mouthed cough, he drew his head back a little, his lips still holding Shara, and looked up at him.

Shara's eyes were shuttered, his long lashes pressed to flushed cheeks; a continuous quiver ran through his tensed, glistening body, cording the sinews of his thighs, clenching and releasing his abdomen with each shallow, rapid breath.

Yngvi stared. Shara, in this moment of vulnerability, was exquisitely on the edge. Yngvi held there, lips wrapped around the head, torn between drinking in Shara's wild beauty and wanting him to remain in his private bliss until the end. He would use his hand the next time, if there were a next time, and watch Shara.

Drawing in a deep breath through his nose, Yngvi relaxed his throat and took Shara all the way inside until his lips were moving in soft hairs. Then he swallowed with a groan. With a single warning jerk and a bitten-off cry, Shara spilled into Yngvi's waiting throat. Yngvi took it all in, stopping only when Shara's hand tugged his head up.

His own body, hard and aching, craved completion.

"I want you," Yngvi said, helplessly.

Shara was still trembling beneath him, in the aftermath of climax. His lips were parted, his breath shivered.

"Shara, I need to be inside you," said Yngvi, curling his fingers around his own hardness.

Shara glanced at Yngvi's hand, then met his gaze. "Inside me, yes," he said, readily compliant. "Show me what to do," he murmured through flushed lips, his eyes unfocused and glassy. His body moved against Yngvi's.

"Yes, that," said Yngvi, with a soft laugh. "Not yet, but soon." He reached over to the table for the vial and popped the stopper with his thumb. "I need to open you first, with my fingers."

Shara looked at Yngvi, then at the vial, questioning.

"I'm going to use the oil," Yngvi said, and reached between Shara's legs, gently parting his flesh and putting his hand where they would be joined. Seeing Shara's gaze darken, he dipped the tip of a finger inside in unequivocal instruction.

Shara nodded a few times, but his eyes could not mask the nervousness of inexperience.

"Shara…are you sure—"

"I'm sure," said Shara. As proof, he put his arms above his head and spread his thighs, leaving himself open to Yngvi's gaze and fingers.

Yngvi poured out a little oil and let it flow down the fingers of one hand. Reaching again into the shadow between Shara's legs, he sought. And found.

Desire rolled over Yngvi in a wave, hot and damp. Then he pushed in.

Shara hissed in a sharp breath, then closed his eyes with a sigh. The pressure around Yngvi's fingers was not new but with Shara, it felt different. How often he had done this to his lovers, and how often he had wondered about the sensations that it gave them. Another push. Two fingers where there had been one. Shara made a breathless sound of pleasure. Another finger, careful and slow. It was so tight. Easing a little. Deeper. There.

When Shara had taken three fingers comfortably, Yngvi became audacious, twisting his fingers inside to make Shara seize and quiver. He leaned down for a kiss and Shara panted into his mouth. Their tongues slid over each other as they kissed, deeper, slower.

Yngvi lifted his mouth and whispered into Shara's neck, "Now?" as he slowly drew his fingers out.

"Yes," Shara gasped.

Yngvi sat back on his heels between Shara's legs and used his glistening hand to slick himself up. Then he clasped Shara's knees and pushed them out and up. Shara understood and bent his legs all the way.

"That's right," Yngvi murmured, feeling the warmth of Shara's thighs as they slid against his hips.

"I want you inside me," said Shara. The words were raw and rough with desire.

Yngvi could do no more than nod. Using one arm to support his body, he guided himself in with his other hand.

Shara's head fell back with a low groan. At once, Yngvi froze, but Shara locked his ankles behind Yngvi's back and invited him in. With a long, firm slide, Yngvi pushed again.

When Yngvi was all the way inside, Shara slipped his arms around Yngvi's neck and tugged him close. "Don't move," he murmured, and Yngvi stilled.

They gazed at each other, and Yngvi was engulfed by the wonder, the gratitude in Shara's eyes. Shara was gazing at him as though Yngvi was a marvel Shara had been allowed to touch, and Yngvi wanted to laugh at the absurdity of that.

A very different kind of affection rushed through him, a want deeper than he had known with any previous lover, because Shara was the marvel, and gratitude was Yngvi's to offer.

He ran his fingers through Shara's hair, feeling its silkiness, then gently tucking the long strands behind Shara's ear. They trailed over the pillow and along his neck, white against blue.

"You are lovely," Yngvi murmured. "So lovely. Like this. And like you were in Midgard."

"You are, too," said Shara, smiling. "Maybe *lovely* is not the word for you"—he drew his fingers over the rasp on Yngvi's jaw—"but pleasing." He let out a soft breath of laughter.

"Go on. Have some fun at my expense," said Yngvi.

Shara smiled up at him. There was a teasing light in his eyes. "I mean it. With your golden hair, and your deep blue eyes, and your pleasing form, your very pleasing form? I think you are *very* pleasing."

Yngvi had not forgotten. "I thought I had you under me, not Ares," he said, burying his face in Shara's neck, laughing, and Shara laughed with him. But the question remained. "Do you mean that?"

Shara lolled his head to the side and flicked his gaze down their tangled limbs. "Do you think I'm in a position to lie?"

Laughter bubbled out of Yngvi; the movement travelled down his body and into Shara, where his cock must have jumped and tapped a very specific spot because Shara's back arched. He cried out. Yngvi stilled at once, and Shara's back slowly flattened.

"What was that?" said Shara, when he could speak again. He was still shaking.

"Just a taste," Yngvi teased. He traced a finger over Shara's eyebrow and the planes of his face from his cheekbone to his jaw. "I've never known anyone like you."

"Kiss me."

Yngvi was happy to kiss for as long as Shara wanted; it was a lengthy interval before Shara slipped his mouth off and buried his face in Yngvi's neck.

"Give me another taste," Shara said, nipping his earlobe.

Yngvi moved, slowly. Shara swore. Yngvi moved again.

At first, their movements were uncoordinated, lurching. Shara squeezed his thighs around Yngvi's hips and reproached him for being clumsy, but his words were teeming with fondness.

In retaliation, Yngvi thrust again.

Shara groaned. "Where are you trying to go?" he muttered.

"Inside you."

"You *are* inside me," Shara informed him, struggling to keep his voice level. "I think you're trying to go *through* me."

Yngvi went still, then lifted his head. And because Shara was right, they laughed again, an unsteady chorus of delighted wonder.

Yngvi couldn't believe how closely they were tangled, how little space remained between their bodies and how hateful even that small bit of separation was to him. Happiness was pushing its way through his skin and into every part of him. He wanted desperately to hold onto this moment, to the image of Shara gazing at him with the light of the stars reflected in those pale eyes. And there was also pain in the knowledge that he might not have this again and it was not enough. It would never be enough.

They were joined above and below, and the heady harmony between their mouths, the curving slide of Shara's tongue against his, left Yngvi desperate for even more closeness where he was inside Shara a different way. He moved, then Shara moved, again and again until their bodies found their rhythm—a rocking, undulating union that became a hard, driving phase of push and drag.

Gasping words were scattered over choked silences. Yngvi's fingers pressed hard into Shara's back and hip, he pulled Shara's choked groan into his own mouth as their rhythm faltered, and he held Shara through the shudders as he spilled on his stomach and Yngvi's chest.

Moments later, Yngvi's body pulsed, and he cried out as he found his own shaking release inside Shara.

He didn't know when they had separated, or when they had rolled over, but Shara was lying over him, as if it was Yngvi who had been fucked.

By the time Yngvi's breathing evened, the evidence of Shara's pleasure had begun to dry on his skin. It took longer for his tongue to untangle from Shara's and become his own again. Their mouths separated and Shara's slaked kisses trailed along Yngvi's jawline until he finally settled his lips into the damp nook between Yngvi's neck and shoulder. Yngvi ran his fingers through the silken white hair that was fanned out over Shara's back.

Shara nuzzled the skin behind Yngvi's ear. Tickled, Yngvi squirmed, but Shara held him tighter. His entire weight rested on Yngvi.

"I think I'm being crushed by Mjölnir," Yngvi groaned.

Shara's body shook with breathless delight. Yngvi pretended to cough, then drew in theatrically deep, gasping breaths until Shara moved off to lie on his side.

Propping himself up on an elbow, Shara rested his head in his palm. His other hand traced the leaf mark on Yngvi's stomach while his silent, pensive gaze held Yngvi's.

Every long caress of those slender, warm fingers left Yngvi less and less capable of forming words that were not *Shara*. It became imperative, therefore, that his first coherent sounds conveyed the vital discovery he had made. But Shara spoke first.

"Was that…"

"Proof," said Yngvi.

Shara blinked because they both knew that was not what he had meant.

Yngvi's breaths came in long, slow cycles. He was smiling, lost in Shara's heavy-lidded, dark gaze. "I have proof that you're an Anunnaki."

The corners of Shara's mouth tipped up; he was tracing patterns over Yngvi's front. "Really."

"Anunnaki," Yngvi insisted, with a decisive nod and the sated burr of a thoroughly fucked warrior. "That was Anunnaki-level fucking."

Their eyes held. Bliss was a bright heat welling inside Yngvi.

Shara looked very solemn for a moment. In the next, he was face-down on Yngvi's shoulder, laughing.

It was so heartfelt, so sweetly spontaneous that Yngvi's own delight was swept away by an unfamiliar emotion, fierce and raw. It smothered him in its enormity. Without a word, he pulled Shara into an embrace and took his mouth in a fevered kiss, desperate to capture forever Shara's guileless joy and the absurd lightness it created in himself.

Shara pressed his lips to Yngvi's shoulder. "Thank you," he said.

"For what?"

"For giving me this."

"And what is that?"

Shara kissed his chin. "Confirmation that I can fuck like the Anunnaki," he said, amusement glittering in his eyes, "whose talents in bed you have somehow assessed."

Yngvi laughed, and their mouths met again, drawn together by some invisible force that grew stronger every moment they were not touching. Lips and cheeks and eyes and neck and forehead, everywhere they could reach. But Yngvi sensed a subtle change in Shara's caresses. They had grown less playful.

Shara turned his head and rested his cheek in the dip between Yngvi's shoulder and chest. "I'm glad I had this night with you." Very gently, he nuzzled his face in, causing Yngvi's skin to tingle under the light scrape of his cheek. "I will remember you. Always."

Yngvi held very still, wanting nothing more than to cover Shara's mouth with his own and tell him luminous, wonderful things he had never thought to say to anyone, let alone a stranger from another world, a man he had known for a month. It made him feel vulnerable and exposed to want someone this much. Someone who might, tomorrow or the day after, or the day after that, and with no explanation, spurn him again. Which was why he retreated to the familiar safety of casual flippancy.

"And that's the danger in tumbling an innocent," he said, with a harsh chuckle. "A good fuck might evoke sentiment."

He knew, as soon as the words had left his lips, that it was the wrong thing to say. But Shara weathered the rebuff with admirable poise. Mustering a self-deprecating laugh, he disengaged from Yngvi's embrace, ostensibly to assume a more comfortable position. He lay on his back, his shoulder touching Yngvi's.

An endless moment later, sickened by his own hesitancy, Yngvi leaned over and forced Shara's head towards him.

"Look at me," he said.

Shara did, and what Yngvi saw on his face felt like a knife-strike to his chest.

"I was wrong to say that."

Shara gave an almost imperceptible nod. "I've said worse things to you."

They kissed, and Yngvi's mouth was soft with apology. After, he held Shara's face in his hands and gave him the fierce, distilled truth of that moment.

"How can I ever forget you? I've never known anyone like you," Yngvi said, unsmiling. "It's never been like—like this for me. I find myself wishing for too many things, impossible things—" He gave a bitter laugh. Magne was right. He should seek constancy, not this kind of parlous sport with life and heart.

"Impossible things," said Shara, as though he understood. "Yes…"

"But we have time, don't we?" said Yngvi, his unease growing with each passing second of waiting for Shara's answer. "There's tomorrow, and the day after that. And…"

Shara was watching Yngvi, his solemn, forlorn gaze seeming to want to penetrate Yngvi's thoughts.

"There's tomorrow," Shara said at last, "and the day after that."

Enough of this.

"All right, we should sleep," Yngvi said, gruffly, "before that marvellous fuck makes me even more sentimental and I start spouting nonsense to you." He held his arms open.

Shara leaned his body over Yngvi's and hesitantly rested his head on Yngvi's chest, running his fingers over the swell of Yngvi's pectoral muscle.

Yngvi wrapped his arms around Shara and held him close, his lips in Shara's hair, breathing in its scent. He felt Shara's warm breath against his okin.

Soon, Shara's breathing evened and his hold on Yngvi loosened with sleep. But Yngvi lay awake, wondering what he had done to deserve this glimpse of happiness even as hope dwindled that the coming days would cure him of this impossible infatuation.

Because he knew what he would do in the morning.

CHAPTER TWENTY-NINE

IT WAS EARLY afternoon when Yngvi woke.

He was smiling, and for good reason. He was alive, he was uninjured, and he was in bed with Shara. Last night had been... Why not tell Shara that? He patted the mattress beside him, expecting a warm body, but his hand encountered the cool, flat sheet.

"Shara?" he called, thinking that Shara was perhaps bathing in the curtained bath chamber. When there was no response, he got out of bed, wrapping the sheet around his waist, and stood outside the curtain. "I'm coming in," he said. Waited a few moments before lifting the curtain. The bath chamber was empty.

No, no, no. Not this again.

He cast his gaze about the room, looking for signs that Shara was returning. There were none. Shara's boots were gone; he looked in his clothes bag and found that the ka jar was missing; Enki's sword was gone. And most telling, the leaf-amulet was laid out on what had been Shara's pillow.

Yngvi felt the strength leave his legs. He sat down heavily on the bare mattress, his hands on his knees, clutching the sheet tightly.

Shara had left him to go to Nibiru with Enki's essence captured in the jar. But he could not get there without the leaf-amulet, could he? Did he not need it anymore? Or would he return for it? The leaf-amulet was neatly laid out on the pillow, as though Shara had left it for Yngvi to use to return to Midgard. He knew that Yngvi knew how to use it. Yngvi felt his hope gutter and die.

Shara had allowed Yngvi one night together.

But after last night, Yngvi had thought they would— He jammed his fingers in his hair and pressed down on his scalp. What had he thought would happen? How many times would he have the same foolish expectations and watch helplessly as they were shattered? Had he really thought they would go together to Nibiru and explore the tablets in the Library to discover how they could imprison Enki for all time? That perhaps Shara would come back with him to Yggdrasil to speak to Odin and Thor and Magne? That he might even stay back on Midgard for a while? Or longer?

His reputation with the Aesir, his Captaincy in the army, his life in Midgard—all the things that had been important to him—did not hold the same meaning they had when he had left Midgard. Because, after everything that had happened, what he wanted most was to see Shara again.

A knock sounded on the door. Had Shara returned? Hope quickened Yngvi's steps. He pulled the door open and was greeted by a bright face and even brighter voice.

"You're awake at last!" said Hippocrates. He did not enter, but his keen eyes darted about the room, with infinitesimal pauses here and there, as if registering the crumpled sheet around Yngvi's waist, the empty bottle of oil, Shara's evident absence.

"So, you did bring your pollux with you. I knew it."

Pollux. That word again. "What does that mean?" Yngvi asked, but Hippocrates didn't seem to have heard him.

"I must see to my other patients. And since you are recovered enough to have done...well...that"—Hippocrates gestured to the bed—"you're recovered enough to leave. I wish you well, young man. Do try and stay alive." He grinned, then turned sharply and was gone before Yngvi could thank him.

"Apollonius, my boy!" the physician called out in the corridor. "Your charge is ready for you!"

Moments later, Apollonius appeared in the doorway holding a bulging pouch in one hand, and a fresh folded chiton in the other. As before, three youths trailed in with buckets of hot water which they emptied into the tub, then left the room.

"Brother Nikos," said the boy, "asked me to prepare the bath for you when you woke."

"Where did he go?"

"He didn't say."

"Did he say when he would return?" Yngvi knew the answer already.

"He—didn't say."

Yngvi nodded slowly.

"Is something the matter?" Apollonius placed the pouch and chiton on the bedside table.

"No—nothing's the matter. Your father… He said that I brought my pollux with me. What did he mean by that?"

The boy's eyes lit up. "Oh! That is one of Father's favourite tales."

"And yours, too?" said Yngvi. "Tell me."

"Pollux and Castor," Apollonius began happily, "were twins borne by the same mortal mother. But Pollux's father was a god, and Castor's father was mortal."

"I don't like where this is going," said Yngvi.

"I promise, it ends well!" Apollonius assured him. "The brothers loved each other, and when Castor sustained a fatal wound, Pollux could not bear the thought of his brother dying—"

Yngvi had heard a tale like this before. Shara had, too. In Saqqara. Perception was like quicksand, pulling him deeper with every new pulse of understanding. *Please, let this end differently.*

"—and asked the gods to allow him to share his immortality with Castor. Are you all right?"

Stop. Gods, stop, please. Yngvi was sinking into despair, and the only man who could draw him out had left.

A concerned pause. "Are you well?"

Yngvi managed a half-nod. But he was not all right. His stomach lurched, like he was going to vomit.

"I—," he bit out as he fell forward, elbows digging into his knees, grabbing his hair so hard it hurt. He understood now.

"Brother Inachus!"

Yngvi understood it all. It was the same across realms: tender-hearted immortals, and the disproportionate gifts they gave the mortals who loved them. He wanted to scream at the stupid, stubborn, infuriating man— immortal—who had left him here.

Apollonius was kneeling before him. "Should I call Father? You don't look well."

Yngvi did not know how long the boy had been calling to him before he lifted his head. He knew what he had to do.

"I'm all right. I—I need to be alone. Would you mind very much if I bathed myself, Apollonius?"

The boy rose at once. "The bath is ready for you. If you would call for me when you are finished, I will bring your meal."

Yngvi forced himself to smile at the boy, because he was crumbling inside. "You have been most kind to me, Apollonius. I will remember you always. This is for you." He handed the boy Apollo's mask. "I hope you like it."

In Apollonius's sweet face, brighter now than the mask he held, Yngvi saw the boys his nephews would grow up to be, all sweet-natured with sweeter smiles, hair of gold and eyes of forest-green. His hand rose of its own accord to ruffle the soft gilt hair.

"Thank you, Brother Inachus," Apollonius said a little breathlessly, hugging the mask to his chest. "I will remember you also. Please, call for me when you are ready." Then he bowed, and turned to leave.

"Apollonius, wait," said Yngvi. "What is in the pouch?"

"I forgot to tell you! Father would have never forgiven me!" The boy wore a relieved and grateful smile. "It contains a small waterskin, powders, salves and bandages. Brother Nikos asked Father if we would prepare an assortment of medicines for you to take with you. He said you had a tendency to get injured, too often and too critically."

"He was right."

"The powders—just a pinch, they are very potent—are to be taken with a spoonful of the water: red if you feel faint from bleeding, green if you feel bilious. The salves are to be applied only after the wounds have been thoroughly cleaned, and the bandages—" He stopped and spread his hands, the use of bandages being obvious.

"And the water?"

"That water was taken from the spring that flows behind Asclepius's temple. Its healing properties enhance the efficacy of the powders." He smiled at Yngvi, a little bashful now. "I have also put something in there from me."

"You have?" said Yngvi. "What is it?"

"A pendant shaped like the Rod of Asclepius. It will keep you safe if you wear it around your neck."

"Then I shall wear it and never take it off." Yngvi glanced at the pouch, then back at the boy. "Thank you, Apollonius," he said, when he had swallowed down the emotion rising inside him.

"It is my hope that you have no need of the contents of the pouch, Brother Inachus."

"That is my hope as well," said Yngvi, with a faint smile.

He shut the door behind Apollonius and stepped into the bath chamber.

The boy had prepared a tub with clean, hot water and soaps and towels.

Yngvi remained submerged in the water until the heat had permeated so deep into his body that even his bones felt warm. He sat with his legs bent and his elbows on his knees, the heels of his palms pressed into his eyes as he rocked back and forth, thinking of what he would do, could do.

He had assumed they would be together till the end, but if Shara thought he could leave Yngvi behind with no choice, even in the matter of Yngvi's own life, he would be pleased to show Shara how wrong he was.

He thought of last night, of the laughter and delight of their first coupling, and Shara's quiet despair the second time. Yngvi had been asleep when the feathery touch of Shara's blue aura had stirred him to the dreamlike state between sleep and wakefulness. It had felt like an impossible fantasy, languid and evanescent, when he had reached for Shara in the darkness, guided by need and touch alone; they had kissed, and he had lain on his back while Shara had shifted above Yngvi and given himself again. They had held each other as the shudders slowly subsided. Yngvi should have known then, but he could not think beyond the fact that Shara was in his arms, that he was inside Shara, and that he never wanted to let go.

He ran his fingers over his torso, dipping below the water to trace the path of Shara's lips over his chest and navel, and even lower, where— It was too much. He wrenched his thoughts back to the present, cursing himself as a damned fool for wanting more. One night changed nothing. He should have known that. No matter. He still had options. Shara had left the leaf-amulet behind, but he was not here to make sure Yngvi used it to return to Midgard. And Shara might be finished with Yngvi, but Yngvi wasn't finished with Shara.

He bathed and dressed in a clean pair of tunic and pants; pulled on his boots; fastened his sword belt, which was lighter now without Enki's sword. He picked up the carving knife Apollonius had brought the previous night for the meats, wiped it clean with the sheet and tucked it into his belt. Then he enfolded the masks of Athena's owl and Cerberus in the blue chiton, and placed the bundle and Apollonius's pouch in his clothes bag.

He sent a silent thank you to Hippocrates, Apollonius and Hecate, a final farewell to Athens and Saqqara, and an apology and his love to Magne, whom he might never see again.

And then he clasped the leaf-amulet around his neck, recalled the images of Shara's home and closed his eyes.

CHAPTER THIRTY

HIS EYES OPENED on Nibiru.

It had felt different to traverse the stars alone. But he was in Mashu forest now, standing outside Shara's lodge. He could hear the stream and waterfall close by. He knocked on the door. "Shara. Are you there?" When there was no answer, he slowly pushed it open. As he had in Hippocrates's infirmary, he said, "Shara, I'm coming in." The door was unlocked. And the cabin was empty. Where could Shara be? Yngvi was thinking that he could not tell how deep inside the forest Shara lived when another memory surfaced.

He left the lodge, and recalling the path Shara had taken, made his way deeper into the forest, accompanied by his long shadow. The evening sun had dipped below the treeline, peeking playfully in sudden, bright flashes through gaps in the thicket. It had rained, the breeze was cool and damp, and he breathed in the scent of wet earth. Distant birdsong and the restless rustle of the undergrowth parting around his legs were punctuated by the cadenced squelch of his boots on the moist carpet of fallen leaves. A short while later, he stood before the large banyan tree where Shara had gone after Nidaba's death.

It was unmistakable, a single tree wider than a small grove. Under its dappled canopy was cool, dark shade. Its roots hung like thick vines right down to the forest floor, giving it the impression of having numerous thinner trunks. And at the base of the thickest trunk, he located the mound where Shara had sat. That was when he had been pushed out of Shara's memories.

But now the tree and its mound were before him, and there was no one to push him away. He sat, as Shara had, with his back to the tree, and lay down on the soft ground so that his head touched the mossy trunk. He looked up at the green shelter, saw the boughs shake over him, as if in greeting, and spread out. And then the tree reached down, the leaves touched the grass and enclosed him.

Yngvi had never seen a tree react to the presence of a man, yet he felt no fear. There was a comfortable familiarity in the way the tree accepted him into its shade, the way the mound seemed to open up around him, causing him to sink a little into its warm, wet welcome. He heard the crackle and crunch of wood as the roots of the tree laced over him, forming a gnarly cocoon that gently enveloped him.

The web of wood around him was turning blue, and through gaps in the netting he could see the deep green leaves paling, the colour leaching out of them until they were white like the grass soughing around him and the burst of blossoms unfurling along the blueing trunk.

He closed his eyes. "Show me," he said, to the tree, to the forest, to the air. "Show me everything."

A shuddering voice whispered, "I have waited so long."

The words kindled something inside him, and a spark of memory caught fire, but these were not among the memories Shara had chosen to share with him in Midgard.

He gasped when invisible fingers stroked his scalp. Or perhaps they were fingernails, because it had started to hurt—fingernails that were digging into his skull and reaching inside his mind.

His whole world narrowed to the point between his eyebrows. His eyes were closed, but he could see. A sudden cold enveloped him and his body shook. His eyes rolled back into his head, his mind slipped inwards and fragmented scenes from someone else's memories crashed into him. His last coherent thought was: *Who are you?*

A glint of steel, a flash of light as a flaming sword swung up and swept down with force.

Pain. Blood. A limb severed. A man's screams rending the quiet of night.

A blade dismembering the man's body with methodical efficacy, first cleaving his legs above the thighs, then his arms at the shoulders. Cutting his torso below the ribs.

Yngvi looked through the man's eyes at a woman crouching behind a curtain. Her hand was clapped over her mouth, stifling a scream. She was a blue-skinned snow-mane, and her stricken pale eyes were wet.

She was staring at a hand with a ring on a long finger. A ring with a curious emblem—two eyes transecting inside a circle.

He had seen that ring before, in Midgard, when Shara had joined their minds and shown him the scene of Nidaba's death. It belonged to the Sky-Father. His heart hammered against his ribs.

Leaving his own weapon sheathed, Enlil took the sword from the murderer, raised it and brought it down again. Yngvi heard the hiss of the fire-blade, felt its heat as it cut through the air and...something else.

The room spun.

One moment he was staring at the ceiling, then, abruptly and in rapid succession, at the wall, the windows, the curtains, and finally looking down at the floor. It took him a moment to grasp that the victim's severed head had tumbled to the ground.

The scene went dark and Yngvi heard the revulsion tear out of him in a terrible cry.

He was breaking loose from the appalling vision but, throttling his own violent reaction, did as the voice pleaded and forced his mind to turn inwards again.

A moment later he was, incredibly, back in the chamber, and a curtain fluttered gently before his eyes. Yngvi knew through whose eyes he was now seeing.

Enlil watched while the first murderer flung the dead man's arms, legs and the pieces of his torso into the ether. The severed head had rolled over the floor and come to a stop by the wall. From this close, the lifeless face and open eyes were a shock to behold.

It was...Shara.

But it also wasn't. Or it might have been Shara, if he was much older.

Yngvi's heart threatened to burst out of him.

If this vision was true, Enlil and someone else would kill Shara far in the future. This is what Shara must have seen in Saqqara. He had to warn Shara that he was in more danger than he had thought.

Then Yngvi remembered the woman whose memories he was reliving. He felt her surprise, her anguish, her fear, and an altogether different kind of ache pulsed inside him.

Shara would have a lover. Or a wife. And she would watch him being murdered, helpless to save him, just as Yngvi was helpless right now. He experienced the woman's grief as if it were his own.

The other man came into view. A sword hung at his waist; it had a blue jewel and an engraving of snakes on the blade.

Enki!

But that gem had shattered. Yngvi had watched as Hermes had broken it. How was this possible?

Enki hurled Shara's head into the heavens and strode to the curtained door. Yngvi heard him call for a guard.

"Brother, look who it is," said Enlil, lifting the curtain. Yngvi found himself looking right at Enlil, through the woman's eyes. "Did you think you could hide, stepmother?"

Stepmother? Ishtar? This was impossible. Unless— Unless he had been looking at it the wrong way.

From a previous image, a small detail pushed itself into the foreground: the dying man's hair was dark, and his eyes were a dark grey. Yngvi felt himself shaking with the horror of discovery, felt the roots of the tree gently tighten around him, holding him in place. In the moments that followed, the haze of obscurity was slowly dispelled. And Yngvi knew this to be not a foretelling of events, but an echo. Enki and Enlil were both murderers, but this wasn't Shara's killing he was witnessing.

It was Anu's.

Enki thrust Anu's sword into Ishtar's hand just as a guard arrived at the door.

Enlil loomed over Ishtar. "You murdered our father, and for that, you will spend your life in chains." He gestured to the guard. "Take her."

Yngvi's body jolted hard as time jumped ahead, like a fold in the horizon, and he was thrown millennia past that night.

The scenery had changed. Ishtar had broken out of a dank cell and was crashing through a dark thicket. She had tarried only a moment to thank the snow-mane who had freed her. Her daughter. Nidaba. Ishtar slowed to catch her breath, palming her way through a grove. Yngvi picked up her memories of the scents of the wild. They were in a forest. She stopped by a tall rock over which a cascade plunged into a stream. Yngvi recognised the location. He had just come from there. But there was no lodge. Because it was not that time in history.

Rushing to the water's edge, Ishtar dropped to her knees beside a small mound covered in gnarled, mossy shoots and fresh blossoms. She ripped at the stalks and tore them off, dug at the thickly packed mud with her fingers, throwing off more and more detritus until she reached something dry and bristly.

Dark matted strands. It was hair.

She gasped, and her hands worked furiously to uncover more of the head under that hair until it was fully revealed.

Anu's head.

His skin had turned pallid, yet even after all this time, it retained signs of feeble vitality. Ishtar picked up her lover's head with care, brushing away the dry locks and cradling his face to her breast.

Yngvi gazed down at Anu through Ishtar's eyes and, astonishingly, found himself looking up at Ishtar. His eyes burned as tears ran down her cheeks and he felt wetness on his forehead as they dripped over Anu's face.

Through Anu's eyes, Yngvi saw that a small section of the dark expanse above had brightened. He discerned the shape of Oruwandil, or Sipa-Zi-An-Na as Shara had taught him. The archer's bow glinted as a light flashed through the archer's starry shape and arced across the sky. It was a fireball with a long white tail, and it seemed to have been shot by Sipa-Zi-An-Na into the darkness.

Yngvi sensed Ishtar calling on something deep within her. His own skin grew hot with the memory of her energy breaking through the confines of her skin to become a cloud of blue around the head in her arms.

Answering her command, water from the stream flowed towards her, carrying with it fallen leaves and mud and grass, and coalesced in a glowing, wet bubble that spun around the cloud.

Surrounded by this whorl of blue, Yngvi felt the head in Ishtar's arms disintegrate into tiny particles that transformed into an uncontrollable, throbbing force. It was Anu's male power, and Yngvi could feel it forcefully, urgently perfuse Ishtar and consume her female force.

The distinction between their essences gradually blurred into a single consciousness that transcended the sum of their individual energies. When the blue cloud dissipated, Ishtar was gone, as was Anu's head.

But their joining had left something behind.

That final image ripped through Yngvi's fractured mind and turned his world black.

Yngvi's eyes fluttered open to a darkening sky glimpsed through gaps in the green canopy.

The tree had straightened, the roots had returned to their upright stance as the stoic guardians of Nibiru's secrets, and his body was free of their woody nest. He sat up, felt himself slowly come back to the present, then stood. He touched the massive trunk.

"Thank you," he said to the tree. The leaves shook in response.

Thank you, said the voice, a woman's voice. Ishtar's voice.

Yngvi nodded at the tree, then turned and made his way in the opposite direction. He had remembered the path Shara had taken into the forest and reversed it. The distance gave him time to think about what he had been shown. Details began to resurface that had been obscured until now.

Take it, take me, take it all back! Shara had shouted in the Graecian Underworld. And Yngvi knew with absolute certainty what Shara had done, how much he had given up. And for what? For Yngvi? Who was destined to die someday?

The memories Ishtar had shared had left him shaken. He knew now that Nidaba's choice of the name *Shara* had not been arbitrary. He understood Shara's ability to command that sword, knew that Anu had been inside Shara all this while, Anu and Ishtar both, and that Anu had reemerged, and he was wrathful. Anu had come back to Nibiru to bring ruin to his own children. He was going to kill them for killing him.

Yngvi thought also of all the times that Shara had vacillated between cruel and considerate. Shara had tried to tell him. Yngvi knew that must have been Anu, who had grown stronger inside Shara until he had finally taken over. But that did not explain last night, because he knew, with absolute certainty, that Anu would not have allowed last night to happen.

It was dusk when the forest started to thin and a city appeared in the distance.

As he neared, clanging noises drowned out the receding sounds of the forest. The sun might have set, but the people of Nibiru were hard at work. Some of them, at least. This, too, Yngvi had seen in Shara's memories: humans toiling over some form of strenuous, digging work while armed guards held up torches in one hand, and with the other, whipped the humans' bare, bent backs. One of the guards, who, from his overbearing manner and embellished clothing, appeared to wield authority over the others, was familiar. He was dark-haired, brown-skinned, and wore an expression of smug superiority. Yngvi's hand curled into a fist. Shoulders squared, he strode up to the guard and tapped him on the shoulder.

"Namhu," said Yngvi.

Namhu spun around, his eyes flitting over Yngvi as he took in his foreign appearance. "Who are you?"

"It doesn't matter who I am. I need to go to the Sky Palace."

"Why?"

"Isn't that where the gods live?"

Namhu laughed. "You are not certain where the gods live?"

Yngvi allowed Namhu a few moments of amusement at his expense. "The Sky Palace," he repeated.

A smirk. "You won't be allowed inside."

"No matter." Yngvi pulled out Apollonius's carving knife and pressed it to Namhu's side, just below the ribs. "You can get me in. And if you think of calling for help—" He twisted the knife a fraction, just enough for the tip to breach the thick weave of Namhu's livery.

Namhu's shoulders dropped. His expression soured. "I was going there anyway."

"Then you won't mind if I go along with you," said Yngvi, amiably.

Yngvi kept close to Namhu, knife pressed into the envoy's side, as he was taken down a grid of streets that might have been familiar in the daytime. A short while later, the streets fell away and they stood on the edge of a vast courtyard, before its towering arched gate. There was no light, save the glow of the flames from Namhu's torch. Their progress was slow and careful under the dim light. Minutes later, Namhu gasped, and Yngvi saw why. The tongues of yellow flame were glinting on the livery of prone bodies. It felt like Ragnarök again.

"*They're all dead.*" Namhu had whispered, even though the courtyard appeared to be empty of life and his words only reached Yngvi. He lifted his torch to Yngvi's face. "Who are you?"

Yngvi returned his gaze. "You wouldn't believe me."

"Your hair. It's yellow. No one has hair like that here. Are you some new breed of snow-mane we haven't seen before? We only have one other like you, but his hair is white."

"You mean Shara. Have you seen him?"

"You know him?" Namhu laughed with undisguised contempt. "Then you know that no one really cares to look in on that mongr—"

Yngvi drove his fist into Namhu's jaw, snapping his head to the side. Namhu took a few stumbling, startled steps back, holding his face.

Yngvi clenched his teeth. "Don't *ever* call him that." Each word was precise and deadly.

Namhu was testing his jaw. A thin line of red was seeping down his chin. He gave Yngvi a vicious look, but Yngvi stared back until Namhu averted his eyes.

Yngvi snatched the torch from Namhu. "Get out of here," he snarled, "or I'll make sure you'll end up like them." He swept the torch out over the yard. "Run."

Namhu ran.

With the guards of the Sky Palace lying insensate on the ground, Yngvi encountered no resistance. He strode up to the gate, the glazed blue bricks spangling under the torchlight. As Shara had done, he passed through the archway and headed up to the sprawling Sky Palace that loomed darkly behind the gate. He recognised the marble colonnade, swept past it, his footfalls echoing as he strode through concentric corridors, silent and devoid of any sign of life, until he stood outside huge oak doors.

Drawing in a breath, he pushed the doors open.

And froze.

CHAPTER THIRTY-ONE

"SHARA!" IT WAS a voice he had despaired of ever hearing again.

Shara turned, and felt the most incongruous of emotions, given where he was, who he was, and what he was doing. In the small part of his mind that remained his, he felt a burst of joy. Because he was looking at the face that he had left in peaceful sleep just hours ago. And he knew what had shocked Yngvi into silence.

It's not me you're seeing, it's Anu!

He had shouted, but there was no sound. His voice was no longer his, nor his body.

Yngvi was staring at the wrathful countenance so much like Shara's, the body hovering in the middle of the hall, hair floating around him like an aura, enveloped in blue fire. Then Yngvi's horrified gaze shifted to the two empty thrones on the dais, and swept over the stricken blue-skinned men and women gaping up from the bottom of the steps where they had fallen. Their weapons were strewn around them, rendered as impotent as their own limbs.

Ninki stared mutely at the ka jar in Anu's hand, which bore the likeness of her husband and juddered with his captured spirit. Her left arm was tight around their quailing son, Ninkur, holding him to her bosom.

Ninlil was a straining mass of pallid flesh in dark velvet. Nergal lay unconscious and spreadeagled on the floor between his parents. And Enlil was closest to Anu, fallen on the floor over his left arm. His right arm was outstretched, its four-fingered hand lying in a small pool of his own black blood. The severed ringed finger had rolled out of his reach. The red jewel at the centre of the ring's intersecting eyes was still intact and gleamed under the flames of Anu's aura.

These were the purest, most powerful Anunnaki—direct descendants of Anu—brought to their knees. The goddess of Death faced with death herself, and desperately holding onto the young god of Healing; the goddess of the Wind, her struggling elemental force tethered by Anu's invisible power; the god of War subjugated by the creator with a single thought; and the head of the pantheon—the Sky-Father—thrown down to the ground before his father.

This was Ki's bloodline. Ishtar was dead, as was her only child, Nidaba.

The death of a god here would send death rippling out to the pantheons on every other realm.

Anu had been moments away from making that happen when Yngvi had entered, and called Shara's name. Shouted it. And the Great Hall had immediately fallen into a fragile, quivering impasse, as though the sound of his name had frozen the divine massacre in mid-strike.

But now Yngvi's eyes widened, and he took a step back, because Anu was holding up the ka jar, which still jerked in his hand. With his other hand, he raised Enki's sword and placed its tip inside the groove between the etched lips of the carving of Enki's face. And they were on Nibiru. If the sword shattered the jar now, Enki would be killed.

Stop! Shara fought the impetus of his own muscles, restraining where Anu tried to release. It caused Anu to jerk, but only a little—

"Stop!" Yngvi shouted.

Incredibly, Anu listened. He lowered the sword and turned his fulgent attention to Yngvi.

"You! What are you doing here?"

"Don't do that. Please! Don't kill Enki!"

"Enki is going to die today," said Anu. Shara felt the blue flames flare. Anu was angry.

"No, no, please," said Yngvi. "Please! You know if you kill Enki, the gods of the Underworld everywhere will die."

"I do know that. I know everything," said Anu. "And after I kill him, I will kill my other son, his murdering family and every last cowering traitor who supported him."

"I know what it's like to seek revenge," said Yngvi. "I killed Loki for killing my parents. But that didn't turn back time. They were still dead. Even someone as powerful as you must tire of all this bloodshed."

Anu laughed, and the blue aura dimmed a little. "I commend your courage. Or is it simply recklessness? For no one has dared speak to me as you do."

"I dare nothing," said Yngvi, haltingly. "I only plead with you to spare the Anunnakis' lives. Your children's lives." Another pause. "Great Anu."

Shara could sense the struggle in Yngvi as he clamped down on the biting accusations he would doubtless have wanted to fling at Anu, and employed, instead, the supplicative manner of an awed mortal. But everything Shara knew about Yngvi was known to Anu as well.

"Great Anu," said the creator. He made a derisive sound, part laugh, part snigger. "You needn't pretend with me, Yngvi Ecklundson. I am well acquainted with your...unorthodox opinions about gods and their fallacies. It might surprise you to learn that, in this case, we are in agreement. The gods, the Anunnaki in particular, are flawed beings. They were made to be greater and more powerful than man. Better in every way." He directed a withering look at his family. "Yet they exhibit all of the humans' weaknesses, but only wield more power. They are unworthy of their creator. And I will end them."

"Unworthy of their creator," said Yngvi, adding, carefully, "unworthy of you."

"Unworthy of me," said Anu.

"And yet, wouldn't the creation of imperfect beings imply imperfection in their creator? You must, then, end yourself."

Shara felt Anu's eyes narrow dangerously, felt the flames around his head flare brighter, and begged Anu, wordlessly, to spare Yngvi, because he might well be burned alive by Anu's wrath.

But Anu only laughed, sounding pleased with Yngvi's audacity. "You are craftier than I thought." He gave Yngvi a patronising glare. "I was never born and therefore I cannot die. And you should be glad, because if I did, everything would die; every realm, every god, every mortal. Immediately."

"I know," said Yngvi.

He ran a hand through his hair, a mannerism Shara had come to recognise as Yngvi either thinking or preparing to say something outlandish. And Shara had a fervent hope that he was not about to make another reckless proposal. But of course, he did.

"I know of another way," said Yngvi, "a better way."

"You've already asked me to spare these traitors. But they must die, my treacherous sons especially."

Yngvi raised his head and held Anu's gaze. "Death is a very quick and painless end for your sons. Far too kind for what they have done to you."

"They must suffer as I have," said Anu. "They must pay with their lives."

"They will. But they don't need to die."

"It would appear you took leave of your sanity in Graecia. You cannot spare a life and also take it away."

That was true. And yet Shara stopped worrying for a moment, because he was intrigued. He could not envisage whatever brazen idea Yngvi was about to propose. He caught a spark in those deep blue eyes; the lips he had kissed were curved in a faint smile. A small glimmer of hope peeked through the cloud of dread inside Shara.

"Make them exist together for all eternity," said Yngvi. "Imprison Enki's spirit inside Enlil's body."

Yes! Do it!

You want me to do what he says, Anu thought back at him. *How unsurprising. Now, calm down.*

I mean it. If Enlil hates Enki inside him even half as much as I hate having you inside me, it will be worth it.

Anu gave a long, unrestrained laugh. Inside him, Shara felt his own relief. "That is rather…inventive," the creator acknowledged. "My dastardly sons who hate each other, trapped in the same body for eternity."

"Yes! Do it!" Yngvi urged, seeming encouraged by Anu's good humour.

"Calm yourself," said Anu, but he was smiling when he pressed the tip of Enki's sword to the floor, rammed his foot down on the blade and shattered the steel, the shards clattering on the marble. His face grew cold when he curled his fingers and jerked his hand, as if tugging on an invisible rope.

Enlil's body rose limply from the ground, his neck stretched as if a hand held him there, feet trailing the floor as Anu dragged him close. He seized Enlil's jaws in one hand, forcing his mouth open. Then he snapped off the lid of the ka jar and rammed it between Enlil's teeth.

Enlil's hands flew to his throat; he made a retching sound, convulsing hard, forced to swallow over and over as Enki's spirit poured into his body. Then Anu crushed the jar, opened his hand, and blew off the fine red residue into the still air of the Great Hall.

Enlil crashed to his knees, mouth contorted in horrified disgust. A worm-like ripple slithered into the inky blackness spreading through his startled grey eyes, and Shara knew Enki's spirit was inside Enlil.

A pitiless smile played on Anu's lips as he watched Enlil quiver and thrash on the floor, wild hands tearing at his hair. He made no move to stop Enlil when the Sky-Father, now carrying his hated brother inside him, leapt to his feet with a tortured bellow and tore out of the Great Hall through one of the smaller doorways.

Anu redirected his blazing attention to the cowering gods. "And you, murderous family of mine, that is what awaits you if you dare cross me again. I will not think twice about wiping out all the Anunnaki and creating a new line of descendants. Now get out!"

Ninki hurriedly pulled on Ninkur's smaller body, helping him to his feet, and as soon as the youth was upright, mother and son stumbled out of the hall as swiftly as their wilting limbs would allow.

Meanwhile, Ninlil shook Nergal urgently, exhorting her inert son to wake up. With Anu's death-hold on them released, Nergal regained consciousness within minutes. They stood with effort, using their left arms to push themselves up. Ninlil held on to Nergal's lifeless right arm for support as they staggered out of the hall through the same doorway Ninki and Ninkur had taken.

Ninki and Ninlil had not dared protest their husbands' fates. All four had kept their eyes on the floor. They had not dared make a sound, not even a whimper, even though they were in obvious pain. They had needed no incentive to flee Anu's rage. And Shara doubted that they, or any of the lesser Anunnaki, would ever be seen or heard from again.

When the Great Hall was finally empty of Anunnaki, Anu turned to Yngvi. "Well done. I would not have thought you capable of such exquisite cruelty." Seeing Yngvi open his mouth to speak, he held up a hand. "You're about to thank me for saving the other pantheons."

"Yes," said Yngvi.

"Would you still thank me knowing you'll never see Shara again?"

"I would, but I still see him inside you."

"I should have known you would follow him here. He has been plagued with your presence since Midgard."

"And with yours since his birth," Yngvi retorted. "Nidaba knew. She named him for you."

Shara gasped soundlessly. All other reactions and impressions, even the gladness inside him that Yngvi had come, were now secondary to his fear for Yngvi's safety.

"He has always been a vessel for me," said Anu. "But you seek something else from him."

"Nothing that I would not give him myself. And he is not a vessel; he is a man you have invaded."

"He is a man I have *created*. Without me, he would not exist. That makes him mine to use."

Anu's casual, abject diminution of his entire being made Shara recoil hard enough that Anu's body shook.

"*Use?*" Yngvi's lips twisted. "No," he said, shaking his head. "No! He is not your puppet. And you are not alone in creating him."

"Then you know I will never give him up. He is all that remains of her."

"That is not true," said Yngvi. "She lives, she is there, in the forest."

"You dare lie to me? You forget who I am."

"I know who you are…" said Yngvi. "Shara said you are the creator of life. I know that without you, none of the realms, none of us would exist. I know that *Shara* wouldn't exist. I know that."

Shara felt his heart breaking.

"But he exists!" Yngvi's voice shook. "He is… He…is. Leave him in peace."

Anu grew quiet. He closed his eyes briefly, then said, "You have good intentions, but you are too late. Shara is gone."

"I don't believe you. He's still inside his body. He *has* to be there. You have been tearing him apart. And now you have pushed him aside, but he is still there."

Shara struggled to tear free of Anu, to rid himself of this body and stand before Yngvi. Anu only jerked his head minutely.

"He still fights you," said Yngvi. "I can see it!"

Anu floated down to the floor and faced Yngvi. Shara could feel the blue fire simmer with restrained displeasure, and even he did not know when it might erupt. He felt Anu's eyes flash.

"I know who he is. I know what happened to you."

"Is that so? Impress me, then."

Yngvi said, "You survived your sons' attempt at murder."

"That much is obvious if I am talking to you now."

"You continued to exist in the realms that rose from your body, when they scattered your pieces into the heavens."

"Six manifestations of my energy—Nibiru and its five echoes— scattered across the universe."

"There was a seventh," said Yngvi. "Your head. It was not on Tausret's false door. And in my vision, Ishtar found it in Mashu forest."

And Shara knew that Yngvi knew.

"But my sons didn't know that. No one did," said Anu. "I can never be sundered from Nibiru. It is in me and I am in it. My head waited in Mashu forest for millennia until Ishtar escaped Enlil's prison a mere twenty years ago." A wistful smile touched Anu's lips. "She found me, and together with the life force of Mashu, we created Shara, the newest immortal. But he is the most primal, more powerful than them all. A pure seedling, born of my consciousness and Ishtar's. You wondered about the elegance of his features. He gets his beauty from her."

"Already he looks less like himself and more like you. Let him go. He doesn't deserve such an end to his short life."

Anu's head jerked as Shara thrashed inside him. His eyes closed, his lips tightened.

"He fights you even now," said Yngvi.

"He will give up, in time. And you should, too. He has no need of you, but it shouldn't come as a surprise. After all, you've brought him nothing but suffering and sacrifice. He found you diverting initially, but you became a liability later on. An impediment."

No! You're lying! I never thought that about him! Shara was shouting, but he could not hear himself. Anu jerked his head, and Shara found even his thoughts muzzled.

Yngvi held himself straight, chin lifted in defiance. "He has said that to me, many times and in many different ways. And each time, he sounded exactly like you did just now. I think that was you."

Anu did not answer immediately.

Yngvi said, "It was almost as though, with each realm he visited, you grew stronger inside him."

This time, Anu answered. "You are correct, Yngvi Ecklundson. My sons may have flung my body into the heavens, but that did not kill me, because my head, the seat of my consciousness, remained on Nibiru. It was Enki's killing of the gods that awakened me in Shara. And I grew stronger as Shara took me to each of my realms."

"If the realms are yours, the gods are yours. The gods Enki murdered—they had no part in all of this. Can you bring them back?"

"You mean like Shara brought you back?"

Don't do this, Shara begged Anu.

"No," said Yngvi, dropping to his knees. "No, not like that."

"Your body is now marked like his."

"I know." Yngvi's hand strayed to his stomach.

Shara remembered tracing the silver outline of the leaf around Yngvi's navel with his lips, the mark that now was as much a part of Yngvi as the rest of his golden skin. *Please, don't tell him! He never asked me to bring him back. He won't forgive himself for the rest of his life.*

It was your life first, Anu returned silently.

"It is the mark of Mashu forest," Anu said to Yngvi, "and only one other man in all the realms has it. It was his gift to you when he gave up his immortality to save you. A life for a life."

"I *know.*" Yngvi looked nauseated.

"You died that day on Graecia," said the cold, implacable creator. "You should have stayed dead. I told him what it would cost him. I tried to stop him, but he would not listen to me."

"I know! I know all that."

Anu gave Yngvi a long, scrutinising look. "So, that's really why you are here...isn't it? You have come here to give it back."

"Yes," said Yngvi, his voice scarcely louder than a whisper.

"It is the force of *his* life that flows inside you. You care so little for his gift?"

Anu's words seemed to break something inside Yngvi. He hunched over, holding his head in his hands.

"He's a fool, a damned fool!" He sat back on his heels, a haunted look in his eyes. He was blinking rapidly. "He knew I was already dead. Please, take it from me. Give it back to him."

Anu's laugh was a short, harsh sound that held no amusement. "Don't kill the Anunnaki! Bring back the dead gods! Take back a life from one body, put it in another! Do you think this is a game? There are consequences, and they are irreversible."

"Even by you?" Yngvi challenged, his voice shaking.

"Even by me. A sensible man would have gone home, back to his ordinary life and his ordinary world to live out the rest of his days. But you chose to come after him. Why? Is it guilt, or is it that you can't forget the night you spent together?"

"Get out of my head," Yngvi snapped.

"It's only fair," Anu countered. "You have been inside mine."

Yngvi thrust his hands into his hair, and held his head a moment. "What happens to Shara with you inside him?"

"As long as I am inside him, Shara is immortal. He is a god. But if I abandon his body, he will be no more than a man. He will age like a mortal; his flesh will fail and he will die. Do you wish that for him?"

Give me that choice, and I will take it.

"No! I—I never did, and I never would," said Yngvi, immediately, his eyes closing. "He gave up his immortality once already for me. But—" He looked up at Anu. "It was his choice then, and it should be his choice now."

"It *is* his choice," said Anu.

Shara saw Yngvi absorb Anu's words. Yngvi nodded a few times, as though he understood.

Anu laughed. "It's not what you think. He won't tell you this…he can't speak anymore…but he begged me for one night with you. A single night, as himself. I gave it to him. And in exchange, he gave up his body to me. So you see, I am not actually arrogating his body. It was our bargain, Shara's and mine."

"Bargain?" said Yngvi, bitterly. He held himself like a man who had been beaten to the point of numbness, his head dropped, his shoulders slumped. He was shaking his head.

"Shara and I are one," said Anu.

Yngvi jerked his head up. "Shara is *more* than you. He was born of you and Ishtar, yet he is himself. If it must be a choice between immortality and independence, he must choose. If you stay inside him, you reduce him to a frame of flesh and bones."

Shara felt the intensity of Anu's cold gaze settle on Yngvi. The creator's blue halo was agitated; he was displeased.

But Yngvi persisted. "Let him decide."

"*I* have decided," said Anu. "I will not give him up. I cannot." His voice dropped. "He is all that remains of Ishtar. She lives through him."

"She lives in Mashu forest!" said Yngvi. "She's in the trees and the grass, she is in the mound under the banyan tree. How do you think I know about Shara? She spoke to me! She showed me your past."

Anu hesitated, and Yngvi pressed on, recounting what Shara had told him. "Your legends say that the trees came from her hair, the hills from her breasts, the rivers from her tears, the first humans from her womb. She is as much a part of Nibiru as you are, as much a part of Mashu as Shara is. She *is* Mashu."

Anu was listening, and Shara was, too.

"But she is not Shara. And he is not Ishtar."

"I am all he has," said Anu, dismissively.

"He has me!"

"He has you?" Anu was paying attention now. "Are you asking him to go with you to Midgard?"

"If he did," said Yngvi, carefully, "he would be welcome."

"Would he? What do you think his life would be on Yggdrasil, Yngvi Ecklundson?"

"I think…" Yngvi said in a faraway voice, looking at the floor. "I think…Odin and Thor would give him their gratitude and their welcome. Magne would be a brother to him, and in time, Ulla a sister. The children would adore him. Halli and Vidar and the others would be his friends."

Shara allowed himself to picture Yngvi's words, and found that he wanted the possible future they showed him. *And what would you be, Yngvi?*

"And you? What would *you* be?" Anu asked.

Yngvi whipped his head up. "Me?" He gazed at Anu for so long that he might have been seeking Shara behind the creator's eyes. "A,,,friend? A companion? I don't know…I would be whatever he wanted me to be."

Shara went still as the struggle left him.

"I think it would have made him happy to hear that."

"Is he happy?" Yngvi asked.

"He will be," said Anu. "He is where he belongs, on Nibiru." Anu's halo calmed, and Shara had the sickening realisation that the creator pitied Yngvi. "He is a god and always will be. You are not and never will be. Use the time he has given you to find happiness with a good woman or man."

But Yngvi shook his head and stood. "Don't presume to tell me what to do."

Shara could tell that Anu was peering into Yngvi's thoughts, but he couldn't see what Anu saw. He could only sense Anu's amusement.

"Not even I can predict the future," the creator said, laughing softly. He lightly yanked the leaf-amulet from Yngvi's neck. "You won't be needing it anymore. And I don't need this anymore." He reached under his tunic to pull out the second ka jar that Tausret had made for Shara and tossed it to Yngvi, who caught it in cupped hands. "You can have it. There. A souvenir from Aegyptus. Now go."

"Shara, please! Don't let him—!"

Those were his last words, because Anu touched Yngvi's shoulder.

And Yngvi was gone.

CHAPTER THIRTY-TWO

THE FOREST PASSED them by, a rolling vista of green and brown, yellow and red and white.

The blossoms, all bright colours and sweet scents, stirred and bobbed on their slender stems, and the tall grass rustled in the breeze as Anu made his way through Mashu forest.

He sat under the banyan tree for hours, calling for Ishtar. He lay on the mound, waiting for Mashu to reach for him, for Ishtar to speak to him, but when there was no change, he rose and stomped around the tree, angry at its impassive presence. Every minute of those hours, Shara fought to break free of Anu.

He would wait for Anu's attention to drift, then conjure up his—Anu's—sword and try to impale himself, but Anu would move his fingers and the sword would vanish. Shara did this, again and again, until opposing the impulse of his own muscles left him drained. He decided to use his words.

You lied.

"Oh?" Anu sounded amused. "How so?"

You said no one would come. Yngvi came. He came for me.

"That young man was very resourceful. Far more than I expected a mortal to be. And surprising. I liked being surprised. But Shara, that does not change anything for you. You were never meant to exist," said Anu. "You do realise that?"

Then let me die.

"Die?" said Anu. "You're immortal. Or you *were*, until you foolishly gave up eternity for a mortal. But you have me now."

I have you? I am nothing to you but an inconsequential little remnant of Ishtar. I don't want this! Let me go.

"What of your immortality?"

What of it? An endless existence inside you and never being able to be myself? Why would I want that? Why would anyone?

"What is the alternative?"

Are you giving me an alternative? Because if you are, I would ask for my body, my mortal body. I would choose companionship for a limited time over an eternity of isolation. And if I could not get that, I'd choose death over this undying existence.

"You miss him."

The legends were true. You do know everything.

If he had hoped to rile Anu up, it did not work, because Anu only laughed. "You gave up so much for someone you knew for such an insignificant amount of time."

And yet, in that time, I lived and felt more alive than I had in all my years.

Shara did not know when the day had passed, and night had crept up on them. Distantly, he remembered the stars coming out in ones and twos, and by now, countless little lights dotted the dark sky.

"I don't understand you, Shara. Mortals go to great lengths, punishing lengths, to ask the gods for the boon of immortality. It was given to you, and yet you gave it up. Willingly."

Boon? They are fools. Immortality is a curse if it must be spent alone.

"Now you are speaking the truth. I thought I would have Ishtar by my side. Ishtar!" he called into the night air. "Where are you? He said you were here. Ishtar!"

The forest came alive, shaking its susurrating leaves. And then, a voice, a woman's voice, spoke to them.

"I am here, my love."

"Ishtar!"

The forest floor around Anu had turned a luminous white, as if each blade of grass carried Ishtar's light within. Small flowering shoots were twining around the broad trunk which was now blue, its leaves as white as the grass. Its vine-like roots swayed in the gentle wind as they, too, turned blue.

Ishtar was all around them.

"My love," she said again. *"Shara, my son."*

"Ishtar! I can hear you!" Anu reached up with his hands to stroke the trunk of the tree; it glowed under his touch. "Come back to me."

Ask him to let me go, Shara said to Ishtar. *Please. Let me go.* He was looking up at the boughs, now blue and bright white in the dark night.

No one was listening to him. Yet he was able to hear Anu's and Ishtar's endearments to each other, a rush of words, and sighs of love and longing after spending ages apart. He turned his mind inward, to the solitary solace of his memories.

Let me go. It was a feeble thought, expressed for probably the hundredth time in his seemingly endless silent observation of the reunited lovers. *Let me go.*

This time, Anu answered. "You are my only physical vestige of Ishtar, Shara. I cannot let you go."

"Anu," said Ishtar. *"I did not think you were cruel."*

"If I lose him, I lose you. I see you in him. I miss you, Ishtar. I miss you."

"But he is our son," said Ishtar. *"Shara, my child—"*

"Son?" Anu hissed. "We are where we are because of our sons!"

"Your sons with Ki," Ishtar reminded him, gently, cannily. *"But Shara is not Enlil or Enki. He is the only reason you speak to me today. He and Yngvi. Is it fair to keep them apart? I will always be in Mashu. You know that. You must let him go. You know that, too."*

"I won't. Don't ask me again. What must I do to bring you forth? Why are you not in my arms already?"

"I do not know, my love. But look," said Ishtar.

The flowers creeping up the trunk opened their white petals, fanning out around black centres, like eyes. The air was sweet and fresh with their scent.

"I see you. Do you see me?"

"I do, I see you! Please, come back to me."

Anu's despair felt as real to Shara as his own. *Please let me go,* he pleaded.

"You will be quiet," said the creator.

"Anu... Let him speak," said Ishtar. *"Tell me about him, Shara. Tell me about your young friend."*

Her words evoked a strange feeling, one that Shara had never experienced before. It was sanctuary—a comfort he had never known, had never expected to know. Ishtar's voice was gentle and calming, like a mother's hand in his hair.

They misunderstood him, his gods. They wouldn't listen. I was there. He told them the truth, but they still blamed him for the attack on Asgard. Even his brother doubted him. They didn't know it was Enki's doing. They think he's reckless. I thought he was reckless. But he is brave, and loyal. He's kind and—

"—mortal," Anu interjected.

"Go on, Shara," said Ishtar.

He came with me to redeem himself. He knew the only way he could do that was to stop Enki. I could have taken the sword from him, I didn't even need to kill him, but there was something about him.

"You wanted to know him, too," said Ishtar, a smile in her voice.

"You're as reckless as he is," said Anu. "You showed him everything. You showed him all our secrets."

Your secrets. I have no secrets, and no one to keep them from. Not anymore.

"You—"

"*Anu, when Enki killed our daughter,*" said Ishtar, "*he took away the only person who had ever loved Shara. And then you sent Yngvi away. Let him speak.*"

Anu closed his eyes.

He loves his brother. And his brother loves him. I gave Magne my word. But I let him die. I have never missed. But that day…it was my arrow that—

"Hecate cheated."

What?

"You didn't know?" Anu laughed. "She was desperate. She needed you to lose. So, she blew your last arrow off course. No, don't be angry with her. It was Hermes who made certain the arrow entered Yngvi. They both knew Yngvi was dying. And Hecate did give you Hermes's wand, didn't she?"

That doesn't excuse what she did! If he had died in Graecia, his brother would have been waiting for him forever.

Anu pushed out a breath of exasperation.

I could not have done this without Yngvi. I'm only here, you *are only here because of him.*

"I'll grant you this: he is brighter than the average mortal."

He is…

"Brighter than the sun?" Anu sniggered. "Isn't that what you were about to say? You have lost your head over a mortal. Although, he did lose his head over you first."

The white flowers craned their stems and leaned eagerly towards Anu. *"Did he?"* said Ishtar. *"What happened?"*

Shara was silent. He remembered how Yngvi had looked at him that first day in Midgard. Yngvi had smiled at him while the other Midgardians had sneered.

"He couldn't look away, Ishtar. That young man was fascinated with Shara's dark hair and pale skin."

He liked me as myself, too.

Anu snorted. "He must have liked you very much as yourself. Enough that he hit Namhu."

What? Why?

"He found Namhu in the city and forced him, at knifepoint, to bring him to the Sky Palace. Namhu was starting to call you a mong—

"Anu," Ishtar cautioned.

"—what he usually calls you, and your Yngvi hit him and warned him to never speak about you like that again."

He's not my Yngvi.

"But you'd like him to be?" said Ishtar, with a mother's insight.

The flowers were—Ishtar was—beaming up at him.

Doesn't matter what I want. But…he kept his word.

"He did. He kept surprising me, your Yngvi."

Shara sighed soundlessly. *He kept surprising me, too.*

"That's why, when you asked for one day, I gave you one day. I stayed away that day in Athens."

You did. But…

"But?"

Before that, you also made him think I despised him. Over and over. And yet he helped me. He had no reason to, in Saqqara. He could have let me—

"Fondle the door handle? Perform the ritual with Tausret?" Anu's shoulders shook.

The grass around them stirred curiously. *"What door handle?"* Ishtar asked. *"What ritual? Who is Tausret?"*

"My love, there's so much to tell you!" Anu was happy to recount those events for his disembodied lover. When he finished, Ishtar's delighted laughter rustled through the undergrowth.

"He is amusing, that boy," she said. *"And irreverent."*

He is many things.

"He was getting a little too fond of you for my liking."

Ishtar laughed softly. *"Is that so bad? Do you not want that for our son?"*

"Your son," said Anu, "has been living on his own, traversing the realms—"

To find your killer—

"—and giving his body to strange men."

One man. And he's not strange. Not anymore.

"All right, one man. But to me, you're a child. A child who did wicked things disguised as an Aegyptian maiden. What do you think he would say if he found out?"

He won't.

Anu chuckled. "He already knows."

What?

"Do you remember if he looked at Tausret at all?"

No.

"That's because he didn't. His eyes were on you the whole time. Do you remember that?"

I remember that.

"I think it is guilt that's making you want to see him again. You should have let him fight the Graecians. He would have died, and it would not be on your head."

I did not want him to die. I could not let him die.

CHAPTER THIRTY-THREE

SHARA WAS DRAINED.

He had been listening to their voices, his *creators'* voices, for hours. It was strange to think of himself as their son. For twenty years, Anu and Ishtar had been no more than names he had heard from Nidaba, long-dead gods from Nibiru's long-ago legends. For all that time, his only refuge had been Mashu forest, and if he could, he would return to its welcoming earth.

His thoughts were drifting, his energy waning. He was being subsumed into Anu; his voice inside the creator would soon be silenced and he would lose the last of his memories.

Keep this body, but let me go.

"You'd give it up to me?" said Anu.

Shara wished he could scream. *What use is a body that is not in my control? You were inside me all these years, and now I'm inside you. I'm the uninvited guest now. Please, let me go. You have no need of me.*

"Shara...you know what it means for you if I take this body over."

Yes. I want that. I told you. Unchanging, dependent deathlessness like this is a torment I don't want. Please. Keep this body. But let me go.

"*Shara...*" said Ishtar.

Return me to the forest. Mashu will have me back. I have... I have lived a life. I have made memories. If I cannot live with them, then let me take them with me to my death.

"*Anu,*" said Ishtar. "*You must let him go.*"

"I won't. He is a god!"

"*He is also our child, and he's unhappy. Can't you see how unhappy he is?*"

Anu shook his head at the tree. The white flowers on its trunk glared back at him.

"Do you want him to be mortal?"

"*I want him to be himself.*"

This went on for a long time. Shara gave up trying to follow the ebb and flow of the argument, and retreated into his thoughts while they were still his. He remembered the tavern, the battle, the ritual, the contests, death in the Underworld, the night after, the light in Yngvi's eyes before he had shuddered over Shara's body, Shara's name on his lips—

"I can hear your thoughts, you know?" said Anu, interrupting Shara's musings.

And I had to listen to you all this while, Shara retorted.

Anu laughed, but his words sounded weary. "All right, I'll let you go. I will miss you, I think."

Probably not.

"Probably not," Anu admitted. "I'm only doing this because Ishtar thinks it might allow her to emerge."

Shara knew that. He had caught the part of the exchange when Ishtar had convinced Anu to try.

"*A life for a life, isn't it?*" she had said to Anu, reminding him of his words to Yngvi.

But Shara had also known somehow, deep inside him, that it was only her affection for him that had made her suggest that. It felt strange to know that he mattered. Since Nidaba, he had been important to only one other person, a man he would never see again. It was time to surrender those thoughts to what awaited him.

Anu stood before the tree, touching its trunk. The wood glowed under his palm.

"You held me, Mashu, and kept me safe. For that I thank you."

The tree dipped its branches, as though bowing to the creator.

"And now I return Shara to you."

The leaves whispered loudly.

"Shara, my child, I want you to be happy," said Ishtar.

"Keep him safe, Mashu," Anu said.

"I will," Ishtar answered.

And Shara remembered Yngvi imploring the creator to seek Ishtar. She *is* Mashu, he had said.

Anu lay down on the mound as the white grass rose up to enmesh his body. He closed his eyes.

Shara felt himself sink into the soft earth, heard the voices inside his own mind subside and go quiet. He felt himself fade from his body. He said the silent words: *Be well, Yngvi. I will miss you.*

He closed his absent eyes, but he could still see. Nothing happened for a while.

Nothing happened for eight days.

For eight days, Anu lay on the mound as the sun sank behind the treeline and Ishtar reemerged and suffused the forest around them with her light. She enveloped Anu, and they attempted to return Shara to the forest and draw Ishtar out. A life for a life, even in the forest. The whole night passed like that. But with the first blush of dawn, Ishtar retreated into Mashu's bosom, restoring the forest to its colours, and waited for Anu to return in the evening, when they attempted it all over again.

Shara had gone silent since that first day, reconciled to disappearing into nothingness like one who was never meant to exist.

By the ninth night, the last, stubborn flicker of hope in Shara was nearly extinguished. As before, Anu lay down on the mound. As before, Ishtar rose from the forest and covered him with her white roots. And as before, the stars came out, winking like faraway gemstones strewn over the dark dome of sky.

But on this ninth night, that vista had begun to change. A single constellation glowed brighter than the surrounding stars. It was Sipa-Zi-An-Na. Shara felt a pounding where his heart had beaten when he had been alive. He knew this sky, knew what came after. The inky expanse flashed as a fireball shot past the archer's bow, a beacon of brilliant white that drew the eye across the sweep of the firmament. He hoped it was a sign that he would die tonight, twenty-one years after he was created.

And then he saw it: a stream of fluid energy, bright and crackling, rising sinuously from Anu's body. Shara knew it as his own force, the thing which made him uniquely himself. The sundering from Anu was a twisting, painless agony that left him feeling unmoored, yet also unshackled. The grass around Anu, that he had felt around himself, had withdrawn.

He appeared to be fully separate from the creator's body, because he was facing it. What used to be his face was now harder, older, more angular; his skin a darker blue, his body bigger, his form now fully inhabited by the ageless being who had made him. Or beings, because Anu's appearance was shifting, his whole body was transforming. It was like two beings in one physical casing, their forms blending and separating over and over. Anu's hair was dark one moment, white the next, the angles of his body softening out into breasts and curves, then flattening again. The forest was brown and green again; the light had left the leaves and grass and flowers. And Shara knew that Ishtar had risen from Mashu into Anu's body.

Yet, impossibly, Shara was still extant as himself, persisting separate from the forest he had expected would assimilate him. A change was occurring inside; he did not feel weightless any longer. There was, incredibly, a mass to himself.

He could feel his limbs. A phantom sensation, he assumed, but the ground under his legs felt wet and soft, as real as if he were kneeling on it. He lifted a hand, expecting to see nothing, but saw a palm, fingers, nails, a wrist. He looked down at himself and saw arms and legs. Touched his face, felt skin. Touched his chest, felt the beat of his heart inside, rapid, excited, strong. Closed his eyes, searched his mind, let out a shuddering breath when he realised that he was alone in it.

How could this be?

He rushed to the stream and leaned over. The face in the water looking back at him was his face from Midgard. Pale skin, hair the colour of dark ash. But vestiges of Nibiru were visible from certain angles under the dawning sun: the blue tinge of his skin, glimpses of the silver sheen of his hair, the leaf birthmark around his navel, the ice-blue of his eyes.

"I think he'll like you like this."

Shara sat back in shock. He heard footsteps on the wet riverbank behind him, and looked back at his erstwhile body, at Anu, gazing at him with dark grey eyes. Ishtar stood beside him, inhabiting her own physical form, brought forth by Anu's creative power. Her pale eyes were soft with kindness, and a mother's indulgent affection. Shara looked down at his body.

"This is close to how he first saw you, isn't it?" said Anu.

"Yes," said Shara, and heard himself. He was no longer voiceless. He ran his hands over his arms and legs, felt the living warmth of his skin, the responsive muscles shifting smoothly with his movements. "I'm alive." He looked again at Anu, at Ishtar. "I am myself."

Anu smiled. "Yes. And now you won't have to change your appearance."

Ishtar bent forward to put a hand on Shara's head; she threaded gentle fingers through his hair. "We could not be with you before, but I am glad that your sister found you. You carry us both inside you. There is goodness in you, and courage and loyalty. You are our greatest creation, Shara. And if this is what you choose, we will not stop you."

"You should go," said Anu, "before your Yngvi succeeds in losing his life again."

"What?"

"The heartbroken young man was imagining his own death when I sent him back," said Anu, laughing. "I told you, mortals are foolish. And yours was also a little melancholic at the time." He held out a hand. Shara took it and stood.

"Now go home and put on some clothes before you leave," said Ishtar. She kissed his cheek. Her lips were warm with life, and soft against his skin. "Anu, will you get him to Yngvi?"

"I could. Or he could use this." Anu opened his other hand. A leaf-amulet sat on his palm. He smiled at Shara. "You'll need it if you ever wanted to come back."

"Be safe, my child," said Ishtar. "Be happy."

Shara felt an emotion he had never expected to feel again. There was a brightness inside him, like he had swallowed the rising sun. It was hope.

He looked at Anu and Ishtar, the beings who had created him, and grinned.

EPILOGUE

THE SUN HAD SET on Midgard.

Yngvi slogged home from another humiliating session in the arena. He had dropped his shield, let his sword be knocked from his hand. But he had trained Vidar too well. Vidar had withdrawn immediately and lowered his sword and shield, and Yngvi had been silent when the young soldier had enquired, hesitantly, about his dwindling enthusiasm. And so, he was still alive. Either he hadn't reached the bottom of his pit of despair or he was not being allowed to die. Or he was still hopeful.

He had seen it clearly in Nibiru: a fight in the arena with real swords. Haunted by the memory of crystalline eyes, he would falter and his shield would be knocked from his hand; he would lower his sword in a miscarried feint and leave his chest exposed to his opponent's competitive instincts. He hoped it would be clean and quick.

His last thought, as almost every thought had been since he had left Nibiru, would be of Shara. He would wish Shara happiness. His spirit, if he still had one, would begin its journey to the Afterlife, to join his parents. And his life, if it were possible, would return to the man who had given him a reprieve from death.

Magne had been overjoyed to see him. His embrace had been tight and long, as if he did not want Yngvi to leave again. Even Ulla had kissed his cheek briefly. His nephews, only then noticing that he had been absent for some time, had asked if he had brought anything back for them from his travels. He had. They trilled happily, and ran about the house, hooting and growling, one looking like an owl, the other like a three-headed hound.

When he returned home, he crushed the blue chiton against his chest. Placed it back on the bed beside the empty ka jar before answering the door.

"Vidar," said Yngvi, "what is it?"

Vidar was panting. "You must come with me to the arena."

"We were just there. What is it now?"

"Please, Captain. It's Halli…and—"

"Halli's back from Valhalla? What has your brother done now?"

Yngvi fastened his sword belt, weighed down by a new blade, shut the door behind him and headed out to the arena with Vidar.

Halli's horse was tied outside. Vidar pushed the arena door open and held it for Yngvi to follow. Yngvi stepped in, and stopped short.

Halli was sparring with a man, a pale, dark-haired man who had first looked into Yngvi's eyes outside the seaside tavern in Midgard's square. A man he thought he had lost forever.

"Halli!" Yngvi called out.

Halli froze, lowered his sword, and turned his head to Yngvi.

"Out," said Yngvi. "You, too, Vidar."

"Come on!" Vidar urged his brother.

Halli placed the training sword and shield on a nearby table, and hurried out with Vidar.

"Idiot," Vidar muttered.

Yngvi closed the door, stood rooted to his spot. He took in the scattered training weapons, the footprints and tracks left in the sawdust, and visualised the fighting patterns employed, the manoeuvres he remembered from Athens. He lifted his eyes and met that pellucid gaze. The silence stretched out.

Yngvi swallowed. "You're here," he said thickly, hearing the incredulity in his voice.

"Yngvi…" Shara dropped his sword and shield to the ground. His dark pants were tucked into boots, and his long-sleeved tunic hung loose down to mid-thigh because there was no belt around his waist. But he had never needed a scabbard.

Yngvi could not breathe. His throat ached with all the things he wanted to say. He watched the play of light on Shara's skin, glimpsed the tinge of blue in the planes of his face. "Is this what you look like now?"

"Yes," said Shara. "Anu thought...you might like..." He came forward half-way, and waited.

Yngvi crossed the distance that still separated them, each step seeming even more impossible because it led him closer to Shara. He stopped when he was near enough to see the creases in Shara's tunic, the weave of the fabric.

"Do you not like it...me?" Shara's eyes were wide and dark, almost black.

Yngvi raised the hem of Shara's tunic with a finger, saw the leaf birthmark, dropped it. Lifted his hand to Shara's hair, untied the leather that held it so that it fell loose about his shoulders. Ran his fingers through the soft strands, saw them catch the last of the light and shine silver in the gloaming. He stroked Shara's cheekbone, tracing the blue in the angles. "Still magnificent," he said, his voice quiet. He pulled out a knife from his boot, took Shara's hand in his own, and nicked Shara's palm. A bead of blood quivered over the cut. It was red. "For a fool who gave up his immortality."

The emotion in Shara's eyes darkened to irritation. "Are you going to argue about that? You know it's not going to change anything."

"Why! Why did you do that? How could you give up *everything*?"

"Not everything."

Yngvi shook his head silently. What could he say that Shara had not already heard him say to Anu?

"Yngvi... You wanted Anu to ask me what I wanted. *This* is what I want."

Yngvi nodded, because he understood and because his own words were exhausted. But Shara was still speaking, and Yngvi let him. He listened to what had happened on Nibiru after Anu had sent him back to Midgard, but mostly he listened to Shara's voice, watched Shara's lips form words, watched the expressions shift on his face: desperation, anger, hurt, relief. And felt the hard ache of longing in his own chest.

"So, Anu has let you go now? He won't come back to claim you?"

"He has his own body now. And Ishtar. They don't need me."

"Good. That's good." Yngvi passed a hand over his face, rubbed the back of his neck. A thought arose, sudden and tangential. He looked up. "When did you come here?"

"A day ago." Shara must have caught Yngvi's interrogative look, because he quickly added, "I had things to do."

"Things to do," said Yngvi. "Things to do?" He grabbed Shara's tunic at his neck and yanked him close. "Did you think that I might be waiting?"

Yngvi's exasperation was, maddeningly, making Shara smile. There was a softness in his gaze, and Yngvi thought there was relief and understanding and fondness in the clear blue.

"I hoped you would." The words were quiet and intimate, as if they were alone—not in the arena, but in Yngvi's house, where no one would interrupt them. Shara covered Yngvi's clenched hands with his own, stroked Yngvi's knuckles with his thumbs. "I was with Odin and Thor. I went there to tell them what had happened."

"You did?"

Shara nodded. "They were wrong about what they thought happened, wrong about you."

"And?"

A light breeze had sprung up and brushed along Yngvi's cheeks, playing with his hair and spilling it over his forehead, the ends tickling his skin. Shara lifted a hand to push the stray strands off Yngvi's face and tuck them behind his ears.

"They didn't believe me at first. They said they hadn't seen you since the battle. They were still upset with you, but that changed after I told them…showed them what had happened."

"You went to Valhalla." Yngvi shook his head, closed his eyes. He ran a hand through his hair, keeping the other in Shara's tunic to hold him in Midgard. "I thought I'd never see you again. You didn't think to come to me first?"

"I did, but you didn't answer the door. I went to the tavern next, but they hadn't seen you for weeks. Finally, I went to Valhalla because I thought you might go there, and I knew how to get there."

Shara was solemn and unsmiling as he laid out his practical considerations while Yngvi listened, taking quiet pleasure in watching Shara navigate the absurdity of the situation. And just like that, past all the hurt and the waiting and the hopelessness, he felt a wellspring of happiness inside him. He heard his own breath of disbelief, of amusement, of brimming affection.

He schooled his features into a semblance of seriousness. "So you went to Valhalla."

"Yes. I…I saw Magne there," Shara was explaining, his face and hands animated, and Yngvi was losing himself in that clear, earnest gaze. "He crushed me in his arms as soon as he saw me. I didn't know what to do, so I embraced him back. He said he would take me to you after he finished his work with Thor. But then Halli said that if I didn't want to wait, he could take me to the arena because you came here almost daily. So we rode Halli's horse back to Midgard."

Yngvi frowned, as he tended to when Halli was involved. But he must have been at the arena with Vidar when Shara had gone to his house.

"Halli said we could wait for you here for a little while, and if you didn't come, I could go back to wait outside your house. He suggested sparring while we waited. I thought, why not? But he seemed to be taking it very seriously. I had to fend him off a few times. Then Vidar found us here. He warned Halli about what you might do to him when you found out, then left. And then he came back. With you."

"Vidar was right to be worried," said Yngvi, with an inauthentic smile.

"Oh?"

"I am going to kill Halli." Yngvi had managed to say it with an even voice and wider smile.

"Oh no." Shara stopped speaking.

Yngvi gaped at Shara, at his grave eyes, and shook his head. He was laughing now, all his irritation at Halli drained out of him by Shara's blown eyes that were on him silently, waiting.

"I missed you," he said.

"I hoped you would." Shara took a step closer.

"So much," Yngvi added. Then he took Shara's face in his hands, and kissed him.

Shara's mouth opened under his, his arms slid around Yngvi's neck, and they kissed, with longing and laughter and delight. Yngvi ran his hands down Shara's body, reclaiming the planes and dips and the taut swells of muscle that he had traced with his mouth in Athens. They pulled apart to look at each other, incredulous and blinking hard, and then kissed again, because it was too painful not to.

It was a long time before Yngvi lifted his mouth from Shara's.

"I'll set things straight with Halli," he murmured into the skin behind Shara's ear. "But you should be careful around those boys. They like to play pranks on newcomers."

"All right," said Shara. And kissed him.

However long he had been pressed against Shara was not nearly long enough. Which was why, when a throat was cleared, strident in the hollow arena behind him, Yngvi disengaged from Shara with extreme resentment and turned to confront the interloper. He bristled when he saw who it was.

"What do you want?" he asked.

"So, you found him after all," said Magne, with a grin so infuriatingly sunny that Yngvi wondered whether Apollo had possessed him.

"State your business and leave."

"State your business and leave," Magne repeated, puckering his lips in an exaggerated impression of Yngvi's hostile manner. "And I was talking to Shara, not you."

"Magne—"

"You know, brother, I was right to worry that there was no one left on Midgard to hold your fancy." Magne's hearty laugh echoed in the empty arena. "I never imagined we'd have to go beyond even *Yggdrasil* to find someone for you."

"Magne! Can you, for once, not be so irritating?"

"Oh, all right! You never let me have my fun with you," Magne groused. "In any case, I'm not here to pass the time. I'm here to tell you that you've been summoned to Valhalla. And before you ask, no, it's not Thor. This comes all the way from the top."

Yngvi swung his gaze to Shara, then back to Magne. "What does Odin want with me now?"

"You can ask him yourself," said Magne. "Or should I tell him you're *going* to be busy?" He winked, not at Yngvi but at Shara.

"Yes, do that."

"You know I won't!" Magne assured him. He waved a cheerful hand as he turned to leave. Looking over his shoulder, he said, "Odin doesn't like to be kept waiting." He closed the arena door behind him, leaving Yngvi alone with Shara again.

"Odin can wait." Yngvi tipped Shara's chin up, but Shara held his shoulders and took a step back.

"I think you should go to Valhalla," Shara's face was sombre. "You should see Odin and Thor."

"They cast me out." The words came out sounding bitter. It still hurt.

"I know." Shara clasped Yngvi's shoulders tighter. "But don't leave it on those terms. They didn't know the truth then. They do, now."

Yngvi gazed at Shara for a long time in silence.

"They realise now that they were wrong, that they were unfair to you and want to set things right."

"They *said* that?"

Shara nodded. "They said that. They want their Captain back, Yngvi. They want *you* back."

How easy it was for them to call him back. They knew nothing of the wound that still flared inside him now and again, that gnawing desire for the exculpation he had not thought he would ever receive. But Shara, godlike Shara, sweetly thoughtful Shara, had come back to Midgard to give Yngvi just that, to lift the pain that had weighed him down like the ruins of his reputation since the night of Ragnarök. Shara stood before him now, the ghost of a smile curving his lips, waiting benignly for his answer. And Yngvi wanted to give it, so badly.

He said, "All right, I'll go. But I want you to come with me." *I want you to stay with me.*

"All right, I will," said Shara. Then, as if reading Yngvi's mind, "I'm not going to disappear again, you know."

"Do I know that?" Yngvi asked, lifting helpless fingers to touch the leaf-amulet around Shara's neck.

Shara touched the leather cord around Yngvi's neck. "What's this?"

The pendant was tucked inside Yngvi's tunic. He pulled it out and ran his fingers over its shape. "It's the Rod of Asclepius. A gift from Apollonius. It's meant to keep me safe." He lifted his eyes to Shara's. "Apparently, someone told him I get injured too often, and too critically."

Shara grinned. "It's true, isn't it?" He untied his leaf amulet and reached under Yngvi's hair to knot the leather behind his neck. "Now you have a gift from me, too. I'm not going anywhere."

Yngvi looked down at the leaf-amulet he held between his thumb and forefinger, feeling its striations and pointed tip. The ka jar and chiton sat on his bed, mementoes from two worlds he had never imagined existed. And now this, a token from Nibiru, while Shara stood before him in the flesh. For now.

"You left this behind when you left Athens. You didn't need it."

"That was Anu. But *I* need it."

They gazed at each other for a long moment.

"I'm not going anywhere," said Shara again.

"Unless we go together?"

"Unless we go together."

"Good." Yngvi nodded a few times, then took Shara's hands in his. "So, what happens now? What will you do? What do you want to do?"

Shara glanced down at their joined hands. "I don't know. I hadn't thought about it, but Odin expects that Hel will regroup to avenge her family eventually, and Asgard needs to be ready. He said that Asgard stands alone now, with the support of only Midgard's mortal army."

Yngvi knew from Magne that Odin would never forgive the Vanir, the Elves and the Dwarves for abandoning Asgard in its time of need. That trust, that alliance, was forever shattered.

"He asked if I would join you and Magne in training new recruits. He also wanted me to be his Captain. Since Tyr…"

Yngvi nodded. "And what did you say?"

"I said I needed to talk to you first."

Yngvi nodded again.

"I could do all that, but I don't have a sword now."

"I'll have one made specially for you."

"I'll need a place to stay."

"You can stay with me," Yngvi said without hesitation.

"There are also…other things I want from you—" Shara's gaze had dipped "—things that can't happen here."

"No, they can't," said Yngvi, a smile trembling on his lips. "But I can give you those things, too."

Shara smiled. "Then we should go to Valhalla. We have time, don't we?"

When Yngvi tipped Shara's chin up again, Shara let him.

"We have all the time we want."

THE END

CHARACTERS AND PLACES

YGGDRASIL

Places

YGGDRASIL, the invisible cosmic tree that connects the nine Norse realms

MIDGARD, realm of the mortals

ASGARD, realm of the gods.

VALHALLA, Hall of Fallen Heroes and abode of the Aesir

Mortals

YNGVI, Captain of the Midgardian army of Thor Odinson, Warden of Loki

MAGNE, Yngvi's elder brother and General of the Midgardian army of Thor Odinson, Warden of Loki

HALLI, soldier in the Midgardian army of Thor Odinson and occasional lover of Yngvi

VIDAR, soldier in the Midgardian army of Thor Odinson and Halli's brother

ULFE, another Warden of Loki

The Gods

ODIN ALL-FATHER, principal god of the Asgardian pantheon

THOR ODINSON, Asgardian god of Thunder and Lightning, and son of Odin

LOKI, stepson of Odin, and renegade god who brings about Ragnarök, the Twilight of the Gods

HODUR, blind son of Odin

VÖR, goddess of Knowledge

AESIR, gods of Asgard

SIF, goddess of Destiny and wife of Thor

TYR, god of War

HEIMDALLR, Guardian god

SIGYN, wife of Loki

JÖRMUNGANDR, sea-serpent son of Loki

FENRIR, wolf son of Loki

HEL, ruler of Helheim, and daughter of Loki

MANI, god of the Moon, swallowed by Loki's monsters during Ragnarök

SOL, goddess of the Sun, swallowed by Loki's monsters during Ragnarök

BABYLON

Places

NIBIRU, the realm of Shara's origin

MASHU FOREST, home to Shara

SKY PALACE, abode of the Sky-Father, Enlil, and the Anunnaki

APSU and MARDUK, the first two realms whose pantheons were destroyed by Enki

Mortals

SHARA, blue-skinned snow-mane orphan living alone in Mashu forest

NAMHU, envoy to Enlil in the Sky Palace

The Gods

ANU, the first consciousness. Male energy

KI, Anu's wife, created by Anu. Together, Anu and Ki were the first primordial beings whose children and grandchildren were the original Anunnaki

ISHTAR, snow-mane sister of Ki, born spontaneously from Ki's creative essence

ANUNNAKI, the pantheon of gods on Nibiru

NIDABA, goddess of Knowledge, snow-mane daughter of Anu and Ishtar

ENLIL (Sky-Father), god of the Heavens, and son of Anu and Ki

ENKI, god of the Underworld, and younger son of Anu and Ki

NINLIL, goddess of the Wind, daughter of Anu and Ki, sister-wife of Enlil

NERGAL, god of War, and son of Enlil and Ninlil

NINKI, goddess of Death, daughter of Anu and Ki, sister-wife of Enki

NINKUR, god of Healing, son of Enki and Ninki

AEGYPTUS

Places

SAQQARA, location of Wadjet's temple

THE NECROPOLIS, City of the Dead, where Pharaohs were laid to rest

Mortals

PHARAOH DJOSER, ruler of Aegyptus

HEMIUNU, head priest and chief architect of Pharaoh Djoser

TAUSRET, daughter of Hemiunu; priestess to the Sun god, Ra

SHAI and INENI, local youths in Saqqara

The Gods

SESHAT, goddess of Knowledge and wife of Djehuty

WADJET, oracular goddess whose temple is situated in Saqqara

MIN, god of Fertility, husband of Wadjet and son of Osiris

OSIRIS, god of the Underworld and father of Min

DJEHUTY, god of the Moon and Healing

RA, god of the Sun

GRAECIA

Places

MOUNT OLYMPUS, abode of the Graecian pantheon of gods

ATHENS, city of Athena

Mortals

HIPPOCRATES, foremost physician in Graecia, based in Athens

APOLLONIUS, son of Hippocrates, named for Apollo

The Gods

ATHENA, goddess of Knowledge

HERMES, Messenger of the gods, god of boundaries, Shepherd of mortal souls to the Afterlife

DIONYSUS, god of Wine

APOLLO, god of the Sun and the Hunt

ARES, god of War

HECATE, demi-goddess of the Underworld

HEPHAESTUS, god of the Forge

ASCLEPIUS, god of Healing

CASTOR and POLLUX, mortal and immortal twins born to the same mother from different fathers

ACKNOWLEDGEMENTS

Thank you for reading Echoes of the Gods – A Punarjanman Novel. I hope you enjoyed it!

"Punarjanman" is the Sanskrit word for reincarnation. Having grown up on mythology (primarily Indian and Greek, but also Norse and Egyptian), I am fascinated with the concept, and repercussions, of reincarnation (for gods) and rebirth (for mortals). My story ideas tend to be based on the theme of reincarnation, and if the stars align, my muse cooperates and these ideas end up spawning new novels, those books will also be Punarjanman novels.

This almost completely revised edition of Echoes of the Gods, with all its new characters, myths and plot twists, is the story I wanted to write the first time around. Rewriting Echoes was a labour of love for me, and also a challenge, because I returned to writing after five fallow years, convinced that I'd never write again. But I'm thrilled with how it has turned out.

I've taken gleeful license with the myths referenced herein, and could have lost my own plot were it not for the beta reviews by Barbara and Rhonna, my friends and trusted beta readers. They gifted me their gold-star patience and unflagging enthusiasm for this story for a second time, even though they already knew how it ends! Thank you for your friendship and for celebrating this book with me (again)!

Huge thanks are owed to May Peterson, whose insightful edits showed me what this story could be, and who helped me polish this novel into what you've just read. After every round of May's sobering, but unfailingly kind and encouraging, emails, I would bandage my wounded ego, channel my inner Bryan Adams and sing to myself: "*Now it cuts like a knife, but it feels so right.*" Thank you, May, for your support of me and this story!

And once I'd gone cross-eyed from reading the same words so many times I could recite them in my sleep, Nerine Dorman's eagle-eyed edits helped catch all the lingering little 'gremlins', as she calls them, and a few plot oopsies that I had overlooked despite numerous rounds of self-review. Thank you, Nerine, for your instructive feedback and generosity!

Of course, I have a tendency to tweak things until the last minute, so all wonky elements are down to me alone.

The beautiful new cover was designed by Noor Sobhan, my dear friend, who patiently worked through countless iterations to design and produce an image that truly captures the cosmic and mythological essence of Echoes of the Gods, teasing clues to its theme. Having observed the real-time evolution of the cover, I have a new appreciation for the amazing vision and tremendous effort that goes into creating something this lovely. Thank you, Noor, for your friendship and this amazing cover!

My husband, R, is my rock.

And finally, thank you to everyone who read Echoes of the Gods. I am so glad that you joined Shara and Yngvi on their celestial adventures!

Word-of-mouth is critical for self-published authors, so I'd really appreciate it if you took a moment to rate and review the book online on Amazon, Goodreads and other online forums.

AUTHOR BIO

Gaia Sol lives with her husband in Toronto, Canada. Her adventures in creative writing began with a 9K-word story in 2013, as a much-needed diversion from her day job in finance and technology.

Over the next three years, she wrote longer and bolder stories that explored her love of the legends and myths of the past—Camelot, Robin Hood, the Holy Land—and even the parallelism of ancient mythologies. That last one eventually became Echoes of the Gods which she published under the pen name "Gaia Sol" to combine the Greek and Norse mythological equivalents of her real name and surname (she was very pleased when she came up with it).

She's now researching India's myths, cultural past and heritage to plot her next story. If her muse cooperates, she will publish that novel sometime this decade.

Say Hi!
X: @GaiaSol_writes
Website: https://www.gaiasolwrites.com